Also by Carol Marinelli

The Midwife's One-Night Fling
The Nurse's Reunion Wish

Those Notorious Romanos miniseries

Italy's Most Scandalous Virgin
The Italian's Most Forbidden Virgin

Also by Marion Lennox

Rescued by the Single Dad Doc
Pregnant Midwife on His Doorstep
Mistletoe Kiss with the Heart Doctor
Falling for His Island Nurse

Discover more at millsandboon.co.uk.

UNLOCKING THE DOCTOR'S SECRETS

CAROL MARINELLI

HEALING HER BROODING ISLAND HERO

MARION LENNOX

MILLS & BOON

Published in Great Britain 2021
by Mills & Boon, an imprint of HarperCollins*Publishers* Ltd,
1 London Bridge Street, London, SE1 9GF

www.harpercollins.co.uk

HarperCollins*Publishers*
1st Floor, Watermarque Building,
Ringsend Road, Dublin 4, Ireland

Unlocking the Doctor's Secrets © 2021 by Carol Marinelli

Healing Her Brooding Island Hero © 2021 by Marion Lennox

ISBN: 978-0-263-29772-0

08/21

MIX
Paper from
responsible sources
FSC® C007454

This book is produced from independently certified FSC™ paper
to ensure responsible forest management.
For more information visit www.harpercollins.co.uk/green.

Printed and bound in Spain
by CPI, Barcelona

UNLOCKING THE DOCTOR'S SECRETS

CAROL MARINELLI

MILLS & BOON

PROLOGUE

'YOU'LL BE NURSING here tomorrow night!'

From the ambulance bay, Lina Edwards looked towards the bright lights of The Primary Hospital. She was now back in the driving seat after completing the handover for a patient they had just blue lighted.

'At least I'll be warm.'

It was a wet and cold Thursday night, and they really hadn't stopped since the start of their shift. Brendan held her coffee while Lina re-tied her long, damp black hair and tried to both dry off and warm up as they took a moment for a welcome break after a long and busy night.

As well as being a paramedic, Lina was also a registered nurse and did the occasional shift in Accident and Emergency, not just to keep her registration current but also to keep her hand in. 'You might be here too,' she pointed out to her colleague. Brendan's wife, Alison, was booked to have their first baby here. 'Or rather you might be up on Maternity!'

'Fingers crossed that it won't be for another three weeks,' Brendan said, 'although I swear that Alison's in labour.'

'You've been saying that for the past fortnight.' Lina smiled as she opened up the foil on her egg mayonnaise sandwiches.

'God, not them again,' Brendan groaned, and wound down the window a touch. 'If it isn't eggs then it's tuna.'

'What have you got?' Lina asked, because, well, they always asked, and food was an especially big topic at the moment given that Brendan was on a diet and trying to lose weight.

'A salad wrap, a tub of cottage cheese and an orange,' he sighed, checking his phone for the umpteenth time. 'She was on edge this evening before I left for work.'

'I'm sure Alison would call if anything was happening. There wasn't a light on when we drove past.'

'True.'

Their ambulance station was west of London but of course they went where their shift led them and sometimes they ended up at The Primary, a huge general hospital in the north of London, close to where Brendan and Alison lived and Lina once had.

'I wonder who I'll end up working with tomorrow,' Brendan mused. 'I hope it's not Peter.'

'Perfect Peter,' Lina groaned, because there was a good chance that she'd be working with him when Brendan went on paternity leave and Pedantic Peter could also be Peter's nickname. 'Well, if you do end up with him, just remember that it's only temporary *and* that it's overtime.'

'I certainly need it.'

'Me too,' Lina agreed. 'This shift tomorrow is going to help pay for my next trip.'

'Another one?'

Lina nodded. She loved nothing more than to get away. It was the time she got to not just let down her guard but to think…or not. Her relationship with her family was complex, her flatmate was wonderful but always *there* and as well as that her work was stressful—it required a series of rapid decisions and being assertive, while at other times a lot of aimless killing time, as they were doing now.

Walking, wherever her train or coach ticket took her, replenished Lina. But there was another reason she had been away so much lately—she was seriously considering relocating from London and was quietly working out her options, not that she had told anyone. Soon, though, she would have no choice but to share the news. These days she was all too often on the phone with the bank and estate agents and Brendan had noticed. Aside from that, she had applied for a job in Newcastle and needed a preliminary reference.

'I've been thinking...' Brendan said as he peered into his salad wrap as if hoping some ham and cheese might miraculously appear.

'About what?'

'Your love life.'

'I have no love life,' Lina said. 'So you can save your grey matter, I really am through. Men are a mystery and one I have no wish to solve—I've decided that I'm sticking with Gretel...' Gretel was her needy and demanding ancient diabetic cat.

'Please.'

'I mean it,' Lina said. 'It's been months since I've been on a date and I intend to keep it that way. I'm just sick of...' Her voice trailed off and she looked over at Brendan, wondering if now was the time to tell him the plans she had in mind.

'Sick of what?'

'I don't know,' Lina said, deciding against telling him just yet—she knew Brendan would try to dissuade her and so instead she spoke of other things on her mind— men, or the lack of decent, single ones. 'Being dumped, being let down, being left sitting alone in a restaurant while he makes his escape...'

They had worked together for more than two years and so Brendan knew about her rather disastrous love life, in the same way she knew about his and Alison's difficult journey with IVF and the upcoming birth of their baby.

He didn't know all of it, though.

Lina wasn't sure if it was bad luck or poor judgement that plagued her, but at twenty-nine she didn't have so much as a long relationship to her name, let alone a broken engagement, or anything of note really. Just awful dates or, what she considered even worse, wonderful dates, followed by more dates, and bed—except, just as she got her hopes up, she'd find out he was cheating, or he failed to call, or it all just petered out, or she was told she was too abrupt, too work obsessed, not feminine enough...

'I don't think there are any good guys left,' she admitted.

'Of course there are. You just go into things expecting to be let down. We're not all like your dad, Lina...'

And though Brendan was trying to say the right thing, even that annoyed her—not that she let it show.

Oh, her friends all knew about her father's leaving and moving overseas, they just didn't know the friable scar it had left on her heart—one that bled on contact. Lina kept her deepest feelings well tucked away. Everyone carelessly assumed that she must be angry with her father for leaving them to live in Singapore, when the truth was that she simply missed him, and still, to this day, wondered what she had done wrong. How someone who had supposedly loved her could simply get up and leave and make so little effort to keep in touch.

But instead of telling Brendan the truth she offered a blithe response about her dating life, one she had almost come to believe. 'I just can't be doing with it all…'

'You should try online dating.' Brendan suggested, but she shook her head even as he persisted with the idea. 'That's how Alison and I met.'

'I never knew that!'

'Best thing I ever did.'

But Lina wasn't convinced. While it was true that he and Alison were utterly devoted, Brendan seemed to think that just because it had worked out so spectacularly for himself and Alison, true love was a mere swipe away.

'I did try it,' Lina admitted as she gazed out through the windscreen. The clouds had parted and she looked out at the blue hour, the delicious navy sky that crept in just before dawn. 'Several times.' She gave a tired laugh as she thought of the hours of preparation her beautician flatmate had taken to deem her suitable for a date—her pale skin had been fake tanned, her wavy hair straightened and smoothed, her green eyes framed with fake eyelashes and eyeliner and the photo had been taken at an angle that supposedly slimmed… 'Shona got me all tarted up for my photo.'

'You never said.'

'No, because it didn't work out. I got loads of responses but it would seem I'm a bit of a let-down in the ample flesh.'

'Well, then, put up a picture of yourself as you…'

'I tried that too,' Lina sighed, thinking of the real picture she had put up of herself, dressed in walking gear sitting on top of a snow-capped hill, feeling relaxed and accomplished and at peace. '*She's* nowhere near as popular, at least not with anyone I find attractive.'

It was a fact.

The type of men she liked seemed to like the type of woman she wasn't.

Lina spent most of her life at work and in overalls and steel toecap boots. On her days off she liked nothing better than to take a coach or train and go walking and exploring. There was no real reason for make-up, let alone heels and glamorous outfits, and anyway she felt stupid in them.

She had been raised on her brother's cast-offs and the only real concession that she was female had been that her mother had trimmed her long black hair now and then, rather than taking the clippers to it like she had for her brothers. The only sexy clothing she possessed was her vast collection of *gorgeous* colourful underwear—not that she would be discussing that with Brendan!

'Men *say* that they like independent women…'

'They do,' Brendan assured her, 'though you are a bit bossy…'

'I'm assertive,' Lina corrected. Well, at least she was at work. 'Have a sandwich if you want one.'

'Assertive, then,' Brendan agreed as he took a sandwich. 'Forthright.'

And she was, except what Brendan didn't know was that it was a learned trait.

She had been so sensitive growing up.

Every tease from her brothers had felt like a bee sting, and her mum, whom Lina adored, could be described as tactless at best. The only person who had understood her finely tuned ways had been her dad. Well, she could remember long walks, when her mother and brothers had chosen to stay on the beach or back at the holiday house they'd rented, and she'd tell her dad about trouble at school, or a friend that had turned out not to actually be one…

It had broken her heart when he'd left and since then her walls had gone up.

But that sensitive edge had surfaced again during her nursing training. She'd often considered quitting, and though she'd loved paramedicine, during her grad year as a paramedic on several occasions it had hurt too much and she'd considered simply walking away.

Well could Lina remember a wretched shift, going from a disaster into the mundane and just wanting to pause a moment and cry. She had gone to her mum's, hoping for wise words and comfort—not exactly her mother's forte. Instead, after a brief break when she'd taken a few days off to wander the countryside and gather her thoughts, she'd realised that if she seriously wanted to pursue paramedicine as a career then she had to toughen the hell up—at least on a surface level.

The tough, assertive, wickedly funny Lina had sort of become the norm—except that the tough, assertive, wickedly funny Lina everyone knew wasn't entirely her.

'My last date said I spoke about work too much,' Lina admitted.

'Alison says it's all I talk about too,' Brendan said, and Lina couldn't help but laugh.

'What's so funny?'

'At work *all* you talk about is Alison and the baby...'

'Guilty as charged,'

As Brendan smiled fondly, Lina felt a wave of...not envy, more pensiveness. She didn't mind a bit that he talked about the wonderful Alison all the time—in fact, it rather restored her faith in men.

Close to thirty, Lina was more than a little jaded as she examined her dating past with her colleague. 'The one before complained when I changed his tyre when he got a flat. He said I emasculated him.'

'Ha-ha,' Brendan said.

'I don't really have interests. Well, it's not as if I go to the gym…'

'You have your walking.'

'Yes.' Lina said, 'but I do it so lazily. Remember that guy I met who turned out to be a racewalker! That date nearly killed me!'

Brendan laughed.

'I like food, but even that's complicated. I'm not a foodie…'

'You like cakes and puddings…'

'And sandwiches,' Lina added, 'but only particular combinations.'

'You like antique shops,' Brendan reminded her. 'Though maybe leave that out of your online bio, or you'll be attracting the oldies.'

'Oh, I already do!' Lina sighed.

'Wear a bit of make-up now and then, have wine instead of beer…'

'Careful,' Lina warned.

'Be more agreeable…' He was really teasing her now. 'Ask him if he'd like his slippers warmed…' He turned and smiled. 'Just be yourself, Lina.'

Which was all well and good in theory, except *herself* didn't seem to be getting very far! And she was about to quip the same, but there really was something about the blue hour, that slice of time before dawn, that made you delve a little deeper.

Maybe it was that Brendan had become such a good friend.

Or perhaps she was just tired, but for whatever reason Lina admitted a deeper truth. 'I think it would be harder…'

'What?' Brendan frowned.

'Being completely yourself, only to then have them leave. It's better to hold a part of yourself back.'

Brendan, as he ate her last egg sandwich, respectfully disagreed.

CHAPTER ONE

'WHAT DOCTOR'S ON TONIGHT?'

As he made a mug of tea from the kitchenette beside the staffroom, consultant Garth Hughes could hear the night team chatting away.

'Huba,' said May, the nurse in charge, referring, in her thick Irish brogue, to one of the junior doctors. 'I just saw her in the changing room.'

'Desmond until midnight and Garth through till morning,' someone else chimed in. 'He's back from his leave.'

'Well, hopefully the break has put him in a more cheerful mood,' May said, and then, because she'd just seen him in the kitchen, added loudly. 'And I'd say it to his face if he were here.'

'I know you would, May,' Garth responded as he squeezed out his teabag with a wry smile and then took his mug into the crowded staffroom.

He glanced around for a seat and took one of the few available.

'Well, has it?' May pushed, but then forgot about the consultant on call tonight, clearly delighted by who had just walked in. 'Lina!' She gave a bright smile. 'I was hoping that we'd get you.'

'I thought I was going to be late…' she said, and as he stirred his tea Garth glanced up at the new arrival.

She *looked* late.

Her long dark hair was untied and she was wrapping a stethoscope round her neck and clipping on a lanyard, as well as seeming a little breathless and just…rushing. 'I promised to drop in on Mum and she wouldn't stop talking and then when I got here I couldn't find the scrubs…'

'They've been moved,' Dianne said. 'The surgeons keep pinching them so they're behind the lockers…'

'I know that now,' Lina said as she took a seat next to Garth and bent over to do her runners up. 'But I felt like the new girl having to ask where they were…'

'You're never the new girl,' May said. 'How's Mum?'

'Off out on a hot date,' Lina replied. 'I had to do her roots. She tells them she's mid-forties.'

'If I remember rightly she was mid-forties when you did your training.' May laughed and then added for the benefit of anyone who didn't know, 'Lina did her placements here.'

It was as much of an introduction as anyone really got—the roster was so big and fluid that there were new faces all the time, except it was clear to Garth that, though in his six months at The Primary he'd never come across her, Lina was something of a regular.

Still, the new addition to the room was quickly forgotten by all as May resumed her grilling of him.

'Well, has it?' May said, and looked at directly at Garth.

'Sorry?' He was more than used to a break in the conversation and May's ability to pick up from where she'd left off, but unusually he was completely unable to recall what they'd been talking about before Lina had arrived.

The new addition's arrival *hadn't* been forgotten by all. In fact, Garth was by far too aware of her.

She took up too much space.

Well, she barely touched him, but she'd moved on from doing up her runners to pulling her long black hair into a ponytail and was just this fidgeting ball beside him, filling up his senses, flooding them with newly washed hair and then the sound of a fizzy pop as she opened a can of soft drink and took a sip.

'That's better,' she said, completely to herself—except he had to actively resist responding.

Yes, it was hard to focus as she tapped little chinks of awareness into his usually impervious shield. He checked himself and tried to get back to whatever it was they'd been discussing before this woman who took up too much headroom had taken a seat beside him. 'You've lost me, May,' Garth admitted. 'What did you say?'

'Has the time off put you in a better mood?'

'Of course,' he responded wryly. Garth knew that May was half teasing and half delving.

He'd hoped the break would improve things, and for a while it had, but there had been grey skies and a steady drizzle of rain on his drive back from Wales that had matched his mood exactly. The days were still short and so by the time he had arrived back at his flat it had been dark, and the place that had been bought to provide a new start had felt nothing but cold and empty.

Or was it that *he* felt cold and empty?

It really was a case of one foot forward and ten steps back, but then trips to Wales always did that to him.

'How *was* your break?' Dianne asked.

'Fine.' Garth answered, when in truth the last part had been hell.

A necessary hell, though.

'You had two weeks off, didn't you?'

God, why didn't they let it drop? Garth thought to himself. Yet, conversely, he knew he'd be the first to ask about a colleague's holiday, or how their weekend off had been. As well as that, he'd promised he would make more effort, really give his all to this new start, and so he answered, 'Yes, two weeks.'

'Where did you go?' May joined in the rather one-sided conversation. 'What did you do with yourself? Did you catch up with your family?'

He was tempted to answer honestly, not because he wanted the sympathy, more for the bliss of the silence that would inevitably follow, but instead he deflected. 'No.' Garth gave a shake of his head. 'There just wasn't time. To tell you the truth, I was busy with...'

His voice lowered and he leaned forward a little, as if about to share a secret, and May eagerly leaned forward too, clearly delighted that the very private Garth was about to reveal more of himself. 'Did I tell you that I booked in to have a personality transplant during my leave, in the hope I'd suddenly start sharing with all of you the ins and outs of my private life?' There was the sound of laughter from beside him and clearly Lina got his slightly sarcastic response.

So too did May. 'It didn't take, then.'

'No,' Garth said, 'it didn't take.'

'Oh, well.' May stood up to head out and face the night, as did the rest of the nursing team. 'We'll just have to work with what we've got.'

It was all good-natured teasing, and as the staff, Lina included, stood to leave, he called them back. 'I did bring you these, though.' He placed a ginormous paper bag, all shiny with butter, on the coffee table. 'They're best eaten on the day they were made...'

'What are they?' May asked, picking up the bag and peering into it.

'Welsh cakes.'

'They don't look like cakes.' May frowned as she took one.

'They're called bakestones,' Dianne said as she helped herself to two. 'My gran used to make them for us.'

'Well, I've never heard of them,' May admitted, taking one herself and wrapping it in tissue. 'I'll have one with my next coffee.'

A few others dived in, but he found himself watching as Lina held back, even though she sniffed the air and gave a slight lick of her lips. 'Help yourself,' Garth offered, guessing she wasn't taking one as she wasn't a permanent member of staff.

'Maybe on my break…'

'They'll be gone by then,' Garth said. 'I wouldn't wait if I were you.'

'Well…' Lina said as she took one and wrapped it in a tissue. 'Thanks very much.'

'You're welcome.'

'Don't mind him,' Garth heard May saying to Lina as the nursing staff spread out across the department. 'I'll warn you now, his bark is worse than his bite.'

As their voices faded into the distance, Garth wasn't exactly surprised to hear May's first summing up of him but, yes, it both registered and stung. He'd been determined to come back from his break with a new attitude.

New flat.

New start.

Well, that had been the plan, but instead, when they'd asked about his break, he had fallen at the first hurdle.

May had had a quiet word with him before he'd left. Well, not a word, more she had asked a pointed question. They'd been drinking tea in May's office, going through the mountain of paperwork that was always piling up, when she'd asked if there was trouble at home.

'Trouble at home?' He'd frowned, wondering where the hell that had come from.

'I'm just asking because when I was going through some difficulties with my son, well, I tended to bring things to work a bit. I never meant to, of course. If there is a problem at home then know that you can speak to me—it would never go any further.'

'May...' He'd given an incredulous smile. How the hell could there be trouble at home when there was no one at home? But then he'd swallowed, realised perhaps that he was being told, albeit kindly, that he wasn't the sunniest to have around. 'There's no trouble at home.'

'Good,' May had said. 'It was just a stab in the dark. I mean, I don't even know if you've a family...' Perhaps she registered his frown. 'Okay, I know a little. I was on the interview panel, Garth...'

He gritted his teeth because, yes, there was a large gap in his résumé that protocol dictated he explain the necessary, but from that point on he had refused to discuss it. 'We don't all put photos up on our desk, May,' he had said tartly, glancing at the array on hers. 'Are there any problems with my work?'

'None,' she'd said. 'You're an excellent doctor.' Which might sound like a compliment except there was no elaboration.

'Is that a backhanded compliment?'

'It's an observation, Garth. You're an excellent doctor, and you're great to work with, but I can't attest to much else because you don't give us anything else to go on.'

May's observation he had taken seriously.

Oh, he wasn't about to open up to May. And there was

never going to be any chance of him being all ho-ho-ho, but with the new flat and two weeks' break he had been determined to come back a little more, well, open.

Like Lina.

She remained in his head and that quietly stunned him—and Garth wasn't used to feeling like that.

Aside from the immediate physical attraction to Lina, which was unsettling in itself, were the glaring disparities on display to him. He'd met her for all of two minutes and he already knew more about her life than the entire department knew about his: she had a presumably single mum nearby who lied about her age and dated, and to whom she seemed close, she'd worked at The Primary before and hated feeling like the new girl…

All that gleaned in one breezy conversation, whereas they had to turn the thumbscrews to get information out of him.

Garth knew he was way too remote with them all.

He looked at the stupid cakes, which had been a sort of olive branch, an effort to show that he did appreciate his team.

They knew that, surely?

He told them often enough and he thanked them and debriefed them after difficult cases and *always* had their backs, but, no, he was not going to sit in the staffroom and tell them where he'd been on his days off, or even hint at the hell of the past couple of days.

It was, he had found, far better to leave his private life at home. Except this wasn't a locum position or a temporary role, it was a permanent position, his first since—

Garth closed his eyes.

All these years on and he still could not say it easily, even to himself.

* * *

Lina wasn't quite sure who May was talking about as they headed through the unit.

She hoped the conversation was about Garth, because there had been a prickle of awareness between them and she wanted to know more about him, but May's words about his bark being worse than his bite didn't quite correlate with the man who, while a touch distant, had seemed friendly.

'Who?' Lina checked.

'Garth, the consultant on tonight…'

'He seemed okay,' Lina said. 'Mind you, he did give me a biscuit and we all know that I can be bought for food!'

May laughed. 'Have you come across him before?'

'No.' Lina said, casting her mind back. Her work as a paramedic was so variable that sometimes she could be at The Primary twice in a single day, while at other times there might be weeks in between cases. 'I don't think so.'

'He comes across as the most miserable sort—I mean, grumpy doesn't even begin to describe it—unless you're a patient, of course, *then* he's nice. I've a soft spot for him, though.'

'What sort of soft spot?' Lina nudged, making May laugh.

'A motherly soft spot, you cheeky thing. The trouble with Garth is he's not…well, he doesn't *let* himself be one of us. I'm working on it, though.'

It sounded like an odd statement, but Lina knew what May meant. ED could be a cliquey place at times, and though Lina only did the occasional shift, she kept herself *in*—stopping for a chat when she brought in a patient if time allowed, and attending the Christmas do and such. Now that she came to think of it, Garth hadn't been there—his dark good looks would not have gone unnoticed. A case in point: Lina had noticed him tonight the very second she had come into the staffroom.

Even sitting down, he stood out!

His black hair and unshaven scowling face had had her all flustered when she'd seen that the only spare seat was the one next to him.

Even his voice was sexy, with a deep tone and just a hint of an accent behind his well-schooled accent that she hadn't quite placed until he had mentioned the Welsh bakestones.

Yes, he was Welsh.

'Still, he keeps the place running well,' May added, 'which is all I'm asking for these days. It's good to have you with us for the night, Lina.'

May wasted no time allocating the work when they arrived in Section A. 'You don't need to hear the handover up here, Lina. Can you take Tanya the student and keep Section B open, please? Elise is already down there with the aim of having it closed by midnight…' She peered at the waiting room. 'Though I doubt that's going to happen.'

Section B was for the 'walking wounded', and though Lina would have preferred to be with the main action she was more than happy to go where she was put. Elise and the student were organised and Huba, the junior doctor, clearly knew her stuff, but tended to double-check everything, which rather slowed things down.

'I know you, don't I?' Huba said as she wrote up a tetanus shot and some antibiotics for a hand injury that Lina was about to dress, but not until *after* Garth came to check the wound. 'Have you worked here before?'

'Not for a while,' Lina said. 'Well, not as a nurse. I

think you know me from when we brought in a burns patient a couple of months ago and you were on. I'm a paramedic.'

'Oh, yes.' Her shoulders briefly slumped. 'I do remember you now.'

'Dreadful, wasn't it?' Lina said, but Huba moved the subject away from that night.

'So you're a paramedic *and* a nurse? How does that work?'

'I studied nursing and graduated,' Lina said, 'but my last placement was here in Emergency and I guess that was when I decided that I wanted to be a paramedic...' She didn't get to finish the conversation because Garth had arrived and Huba seemed a bit flustered by that fact.

'Thanks for this, Garth. I just wanted you to check this hand before he goes home. I'm worried that he's not giving us the full story and that it's a human bite.'

'You've put him on antibiotics?' Garth checked as he read through the notes, 'and brought him back to hand clinic for evaluation tomorrow...'

'Yes, but I'd just like you to check for function. I'm worried that there might be a nicked tendon and that he might need admitting.'

Garth took the card and stalked off to the cubicle then turned and looked at Huba. 'Are you coming?'

'Of course.'

They returned just a couple of moments later and he handed Lina the card. 'Huba's right—it is a human bite, not that he's admitting to it. We'll see him in hand clinic tomorrow. Stress again the importance of elevation and that he really needs to come back for review.'

'I will,' Lina said as he glanced around at the thinning-out Section B waiting room.

'And perhaps start to close up here,' Garth said.

Lina started to respond that she was about to, when Huba chimed in. 'May wants it kept open till at least midnight.'

Lina stood up, wearing not quite a frown but a smudge of one, because May *hadn't* said that. In fact, May would like nothing more than Section B to be closed in a timely fashion and all staff working the main section, but of course she wasn't going to correct Huba in front of her senior, so instead she gave a nod to Garth. 'Sure,' she said to his departing back, and she could feel not so much a chill in the air but more a certain tension, and that was confirmed when Huba put down her pen and ran a worried hand over her brow.

'I shouldn't have called him up to check on that hand.'

'Of course you should if you're concerned. And you're right about the human bite—they can turn nasty,' Lina said, though in fairness Huba called Garth up a lot. 'He shouldn't make you feel bad for asking.'

'He doesn't make me feel bad. If anything, he's more than willing to have me run things by him. It's just that I'm always asking these days.' Lina wasn't sure she understood. 'That night of the house fire…' Huba said, and her brown eyes suddenly filled with tears and she shook her head. 'It doesn't matter.'

Clearly it did matter, because Huba went very quiet then, and though curious as to what might have happened, Lina decided it would be unfair to push as Huba clearly didn't want to talk further about it.

It had been a very fraught night, with three little children fatally injured as well as their mother, and though she couldn't recall Garth being there as she herself had rushed the mother in, perhaps he had been around, and, like a lot of people that night, not at his sunniest.

'If you want to talk…' Lina said, and touched Huba's arm.

'Thank you,' Huba said, but she shook her head. 'I'll be fine.'

'Or a coffee?' she offered.

'I would love one.' Huba smiled.

'That I can do!'

She made Huba a drink and there were still a couple of the Welsh cakes in Garth's bag, so she put them on a plate and brough them around, but even as she put them down for a grateful Huba, the intercom buzzed and May asked if Lina could come now for a patient expected in Resus. 'Now!'

It was bedlam up in Section A, with the cubicles all full and stretchers lined up awaiting admission, where Lina would usually be as a paramedic. She headed straight into a very full resus. There was a red-in-the-face two-year-old screaming and a lot of the staff were with him; as well as that, a crash team was working on a young woman but May urgently signalled her to head to the middle bay. 'We've got a STEMI coming in, the second on cardiac team has been paged, but we're tied up with this amitriptyline OD. It's just you and Garth until they get here.'

A STEMI was a very serious type of heart attack and one in which Lina was well versed and trained. 'Does the cath lab know?' Lina asked, but May was back to concentrating on her own patient now, so Lina ducked into the middle bay.

Garth was there, pulling up drugs, and looked a little less than impressed when he saw that help had arrived in the shape of the casual nurse.

'Where is everyone?' he said. 'The patient that's coming in is time-critical.'

As if she didn't know! Still, Lina bit back a smart response and more suitably replied, 'The first on team are tied up next door.'

'I know that,' Garth retorted. 'I called them.'

'The second on team has been paged,' Lina said, while knowing he really meant where the hell were the nursing staff? 'I'm going to check that Cath Lab knows.'

Thankfully, because all her nursing shifts were done at The Primary, Lina had a list of extension numbers clipped to the back of her lanyard and had soon ensured that all the relevant staff had been alerted. She wheeled back a spare IVAC pump to the bay and was opening packs when the paramedic team wheeled in the grey-faced, barely conscious patient.

Annette, one of the paramedics, did a slight double take when she saw Lina, but now was not the time for a catch-up so instead she handed over the patient.

'Walter James, fifty-eight years old, in London on business, no previous history or allergies...' All this was said while the man was moved from the stretcher to the resuscitation bed.

'Mr James, you're at The Primary,' she said as she attached him to the hospital's own equipment, but he was barely responsive. She started running a twelve-lead ECG as Garth examined the one that the paramedics had brought in as they continued the handover.

'Any family?' Lina asked Annette.

'An ex-wife in Nottingham is all we could glean before his BP dropped.'

Lina looked at the man on the bed. Though she was very tough, things still got to her at times...and this was one of those times.

Still, she pushed all thoughts of her dad and the unfortunate timing of his heart attack out of her mind as the paramedics concluded their handover.

'Thank you,' Garth said to them as he worked on the patient. 'Excellent work…'

Well, even if he was a bit bearish, the fact that he thanked the paramedics won Lina onside. She was so used to being ignored when they brought in a critically ill patient; it was a good consultant who actually took a second to thank them.

Then he got back to barking as the patient's heart rate suddenly dropped down to thirty and he commenced cardiac massage. 'He needs intubating,' he told Lina, as if she were a schoolgirl on work experience. 'Can you take over the massage while I—?'

'Fine,' Lina said, not remotely fazed that it was just the two of them. After all, that was how she usually worked.

The drugs were already pulled up and the intubation kit opened, so that even as he spoke she was taking over the massage while he quickly got some drugs into the unfortunate man and then looked around for another IVAC pump.

'There's one there.' Lina nodded as she pumped on the man's chest.

It was all very quickly done, and very soon Mr James was intubated and with the drugs circulating in his system thankfully soon had a decent cardiac output. In fact, by the time the anaesthetist and cardiologist had arrived his blood pressure was improving.

'How are we doing?' May popped her head around the curtain.

'All good.' Garth nodded. 'We're going to move him up to the catheter suite. How's the young girl?'

'They're moving her up to ICU. Garth, can you speak

to her relatives again? They really don't understand just how critical she is.'

'Sure.' He nodded.

'What about this one?' May asked. 'Any relatives?'

'No. There's just an ex-wife so far,' Lina responded, going through his wallet. 'There's nothing on his phone.'

'Well, why don't I take over here,' May suggested, 'while you try and find out some more?'

As she stepped out, Dianne was preparing the overdose patient for her move to ICU. Lina was more than used to working backwards to glean details and so she headed to Reception and Triage and did her best to piece together events, but she returned to Section A a short while later really none the wiser.

Lina found Garth as he came out from speaking with the OD's family and told him the little she had been able to glean. 'The only contact I can find is an ex-wife. I've tried to call his work but given that it's midnight I haven't had much luck…'

'No ICE contact on his phone.'

'No,' Lina said, because she had checked what she could access and unfortunately there were no details. 'I'm waiting for someone from the hotel to call me back, though they weren't exactly helpful.'

'Well, I'd better call the ex-wife,' Garth said. 'I wonder how pleased she'll be to hear from me, though…'

'She'll probably appreciate knowing, but even if not she might be able to point you in the right direction…' She paused. He was a consultant after all and would know all this, but it didn't stop her adding, 'They might have children together.' She gave a pale smile. This patient really was a little close to the bone for her—not that Garth could know that. Her own father had suffered a major heart attack years ago and they hadn't found out until thirty-six hours later.

She didn't want the same for the family of Mr James.

'Well, I'll go and call her. Thank you,' he added. 'Good job.'

'And you,' Lina said, just as she would if it were Brendan, or any other colleague. 'Well done.' She saw May approaching and gave her a smile. 'I'm just heading back to Section B.'

'No, I'm closing it,' May said. 'You go and take first break.' Lina's lips pressed together a fraction—first break was the one no one wanted because it made the rest of the night a very long one.

May must have seen the press of her lips. 'If you don't want first break then come and work for us full time and you'll get your pick of dinner breaks.'

'I'm not that desperate.' Lina smiled and headed to the kitchenette where she made a coffee and took her lunchbox from the fridge. She then made her way to the staffroom, and long before she was hungry opened up the foil on her tuna, lettuce and mayo sandwiches.

'Gawd.' Les, the porter, waved his hands in the air. 'You don't change, do you? If it's not eggs you're eating it's tuna.'

'I need the protein to keep me going.' Lina laughed. 'Do you want one?'

'Might as well if I've got to sit here and smell it,' Les harrumphed, taking one of the offered sandwiches. 'They've had me running up to ICU twice. Running at my age…'

'I can't run,' Lina admitted.

'Well, jogging,' Les conceded.

'I can't jog either. A brisk walk, maybe…' They laughed and they chatted and moaned, but not for long—

Les was soon buzzed to take another patient to the ward. Sitting there alone, her sandwiches done, Lina was too full to contemplate the Welsh cake and, ten minutes before her break ended, decided to head back out to the unit. Before she made it to Section A, though, she saw Brendan, making up a stretcher, having just brought a patient in.

'Hey.' Lina smiled, and given she wasn't yet due back from her break she stopped for a little chat. 'How's it been?'

'Busy,' Brendan said, and told her about a stabbing that had brought them over this way, and then the patient they had just brought in—Mrs Amy Hill. 'She's confused. Just lost her husband over Christmas and keeps asking where he is, poor lady. She was fine yesterday, according to her carer—as bright as a button.' She liked it that Brendan really took the time and care to find out about his patients.

'How are things your end?' Brendan asked as he threw the blankets into the linen skip and then did a double take when he looked up. 'What happened to your eyebrows?'

'Shona tinted them,' Lina said. 'I feel like Groucho Marx '

'Who?' Brendan frowned and then got back to finding out about her night. 'What's it like on the other side?'

'Good!' Lina replied enthusiastically. 'We had a STEMI.' Odd to some, but Brendan gave an appreciative nod as she told him how well it had gone, but she could see his mind was wandering and as he took out his phone to check it, she guessed where his thoughts had gone. 'How's Alison?'

'We were in here earlier. Alison thought she'd gone into labour and we spent the afternoon up on Maternity,'

Brendan said worriedly. 'They put her on the monitor for a couple of hours and then sent her home. The midwife said she didn't think it would be too long. I just hate leaving her on her own…'

'I know you do.' Lina put a sympathetic hand on his arm. Brendan was, she was certain, going to faint when his beloved Alison actually went into labour and she repeated the same platitudes that she had, over and over, in recent weeks. 'I honestly think if something was happening, Alison would let you know straight away.'

'Really?'

'Yes,' Lina said patiently. 'She'd be straight on the phone to you.'

'I know you're right, it's just…'

'You're worried.'

'I'm beside myself,' Brendan admitted. 'And bloody Peter…' He nodded at his partner for the night. 'He's told me to stop banging on. Said he's sick of hearing about it. I tell you this much, I miss you tonight, Lina…'

'I know.' Peter maybe did have a point, Lina thought, but Brendan was just, well, Brendan, and currently, in the moments between patients, the only thing on his mind was Alison and their baby. 'Just ignore him,' Lina said. 'Maybe you could—'

But she never got to finish as her name was being abruptly called by Garth.

'Lina!' There was a bark of command in his voice as he walked towards them. 'When the two of you have finished your little get-together, could I ask you to sort out cubicle five so we can get the patient off the corridor?'

'Sure,' Lina said. 'We were just finishing up anyway.' Not that he was waiting to hear it. Garth was already striding off and she rolled her eyes at Brendan. 'He's not the friendliest, apparently,' she said. 'I'd better go.'

'And he'd better watch it.' Brendan smiled. 'That poor guy clearly has no idea who he's dealing with!'

Garth didn't—Lina was not one to be told off for no reason and stay silent. Working out on the road, she'd long ago learned to be assertive, even if she found it difficult at times. Though it still didn't come naturally to her, she had found it far better to stand up for herself at the start of rumblings than to simply let things slide.

And, for whatever reason, Garth was starting to rumble!

Cubicle five was a mess, but soon it was clean and restocked and ready for the next patient. Lina, though, was cross and when Garth stuck his head in to make sure the cubicle had been prepared, she put in her request: 'Can I have a quick word, please?'

'Of course,' he said, and stepped into the cubicle and gave her his attention.

'I was actually on my break back there when you told me off in the middle of the corridor…' Lina said. 'I don't need to be spoken to as if I've been caught talking in class, when the fact is…'

She stopped, not because she had run out of words, more because she had run out of breath, for it held in her lungs. His dark eyes were as navy as the blue hour, and now that she properly met them, she found they were just as captivating. She caught the very male scent of him, like soapy rain with a hint of citrus that was both subtle and lingering. And for someone who had sworn off men, she was fast finding it wasn't quite that simple.

It was physical, Lina told herself, remembering that she was angry, and with the little breath she could summon she spoke on. 'I have every right to talk to someone, without being told off—'

'You do, and I apologise.' Not satisfied with stealing

her breath, he now took the wind from her sails as he spoke on. 'I was completely out of line.'

'Oh!' She hadn't been expecting that. Lina had thought there would be if not a disagreement, then at least a little snap back from him, or some lecture, but instead he had straight away admitted to being in the wrong.

'Apology accepted,' Lina said.

'Thank you.'

'I'll go and bring in the patient.' As Lina walked off, she found that she was holding her breath and that her cheeks felt warm, as if there had been words…yet there hadn't been.

His apology had been unexpected and she felt all churned up, but not in an angry way.

It was all very polite, and also a little disquieting, in a way she couldn't properly define.

A slight rumbling of her own, perhaps.

CHAPTER TWO

'MRS HILL?' LINA checked the name band and notes and saw that it was the patient Brendan had brought in. Her observations were of concern, as was her blood glucose, which was rather high. She was restless and sweaty and needed to be seen. 'I'm going to bring you through now.'

Mrs Hill was tiny and feisty and over eighty—and very much did not want to be in the emergency department on a Friday night. 'I want to go home,' she kept saying as Lina got her undressed and did a set of obs.

'Well, hopefully you soon shall be,' Lina said, 'but first we need the doctor to take a look.' Only Huba was in the suture theatre with a patient who looked as if he might take a while. 'She really does need to be seen,' Lina explained, a little unsure as to why Huba was suturing when Dianne was assigned to be in here. 'She's febrile and very dehydrated…'

'Could you ask someone else?' she said, and held up her gloved hands. 'I've only just started.'

'Sure,' Lina responded, and as she came out of Theatre she saw May's slight raised eyebrow.

'Is Huba still in there?' May gave a shake of her head. 'Desmond should have finished an hour ago but is still tied up. I think Garth is just finishing up with a patient in Resus.'

'Okay.'

Garth was indeed just finishing up, but clearly had plenty else to be getting on with. 'Where's Huba?'

'Suturing,' Lina said, and watched his dark eyes glance down the packed corridor and the lines of paramedics waiting for their patients to even be assessed. He let out a tense breath and then took the admission card, but still he gave a very nice smile when he introduced himself to the patient. 'How are you, Mrs Hill?'

'Isn't it your job to tell me?' she asked. 'There's no reason for me to be here, I just want to go home.'

'Where is home?' Garth asked, as if politely making conversation while he read through the doctor's letter.

'You know full well where it is,' Mrs Hill retorted. 'It's written on the paper you're holding.'

'Okay,' Garth said, and he was very kind and patient with her as he went through a few other details and checked with her the medications she was on.

'It's all in the letter.'

'Okay,' he said. 'I'm just going to examine you, if that's okay.'

'No,' she said, her voice rising. 'It is not okay. I just want to go home.'

'Where are you, Mrs Hill?'

'Hospital.'

He questioned her very gently and Lina watched as the old lady battled to answer him, deflecting his questions at every turn.

'What does it matter!' she shouted when he asked her the year. 'With the mess the world's in.'

'I think you're confused, Mrs Hill,' he said. 'And trying very hard not to show it.'

'Wouldn't you be?' She sank back on the pillows and tears filled her hazel eyes. 'I don't know what's going on. There were men in my bedroom. They took me out of my bed.'

'That was the paramedics,' Lina said, and took the lady's hand. 'I know it must have given you a dreadful fright, but the district nurse was worried about you when she came to give you your medication for the night and I believe the GP called for an ambulance.'

'How did they get in?' She turned anxious eyes towards Lina.

'Your carer gave them the code.' Lina had seen it so many times, and she took a moment to explain things to the lady who had had such a terrible scare. 'Apparently you weren't yourself.' She looked over at Garth. 'Mrs Hill's just lost her husband.'

'Now, that wasn't in the note,' Garth said. 'I'm very sorry to hear that, Mrs Hill. When did your husband die?'

'It was my first Christmas without him.'

Finally they were getting somewhere.

'You're very dehydrated,' Garth said, checking the skin turgor on her hands.

'Bert used to bring me my tea.'

'It's hard,' he said, 'when those routines change, but we need to replace those fluids and I need to find out what's wrong with you.'

'I miss him.'

'Of course you do,' Garth said. 'What would Bert say if he were here?'

She gave a grudging smile. 'To let the doctor do his job.'

'Then will you let me do that please?'

She did, and Lina liked how he took his time with Mrs Hill, explained things carefully to her, and seemed to understand her proud struggle to hold onto normality. 'Your blood sugar is a little high, as is your temperature…' Now that she let him, he examined her carefully then took some blood and commenced an IV and asked Lina to obtain a urine specimen.

'I hate this,' Mrs Hill said as Lina sorted out the specimen.

'I'm sure you do,' Lina agreed, and listened as Amy reminisced about Bert. 'He never missed my morning tea,' she said, as she told her about all the little things her late husband had done for her. 'I tend to forget, but he never did.'

She seemed a lot more settled by the time Lina left her—with the curtains wide open and in full view of the nurses' station.

'How is she now?' Garth asked as Lina sent off the specimens.

'Settling,' Lina said, and she gave him a smile. Then her choice of word wavered because he nodded, but instead of getting back to his notes there was a brief suspension of time, which was, well, unsettling.

Nicely so.

Just a nod from him and a smile from her, except the small non-event took too long in her mind and when he didn't immediately turn and resume his notes…well, it seemed to take too long for Garth also.

'That's good,' he said.

'Yes.'

'I suspect a UTI. She's probably been neglecting herself a bit.'

'Yes, I think Bert took care of that side of things.' She paused. 'Well, he brought her tea and checked her blood glucose…'

'I'll wait for all the results,' Garth said, 'but she needs a geriatric referral. I'm sure the UTI is exacerbating things but there may be some underlying confusion that Bert was handling.'

Lina nodded. 'Or she's just grieving.'

'Yes.'

It was a completely normal conversation, except it felt different to Lina. He opened his mouth as if to say something, but then clearly decided otherwise and he climbed down from his stool and spoke to May. 'Is Huba still in Theatre?'

'Yes.'

He headed off in the direction of the theatres and Lina stood, a bit *unsettled* still.

'You okay, Lina?' May checked.

Apart from a sudden crush on your grumpy consultant? Lina thought. 'Fine,' she replied.

It was all very disquieting, this odd feeling of hers, this awareness of *them*. At around four in the morning, when the department was slowing down and he was updating charts on the computer and May took the chance for a little catch-up, she *felt* him listening.

'Is it nice to be back?' May asked her.

'It is,' Lina agreed. 'I always enjoy my shifts here.'

'I'm sure we could find a spot on the roster for you. If you ever do decide to come back to nursing you're to be sure and let me know.'

'Come back to nursing?' Garth glanced over.

So he *had* been listening, Lina thought. 'Lina's switched and is now a paramedic,' said May. 'She did all her nursing placements here but still comes back to us now and then…'

'Oh,' Garth said, and their eyes met, just for a second but long enough to know he was perhaps replaying the conversation he'd overheard between her and Brendan.

Lina gave the tiniest triumphant smile, because he *really* had had no right to tell her off.

'Wasn't that your partner in earlier?' May asked. 'Brendan. I thought I saw him.'

Lina nodded. 'He's on with Peter tonight.'

'God help him, then.' May smiled. 'Brendan's baby must be due any day now?'

'No, another three weeks or so,' Lina corrected, 'though Brendan's quite sure it will be tonight. Mind you, he's been saying that for days. Alison's booked to have the baby here, so I'm sure you'll all know.'

'He'll be passing around the cigars.' May smiled again. 'He's so excited.'

Lina didn't carry on the conversation. She was having trouble focussing on it, and that was rare for her, but she felt impatient almost for a pause just to think.

She was all churned up and unsure quite why.

'You're quiet, Lina,' May commented, as she filled out tomorrow's on-call board in preparation for the day staff.

'Am I?'

Perhaps she was, but she was just so conscious of Garth. It was ridiculous really, because he was completely out of her league—and that *wasn't* her being self-effacing.

Garth Hughes was stunning looking, and if her foray into online dating had taught Lina anything it was that she was fair to middling at best.

'Did that STEMI upset you?' May checked, briefly glancing over her shoulder.

'No,' Lina said, 'that's what we live for…' It sounded a bit flippant, but as paramedics it was a condition they were well trained to face. But then her dark humour could no longer deflect, because in truth it had upset her.

Maybe that was why she was all churned up. 'Maybe a bit,' she admitted. 'I mean, following up and trying to find the family and things, it just, well…'

'It reminds you of your dad?'

Lina glanced up. Of course May knew that her father had had a near fatal heart attack years ago while overseas. Well, May knew the gist, though Lina had never revealed to anyone the circumstances that had surrounded it.

May was right—the STEMI *had* unsettled her.

'Yes,' Lina admitted. 'It did upset me a bit.'

Garth found that he was waiting for Lina to elaborate. She did not.

And he found he was grateful for May's nosy nature, and wished for her to persevere with her line of questioning.

Yet she did not.

Instead, May asked a work question. 'Are you on tonight, Garth?'

'No,' Garth said. He was about to return to his notes but, reminding himself that he was supposed to be trying harder to be more sociable, added, 'I'll be unpacking.'

'Unpacking?' May said, clearly so surprised at this snippet of freely given information that she turned around.

'I moved into a flat on my break…'

'Oh!'

'It's very bare,' Garth elaborated, 'and now that all their furniture is out of the place, I'm starting to see that I might have bought a whole lot of trouble for myself.'

'So you've bought?'

'Yes.'

'Where?'

'Close by,' he responded crisply. Lina could almost

feel his reluctance as he answered May's question. 'It's not within walking distance, though,' he added. 'Or you'd be forever dropping in with something for me to sign…'

'I would too,' May said. 'Well, I guess if you've bought then you can't just up and run away.' May smiled, though her eyes met his and Garth knew she had seen his résumé and the multiple work locations over the last six years or so. Scotland, the Midlands, the south. Prior to that it had all been Wales. And, yes, the fact that he had bought a property for the first time in the said six years possibly spoke volumes. But for once May didn't delve further, just gave him a small smile and got back to updating the board. 'Looks like we're keeping you, then!'

'Looks that way. Right.' He stood up and yawned. 'I'm going to have something to eat, but call if you need me. Where's Huba?'

'Hiding in Theatre,' May said.

'Hiding?' Lina checked once Garth was gone.

'She's lost her confidence.' May nodded. 'You were working on the night of the house fire, weren't you?'

'Yes.' Lina nodded. 'I brought the mother in.'

'Well, poor Huba's taking some fallout from it and between you and me it's knocked her for six. Garth is doing his best to help her regain her confidence, but she second-guesses everything, or else she hides. Why do you think I closed Section B? Huba would still be down there now if she had her way.'

Ahh, now things were making a little more sense, and Lina conceded to herself that she had read the interaction between Garth and Huba wrong—he hadn't been reluctant to come down, it had been Huba berating herself for having to ask him.

'Goodness,' Lina sighed. 'Poor thing.'

'She'll get there,' May said assuredly. 'It's good she's got Garth looking out for her. For all I moan about his social skills, there's no one better to have in your corner.'

'Social skills?' Lina checked. 'He seems fine.'

'Sure enough, he's chatty tonight. Perhaps the break did him some good after all.'

With Garth gone and Huba hiding, everyone was busy, so Lina had a couple of minutes while she was restocking to hold a rather tricky conversation. 'May,' Lina ventured, 'I've got something I need to ask you.'

'You *do* want to come and work full time!'

'No.' Lina gave a tense smile. 'I've applied for a job and I wondered if I could put you down as a preliminary reference. I haven't told work yet...' Her lips pulled to the side as May turned around. 'I haven't told anyone.'

'Where's this job.'

'Newcastle,' Lina said.

'That's a long way off.'

'I know, and that's why I haven't said anything to anyone yet.'

'But your family's here in London, you've got friends in London...'

'Yes, but I can't afford a place of my own!' Lina said. 'I'm so over sharing. Dad was born in Newcastle and I've got some family there. I love it... We used to holiday there all the time.'

'But your life is here, Lina.'

'And I can make a new one there...' She went quiet as Huba came in. 'Hey.' Lina smiled.

'Where's Garth?'

'On his break,' May said, and then glanced over at Lina and gave a nod to their earlier conversation about May being a referee.

'Of course…' She nodded, but looked a touch confused rather than pleased.

Lina felt rather the same, but there was little time to dwell because patients were still coming in, and the results from Mrs Hill had also come through. Her potassium was raised so Lina ran them past Huba.

'How is she now?' Huba asked.

'Sound asleep,' Lina said, 'and I think the fluids have helped as she's a little more orientated.

'Would you bring her over to Resus?' Huba said. 'With a potassium that high she should be monitored.'

'Sure.'

'And maybe I should call Garth back,' Huba added.

'Lina was just going to get him to sign for a patient,' May interjected. 'She can let him know the results.'

Having put Mrs Hill on a monitor, Lina headed to the staffroom. She found that Garth was dozing with his head back on the chair, his eyes closed and his mouth slightly open. There was a feeling of recognition that stilled Lina and she stood there, confused for a second, and not quite knowing why.

Oh, that's right, she was to tell him about Mrs Hill.

Only it wasn't that.

Lina had the oddest feeling that she knew him, that she'd seen him before.

Well, of course she had, she told herself. He'd probably been on when she'd brought in patients… except it felt like something more.

Garth must have felt her standing there staring at him, for his eyes opened then and he turned his head and gave her a look.

'Is everything okay?'

'Of course,' Lina said, blushing at being caught looking, so to speak, and still she couldn't shake the feeling that she knew him from somewhere. 'I just need your signature on a couple of things and Mrs Hill's labs are starting to come back.' She ran through the more pressing ones.

'Okay.'

'May's just putting her on a monitor.'

'I'll come around.'

'Sure.'

'You're okay?' he checked.

'Of course,' Lina said, realising she was acting a bit oddly, though he clearly assumed it was for a different reason.

'I would never have known that the STEMI upset you until May said so. You were very efficient back there.'

'Thank you.'

'And if your father…' He gave a grim smile. 'Well, I'm very sorry.'

'My dad's not dead,' Lina said.

'Glad to hear it.'

'He travelled for work a lot and had a heart attack in a hotel in Singapore…'

'Ahh. Now I see…'

Only he didn't see. In fact, not even May, not even Brendan, knew the full story, but she found herself telling him. 'It was how my mum found out that he was having an affair.'

'Oh.'

'Yes. "Oh!"' Lina nodded. 'Well, that wasn't my mother's response, exactly.'

'How did she find out?'

'She didn't,' Lina said. 'Well, not for thirty-six hours. Everyone assumed his girlfriend was his next of kin…' She met his eyes. 'How did Mr James's ex-wife take it?'

'She's on her way now,' Garth said. 'She's probably already here. You were right, they do have children together.'

'Well, it's good that they all know.' She went to turn.

'I'm sorry,' he said, but in a different tone from the one he'd used before. 'It can't have been a great way to find out.'

'No,' Lina admitted.

'Did your mum go?' He was curious, in spite of telling himself to hold back. It was just that she intrigued him so. 'To Singapore, when she heard?'

'No,' Lina said. 'She went to visit a lawyer instead. Odd, isn't it…?'

'Odd?'

'I think I'd have jumped on the plane if only to slap him for being such an idiot to cheat on me… Well, not me, but you know what I mean…'

'I know what you mean.' He almost smiled, just a whisper of one, but Lina found herself wishing that his gorgeous, full mouth might stretch into one.

Oh!

And so rather than stand there wishing and thinking such things, she gabbled on quickly. 'I think we can all count ourselves lucky there was just an ex-wife in the picture tonight.'

She headed back to the unit, where they did their best to get the department in shape for the morning staff and clear the decks as much as was possible.

'And they'll still moan that we didn't wipe the trolleys down or something,' May muttered. 'Thank God I'm back on days next week.'

Her last job for the night was taking Mrs Hill up to the geriatric unit, and though the patient had dreaded it, she was greeted very warmly and soon settled into a bed with a huge warm cover.

'Breakfast is coming round shortly,' the accepting nurse told Mrs Hill, 'but I'll see if I can find you a cup of tea to settle you in.'

'They'll look after you here,' Lina said, glad to see Mrs Hill looking so much more relaxed and knowing that she was in the right place.

By the time she was back on the ward, May was getting ready to start handover. 'Once you've made up the trolley, you can get off,' she said as she signed Lina's time sheet. 'Thanks, Lina, it's been lovely to have you with us…' Her voice faded and then she excused herself from the handover for a moment and pulled Lina aside in a way only May could. 'Call me,' she said. 'If you want to chat.'

Lina was touched that May would actually stop the handover just to reach out to her. 'Thanks, May.'

'And of course I'll give you a reference, but don't go jumping into anything. Talk it through with me, if you like…'

She might just do that, Lina thought as she had a quick freshen up at the sink in the changing rooms. Throwing her scrubs into the linen bin, Lina managed a wry smile as she caught her reflection in the rather speckled long mirror.

Her gorgeous satin amber underwear, her only fashion weakness, would of course go unnoticed, but it always cheered her up anyway.

And that little dash of feminine luxury made her feel, well, better, that was all, even as she pulled on dark jeans and a huge grey jumper and then zipped on her boots. To that she added a large coat and very long scarf and headed out.

'See you, Lina!' Dianne called as she took the short-cut through the department to the exit. 'Nice working with you.'

'And you.' Lina smiled. 'See you.'

'Not too soon, I hope...' May teased, and Lina laughed, understanding that May was referring to the fact that she generally arrived in the department as a paramedic with a stretcher containing a patient.

'Thanks for the sandwich,' Les added, as he dragged a couple of oxygen cylinders for exchange. 'Though put less salt on them next time.'

They were a mad lot and Lina's smile remained unseen as she walked out of the department.

Except her smile was not quite unseen.

Garth Hughes glanced up from a patient's relative he was speaking to as a certain Lina Edwards left the department. His head told him to just let her leave, except he couldn't fully listen to logic right now. 'Excuse me a moment,' he said politely to the relative. 'Lina...' he called.

He watched as she turned, a slight flush to her cheeks, and he looked into vivid green eyes. It had been a long time since he had found himself intrigued by a woman. Aside from attraction, Garth couldn't quite pinpoint what it was that enthralled him, just that if he didn't do something now, he had no idea when or if he might see her again, and that suddenly mattered an awful lot. 'Could I have a quick word before you go?'

'Is there another cubicle you want me to clean?' she teased, and he smiled a wry smile that felt like *such* a reward for a night's work.

For his smile did not come easily, that much Lina had gleaned.

'About that—' he started, but Lina cut in.

'Really, it's fine.'

'Actually, it isn't,' Garth said. 'It would seem that I owe you a double apology.'

'Double?' Lina checked.

'Yes. Do you want to get breakfast once I'm done, so I can better apologise?'

'Breakfast?' Lina frowned as he nodded.

'Yes, and not at the canteen. I'd rather take this conversation away from May's exceptionally beady eyes. There's a café next to the hospital where we could meet.'

'There's a better one around the corner,' Lina said and told him the name. 'One of the perks of my job is knowing where to get breakfast.'

'I'll see you there then,' Garth said. 'Just as soon as I can get away.'

'Sure.'

'I might be a while—it depends what time Richard gets in and how busy we are.'

'It's fine,' Lina said. 'I'm very used to shifts going over.'

'Thanks.'

What she wasn't used to was sexy consultants asking to meet her for a private conversation. It was unexpected and it was unsettlingly nice.

Or, rather, Garth was unexpected and unsettlingly nice.

CHAPTER THREE

'Lina!'

She was known at the café too, although out of her paramedic uniform perhaps not quite so recognisable.

'I didn't realise it was you. The usual?'

Her usual here was a coffee and almond croissant but, though her stomach was pleading for carbs as it always did after a night shift, she decided to wait for Garth and shook her head. 'Just a coffee, thanks, and I'll have it here.'

'Sure.' The barista smiled and then asked the question that was on everyone's lips, because Alison and Brendan lived nearby: 'Has Brendan had his baby yet?'

'Not yet.' Lina smiled back and rolled her eyes. 'I'm sure we'll all know the very second it happens.'

The café was half-empty and she chose a seat by the window and then peered into her bag and looked for something, anything that might freshen up her appearance a touch, despite knowing it was pointless. Unlike Shona, who carried a kit that could transmute her from bedraggled to ravishing in seconds, Lina carried a plastic zip lock bag, the contents of which she'd already used—just a toothbrush and toothpaste, some deodorant and such. There wasn't even a lip balm hiding inside.

So instead of tarting herself up for her unexpected

breakfast date, she gazed out of the window, telling herself it wasn't a date…

Yet she had a feeling that Garth didn't often ask the casual nurse out at the end of her shift.

Or, knowing her luck with men, maybe he did; perhaps that was his modus operandi…

But it would be a while before she found out. Lina was at the end of her second coffee when he arrived, dressed in a heavy grey coat, which he hung on the hook. He had changed into black jeans and a jumper but even casually dressed there was a certain elegance to him.

And sexiness.

She'd been trying to ignore that fact all night, but now, outside work and about to sit face to face with him, it was as if her body finally allowed itself to acknowledge it, and she surprised herself by blushing.

Her blush was, she guessed, as rare as his smile.

'Hey,' he said, and took a seat. 'Sorry I took so long.'

'It's not a problem. I was going to get something to eat before I headed home. It's quite a way…'

'Where is home?'

He raised his eyebrows when she told him it was the other side of London. 'But I lived here when I did my nursing.'

'Have you eaten then?'

'No.'

She ordered her usual almond croissant and, deciding a third coffee might be a bit much if she was to have any hope of sleeping, chose tea. Garth chose the same, as well as a toasted sandwich.

'You were a nurse before you did paramedicine?'

'Well, a student.' Lina nodded. 'I didn't enjoy it as much as I'd expected to, though. I thought I'd made the wrong choice until I did my Accident and Emergency placement, except…' Her voice trailed off, guessing he didn't really want to know.

'What?'

'I found that I was jealous of the paramedics.'

'Really?'

She nodded. 'I found myself wanting to know what had happened before the patient arrived. May was brilliant; she arranged a couple of ride-alongs for me…' Their food arrived and there was a pause in the conversation as they both eyed their excellent choices.

'This looks so good,' Garth said, examining his sandwich.

'They know what shift staff need,' Lina agreed. 'These croissants are delivered at six each morning…' She tore her own open as she resumed their conversation. 'Anyway, I finished my nursing but then went on to study paramedicine and now here I am…' she looked up into those navy eyes '…sitting in a café on a Saturday morning waiting to find out why I'm owed a double apology.'

'I had no right to tell you off when you were on your break. Correction: I had no right to tell you off when I did.'

'We've already covered that.'

'I assumed that he was your partner, or boyfriend, or something along those lines…'

'God, no.' Lina pulled a face. 'What on earth gave you that idea?'

'When he said he was missing you.'

Lina smiled. 'He's missing me because I'm good to work with.'

'You are.'

'Can't have the staff flirting at work,' Lina teased,

and then paused as she realised it was now she who had perhaps misunderstood.

'It irked me,' Garth said.

Her lips began to round to form the W in 'why' and she suddenly wished she'd bothered with that lip balm as his gorgeous gaze fell down to there and realisation struck…and her *why* changed to a surprised 'oh!'

But she was still doubting her own conclusions. Was Garth saying that he liked her or was she jumping ahead?

'It irked me a lot,' Garth said, and then clarified, 'I don't get involved with people at work—deliberately so. I was just wondering if I should make an exception to my own rule when I saw you talking to your partner, who, as it turns out, isn't a partner in that sense… I came over high-handed. I'm not exactly Mr Sociable, but I don't go hauling out the staff for talking. At least, not normally…'

'It's fine.' Lina smiled, and actually it was better than fine. It really was the nicest apology she had ever received. His honesty was refreshing and his complete lack of game-playing as he told her that he liked her meant she felt able to admit to the same: 'I'm glad it irked you.'

'I'm glad that you're glad. I've worked at The Primary for six months now and our paths have never crossed. I'm sure I'd remember if they had…'

'I think they did,' Lina said, because she was sure now that she recognised him, but rather unsure how she could forget such a delicious detail. 'We're often there— well, not often, but…' She tried to place him and then suddenly she thought she had it. 'Were you working the night of the house fire? Huba said you were…'

'Yes and no,' Garth said. 'I was called in, but…' He cast his mind back. 'I think all the patients had been admitted by the time I got there. I'm certain I'd remember you.'

She nodded because she had thought exactly the same.

'What I'm trying to say is that I don't want to wait possibly another six months until our paths cross again.'

'I'm there all the time.'

They ate and they chatted, and while some of it was about work she mentioned her upcoming break, though there was a detail she left out: he certainly didn't need to know about her possible relocation to Newcastle…

'I'm wandering,' Lina said. 'Well, walking, I suppose.'

'Rambling?' he asked.

'No, walking.' Lina smiled. 'I go from one bed and breakfast to the next…'

'Trekking?'

'Walking.' Lina laughed. 'And while I do I come across plenty of trekkers and ramblers and such, but I really am not in that category. In my case there are also a lot of shops involved…' She opened her mouth to tell him about the antique shops and her obsession with vintage toy ambulances and such, but remembering Brendan's words decided instead to hold back a touch. 'I walk with a backpack and sometimes I take a bus or train, and in the evening I go to a bar or a nice restaurant or grab a takeaway. I have a map of the UK and Ireland on my wall and I tick off every town and village I've visited, all the ones where I've had a coffee or meal or glass of wine. Just passing through doesn't count.'

'How much have you covered.?'

'Not nearly enough, but I'm making a dent. I just plan my route and walk and…'

'What?'

'Breathe,' Lina said, 'and think, or don't think…'

'Sounds wonderful.'

She nodded. 'It is. Work's brilliant for it. I'm cramming my next lot of shifts and then heading to the Scottish borders in a couple of weeks.'

'Are you driving up?'

'No, I don't have a car. Anyway, I'll sleep on the train and that gives me four full days of just me and a rucksack.'

'You travel light.'

'Not when you're carrying it. It's just nice to get away, to see the country…' She took a breath. 'To put things into perspective, though…' She stopped.

Slow down, she told herself, because she found herself opening up far too easily where Garth Hughes was concerned.

Find his fault.

Find the reason he's…

She tried to gauge his age and put him in his mid-thirties and, given the flirting, hopefully single.

They hadn't got onto all that. It was just so much fun getting to know each other, except now it was late. Well, it was morning for some, but by night duty standards it was late—late and out of the blue. Lina yawned.

'Am I boring you?' he teased.

It was honestly tempting to switch her seat just to sit next to him, but instead, while the going was so good, it really was time for her to go to bed. 'You know you're not.' Lina smiled and stared back into those navy eyes that looked deep into hers. He tripped the switch in her heart and made flirting, at which she was usually terrible, so simple. 'I just need to go to bed.'

Another mutual smile but, gosh, it would be far too soon when they hadn't as much as kissed, yet… She was going crazy, Lina decided. Too little sleep did poor decisions make, and so she made her excuses and nipped to the loo.

'Go home!' she said to her reflection in the mirror and, as she walked out, she signalled to pay the bill, except the barista told her that it had been taken care of.

She walked over to Garth. 'Thanks,' she said.

'No problem.'

They walked out into rain and sunshine combined, the type of day where you had to squint at the brightness just before the sun dipped behind an angry cloud, and the rain felt cold. It felt so right to give in and face each other.

'You spoiled my line,' Lina said. And then he pulled her towards him and they kissed, something they had both secretly wanted for hours now.

Hours!

Oh, how they kissed.

He put his hands on either side of her face and his touch was so warm and tender. Their tongues mingled and it was like being drawn down a tunnel, into a vortex of delicious want. The sound of traffic seemed to dull and the cold disappeared and the rain felt delicious on their skin. His hands moved down so that they rested on her hips and they kissed slowly and languidly but with a deepening passion.

Nine a. m. kisses on a cold winter morning were surprisingly dangerous.

His eyes really were the darkest yet also the brightest blue, and they were staring deep into her own. There was a slight breathlessness between them, a gorgeous feeling of excitement, as if they were standing on the very edge of a mountain, surveying the view together.

'What *was* your line?' Garth asked.

'When you thanked me for paying I would have said, "You can get the next one…"'

'Ah.' Garth smiled. 'Well, I *am* getting the next one, and hopefully it will be tonight…'

Shona would no doubt tell her she should have said, *No, I can't tonight*, and not appear too keen and free on a Saturday, but feeling his body all warm and toned and pressed against her, it was impossible for Lina to feign nonchalance. 'Yes please…' Between kisses they sorted out the details. 'I really do have to go,' Lina said, 'or I'll be falling asleep on the tube and end up—'

'No,' Garth said, 'I'll drive you home.'

'Don't be daft.'

'Lina, I've kept you waiting an hour after your shift. It's the least I can do.'

Goodness!

Now, this was something she wasn't used to.

Lina's shifts often ended hours after their intended time and she was very used to just accepting the tired ride home, battling not to fall asleep and miss her stop.

It was incredibly nice to be spoiled with a lift.

They walked to his apartment, which actually was just around the corner from the hospital. 'Don't tell May how close it is,' he said, and thankfully he was sensible enough not to suggest that she come up.

Instead, they went to the underground car park and soon Lina was in his lovely warm car and being driven home. It was perfect—well, apart from his terrible taste in music, but Lina felt it was rather too early for her to say so.

But then…

'What *is* this?' she suddenly asked.

'Great, isn't it?' he said, misreading her question as enthusiasm. He glanced over and named some band she'd never heard of. Lina blinked, because it was like having root-canal treatment, but she chose to keep quiet—after all, he'd been so nice to give her a lift home.

And when they arrived at her flat, he kissed her so nicely and slowly goodbye that the boopy-doop music even slowed tempo and curled round her mind.

Bed!

With him!

She wanted to wilt and give in to temptation and invite him in, but she didn't want to endure the rise of Shona's eyebrows if she brought a guy home from work.

They both stared at each other for the longest time, as if a missing person had just been safely returned.

'I'm going up,' Lina said. She looked at the smudges under his eyes and knew he had quite a drive home. 'You'll be okay to drive?'

'I will be,' Garth said, 'but it's tempting to say I might need a lie down first…'

They were both laughing, and kissing, but Lina said again, 'I'm going up,' and this time prised herself off him.

She floated up the stairs and into her tiny flat, then ran to the living room window, and there he was, looking up. She felt like Rapunzel and wanted to let down her hair, certain that if she did he would climb up.

'Uh-oh.' Shona came in from the kitchen, holding a huge mug of coffee. 'I've seen that look before.'

'No, you haven't,' Lina said, because she had actually never felt like this before. 'He gave me a lift home.'

'Really?'

'He's nice—well, except for his taste in music…'

'So when are you seeing him again?'

'Tonight.' Lina beamed, and Shona did the same.

With her flatmate going out, it meant that she had the place to herself.

Or rather to herself and her boyfriend, Marcus.

Lina was positive, *positive* that Shona was about to ask if he could move in. He practically lived here already.

That was the trouble with flat sharing, as Lina had long since found out…

Anyway, she was too tired to think about that now so she had a quick shower and then made a mug of tea to take to bed. As she waited for the kettle to boil, she went to rinse out her lunchbox. But there, nestled inside, wrapped in tissue, was the Welsh cake she had taken last night and forgotten about.

''Night,' she said to Shona, even though it was the middle of the morning.

'Do you want to be woken up?'

'About five if you're around,' Lina said. 'Thanks.'

One of the absolute perks of night shift was closing the curtains on a wet, rainy day and climbing into bed with a huge mug of tea.

And a Welsh cake.

They might, as Garth had said, have tasted better on the day they had been made, but the sweet and spicy buttery biscuit was delicious, possibly more so because it had come from him.

Garth Hughes.

She had a date on a Saturday night, like a normal person, and not with someone who wouldn't match their photo, or who would be disappointed when they actually saw her in the flesh.

Or would he be?

Lina fell asleep thinking about her rather bland wardrobe and utter lack of make-up skills, and wondered how soon he'd be bored by her talking about work and country walks and her penchant for coffee and antique shops and food and, well, not an awful lot else…

CHAPTER FOUR

AND SO IT STARTED!

As a mug of coffee was plonked by Lina's bed, instead of wandering out, as she usually did, Shona hovered.

'Something smells good,' Lina commented, because there were gorgeous herby scents coming from their kitchen.

'Duck in plum sauce,' Shona said. 'It's in the slow cooker.'

'You made it?'

'Of course I didn't. Not that I'll tell Marcus that—you have to give yourself every advantage.'

'What happens when he finds out that you can't boil an egg?'

'He'll never find out, not if I can help it. What time are you going out?'

'Seven.' Lina yawned. 'What time's Marcus coming?'

'He should be home around then.'

Lina felt her nostrils pinch at Shona's choice of word. This wasn't his home, but as Shona sat down on the edge of the bed, Lina knew what was coming. 'You know his lease is up in a couple of months…'

'Shona,' Lina said, and closed her eyes. 'Can I just have my coffee…?'

'Sure.'

As Shona flounced out, Lina's knew that her own hackles were up and she didn't want them to be up tonight. She wanted to just enjoy looking forward to her first date with Garth, not focus on the upcoming expiration of Marcus's lease, and the inevitable conversations to be had.

Except there would be no enjoying tonight because not two minutes later her phone buzzed and she saw that it was Garth. 'Lina, you have no idea how much I hate to do this.'

'You're cancelling.' Lina said it for him, as her face pinched with disappointment.

'I'm working,'

'You're not.' She was her usual direct self. 'You told May you were unpacking this weekend.'

'I did, but I have a colleague who's having a bit of a rough time of it and I've just come off a long conversation with them and agreed to shadow them, which means I'm following their roster.'

'Oh.' He mentioned no name and gave nothing to indicate to whom he was referring, but Lina knew it was Huba. 'I'm suspicious by nature.' She gave a half-smile. 'Comes with the job...'

And with her dating life, Lina thought but didn't add.

'So,' Garth was practical, 'let's reschedule...'

Only the off-duty gods had it in for them: Lina was back on days and he wasn't off until her weekend away, with one exception. He told her about a jazz café near him, and said that he could *try* and get tickets for that trio she liked who were playing on Friday.

'Sorry?' Lina frowned. What trio that she liked?

'When I drove you home...'

'Oh!' The ones who felt like having root-canal treatment. Yet, while she wasn't into jazz, she was terribly into him and so she agreed.

'I am sorry about tonight.'

'It's fine,' Lina said.

It was and it wasn't.

'He cancelled?' Shona frowned as she came off the phone.

'It's no big deal.'

Shona wasn't so sure. 'Your very first date and he cancelled? Doesn't bode well, if you ask me.'

Lina hadn't asked, but even so it left that niggle of doubt wriggling in her stomach.

She felt dumped before they had even started.

He *had* let her down, Garth knew that, but he'd had little choice. And even if he couldn't fully explain the reason to Lina, it was the right thing to do because by Friday he could feel Huba's confidence returning.

'You're starting to get on my nerves.' Huba laughed, and so did he as they came out from seeing a patient.

He took no offence. 'That's the plan.'

It had been a good week workwise and he was looking forward to tonight, though he was rather sure May was onto him as she'd heard him earlier in the week, trying to get two tickets to the jazz café, and it had proved rather difficult. 'Any plans for the weekend?' she, oh, so casually asked.

'Some,' Garth said. 'Though I'll come in tomorrow for a few hours and try and get through some paperwork.'

'So not really here?' May checked.

'Not really here,' Garth agreed, 'so don't go adding me to the whiteboard. I'm hoping that I might finally get my unpacking done.'

'Any other plans?'

'Isn't that enough to be going on with?'

May's lips pursed as she fought to find out his real plans, but he was saved from further interrogation as Reception put through a call to her.

'North East…' May frowned as she took the phone then was of course all smiles and laughed. 'Oh, I wondered what on earth you were calling me for. Yes, Lina Edwards…'

Garth deliberately didn't turn his head, just carried on examining an X-ray image on his computer as he heard what a wonderful student nurse Lina had been before going on to study paramedicine, and she chatted on as only May could!

'She's worked here on and off for years,' May said, and continued to sing Lina's praises. 'I always request her if she's available, though that will have to stop if she's in Newcastle…'

And so the glowing reference continued.

'Yes… Yes… Oh, absolutely, yes… Well, I personally would be very sorry to lose her…'

Garth sat there, pretending to concentrate as May basically said what he already knew—just how wonderful Lina was.

And that she was planning to go.

It rather put a dampener on tonight.

In turn, Lina too was fast losing the magic.

'You have a song!' Brendan teased as they battled rush-hour traffic to get back to base. It had been a busy week and at this rate she might not even make it back in time to go out tonight.

'Yes.' Lina rolled her eyes as they sat at traffic lights.

'We haven't been out yet but we have a song, only I don't know what it is or who it's by…'

She hadn't told Brendan directly about Garth, or rather that her date was a doctor at The Primary, and he was distracted enough by his very pregnant wife to miss that the details were sketchy, and just assumed that it was someone she'd met online.

'But he cancelled on you last week?'

'Yep.'

Lina did not want to get into it with Brendan, especially after Shona's little sniff and doom and gloom forecast.

'Did he say why?'

'Work,' Lina answered, 'and if we don't get a move on I'm going to have to do the same to him.'

It was ten to six by the time she got home and doubts were pinging as rapidly as Shona's suggestions as to what she should wear.

'You can't wear jeans!'

'I've looked it up,' Lina said, running out of the shower wrapped in a towel and carefully selecting her absolute favourite underwear—the most gorgeous satin in kingfisher blue. And truly it wasn't selected with Garth in mind, it just made her feel fantastic when she was wearing it. 'It's casual,' she explained to Shona. 'Well, there's a dressier bit upstairs but we won't be at that…' She hoped not as, aside from the expense, downstairs there were club sandwiches and a craft beer she was hoping to try.

'But don't you want him to think you've made an effort? I mean, you wear jeans to the shops, jeans everywhere really, when you're not at work.'

Lina held her breath.

Shona was actually really nice, but they clearly

weren't destined to spend the rest of their lives living together. That was the trouble with flatmates, Lina had found: you got close, too close.

Shona would be a brilliant friend, if she didn't live in the same rather cosy space.

'I could wear the grey pinafore…' Lina said, running out of time as she searched through her wardrobe.

'Your interview outfit?' Shona scoffed. 'Try that dress of mine I told you about…'

'It's too much,'

'Lina, it really isn't.'

The trouble was, Lina liked Garth enough to try something different because what she'd done in the past had never worked.

Yes, she liked him enough to try on a violet dress that looked nice with black tights and flat shoes. She would wear her hair down for the first time in for ever and put on a slick of mascara too.

'I've got a nice trench coat…' Shona was enjoying herself now, and it was nice to chat and have a laugh. 'You look fantastic,' Shona said, and in truth it looked nicer than Lina had expected, although she wasn't sure about the clunky necklace that Shona had also loaned her. 'Is he picking you up?'

'No, the café is near his place.'

'And it's jazz?'

'Modern jazz,' Lina said, 'I think.' She honestly had no clue and that was *after* looking the trio up!

And then, just when she was thinking that Shona really wasn't that bad, and that maybe things would sort themselves out, *it* started up again…

It being the tricky topic of Marcus.

'Don't answer yet,' Shona said, 'but how would you feel about Marcus moving in?

As Lina opened her mouth to unfollow instructions and answer, Shona hurried to speak. 'It would help out with the rent, and he works shifts so…' Her voice trailed off. 'Just think about it.'

Lina had been thinking about it for weeks—it was the reason after all that she had an interview lined up in Newcastle.

She was so sick and tired of sharing.

The flat was gorgeous but seriously small and the thought of three of them fighting for the bathroom… As well as that, one of the advantages of her shift work meant that there was plenty of time being here on her own. Marcus was a shift worker too, so that would put paid to that.

As well as that, *she* had found the flat.

It should be Shona moving out rather than Marcus moving in.

The tube rattled her, a little late and a whole lot frazzled, towards her destination. Lina further wound herself up with the dread of Marcus moving in until, two stops from her destination, she caught sight of her reflection. She hardly recognised herself and took the chunky necklace off.

It was too much. She just felt all wrong and awkward, and now she was annoyed about Marcus too.

Somehow she made it just on time.

'Hey.' Garth smiled and they shared a brief kiss, which made everything feel a bit better.

'How was your week?' he asked as they walked to the venue. 'Has your partner had his baby?'

'No, we're still on baby watch,' Lina said. 'How was yours?'

'It was good,' Garth said, but he didn't add that it had

been good up until this afternoon when he'd heard she was thinking of leaving.

He knew it was none of his business, and that it was not a subject he could broach, but the news that she was potentially leaving had put a slight pall over him, which he was doing his level best to shrug off.

It was hardly Lina's fault that he'd found out, Garth had repeatedly told himself.

And also it was so nice to see her again.

They stepped into a very nice bar with a stage and gallery with tables where it seemed things were more formal.

Jeans would have been fine down here, Lina soon realised as she looked around. She tugged the dress down as she suddenly felt all awkward and just not herself.

'I've got us a table up there but shall we have a drink at the bar first?' Garth suggested, and her heart sank just a little.

'Sure.'

Lina ordered wine instead of the craft beer she really wanted to try.

She usually tried not to care what others thought, but she rather liked him, and tonight seemed to be about trying something different.

'I am sorry about last week—' Garth said as their drinks arrived.

'Honestly, it's fine,' Lina cut in. 'My flatmate, Shona, thought I was out for the night and had planned a romantic night in. I had to wear earplugs.'

He laughed. They were just finding themselves again, just starting to chat, when it was time to head up to their table. It really wasn't the best place for a first date because, while the food was fantastic, she'd honestly have preferred a club sandwich, and the music was just so loud and so…

…unfamiliar.

It was like an awkward 'met online' date and despite playing them down to Brendan, Lina had had plenty. Still, at least he didn't disappear on her before the first course was served, which she took as a plus. Finally, there was an interval in the music while the band took a break.

'Great, aren't they?' Garth said as the waiter topped up her wine.

'Loud!' Lina said, and then corrected herself. 'But yes…' Well, what could she say? Maybe she could get into the music if Garth wasn't sitting there, but he was so completely distracting—in the very nicest of ways. He smelt all soapy, as he had on the night they'd met, and though he hadn't shaved it was clear he'd had a shower. She liked the scent of him as they leaned across the table to catch what each other was saying.

'May's been trying to get out of me who I'm out with tonight. She overheard me ordering the tickets.'

'May's a white witch,' Lina explained, and Garth nodded.

'I had rather worked that out. She made it look as if I was volunteering information when I told her I'd moved, but she'd have known anyway from the emergency contact list being updated…'

'That's May.' Lina smiled. She thought about May's offer to speak with her about her upcoming decision. She looked over at Garth and considered mentioning it, but why spoil the night by bringing up her tentative plans?

'Do you ever think of going back to nursing?' he asked. Little did Lina know that he was inching towards giving her an opening, hoping that she'd tell him of the plans that she clearly carried in her mind.

'No.' Lina shook her head. 'I love being out on the road,' she admitted. 'Especially night shifts. Sometimes, early in the morning, I feel as I've got London all to myself. Well, apart from Brendan and the patient and ambulance control…'

She made him smile.

And she made him think, because here he sat, wanting more information from her. Yet Garth inwardly acknowledged that he hadn't shared the biggest piece of himself either.

He looked down towards the stage. The band was coming back on and soon the relative peace would be gone. But because there was noise and chatter and laughter, it really wasn't the time to just spill out your past.

And so they went back to silence and to being somewhat awkward until the band finished playing.

'Another drink?' Garth offered, but it felt like a polite offer rather than a heartfelt one and Lina was rather certain that the night was already done.

'Not for me.'

They were all polite smiles as she pulled on Shona's trench coat and he paid the undoubtedly vast bill, refusing her offer to go halves. Even if she couldn't really afford it, Lina liked to pay her way, especially as it must have been an expensive night.

As they stepped outside, Lina was rather certain she was heading for the tube and home—or, worse, a really awkward, long car-ride. It was all such a let-down…

'They were great,' Lina said. 'Thanks, though I wish you'd let me pay.'

'Why?' Garth said. 'I asked you. And, yes, they were

great, but it wasn't the best choice… It wasn't the best place to talk.'

'No,' she agreed, and fully expected him to politely thank her for a lovely night and then make his excuses and walk away, or see her to the station. Except he didn't walk away, and he didn't make his excuses to leave, as so many had before.

Instead he told her what was on his mind. 'It was possibly the most stupid place to take someone you want to get to know…' Lina blinked in surprise and looked up and then smiled some more when he said, 'And I do want to get to know you some more.'

So he wasn't just walking away.

'How about a coffee, then?' Lina said, and even though the sky was black and heavy it felt as if the sun had come out.

'I'd like that very much.'

It didn't matter where, just that they both wanted to be there. They sat in a tiny café on plastic seats—her treat this time, but it had long ago stopped being about the bill.

It was terrible coffee, and stale end-of-day baklava, but the company was back to being divine. In fact, their little plastic seats were side by side as she showed him the route she'd mapped out for her days off.

'It looks amazing,' Garth said. His days off had been spent moving and putting off unpacking and then there had been a couple of hellish days in Wales. How much better it might have been had he thought to plan a couple of days walking, either side of that visit. 'Have you stayed at any of these?' he asked.

'No. I just look at reviews,' Lina said. 'There's a bit of pot luck involved. I splurged with this one…' she pulled up the listing of the tiny hotel '…and got a room with a kettle *and* biscuits.'

'Living dangerously.'

This bad date had just got a whole lot better—though some would say worse because as they stepped out of the café the heavens suddenly opened. There wasn't even a first drop of rain to warn of the impending cloudburst, no warning shower. Instead, there was just a sudden and heavy downpour that had people yelping and dashing into doorways, but she just laughed as he gripped her hand and they ran.

There was water pouring out of the drains and down the pavement, cascading down the stairs into the tube station, but they ran past that too, and she was like no woman he knew because she was laughing and laughing.

No, a bit of rain didn't worry her. She'd seen far worse at work. But although it was fun, and exhilarating, they were soon drenched and cold.

Drenched and in a doorway and wet and…suddenly sexy.

He kissed her hard and she had never felt such violent attraction before.

And as for thunder, it was a paltry effort compared to the power of his hungry kiss.

They didn't need food, or music, or even conversation; they both just needed this…

His hands were inside her coat and she was shivering not with the cold but with want. He simply turned her on in a way no other man had.

But they had to stop—they were trying to stop, to slow down, lest he take her in a doorway, and of course that wasn't going to happen…

'Shall we make a run for it?' Lina suggested. From memory, his flat was five minutes away.

It was a mad run because her shoes went all floppy and she ended up taking them off, and then piggy-backing on him. But it was not to his basement garage he took her to this time—instead it was the agony of an elevator when they both wanted to be in bed.

Shona's stupid coat really was just for appearances as it was totally impractical. As they fell through his door, she was drenched, right down to the thick black tights and azure knickers that she was peeling off while their lips meshed together...

And Garth, who was usually the most sensible person—boring almost, when it came to sexual health— was trying and failing to reach for a condom as she grappled with his zipper and took him out.

Her wet, cold hand should have doused his ardour a fraction but so urgent was their need for each other that he was pressing her against the wall instead.

Lina had never been kissed so hard, so completely deliciously, in her life before, and there was *nothing* tender about the way she kissed him back.

And then he was lifting her, and he took her against the wall, so perfectly that she arched her back and clung on with her legs. It might be *his* neighbours who needed the earplugs tonight!

'Garth!' she was shouting.

'Not yet,' he warned as he thrust into her and *told* her she couldn't come yet ...

For Lina, who normally had to chase her orgasm or— whisper—fake it, and who had never once been required to hold onto it, what a delicious demand that was. She was taut all over and grinding down on him, loving his strength and the pressure of his hands as he held her.

But soon there could be no more holding on because it was coursing through her, and if he hadn't been holding her down, Lina was sure she would have shot out of his arms because he groaned, such a pure earthy groan, as he found his release. A sound came from her throat, one she had never heard before. It was a sort of sob, or a cry, as he coaxed out the last flickers of her orgasm with his own.

He lowered her down slowly and they stood there, heads together and sated. She was so disorientated from the intensity that for a moment she didn't actually know where she was. Her eyes opened to a shadowy room, lit only by the streetlight outside and containing just boxes. As she reached for a sidelight, his hand caught hers. 'Don't turn on the lights.'

'What?' Lina snapped. Suddenly, there was a tiny frisson of fear, because she had, after all, just had sex against a wall with a stranger.

Only he wasn't a stranger—it was Garth. And then she laughed as he admitted, 'I haven't got curtains yet.'

They had a quick tidy up before he turned on the light.

'You really haven't unpacked.' Lina blinked as she looked around.

'No. I swore I'd have everything put away before I started back at work but it's…' He halted and Lina had the feeling that something had been left unsaid. 'I've got a table and couches being delivered but not for another fortnight…'

'It's really gorgeous,' she said as she looked up at the high ceilings.

'But cold. The heating isn't working yet. Well, it is but it's not particularly warm.'

'Maybe the radiators need bleeding,' Lina suggested, and then stopped herself. Suggesting things was something else she tended to do a lot and it never went down well.

'You're probably right,' Garth said. 'I should have thought of that.'

He led her through to his bedroom but, given that there were only sheets up at the windows and not very well secured, he took her through to the bathroom to strip off for bed.

There they undressed, both seeing what they'd just explored and still delighted with each other. Lina smiled approvingly. He really was utterly beautiful, she thought as she traced her fingers down his chest, and that stubbly unshaven jaw was as black as the hair on his chest. She liked the feel of it as she touched it but then she just stood, arms lifted, as he took off her wet dress.

'Do you know…?' he said as he got to her fantastic underwear. 'I didn't expect this…'

'I love underwear…' she breathed, delighted that he approved of the stunning kingfisher-blue satin she had selected with such care.

'No, this,' he told her, and she looked down. 'Lina, you're purple.'

She was!

'That bloody dress!' The dye had leaked and she had been turned purple! Now they were both sort of hysterical with quiet laughter. 'I knew I should have stuck to jeans…'

'I'm going to bathe you…'

'I haven't had a bath in…' She couldn't actually remember how long.

'I've even got this…' He opened a huge cellophane-wrapped basket. 'Housewarming gift,' he explained as he took out oils and candles.

'Who's that from?'

'My friend Boris and his partner…'

She was smiling as he ran the bath because he was

so unfamiliar with it all that he had to read the instructions on the bubble bath!

'More than that!' Lina said as he carefully measured out two lids full. She took over running the bath as he wrapped a towel round himself and headed off to look for glasses and wine.

Yes, the lack of a condom needed to be discussed—and it would be—but... Garth didn't know what was happening between them. It wasn't just the incredible sex, but it had never been so intense, not since...

He shut down that thought process quickly but then as he opened the fridge he was blinded with insight rather than light.

It was because she was leaving, he decided. That was why it felt so insanely intense between them.

Not that she'd told him she was.

But maybe that was what allowed him to be a bit freer with her.

Garth hadn't had a bath since who knew when either, and certainly not a candlelit one with bubbles and wine.

'It's Shona's dress,' Lina explained as he climbed in.

'We should send her a thank-you card,' Garth said as the water engulfed them and they washed each other.

'And to Boris.'

'Indeed,' he agreed. 'If you'd have come tomorrow that basket would have been forgotten in a cupboard or at the Oxfam shop.'

This was them; they were back to the fun and ease that naturally existed between them. They talked between kisses. Yes, she was on the Pill and, no, neither usually went without protection. It had been an anomaly for them both, and one that would hopefully soon be repeated, but for now they just talked lazily, filling in gaps... 'It turned out that it wasn't a casual affair,' she said when he asked about her dad. 'They're married now. He lives there.'

'Do you see much of him?'

'No,' Lina said. 'We were really close when I was younger. I was his favourite…' She gave a pale smile. 'Flights are expensive…'

He said nothing.

'And he's got a new family. Well, they're almost teen-agers now…'

Still he said nothing.

In the past, so many guys had jumped in and pointed out how awful her father was, but his silence was patient, and for once she voiced her deepest thoughts.

'When he left he said that things wouldn't change, that we'd still be close, but then Sally got pregnant…' She looked at him. She didn't want to bring down the fun of their date, but he made it so easy to reach inside herself and just say what she never had. 'He could have made at least some effort.'

'Yes,' Garth said. It was the first comment he had made on the subject, but he saw the dart of pain flash in her eyes. 'But people sometimes don't want to face up to their mistakes, and I'm sure he knows he made one…'

'The marriage was already over.' Lina shook her head, assuming he was discussing her father's affair. 'Now I'm older and can understand things a little better, I can see how incompatible they were…'

'I meant perhaps he knows he made a mistake not keeping properly in touch with you.'

She looked at him.

'It's easy to let things slide,' Garth said, 'except once you have, it makes things harder to pick up. Do you think he regrets not making more of an effort with you?'

She thought for a moment. 'Maybe.' She nodded.

'He's always so awkward when we speak, but then so am I. We used to just talk all the time. I used to be able to go to him with all my problems...'

He kissed her sad mouth, but not to stop her from talking. In fact, it opened her up.

'I miss him,' she admitted. 'He's a nice guy, and I know he hurt my mum but...'

'You are allowed to still love him.'

'Not in my family you're not,' Lina sighed. 'It's agony when he's here. He came back for Daniel's wedding...'

'Daniel?'

'My brother, the older one. It was all so awkward. I mean, *so* awkward... My mum was furious with him still, and both families together...' She closed her eyes at the tension of it and then opened them to his amazing navy ones that were just the nicest thing to look at. 'You read all about these access battles and...' She shrugged. 'Not my dad. I hate it that he didn't even pretend to put up a fight for me.' And there was no real answer to that, so she asked about him. 'What about your family?'

'There's just my dad.'

'Do you get on?'

'We do.' He nodded, and seemed to think about it for a moment. 'He's coming to see the flat next weekend and I believe he's bringing a friend.'

'A friend?'

'Terrible when your parents are dating, isn't it?'

They both laughed and then stopped laughing and found themselves looking into each other's eyes.

'Come to bed,' he told her. She was no longer purple, and the water was cooling off, but more importantly he just had to have her all over again.

Afterwards they lay there, both holding their breath as if waiting for the magic to disperse...except it didn't.

She had never felt so uninhibited with another person, so into another person, and unashamedly so.

They lay there till the heat from their lovemaking left them cool and they shivered as they turned and faced each other.

'If I sleep,' Garth warned, 'I'm going to really sleep.'

'One of the perks of my job—' Lina smiled '—is that I can sleep on demand.'

It was bliss to lie in his bed, to listen to the hum of traffic outside and the pelting rain on the windows, and to know that they had to be nowhere other than here.

'I think I'm going to get drapes the exact shade of your underwear,' he said, and smiled right into her eyes.

'Kingfisher-blue.' Lina smiled back. 'I didn't wear them just for you. I always have gorgeous underwear on.'

'I'll try not to bear that in mind when you bring a patient in.'

'My knicker drawer is like a jewellery box.'

'Really?'

It was her one stab at femininity, the one thing she held onto, and she told him so. 'My mum—and I adore her, by the way—is the dizziest, vaguest... Well, let's just say housework was never her forte...'

He smiled as she spoke, and it was nice to lie in a freezing room and be warm and chatting sleepily.

'So there were never neat piles of washing to put away, it was just a jumble in the airing cupboard.

'I did my own,' Garth said. 'Well, when I was back from boarding school.'

'Oh, stop with the sob story,' Lina said, smiling. 'At least you didn't have to suffer my fate.'

'Which was?'

'Well, the wind blew my school dress up and I was wearing a pair of my brother's Spiderman Y-fronts.'

They laughed and laughed and laughed. She had never done that before, Lina realised, just lain in bed laughing with a man. And then Garth paused, and it was as if, for a moment, he was thinking exactly the same thing.

'So, when I got a job, and pocket money, from the very day I could buy my own underwear I bought the prettiest, brightest, girliest underwear I could, and to this day it persists.'

'I'm very glad to hear it.'

Just before he fell asleep he gave a low laugh, and with her head on her chest she simply knew he was thinking about an eight-year-old Lina in Spiderman Y-fronts, and her most embarrassing moment suddenly didn't burn quite so much.

She felt understood.

Better, she felt completely herself.

It was, she decided, a rather nice place to be.

CHAPTER FIVE

RAIN, RAIN, GO AWAY...

Except they both kind of liked the sound as they woke up in their freezing cocoon, all bundled under the blankets and knotted together. But reality—and their busy schedules—was starting to invade.

'I swore I'd go in and lock myself in my office.' Garth yawned. 'I have a mountain of paperwork after this week...'

'Shadowing?' She didn't say Huba's name and she wondered if he would, but it was a little early to be sharing professional confidences.

'Yes,' Garth said. 'I wanted to get some stuff out of the way before the start of the week, but—'

'Go in,' Lina interrupted, and told him about the *latest* organisation book that she'd been reading, of which she'd amassed quite a collection. 'You'll feel better for it. Well, according to my book. You don't have to do it all, just make a start, but the chances are that once you get going you won't want to stop.'

'I *will* want to stop if I know you're waiting for me here.'

Lina blinked.

She'd rather expected a *Thanks for a great night, but*...followed by a cold journey home on the tube—

or rather a damp and cold journey, given that Shona's purple dress and underwear were lying in a puddle on the bathroom floor.

Except it would seem that, like her, Garth didn't want it to end just yet either.

'Well,' Lina slowly admitted, as she didn't want to appear too eager and terrify him, 'I *am* avoiding Shona.'

'Your flatmate? Why?'

'She's hoping to have "a talk".' Her hands lifted and she made the quotation marks, but then, given the icy air, she shot them back under the covers and toyed with his lovely chest hair as she spoke on. 'She wants her partner to move in with us.'

He pulled a suitably distasteful face and Lina gave a soft laugh.

'I feel the same way.'

'So say no.'

'It's more complicated than that…' It was Lina's turn to yawn. She wasn't avoiding a conversation, but it was also far too early in the morning to be going into the drama of Shona and Marcus and the ongoing saga of living arrangements.

And Garth understood that she wasn't avoiding talking or anything, simply that she was tired. 'Stay if you like,' Garth said. 'I'll bring food back, though I've no idea when.'

'Sounds wonderful.'

'There's a set of spare keys on the mantelpiece if you need to go out, but don't try and start the unpacking…'

'Oh, please.' Lina laughed. 'I'm no domestic goddess, if that's what you're hoping for.'

'No.' He hadn't meant it like that; it was more the piles and piles of boxes that he needed to go through alone. It was something Garth had been putting off, yet now it felt like something he might be ready to start tackling—perhaps he should ask for the name of that book she'd been reading. 'Just rest up, and I'll be back as soon as I can. Do you want a drink before I head off?'

'Not now.' Lina was more than happy to head straight back to sleep.

They shared a lazy kiss and Garth was soon headed out with his tea in a keep-cup, leaving Lina dozing in bed.

And what usually would seem unfathomable—to leave someone in his bed and head to work—felt normal and right.

Invigorating even?

Because for once the pile of paperwork waiting for him felt like something to get through briskly rather than a burden that would stretch out all day.

Lina had no idea when he'd be back and it mattered not; it was just nice to have space, even if wasn't her own. She couldn't find coffee but made a cup of tea instead. The contents of his fridge weren't exactly enthralling, but she was high on last night rather than hungry this morning, and his flat really was freezing.

So freezing that she had another bath just to warm up, and then found a T-shirt of his to put on while she threw Shona's violet dress and her tights over a very tepid radiator, even though the heating was up on high.

Ah, yes! His radiators.

Not your problem.

Lina reminded herself of the guy who'd told her she'd emasculated him by changing his tyre but, hell, it was freezing.

And anyway, she doubted Garth Hughes was capable of being emasculated and so she set to work.

Hanging on the radiator in the lounge room, she found the key, and a couple of hours were spent bleeding the radiators into a Tupperware container she'd unearthed. And it worked, so much so that by the time she was working on the one in the bathroom the place was so warm that she had to turn the heating down!

Then there were another couple of glorious hours lying in bed, just scrolling through the news—all without the sound of Marcus and Shona bonking, or having a row, or knocking on her door and asking if she had a charger they could *borrow*, or if she minded if they used the bacon and they'd get some next time they hit the shops, or Shona wanting to have 'the talk'...

Mind you, a good part of those couple of hours were spent thinking about Garth...

Oh, there was history in those boxes, Lina was absolutely sure. After all, she still hadn't worked out the reason he was mid-thirties, gorgeous and single, but not once was she tempted to snoop.

It was all too new and too shiny and precious, and she didn't need to go looking for a pin to pop their little bubble.

And so when he texted and said he was stuck for the foreseeable future with a broken ankle, she texted back not to worry about grabbing food because she'd sort it.

The violet dress and black tights were far too much for the high street, but she covered them in Shona's coat and was too delighted to care.

Lina bought some dips and fried mozzarella sticks, and ready-made samosas and tiny sausage rolls, as well as some wine. And, given the month, she bought some discounted Christmas pudding, and ready-made custard too. It was all a mish-mash of deliciousness. Certainly there was no domestic goddess involved, or duck in plum sauce that she'd disguised as her own. After the dress debacle, Lina was more determined than ever to simply be herself.

Her damp clothes were back drying on the radiator when he texted to say that he was on his way, and she set up for an indoor picnic.

And Garth, who'd been working up to having a 'talk' of his own—perhaps even opening up about his past—walked into a toasty warm apartment to find Lina in his T-shirt and a blanket spread out on his floor covered in plates and finger food.

'Are we having a party?' he asked.

'Sort of,' Lina said. 'Well, this is my version of a gourmet dinner. All the best bits, without the knives and forks.'

The difficult conversation he had been planning to have flew out of the window. He'd forgotten the feeling of coming home to someone and just stood taking it in for a moment. 'We need candles,' Garth finally said.

Thank goodness for Boris and his basket of goodies because soon they were sitting on the rug with last night's candles set on various saucers and flickering in the low light.

It was romantic, it was fun, but more than that it was all so simple to lie back, completely full, and just look at the high ceilings and the ribbons of light from the melting candles, and listen to the traffic in the wet streets below and talk about, well, not much.

'My flat's so tiny,' Lina said. 'You could paint the ceiling lying down. You'd need a crane to do yours.'

'I might just stick to candlelight,' Garth said, and that made them smile. 'So Marcus wants to move into your tiny flat?'

'Correction,' Lina said, 'I think the hope is that I'll move out. It's a brilliant flat.' She explained the complicated unwritten rules. 'It's actually got a little balcony off the fire escape that's covered, and it's got plants and everything.'

'Sounds good.' He nodded.

'It's perfect,' Lina replied. 'You can sit out there in summer without having to go down to a park, it's just so nice. And I was the one who found it.'

'I see.'

'I lived there for two years before Shona.'

'So she should be the one to move out?' he checked.

'Yes, but who needs a disgruntled flatmate?' They looked at each other. 'Not me.'

'No.'

'But I just can't be bothered finding another flatmate and sharing again…' She stopped herself, lest she reveal her plans.

Except that little bone of contention that had niggled since he'd heard May on the phone faded then as he realised she was possibly just working through her options. 'What did you tell Shona?'

'That I'm thinking about it,' Lina said. 'Which I'll do on my trip. I do all my thinking when I walk. Well, my big thinks.'

'I need to do that,' Garth said. 'Allocate my thinking.'

'You should.' And she told him about another book she'd read—or was it a podcast?—but they never really got to the bottom of it because Lina was precariously close to suggesting he join her on her trip and Garth was wondering what Richard's reaction would be if he suddenly asked for the next weekend off.

It was safer to get dessert.

'What is it?' Garth asked as the microwave whirred again.

'Don't look.' She turned out the pudding, and while she was warming up the custard she opened the tiny

miniature of brandy she had bought and poured it over
the pudding and set fire to it. 'Okay, you can look now…'

Garth didn't know where to look first.

The dancing blue light on the Christmas pudding, her
bare legs walking towards him, the way she smiled as
she carried it over… This Saturday night was up there
with the best he had known.

'Christmas pudding…' he said as she put the plate
down and he watched its fading flames as she headed
off for the custard. 'I don't—'

'Don't tell me you don't like Christmas pudding!'
Lina warned.

'I love Christmas pudding,' he corrected. 'I was going
to say that I haven't had it in years.'

'Why not?' She was aghast at the very thought and
Garth found he couldn't tell her that Christmas had been
placed on hold in recent years, because he didn't want to
bring this perfect night to a screeching halt. She made
him laugh and smile, and it would change things to start
talking about sad things. Selfishly maybe, he just didn't
want to go there right now.

'I just…' He didn't finish and didn't explain because
right now he wanted to hold onto this little bit of magic
and *ease* that she had brought to him.

Not that Lina noticed his silence. 'I live off it in Janu-
ary,' she told him, 'and mince pies…'

Lina knelt up, at first to reach for the custard, but
when he caught her wrist and she looked into his eyes
her sweet tooth was completely forgotten.

'Thank you for this,' Garth said.

'You mean my amazing microwave skills?'

'I adore your microwave skills,' he said as his lips
brushed hers. A picnic in winter and a home full of

warmth—what could be better? As their lips met he ran a hand along her naked thigh and then to her waist.

And then back down, to check something he might have missed, but, no, her knickers really were over the radiator. He groaned as his hand met her bare bottom.

It was not their first kiss together—after all, they had been entwined often since last night—but this was the first kiss for them both where time seemed to stop, where they actually met, because it was such a slow and deeply intimate kiss. They both opened their eyes just to witness the other's pleasure.

He scooped her towards him, and though a tiny plate of mini sausage rolls was knocked over courtesy of her foot, it was of such little significance that it didn't merit either a look or an interruption to acknowledge it. Instead, she sat on his lovely solid thighs and stared into his face and wondered how the hell she could ever have considered him grumpy because Garth Hughes was simply too delicious for words.

She approached his open heart with ease and did not even have to check her words as she spoke, for he accepted her.

'You need curtains,' she told him as she stared into navy eyes, and he pulled her indecently close so that he pressed into her.

'I know,' Garth acknowledged, and he kissed her again, because it was so much easier to do than to get up right now. But somehow, and with mammoth effort, he unlatched their locked lips and peeled them apart. He stood up, holding his hand out to help her up.

'You really, really need curtains,' Lina grumbled as they made their dash to the privacy of the sheeted windows in his bedroom.

'First thing on my list,' Garth said when they got

there. 'No, second,' he said as he peeled off her T-shirt—which was actually his, but neither cared right now.

'What's first?' a naked Lina asked as she pressed her body against his clothed one and kissed him as if it was the most essential, necessary, most vital thing in the world.

'You are.'

For Garth it was as if the sky had split open and the air was suddenly clear because for this blissful time there was nothing on his mind other than Lina.

Nothing other than her skin, and how necessary it was to undress himself so that every inch of him could be pressed against every inch of her.

He stripped and she laughed in delight and called him a magician, because one minute there was a belt and socks and a tie to contend with and the next, his body was hers to behold and hold and together they tumbled onto the unmade bed.

Yes, unmade, because she was no domestic goddess, but who cared? Not Garth.

He made her skin tingle and the weight of him pinning her down made her feel tiny when she was certainly not.

His jaw was rough on her skin and his hands were firm and she loved it. She had never known a kiss could be so exquisite and perfect as he kissed every inch of her skin.

They were just so into each other, so wanting each other. She lay back as he kissed her all over then rolled her over and kissed her spine. She had never known sex could be so slow and so good, or so honest.

He made her feel gorgeous by the roaming of his hands and the soft attention of his mouth.

'What are you doing to me?' she groaned.

'Hopefully the same as you're doing to me,' Garth said, and they sank into the bliss that their bodies gave to each other.

It did not feel too soon to be so adoring of him. If anything, as she lay beneath him, Lina wondered how she had survived to near thirty without knowing the bliss of being properly made love to. Oh, he wasn't her first, but he was the first to make her feel as important and as cherished. This was how it should be.

His body was warm under her hands and she was just this knot of hot desire. The scratch of his jaw on her cheek felt sublime, and he panted into her ear as he entered her.

Oh, where were the condoms? she thought as he thrust into her, but then she remembered that they were past all that. They were in this place, without vocal discussion, where they were here together, and it was just them.

They were locked in an embrace and in a place where no one else would be invading.

'I raced.' he said as he took her higher.

'Tell me,' she said as she dug into his buttocks with her stubby fingers that had chewed nails, but in her mind she was dizzy as she galloped alongside his chain of thought.

'To get through it…'

'I know,' she gasped, because she knew that today he had been on fast forward to get through his paperwork and it excited her, it *excited* her, that she had been on his mind all day. 'I was the same.' This delicious day had been all about filling her trolley with goodies for them and the thought of a night with him.

'I wanted…' She wanted to tell him how she'd wished to turn the hands on the clock, just so it could be now, but words had left her because he took her so deeply and so intently, and there was nothing in the world she could focus on now other than the pounding of her senses and the absolute certainty that she could hold on no longer.

Her head was to the side, just trying to breathe for a second, to hold onto the surge that was flooding her body, to relish this solemn man and the sudden abandonment of anything else but this moment with a mutual lack of restraint.

Finally, she could hold it no more, and her climax arrived so spectacularly that he drowned in her pulsing body and the tension of her limbs. When she sank in relief and was pliant beneath him, he took her so hard against the pillow that it felt as if she had melted and she had the succinct pleasure of watching and feeling the rush of his come.

It made her want to weep because it felt so sublime—and so did the long, slow kisses afterwards as they tried to gather their breath. And then came a blissful minute of silence. Garth was still on top and inside her, and they stared at each-other in wonder.

It was the most treasured, intimate moment of her life.

For Lina, it blew every previous pathetic attempt at a relationship out of the water.

For Garth, it felt as if he'd climbed onto a life raft.

It was beyond words or logical thought.

And then they rolled apart and lay there smiling to themselves before Garth got up and, wrapping a towel around his hips, retrieved the essentials.

Cold Christmas pudding and custard had never tasted so good.

CHAPTER SIX

Why, when life felt so close to perfect that she could almost reach out and touch it, could Lina not sleep?

Garth lay beside her, and though her body was all floaty and relaxed, her mind remained wide awake. Was it just the buzz of adrenaline in her veins, as she replayed the best weekend she had ever known, that kept her from drifting off? Or was it a stupid question that kept popping in uninvited as she lay there: why hadn't he had Christmas pudding in years?

It had her frowning into the darkness as she tried to answer it.

Maybe he worked each Christmas, Lina reasoned. After all, a lot of health workers did, and she had certainly done her share of working through the festivities.

Except, no matter how unsociable the hours of her work were, there was always a Christmas dinner and pudding and all the trimmings waiting for her at her mum's, even if she didn't get there till Boxing Day. She hadn't been able to get there until New Year's Eve once! Yet they had still had their own little celebration.

Maybe it was just her family, Lina thought.

Perhaps others didn't cling onto those traditions so fiercely…

Not quite satisfied with her own answer, Lina lay

there, still unable to sleep but bathed in the streetlight that came in through the sheet. She didn't mind being awake in the least. The world hadn't felt so right in a very long while and she didn't want to miss a moment, for it felt too good to be true.

Too good to last?

She disregarded that thought, simply shrugged it off and put it down to the eternal pessimist that resided within her. Well, she wasn't listening to that voice tonight. Instead, she listened to the swish of cars below and the soft sound of Garth asleep by her side.

He even *breathed* nicely for someone who was asleep on their back.

She wanted to reach out and touch his flat stomach, to wake him up in the nicest of ways. She was smiling to herself at the thought of that as she looked at his gorgeous features.

But then it happened again, that flash of recognition: she knew him. Lina was sure of it.

Oh, where had she seen that profile before?

She had felt it that first night they'd met when she'd walked into the staffroom and seen him sleeping upright in the chair—a jolt of recognition had shot through her.

And now it was happening again.

The straight aquiline nose, lips slightly parted…

It was like trying to recall a dream, Lina thought as she turned on her side and raised herself onto one elbow.

A car's lights cut through a gap between the sheet and the window and cast a sudden, fleeting flash of light on his face…

But instead of the white light flashing into the bedroom, for a moment there Lina saw blue. Or rather she recalled seeing that gorgeous face momentarily lit by blue emergency lights, then red…and she wished at that moment that she had never tried to chase the memory of his face because suddenly she remembered. She remembered him, and it was awful.

Her breathing started to come too fast and too shallow and she rather hurriedly turned onto her back and lay there feeling shaken, blocking her eyes with her arm, trying to forget what she had once seen.

She'd been to so many accidents, but there were some that stood out more than most and that were etched into her memory.

Garth hadn't been her patient, though.

Her patient had been his wife...

CHAPTER SEVEN

'COACH VERSUS MULTIPLE VEHICLES…' Wendy said.

Wendy was driving along the hard shoulder of the wet motorway with lights blazing and sirens blaring as updates came in. A major incident had been declared and Lina's pulse was rapid, her head trying to slow down and go through all she had learned as this was her first major incident.

'Jesus…' Wendy said as she slowed down on approach, and Lina quietly swallowed.

There was a coach and cars all knotted together, and dazed people walking around the motorway, being shepherded by emergency workers who were starting to bring order to the chaos.

Lina and Wendy were waved through. Many first responders were already there and as she and Wendy disembarked, they were told to take over with the driver of a car, while another team dealt with the passenger.

One look at the crumpled metal told her this was far from good and Vos, the doctor, told her the same. The steering column, he told her grimly, was embedded in the patient's chest and it was going to be difficult, if not impossible, to save her. Extraction crews were working on those with a better chance of survival for now.

'You've got this,' Wendy said, and Lina was grateful for her crewmate's encouragement as they approached.

The door of the car had been ripped off and the patient was angled terribly, but they had already managed to get a cervical collar on her and she was attached to a monitor with an IV line in. Wendy took over holding the bag of saline as Lina reached in to the woman.

'Is Garth okay?' the patient begged as Lina peered in to make her own assessment. 'Please, will someone just tell me. Please…' she begged. 'Can you just help my husband. He's not making a sound…'

'There's a team with him now,' Lina assured her, not even glancing over, her focus fully on the woman who was pinned. 'It's Carrie, isn't it?' she checked as she started to take her vitals.

'Yes.'

'I'm Lina. Carrie, I need you to listen to me. We're going to get you and your husband out just as soon as we can, but for now I need you to stay very still.'

Carrie had on long silver earrings, a silver-grey velvet dress, and red lipstick. All these things Lina noticed in great detail, because her blusher was far too garish and severe for such a very pale face, but she was so polished and elegant that Lina knew she hadn't made a mistake with her make-up. Her skin was a horrible waxy colour that concerned Lina deeply; this alone—outside the handover information—told Lina that this patient was desperately ill.

Her vitals were better than she presented, but that brought little comfort—she was young and healthy and would hold her blood pressure better than most.

'I'm just going to get another line into you,' Lina said, 'so we can give you more fluids, while—'

'Please,' she whimpered, pulling at the oxygen mask

to speak more clearly. 'Tell me how my husband is. I'm a doctor, I'm not stupid…'

'Of course you're not. Carrie, keep the mask on.' Lina's voice was firm, but she did glance over towards the passenger.

'Is he dead?' Carrie asked her bluntly. 'You have to tell me the truth!'

'No, he isn't dead,' Lina told her patient, but any more than that she honestly didn't know. She took a moment to look and assess the situation for herself.

His head was resting back on the headrest, and there must be a wound in his scalp because there was blood pouring down his face. He was unconscious but breathing, and a paramedic was wrapping the head wound and flashing a pupil torch into his eyes.

'He's breathing,' Lina told Carrie. 'He has a head wound that I can see, but he's breathing.'

'Garth.' Carrie summoned her strength and ripped off the oxygen mask, calling out to him. 'I'm here.' Her frantic pale blue eyes met Lina's. 'Can he hear me, do you think?'

'I think so.' Lina wasn't one for placating people for the sake of it. This couple were both in a terrible way, but she saw his arm lift slightly to the sound of his wife's voice. 'He just moved his hand when you spoke.'

'Hold on, Garth,' she urged him, except her voice had gone gurgly. Lina's attention left the passenger and returned to the driver.

'I'm pregnant,' Carrie told her. 'Just.'

'Okay,' Lina said, and she relayed it to Vos, who had come back for an update.

'Garth doesn't know…' Carrie cried. 'I was going to tell him tonight when we got home. I bought champagne.

Oh, God…' She started to sob, but couldn't get the air in, and it turned into a rasp. 'My baby…'

'Let's take care of *you* now.' Lina sought to calm her. 'And then we'll worry about the baby. I want you to take some nice deep breaths.'

'I don't like the mask…'

Lina turned at the sound of a voice beside her. Vos was saying, 'We're going to get the passenger out now. Once he's out we can get a better angle on her. Try and keep her calm and pain free.'

There was blood spreading over her dress and pooling in her lap now and Lina knew they were losing her.

'Carrie,' Lina said calmly, replacing the mask, 'I really need you to stay calm and keep the mask on. They're just about to move Garth now.'

But Carrie wasn't following orders and again tore off the mask. 'I love you,' she called to him. 'Garth, I love you.'

Liana saw the blue ambulance lights flash over his pale face and Lina knew that if he did wake up it would be to a world that had changed for ever.

'We're going to get you out soon,' Lina said. 'Garth's on his way to hospital now.'

'That's good.' She closed her eyes as if in relief, but then failed to open them.

'Open your eyes, Carrie,' Lina urged. 'Tell me, how's your pain?'

'No pain,' Carrie said. 'I can't really feel anything much. Please, take the mask off. I feel like I'm suffocating…'

'You need it.'

'I'm so dizzy.'

'We're getting some fluids into you,' Lina said. 'Wendy is putting another line in and we'll have you out soon.' She looked over at Wendy, who was handing her nasal prongs to use instead of the mask; they were both doing all they could to keep her comfortable. 'There,' Lina said as she put the nasal prongs on. 'Is that better?'

'Yes.' She took a couple of breaths then spoke. 'I want the same hospital as him,' she asked. 'Please.'

'I…' She was about to say that it wasn't up to her, but Carrie just needed comfort right now. 'I'll do all I can,' Lina said.

'I want to be with him.'

'I know you do.'

'He'll hate being a patient,' Carrie said, and breathed for a moment, then she told Lina everything.

They sat on a cold, wet motorway with the traffic halted, as Lina did her best to make Carrie comfortable. The roof was being taken off another vehicle and the noise from the Jaws of Life was deafening even here, but in the pauses between the noise of the saw they talked.

'How long have you been married?'

'Two years.' Carrie closed her eyes and smiled.

'Did you have a honeymoon?'

'Maldives,' Carrie said. 'It was just us, and…'

'Tell me,' Lina said, trying to keep her warm with memories.

It was a disjointed conversation, but she kept talking and Lina kept listening as she delivered drugs and fluids.

An emergency doctor was in the passenger side now, as well as two firefighters, all trying to decide on the best method to extract her from the steering column as Lina focussed on keeping Carrie still and calm.

'My parents…' she whimpered, clearly imagining all the awful scenarios playing out. She was a doctor after all, and, unfortunately they weren't just imagined scenarios Carrie was envisaging. They were real. 'They mustn't call them. They hate the phone…'

'Let us take care of that.'

'I want Garth to tell them. Please…' She was starting to talk nonsense, how Garth had to be the one to go and tell them, even though he was probably in the resuscitation bay by now. 'They'll listen to him.'

'Carrie,' Lina said. 'We're going to start cutting soon. It's going to be noisy, but I'll stay with you the whole time. 'Carrie?' she said. 'Carrie!' More loudly this time, 'Stay with me…'

'They gave me such a wonderful childhood…'

She spoke about a pony and a tiny school and how her mum always put down what she was doing when she got home.

'It wasn't like that for him,' Carrie said.

'For Garth?'

Carrie tried to nod, but the collar prevented it. 'I'm so thirsty…'

Of course she couldn't drink but Lina asked for a water bottle, and wiped Carrie's lips and tongue. As that bright red lipstick came off, it was replaced by white lips and a white tongue. Lina ducked away for a second then so that Vos could take another look and when he stood, his face was grim. They both knew how dire this was. The only think keeping Carrie from completely bleeding out was the steering column that was buried in her chest. 'Are you all right to keep talking to her?' Vos checked.

'Yes.' She nodded as she glanced around. There were still other patients being freed, or being urgently treated in the field or in the emergency vehicles that were all lined up. There was the smell of burning rubber and petrol in the air, so she took a quick gulp of water herself and then got back to the job.

And kept talking.

Or rather Carrie kept talking, in breathy tones, as if it was imperative that she speak.

'He's like a son to them,' Carrie said.

'Garth?'

'He couldn't take it at first,' she gasped. 'His father's such a cold bastard.' She coughed and Lina saw that it was blood. She wiped it, trying not to let Carrie see as she resumed talking...

About how they'd met at medical school.

How she'd been a virgin.

Lina listened to the details of a life that was ending, and did her best to be present for her.

They'd just been to her favourite restaurant—well, second favourite, because he didn't like pasta...

All the little details of her treasured life.

'I'm cold.'

'Let's wrap this round you,' Lina said, as Wendy passed her another blanket.

She told Lina everything, really, the important and the trivial and the vital parts of her world, and all in a disjointed, broken kind of way, and Lina was right there with her. They were getting a dog because he hated cats, oh, and coffee...

She told her about her first horse.

She told Lina all that mattered in her world, and she reminisced and closed her eyes.

'I hope it's a boy...' she said, her voice fading. 'Or a girl...'

'It will be beautiful,' Lina said.

'Yes.'

Carrie's eyes opened and she mouthed, 'Same hospital?'

'Yes,' Lina said, and stroked her face. 'Same hospital as Garth.'

* * *

Lina could still remember standing roadside, looking at the covering on the body still pinned by the steering column that they hadn't got out.

She'd thought of the parents in Wales, and the husband who might wake in hospital, only to be told that his beautiful wife had died.

'That was a tough one,' Wendy had said as they did their own little debrief.

'If we'd got her out maybe…'

Wendy shook her head. 'If we'd got her out then she'd have died sooner. The only thing keeping her alive was the steering wheel.'

Lina had known that, even if she'd tried to deny it to herself as she'd done her best to keep Carrie comfortable.

Vos said the same.

'If there had been a fully prepped theatre next to the motorway, the outcome would have been the same.'

'I know.'

And now, years later, Lina lay on her back, recalling with precision the desolation of the scene, and how she'd got through the rest of her shift.

Another car accident on a dark, rainy night.

A drunk driver this time; he had been fine, apart from a few cuts. She could recall the taste of her own tears at the back of her throat at the injustice of it all and knew in her heart that it wasn't her place to judge. She'd actually landed on her mother's doorstep that very morning, which had been a waste of time.

'It's part of your job, though,' Jeanette Edwards had said as she'd handed her coffee and toast, somewhat bemused by her daughter's visible distress. 'Maybe you should think of something else if it's going to upset you this much…'

'But I'm good at it,' Lina said. 'I like what I do.'

'Well, it's clearly taking its toll.'

Her mum hadn't got it then and she didn't get it now. It was a job Lina loved, even if at times it upset her. It was then she'd realised that if she was going to survive this job she somehow had to toughen the hell up.

'I've got some days off,' Lina had said. 'I might—'

'Do you want to come here for a few days?' her mum had offered. 'We could go out, do some shopping…'

Only it wasn't retail therapy Lina had needed.

Somehow, she'd found herself walking on the stony beach at Brighton in the middle of winter, being whipped by the wind and frozen to the core, but actually, finally, able to think.

She'd been young but already a little bit beaten down by the blows her work delivered. And she had known that if this was the career she wanted to pursue, she couldn't take each case home with her—and certainly not to her mum's. And if there were shards that remained in her heart, she must learn how to hide them better.

And for years she had.

Except Garth Hughes had brought everything she'd ever buried to the surface, both the good and the bad.

Now she lay in bed with a man she barely knew, but about whom she knew so very much.

Too much.

As a sleepless night rolled by, she lay there thinking about Carrie and how beautiful she had been, and thought what a dreadful waste of life her death had been. That night had hurt Lina enough; she could not fathom Garth's hell. She lay there, recalling all the worlds that Carrie had described, all the snippets that she'd buried and never unearthed. But now that time spent with her patient on a cold, wet night all came rushing back with painful clarity.

Dawn came at last. Except things didn't look better in the cold, grey morning. To Lina, they looked a whole lot worse.

'Hey.' Garth stirred beside her and his voice broke into her thoughts. 'You're awake.'

'Yes.' Her voice came out all high and all wrong. 'Yes.' She tried to right it.

'You okay?' He frowned.

'Of course.'

She was like some gauche teenager, awkwardly regretting things—except it wasn't that. It wasn't that!

'Do you want tea?' he asked.

'Coffee,' Lina said automatically, and then added, 'Please.'

'I hope I've got some,' Garth said, and hauled himself out of bed. 'I don't really drink the stuff…'

I know you don't, Lina thought as he headed off to the kitchen.

In their brief time together, *coffee* had never come up.

She'd been too full of it back in the café and so had drunk tea, and the nights had been about wine and romance.

But now the real world was starting to arrive: their likes and dislikes…and their pasts.

Oh, God, it was all coming back, all the things Carrie had said on that cold, dark night. He loathed coffee, pasta, his dad, cats… The memories played back in her head.

And she simply didn't know what to do with what she knew.

'I had some after all.' Garth came into the bedroom then and handed her a mug of coffee.

'Thanks.'

She blew on her coffee in an effort to cool it down so she could drink it quickly and go home to think. 'I do need to get back.'

'You don't want to go and get some breakfast first? Or we can have a picnic...'

'Not for me. I really ought to go.'

'Is everything okay?' Garth checked. 'You're not...?'

'I'm fine.' Lina smiled. 'Shona's out and my cat is going to be screaming to be fed, poor thing.'

He hated cats!

Yikes.

He was a dog person, but to her surprise he didn't pull a face or declare to her that he was actually more of a canine kind of guy.

'Cat lady, me,' she said. It was the most ridiculous thing to say, but her mouth was like a runaway train. Was she testing him? No.

Maybe.

She didn't know. Her head was a jumble.

'What's his name?'

'Her,' Lina said.

'What's her name?'

'Gretel.'

He smiled and she waited for him to add that he didn't like cats, but he didn't.

She was all dizzy and confused by her insights because hadn't he told her last night that he got on with his dad?

She had talked about herself and really he'd told her nothing of him...

Was he just keeping things light?

Keeping it...just sex?

It felt more than that for her, though.

She needed to get away; she needed to think.

'I really ought to go,' Lina said again. She felt wooden. All the ease and the promise that had followed them into the bedroom had vanished.

'I'll drive you.'

'No, really…' She pulled on her clothes. 'I said I'd drop in on my mum while I'm over this way…' They both knew it was a lie, but out of politeness nothing further was said.

'Lina!'

Jeanette Edwards clearly wasn't expecting her daughter's company at eight on a Saturday morning, but thankfully the place was clear of whomever Lina's mother had done roots for and she was soon sitting at the kitchen table, nursing another coffee.

'What happened?' her mum asked.

'I met someone,' Lina attempted. 'Well, we've barely been out, but…' She tried her best to explain it. 'It feels like a whole lot more. I mean, it feels as if it could be something special.'

'Then what are you doing here?' Her mum laughed and then stopped herself. 'Sorry. Go on.'

Lina loved her mum, she truly did, and her mum was a wonderful person and great company.

If you were in a good mood.

Planet Jeanette, her dad had called it, often with a slight edge to his tone. It was a happy place, if slightly oblivious.

Lina's mum didn't like to talk about her daughter's work. 'It's a bit depressing really, isn't it?' she'd say, and find some chocolate biscuits, or a nice bottle of wine, or something funny on the Internet that she'd been dying to show her.

Her mum's answer to most problems was to simply cheer up and God alone knew that Lina wished she'd inherited at least some of that trait.

Her answer to Lina's being bullied at school had been, 'Stand up to them then.' Or, 'Stop being so sensitive.' Or, 'Well, I'll speak to your teacher…' which had brought Lina out in a cold sweat.

Really, Jeanette Edwards's level of TLC was the equivalent of Lina handing over her medic pack and the defibrillator and telling the patient they could take it from here.

Oh, and telling them they should come and watch this clip on YouTube once they were sorted.

Still, Lina badly needed some advice. 'Do you remember that patient who upset me a few years ago?'

'Sorry?'

'When I came here crying the morning after my shift…'

'Lina.' Mum blinked. 'From what I can remember, you were always crying after your shifts. That's why you left nursing.'

'No, not when I lived here, the one when I was in my grad year and there was that huge crash on the M25…'

'Not specifically, but then there have been a lot…'

'There was a woman, and she was pinned to the steering column and if we moved her—'

'Lina.' Jeanette stopped her then. 'I can't stand your stories. I'm sorry, I just…' She put up her hand and gave a little shake of her head. 'Did she die?'

'Yes!' That was the whole blessed point. Carrie had died and now six years later Lina was head over heels with her husband. 'She did die and—'

'I can't do this, Lina. I know you love your work, but, really, I don't need to hear about motorway crashes and things on a Saturday morning. I told you that. I can't take the drama of your job…'

The oddest thing was that Lina could remember a similar conversation, but between her dad and her mum, when he had come home worried about redundancies or something…

'You'll be fine.' Her mum had smiled to him.

She could clearly remember her dad's somewhat befuddled expression, because it was the same one that Lina was wearing now.

'So what about this fella?' her mum asked.

But instead of telling her, properly telling her, Lina made some vague comments and had four chocolate biscuits instead.

The journey back to her flat passed in a blur of jumbled thoughts.

'Whoo-hoo,' Shona said as Lina let herself into the flat, but then saw her pale face.

'Don't tell me…' Shona rolled her eyes. 'He's actually a visiting salesman with triplets…'

'Nothing like that,' Lina said, and she gave a tired smile.

'Then what's wrong?'

'I just…' She didn't know how to explain it, even if she'd wanted to. Lina settled for, 'It was a nice weekend. I just don't think we're particularly suited.' She gave a pale smile as she turned and headed off to her bedroom. 'Come here, Gretel,' she said, and lay with her friend purring on her chest. But it wasn't a new flatmate or the thought of finding a new place to live that consumed her; she would save all that for her walking trip.

Garth could not be cast aside until then.

Or rather Garth and Carrie.

The life he had once lived.

Did he ever find out that she had been pregnant? Lina wondered, and decided that he must have. And then her eyes filled up with tears, thinking of that.

Just that.

Garth alone and finding out he'd lost not just his wife but their baby too.

Might he blame her?

And later, an hour or so later, as she lay dry-eyed on her bed, a text pinged in from Garth.

It was a really nice text and she held her breath as she read how much he'd enjoyed their nights. It was flirty and sexy, and normally she'd be dancing around the room, but the perfect bubble had burst on them.

Then another text pinged in.

He'd really like to see her before she went on her trip, if that was okay.

She just stared at it for ages and guessed that this would be when he'd tell her about the life he'd once had...

How the hell was she supposed to tell him she already knew?

They either started on a lie or she ended it now...or she told him.

But how?

They'd been destined to end anyway, Lina told herself. She knew her own track record, and that was in a relationship without a dark past to deal with. How the hell could she have hope for this?

Her faith and skill in relationships were zero at best, but there was another dark niggle too, one she didn't want to examine.

Carrie had been stunning, all polished and elegant— even when she'd been dying!

That jazz-loving, wine-sipping, purple-dress-wearing

woman that Garth had taken out on Friday night wasn't the real Lina.

She knew his likes and dislikes. In fact, she had the cheat sheet on him and was terrified she might use it.

And so, instead of sending a flirty message back, as she usually would, she sent him a thumbs-up emoji and then turned off her phone and cried.

They were over, Lina realised, before they'd even started.

CHAPTER EIGHT

By morning Lina had rallied somewhat.

As she boiled the kettle in her freezing kitchen and made her sandwiches for work, Lina knew that she needed advice.

Male advice.

Certainly not from her brothers.

It had been Daniel's second wedding that she'd spoken about to Garth, and as for the other brother...well, suffice it to say she wouldn't go to either for relationship advice!

She was on morning shifts this week so Brendan would have to hold off on his phantom contractions for five minutes, Lina decided as she took her tear-streaked face to work.

And what did she get?

Kind, overly anxious Brendan and his endless patience? No, she got Perfect Peter who told her, 'Brendan's on paternity leave.'

'He didn't call me,' Lina frowned. 'What did Alison have?'

'She hasn't had it yet.' Peter rolled his eyes. 'In fact, they're not even at the hospital. It's probably another false alarm!'

And so she spent the day with Perfect Peter who,

though less qualified and less experienced than her, thought he knew absolutely everything.

'Let's run through some scenarios,' he said as they waited for their next case.

Please, no, Lina thought, but didn't have the energy to debate so went along with it until thankfully her phone rang. It was Brendan, pacing the floor as, presumably, Alison did the same.

'The hospital said not to come in yet and that we should wait till the contractions were a bit closer, but honestly, Lina…'

'She's going to be fine.' Lina smiled and it was a genuine one, because there was extra space in a breaking heart and she was so excited for them. 'Enjoy every second, Brendan. Hold her hand, you're both going to be wonderful…'

Right when she needed to be busy, it was the longest, quietest day of her working life, interspersed with regular texts.

Two centimetres dilated!!

Lina smiled—it was certainly early days yet!

And then she didn't smile as Perfect Peter kept on with his scenarios.

Waiting for an epidural.

That was the text that arrived at midday.

Finally back at home, Lina checked her texts and found that Alison had got to five centimetres…

Five centimetres!!!!! Alison is so amazing, she's on the phone to her mum!

And that evening as Lina sat with her grilled cheese on toast, which reminded her of Garth, the exclamation marks kept pace with Alison's cervix—by chance, she was sure, but she counted them anyway.

Eight centimetres!!!!!!!!

And then:

She's ready to push!

His excitement made Lina teary.

Brendan's love for his wife made her own love life feel so disastrous that she wanted to weep.

She should never have slept with Garth. They should have gone the old-fashioned route and held hands and got to know each other at a far slower pace and then he could have told her about Carrie in his own time.

Yet that didn't really help, because now, with her cheese toastie long since gone cold, there was a deeper reckoning to be had.

Garth didn't know her.

At least, not the real her.

She wasn't all polished and sophisticated, even if she'd tried to present herself as such on their date. Carrie had been the love of his life and it was hard for Lina to believe that she could ever hold a candle to that.

Her scars from every relationship she had ever attempted felt newly raw and exposed, and the honest truth was that, quite simply, she felt not good enough.

And then the text came that she'd been dreading all day.

Lina, is everything okay?

She stared at the phone. It wasn't Brendan; it was Garth.

She replied that everything was fine, and said she was just busy at work and she was on her way to a job so had to go.

And at midnight, freezing cold and so sad, she crawled into bed. Her phone bleeped again.

Somehow, she knew it wouldn't be Garth.

She had frozen him out enough.

It was happy news, though: Alison and Brendan had just had a healthy baby boy!

She did all the happy faces and emojis, even as tears streamed down her cheeks, and then she reached for Gretel and wept.

CHAPTER NINE

THE PRIMARY HOSPITAL was the very last place that Lina wanted to be.

Only that wasn't quite true.

She was so excited to see Brendan and Alison and their new baby, and a deeper truth was that, even if she was avoiding Garth, there was a painful conflict raging within her because she ached to see him.

In her lunch break she had bought the cutest little bodysuit and socks for the baby. As well as that she carried a floral arrangement with blue balloons and even an ambulance balloon, from all the guys and gals back at base.

She felt like a fugitive, dashing past Emergency with her head down and hopefully hidden by the flowers and balloons. She was just breathing a sigh of relief when she made it to the elevators, only to see Garth stepping out of the one she was going into.

'Lina.' He said it almost wearily.

'Garth!' She jumped at the delicious sight of him and her senses shot into overdrive as she did her level best to appear calm.

He was wearing navy trousers, a white shirt and a dark tie and had pagers clipped to his pockets but was looking very polished and smart.

And Lina, who didn't usually blush, could feel herself going bright red. She hoped it could be blamed on the heat of the hospital and on the fact that she was wearing a scarf and coat. 'I was just on my way to—'

'Maternity!' Garth stated the obvious on her behalf as he glanced at the large cloud of balloons and flowers she held.

'Yes.'

'So your partner had his baby?'

'Well, Alison did all the work but, yes, they just had a little boy. Yesterday,' she added.

'That's nice.'

'Very.'

He waited—not even a second, but it felt like if not a minute passed then certainly he left enough of a gap for her to explain why she hadn't returned his call, or to say that perhaps they could catch up again. Or...

She stood there awkward and silent.

'I should let you get on,' Garth said.

'Thanks,' Lina said, and hurried into the lift. 'It was nice seeing you.'

He gave her a slightly wide-eyed look that told him they both knew she'd lied.

Except, as the lift doors closed, Lina knew it wasn't a lie—it was so nice to have seen him.

And so painful too.

She wanted to press the ground floor button and plunge down and dash after him, and say...

What?

Suggest they go to the canteen and somehow tell him what she had remembered? But how?

The guy was trying to move on with his life and Lina had pegged herself as a transition gal at best.

Visiting hours for Maternity had commenced, and

she was guided down the corridor towards a single-bed room where she knocked on the open door.

'Lina!' Alison was sitting up in bed and wearing a big smile, as Brendan paced with their baby.

'Congratulations!' Lina gave her a kiss and handed over the present and balloons and flowers. 'How are you?'

'So happy,' Alison said. 'Everyone has been so nice. I'm so tired, though.'

'I won't stay long.'

'Don't be daft.' Alison smiled.

'Can I peek?'

'Go ahead,' Brendan said. 'You can even hold him.'

'Oh, my goodness,' she said as she took the tiny, perfect bundle of love. He was all fat and chunky with blond sticking-up hair and he was absolutely so gorgeous that she thought she might cry. 'He looks like you!' she said to Brendan. 'Well, he's got more hair.'

'A mini-me.'

'I want one,' Lina admitted.

'Well, this one's taken.' Brendan smiled. 'Hey, did you know Richard's wife is a midwife here?'

Richard was one of the ED consultants. 'No.'

'Well, she is and she delivered him.'

And then they went into all the details that new parents did, but Lina didn't mind a bit because she was holding the warm bundle of baby. She gazed at his little red face as Alison told her that they were going to get him christened soon.

Very soon.

In fact, the weekend after she got back from her trip.

'We're waiting for you...' Brendan said.

'Thank you.'

Alison spoke then. 'We want you to be his god-mother, Lina.'

It was the nicest surprise, just the absolutely nicest surprise, and it was soon followed by another, because when she stepped out of the elevator Garth was wait-ing for her.

Lina honestly hadn't been expecting that.

Usually guys seemed to melt away, right around the very second that Lina started liking them. Not this one, though. He was leaning against the wall, but stood up straight as she got out of the lift.

'Hey,' Garth said.

'Hey.'

'How was the visit?'

'Really nice,' she said. 'They've called the baby Mi-chael. He's very cute.'

They walked together down the long corridor and the silence between them was strained. It was broken by Garth. 'Your self-help book was right.'

'Really?' Despite trying to play it cool, she could not hide her curiosity and turned and smiled. 'Did you fin-ish all of your paperwork, then?'

'Better,' Garth said. 'I got started on the unpacking and it's finally done. Well, almost, but I've been put-ting it off for ages.' He took a breath. 'I don't like how we left things, Lina.'

'Sorry?' She attempted to sound as if she had no idea what he was referring to, despite it having been excru-ciating and never off her mind ever since.

'You're making me feel like a stalker.'

'What do you mean?'

'What do you *think* I mean? You're avoiding me.'

They were outside Emergency.

'No, of course I'm not.'

'Yes,' Garth said. 'Absolutely you are. You jumped out of your skin when you saw me beside the lift.'

'I didn't.'

'Yes, Lina, you did,' Garth said. 'You sent a thumbs-up emoji when I texted that I'd enjoyed our day in bed.'

'I'm sorry.' She blew out a breath. He would never understand how much thought had gone into that, even if it didn't translate as such. 'Look, it was lovely and everything…' She tried to end it in the same way so many had with her.

'But now it isn't?' Garth checked.

'Yes,' Lina admitted, because that at least was true. The simplicity of their desire for each other had turned into something very complicated, and she truly didn't know what to do for the best.

She didn't know how to, or even if she should, tell him.

She looked at his gorgeous face, and his navy eyes were searching hers.

She was tempted to suggest they go for Greek, his favourite—or should she say Italian to put him off?

She wanted to return to their simple world of toasted sandwiches and almond croissants and never have remembered the truth.

'I don't like jazz.'

'Excuse me?'

'I just don't think we'd work.'

'Because you don't like jazz?' He looked at her incredulously. He clearly thought he had her pegged as he said next, 'It was just sex you wanted?'

'Yep.'

Unlike most men she knew, he didn't smile and suggest a repeat. Instead, he fixed her with his eyes and responded tartly, 'Well, I'm glad to have satisfied.' And then his lovely face got back to the grumpy one she'd first met, and the nicest guy she'd ever been with turned and stalked off.

She was tempted to run after him, to tell him she was doing this for him and trying not to break his heart twice.

Except that wasn't strictly true.

Lina was terrified of baring her soul, of sharing what she knew just to have him ultimately walk away. But even so, it was eating her up, and it made her feel wretched.

Brendan was right: she went into things expecting to be let down. No, Garth was nothing like her dad. He was solid and dependable, she could feel it in her bones. But she was so exhausted trying to navigate this world on instinct alone, and had read men wrong so very many times.

She needed advice, but from whom?

Brendan was floating on the pink cloud of parenthood. She thought of May, but then immediately discounted that idea. After all, May worked with Garth.

For better or worse, Lina found herself back at her mum's.

'When does the baby come home?' her mum asked as she filled the kettle.

'Tomorrow,' Lina said. 'Brendan's coming back to work for a couple of weeks while Alison's mum's staying there, then he's going to take a full month off.'

'More than your father did.'

Lina took a breath and decided it was safer to just let that one go. 'I've been asked to be godmother,' Lina said as her mum plonked a cup of coffee down in front of her.

'That's nice.'

'Mum,' Lina said, 'you know that guy I was telling

you about…' She looked at her mum and faltered. She didn't know how to give her the whole picture without including the sad part, so she told her the difficult part instead. 'The thing is, I've applied for a position in Newcastle.'

'Newcastle?'

'Yes,' Lina said.

'Why on earth would you want to move away, Lina? You love London. Your family's here…'

'I know all that, but I can't afford my own place. Maybe if I moved in here for a few months and saved like crazy…' Even as she said it Lina knew it was the most ridiculous idea.

Her mum agreed! 'Lina, I had three children by the time I was your age and I wasn't asking to move home every time the going got tough.'

'I know.'

'And what's all this got to do with this man you like?'

'Nothing,' Lina admitted. 'Nothing,' she said in a more resolute voice. After all, if she couldn't make a relationship work from the other side of London, what hope was there from the other side of the country?

She was scared, scared to stop and admit just how much she liked him, only to be served another lecture on how men always let you down in the end.

And there was something else, something she hadn't told her mum, let alone admitted it to herself.

Garth Hughes was, she was certain, completely out of her league.

It wasn't about pasta or cats, or jazz, it was about Lina, who would surely be a let-down when he got to know the real her, so she looked at her mum and simply said, 'I think it's time for a fresh start.'

CHAPTER TEN

BREAK-UPS HAD HURT her ego in the past, but this one hurt at a level she'd never known before.

It actually hurt her heart.

It was as if there was a knot in her chest and her lungs could not quite fill. Her shifts couldn't end soon enough and work wasn't exactly brilliant either.

She was invited to attend an interview in Newcastle, and given it was on the way to the Scottish borders, she arranged it for Friday morning and juggled around her reservations and train tickets.

She even made an appointment to view a couple of flats and a house.

Perfect Peter was his usual annoying self, insisting they go through scenarios during their down time, and actively questioning her choice as to whether to call in advanced practitioners in front of a patient's family at one point.

Lina, who had learnt to be forthright and stand up for herself, found that she struggled to do so in this case.

'Don't ever do that again,' she said once the patient was in the care of advanced practitioners and was being blue lighted to the nearest emergency department.

'Do what?'

'Speak down to me in front of a patient. It does nothing for their confidence.'

'I wasn't questioning you…'

'Well, it sounded like it.'

'I was questioning myself,' Peter said. 'He didn't quite fit the protocol.'

She looked over and saw his tense features. She thought of Huba and the way Garth had supported her by shadowing her for a few days… Gosh, why did all roads in her mind lead to him?

'I know that,' she said, 'but by the time they got there he did.'

'Yes, but…' He took a breath. 'I'd wanted to call them earlier…'

Lina blinked in surprise She'd actually thought he'd been opposing her calling for assistance.

'I was trying to remind myself to stick with the protocols. I just struggle with acute asthmatics, *okay*?'

His *okay* was curt, a warning to end the conversation, but she looked at her colleague and knew now that his abruptness might be less about his colleagues and more about his own demons.

'Look,' Lina said, 'why don't we run through it together when we get back to base?'

He nodded.

'And,' she added, 'for what it's worth, I found that patient really tough. It's not always black and white. Yes, we called for back-up a bit early, but it turns out we were right to do so.'

They got on a bit better after that. The days ticked by and life carried on—except she didn't like the world as much as she had when Garth had been in her orbit.

Not even Brendan's return, on her final night before

her break, brought back her easy smile, though she tried. 'What happened?' he asked in a lull between patients.

'Nothing.'

'What's going on?'

'Too much time working with Peter,' Lina said, hoping that would end the questioning.

'You can handle Peter, Lina,' Brendan said. 'Is it the jazz guy?'

'Leave it.'

'Who ended it?'

'Nobody ended it,' Lina said. 'We barely even got started. I don't like jazz and he hates cats.' Usually this would be enough said, but still Brendan stared. 'It just didn't work out, *okay*?' She used the same 'okay' that Peter had, the same 'okay' that said, *Leave well alone... this hurts too much to discuss.*

Except Brendan seemed not to hear it and asked, 'So why are you still moping about?'

'I'm not moping,' Lina snapped. She was still trying to recover from the loss of all she had felt for him and there wasn't a person in the world she could tell who might understand that she felt as if she'd touched love. 'Can you just leave it, Brendan, please?'

He didn't answer, just munched on his orange segments.

'How's Michael doing?' she asked, hoping to change the subject.

'He's got reflux,' Brendan said, 'so we're trying him on this new formula. God, I used to think I'd be calm. I mean, we've seen the lot, but it just changes things, Lina.'

'I know.'

'But you don't know.'

This annoyed her. Just because she didn't have a baby,

she couldn't possibly know what it meant, and so she sulked and looked out of the window.

'What's really going on?' Brendan asked.

'Nothing,' Lina answered sarcastically. 'And even if there were, how could I possibly know, given I've never had a real relationship?'

'All right, my five days of fatherhood doesn't make me an expert on being a parent, but I know what I'm talking about when it comes to relationships.'

'Leave it, Brendan,' she warned.

'Nope,' he said. 'I won't.'

'You've had one serious relationship.'

'And that number has stayed at one because we both work at it,' Brendan responded, and that made Lina catch her breath because he and Alison really did work at it. They fought for their relationship, but she didn't know how to do that.

'Please, Brendan,' she asked, 'can you just let it go?'

Thankfully, he had no choice but to leave it as they were called to a job. Unfortunately, it was one of the patients that got to Lina the most.

Not a patient who was desperately ill, or a situation involving high drama, just a person who really deserved better.

William Carter, known as Bill, aged eighty-six, had been on the floor for some time.

Lina didn't know why it was these patients that upset her the most, just that they did.

'Hello, Bill,' she said as she looked around his tiny flat. She saw the large chair that he'd fallen out of and the spot on the floor where he had lain for several hours after inching across the floor enough to reach his phone.

'I'm frozen,' he said, 'and I haven't fed Blinky.' As Brendan started to look him over, Lina went and found a large blanket to cover him with and turned on the small heater too.

They did a thorough examination, although Bill kept insisting there was nothing broken except his pride. 'Just get me back into the chair.'

'Is that where you sleep?' Lina checked.

'Yes.' Bill nodded. 'It's easier than getting in and out of bed.'

'Do you have anyone come in and help you?'

'Sandra, my daughter, comes in a couple of times through the week, and drops off my shopping and things. She does my washing too. She wants to do more, but she's got MS…'

'What about carers?' Lina pushed for more information.

'I don't need any of that,' Bill huffed. 'I just need you to get me back into my chair. I don't want strangers in my home when I can manage fine by myself.'

He clearly wasn't managing.

And tonight neither was she, but she blew out a breath and pushed back the threat of tears. 'We just need to check your heart before we move you,' Lina said, but that wasn't what Bill wanted.

'I want to get back in my chair and have a cup of tea,'

But a cup of tea wasn't going to fix this.

'Bill, we really do need to take you in,' Lina said as she looked at the monitor. 'Your heart isn't behaving.'

'If you'd just fetch me my blood pressure tablets…'

'Bill,' she said, looking at the hopeless surroundings and this proud old man trying to battle on.

'Why don't you let us take you to hospital for a check-up?' Brendan took over then, trying to persuade him to go to hospital, but Bill was having none of it and insisted he would be fine here.

'I just need a tea and a couple more of my tablets.' He thumped the floor in frustration and Lina could see angry tears filling his eyes. 'And if you can feed Blinky, then I'll be fine.'

Blinky was a budgerigar who was chirping away under a sheet. Lina found herself in the little kitchen-ette attached to the lounge, searching under the sink, while Bill shouted instructions. Finally, she located the bird seed and as she did, she paused, took a little breath, and closed her eyes.

'You okay?' Brendan checked as he came over to fill the kettle and give Bill his tea.

Yes, she was about to say, *I'm fine.*

Like Bill, just soldier on and pretend things weren't falling apart.

Perhaps that was why patients like Bill got to her so much—they were too used to going it alone.

She thought of May, offering to talk, and Brendan extending the hand of friendship, but like Bill she'd re-fused.

She was tired of being too tough and too scared to reveal herself, but tears were so close that she had no choice. 'I'm not great,' she admitted bravely. Out of the corner of her mouth she told him the truth. 'It is the jazz guy… Garth Hughes.'

Brendan shook his head. Clearly Garth Hughes wasn't the centre of his world, or even in his orbit.

She'd hid it so well.

'The consultant at The Primary.'

'The miserable one,' Brendan said, dunking the tea bag. 'You really know how to pick them. We'll talk later.'

'Thanks.' Lina nodded.

'I won't forget.'

They headed out to deal with Bill and the tough old

Lina was finally back, even if she was holding a box of birdseed! 'Bill.' Lina was firmer this time. 'Your blood pressure is dangerously high, your tablets haven't brought it down, and neither has the patch. What if you hadn't been able to reach your phone?' She told him the bitter truth. 'You could have had a stroke.'

'I'd have been fine,' he insisted.

'When is Sandra coming in again?' She asked.

'Monday.'

'So on Monday Sandra would have found you.' She watched as he closed his eyes, despondent at the thought of his daughter finding him on the floor, no doubt in a worse condition than this.

'She'd have called before then and if she'd got no answer...' His voice trailed off and then he admitted some of what was on his mind. 'But what about Blinky?'

'I'm going to feed Blinky and then Brendan and I are going to take you to hospital. Bill, you need your medication to be reviewed,' Lina said, 'and hopefully the hospital can sort some proper home help and support for you...' She looked at the undressed ulcers on his leg. 'There's so much more that can be done for you, but you have to let us help.' He wasn't arguing now, Lina noted. 'Brendan and I can't do it all from this end. We can call your GP, but, really, you're not well enough to leave on your own tonight.'

'Fair enough...' Bill mumbled. 'Careful when you—' But he was too late. The cage door opened and Blinky took his chance and flew out. Even Bill joined in laughing as he watched Brendan's attempts to catch him.

Blinky sat on the curtain rail, surveying them all. In the end, Bill whistled and the little blue bird flew onto his shoulder. 'Why didn't you do that in the first place?' Lina smiled as she returned the escapee to his cage.

'He needs his exercise before I go,' Bill said. 'I might be gone a few days.'

'You'll be back soon enough,' Lina said, glad that Bill had accepted he needed some proper help.

'Should I put the cover back over him?' Brendan asked.

'I don't know,' Bill admitted. 'Sandra might not get here till Monday…'

They both looked at Brendan, who was clearly to be the budgerigar expert. 'Well, it might not be fair to leave him in the dark till then.'

'Why don't we leave the radio on for him?' Lina suggested, so the radio went on and Bill said goodnight to Blinky. She had the craziest job in the world at times!

'Am I going to Barnet?' Bill asked as they got him settled into the back of the ambulance. It was Brendan's turn to drive and Lina sat with Bill while Brendan waited for instructions.

'Let's find out.'

It was a busy night this side of town, though, and Brendan gave her a knowing look when they were cleared to take Bill to The Primary. 'Your favourite place.'

Not.

She was like a cat burglar every time they ended up there, but thankfully, so far, Lina had avoided seeing Garth again.

'Well, this is nice.' May greeted them all with a smile.

'I thought you'd finished with nights,' Lina said, surprised to see that May was on duty.

'So did I! So what have you got for me?'

'William Carter,' Lina started, but Bill butted in before she had a chance.

'Bill,' he said. 'And I'm hoping for some tea before you leave me to wait.'

'Well, lucky for you we're not too busy tonight.' May smiled and guided them straight to a cubicle.

'You're lucky we're not here with a bird in tow,' Brendan quipped.

'Oh, I've had worse,' May said, and she clucked around Bill and chatted to him as she always did, but managed a quick word over her shoulder to Lina. 'Can I have a word before you go?'

As Brendan changed the blankets, May and Lina stood in the corridor, waiting. 'I did that reference.'

'Thanks.' Lina pushed out a smile. 'I'm heading up there in the morning and then I've got an interview the next day…'

'You're taking the train?'

'As soon as I finish my shift. I had to fiddle around with the bookings for my trip, but it worked out really well.' She could see Garth at the nurses' station and he glanced over; Lina quickly looked away. 'I really do have to go, but thanks so much, May.'

Lina sat in the bright foyer on the jump seat. For once she just let Brendan do all the work to restock the ambulance while she just sat there, wondering what to do.

'He was looking right at you,' Brendan said. 'That Garth.'

'I know,' Lina said.

'So what happened?'

'Not here.'

'Yes, here,' Brendan said, 'or something will come up and we'll get called to a job and before we know it morning will be here and you'll be on your trip.'

And looking at houses and being interviewed for a job she wasn't sure that she wanted.

'It was just a short-term thing…' Lina attempted, as that was what she kept telling herself, but this time her eyes filled with tears. 'It just felt like more at the time.'

Could you glimpse for ever in a single weekend? Was there really such a thing as love?

'I've never seen you like this, Lina. I've never seen you cry…'

'He's a widower,' Lina gulped.

'He's not over his wife?' Brendan asked, trying to hazard a guess as to what had gone wrong.

'No,' she interrupted, 'I don't know. He hasn't even told me he's a widower yet.'

'So how do you know?'

Before she launched into the story, she said, 'You can't tell anyone…'

'I'll tell Alison.'

And that made her cry even harder, and made her trust him even more. So she told Brendan that she'd realised that she'd cared for Garth's wife when she'd been dying, because she trusted him as both a colleague and a friend—and the nicest thing about Brendan was that tears filled his eyes as she explained what had happened.

'How long ago did she die?'

'I was a grad—so nearly six years now. You'd never really get over it, though…'

'I wouldn't,' Brendan said. 'I'd be a miserable old git without Alison.'

'He is…' Lina smiled '…but then suddenly he isn't…' She couldn't quite explain, and neither would she try to articulate the reward of his smile and the pure happiness they'd glimpsed together.

How he hadn't cared that she'd turned purple—and neither had she.

How she'd told Garth about her dad and how she missed him, when she'd never told that to another soul.

'When did you realise that you'd looked after his wife?' Brendan asked.

'He seemed familiar but I couldn't put my finger on it. And then…' She didn't want to admit that it was just after they'd made love, as that seemed too personal. 'Maybe I should have recognised him sooner, but—'

'Lina,' Brendan interrupted, 'we get called to so many accidents, and there are so many patients, we'd go crazy if we remembered the details of each and every one.'

'I do remember the details of this one now, though. Should I tell him?' Lina said. 'I mean, would you want to be told?'

'I don't know,' Brendan admitted. 'If it's just a short-term thing, probably not, but if…' He blew out a breath and pictured Alison rather than Carrie. 'I actually don't know what to say here, Lina.'

'Some expert.' She gave him a watery smile. 'I know too much about him. And talking about it is going to really hurt him. I think he was working up to tell me he was a widower and he was already struggling enough with that…'

'You have to have the difficult conversations, Lina.'

'And hurt him in the process?'

'Sounds like you're managing to do that already.' He gave her a tissue and she wiped her eyes. 'You do know how to pick them,' Brendan said, and she laughed grudgingly.

'Thanks for listening,' Lina said.

But Brendan wasn't content with just listening. 'I

think you need to talk to him. He knows you're avoiding him.'

'Yes, he does!'

They both jumped at the sound of Garth's voice.

Lina froze.

'Are you going to tell me why?'

Brendan offered to make himself scarce. 'I might go and try to find a coffee before we clear. Do you want one, Lina?'

'Please.'

As Brendan headed off, Garth climbed into the ambulance and stood in front of her. One of the things she really liked about Garth was that he was direct. 'Did we take it too fast?'

'No.' If only it was as simple as that.

And then in the midst of her misery he made her smile with his next question. 'Am I dreadful in bed?'

She let out a short, watery laugh but her eyes filled with tears. 'You know you're not.' In his arms, life had been as close to perfect as she had ever known.

And clearly he had felt that way too, because he was here, trying to work out what had gone wrong. 'Well, between that and waking up, something happened, Lina.'

After days of mulling it over, and finally telling Brendan everything, she still didn't know what to say.

'I'm pretty good at reading people,' Garth continued, 'and knowing when things are going wrong. God knows, I've had practice. But one moment we seemed fine—better than fine—and I know I haven't felt like that in a long time. Not since...' Lina looked down at her boots. She couldn't meet his eyes as he spoke on. 'I haven't been completely upfront with you, Lina. I was married...' He must have seen her pale face and assumed she was thinking the worst—that he was in the middle

of a torrid divorce or had ten children or something…
'I'm widowed.'

'I'm sorry.'

She felt a little bit sick, along with that guilty feeling that made you swallow.

'I didn't tell you at the time,' Garth continued, 'but I was about to. I wanted to get unpacking the flat out of the way first…' She sat there, saying nothing. 'There's no logic in that, I guess, but I've been struggling with where to put things…' His voice trailed off.

'I get it,' Lina said, and then thought about her words with Brendan. 'Well, inasmuch as I can…'

'Maybe we did take things a bit fast,' Garth went on. 'Maybe I should have told you sooner, but it tends to put a dampener on things and also…it's not something I talk about easily.'

'I understand,' Lina said.

She did.

Life and love weren't like a medical handover.

You shouldn't have to introduce yourself as the widower who had lost the absolute love of your life, straight off the bat. Or the not girly enough dating disaster… They had been at the beginning of all that, yet in other ways they had been so much closer than that… But actually, understanding his explanation as she was reminded of the mountain of boxes in the bare flat, and how hellish it must be to shed little pieces of yourself with each move.

'I always knew the second I'd upset her, though,' Garth said. 'And in all failed attempts at relationships since, well, I can pinpoint the second it goes wrong— although it's usually about fifteen minutes in…'

'Because they weren't her?'

'Yep,' he admitted. 'But I've worked on myself and

I got past that, and then along came you, but for the life of me I just can't figure out where it all went wrong. I mean, I know now you're not into jazz, and maybe it wasn't a great venue for a first date, but we were fine afterwards…'

'It wasn't that.' She felt a hot tear trickle down her cheek. 'It wasn't your fault.'

'Please don't tell me it's not me, it's you…'

She smiled. 'It's us.'

'I don't get it.'

'I remembered something, Garth.' Her voice was strained because even that relegated what had happened to him—the most life-changing, devastating, event of his life—to no more than a difficult shift for her. 'The first night we met,' she said, 'I walked into the staff-room and you were asleep in the chair.' Garth frowned; clearly he had no idea where this was going, and that, of course, was the issue. 'I felt as if I'd seen you before. Then later I put it down to having bumped into you at work or something.'

He was very quiet.

'Then after we…' Now it was Lina who fell quiet for a second, remembering the bliss of his bed and the joy they had found before reality had invaded. 'I realised… I remembered…'

She took a deep breath. It was now or never.

'Garth, I was working on the night of your accident…'

'Sorry?' He frowned and for a wild second Lina dreamt that she was mistaken, that she had mixed him up…but of course it was just hope clouding her senses, for she actually watched the colour leach from his face. She watched the thwack to his head as she sent him back into hell, the same hell he must have fought to claw his way out of. 'Were you working in Emergency?'

'No.' Lina shook her head. 'As a paramedic.'

'You saw…' His voice was croaky. 'I was unconscious the whole time. I don't remember… Did you take care of me?'

'No.' She shook her head and said the hardest part. 'I took care of Carrie.'

He sat down on the stretcher and she watched this big bear of a man put his head in his hands and drag in deep breaths.

She was crying but silently. Perhaps it wasn't even her place to cry here, but she couldn't stop tears from falling.

'You were with her?' Garth checked.

Lina nodded. 'Well, I was part of a team but, yes, I was with her.'

'I know that she was conscious for a while…' He swallowed. 'Did she speak to you?'

'Yes.' Lina nodded. 'She spoke about you and…' she swallowed '…her family and childhood, and…' She finally looked right at him. 'You. She spoke a lot about you.' He didn't look up and she didn't know how to fill the silence, but she had to go on. 'I didn't know how to tell you, or even whether I should.' She had been privy to details not by choice but by the nature of her work. 'She told me things…'

'Things?'

'Big things…like about your honeymoon. And little things too—you don't like coffee…' Her voice trailed off. 'I am so sorry.'

'You have nothing to be sorry for.' He said it, except it sounded more like an automatic response than a heartfelt one. Just a stab at politeness as he negated what she'd revealed.

'No.'

It just sucked.

'I don't know what to say here, Lina.'

'Neither do I.'

He looked up then and she could see the agony in his eyes.

Did Garth even know that she'd been pregnant? He must because it would have been in the coroner's report, yet it was another thing a new girlfriend should not yet know.

'It messed with my head,' Lina admitted. 'I'm not very good at relationships. I always seem to get things wrong, or say the wrong thing…'

'By telling me about Carrie?' He frowned. His face was so pale. She guessed that he was still reacting to the fact that they were in a cold, bright ambulance talking about his late wife's death, and so she attempted to pull on her professional hat. 'If there's anything you want to ask, about Carrie, I mean, about that night…'

He stared back for the longest time before speaking. 'I'm sure I should have some questions. And of course I do. It's just…'

'A shock?' Lina ventured.

'Yes. Of all the things I thought had gone wrong between us, I never thought it might be that…'

'No.'

Neither really knew what to say. There were questions that might or might not need answers, and there was more trouble that a couple at the very beginning of a relationship should have to face.

His past sat between them, and it would seem that neither knew how to deal with that.

'I ought to get back in,' he said. 'May's going to be wondering where the hell I've got to.'

It sounded like a normal conversation except his skin

was the colour of putty and for the first time ever he was completely unable to meet her eyes.

Lina too was brilliant at noticing the very second things went wrong, because as he stood up and gave her a thin smile, Lina knew that it would be Garth avoiding her now.

'Garth?' She called him back, but for a second it looked as if he was going to keep right on walking, but just as he reached the doors, instead of stepping down, he halted and slowly turned around.

'I wanted to tell you.'

'But you didn't.'

They were the three hardest words that Lina had ever heard and they were laced with accusations that she didn't want to interpret. It seemed he was taking back his earlier words and that she did have something to be sorry about. 'You could have told me in bed. You could have called. You could have done it so much better than you did. I'm at work…' And that made her breath hitch in her throat as he put up his hands. 'I can't deal with this now. I've got a department full of patients and a night shift to complete…'

He was angry.

Not with her.

Yes, with her.

And he was embarrassed as he made his way back to the department.

Embarrassed because he didn't want anyone to have seen him like that, soiled and bleeding and helpless, as the woman he'd loved had lain dying by his side.

It was private.

'Garth?' May called to him. 'Can I get you to cast your eyes over—?'

'Get Huba,' he snapped.

Yes, he was angry. Huba was fine now, her confidence restored, while he was back to where he'd started—or rather back to where his life had ended and in that dark pit of grief.

'Garth?' May found him standing in his office. 'What on earth…?'

And May, who for six months had been needling him for information and getting nothing, didn't even try to find out what was wrong, because she knew agony when she saw it, and his was pure.

She was watching him drowning.

'Can you call Richard and ask him to come in and cover…?' Garth said in a voice that was struggling to form words, coming from lungs that had forgotten how to breathe.

'Of course,' May said. 'I'll do it right now.'

'And if Huba needs me, I'll come round but—'

'She's fine,' May said as Garth looked around blindly for a chair as if he had no idea where it might be located. 'You did too good a job with her. She's a bit arrogant now really.' May nattered on as she guided him to the said foreign object and somehow he managed a small smile at her words and then sat there, numb. Not once did May ask him why, or what was wrong,

She just accepted that it was.

Completely wrong.

The same way the world had been wrong when he'd started coming to and found himself in hospital, his father, who he didn't get on with, sitting by his bed.

And still sitting there that evening when he'd briefly opened his eyes.

His father had still been there the next morning as he'd flitted back to the world.

Garth had known, therefore, that Carrie was dead before he'd been told.

Now May made him tea, and he stared at the muddy brown liquid. Even a cup of tea was more complicated now, because he was remembering that morning, the very second he had pegged that the Lina he had gone to bed with wasn't the same Lina that had woken up beside him...

He sat in his office, hoping no serious cases came in, and then nodded in weak relief when May told him that Richard had arrived, but then added that there was no way he was driving home.

'I can walk it,' he told her.

'Not yet you can't.'

May was right.

And so he sat there some more.

CHAPTER ELEVEN

THE NIGHT DRAGGED on and on. And, no, he didn't call.

And Lina, who was more than used to checking her phone for guys who didn't call, this time found that the lack of contact made her feel ill.

His silence was agony.

Her handling of the whole thing had her spinning as she packed for her trip and she wished she could take it back, wished she'd told him more gently. Sooner perhaps?

Why did he not just call?

Except in this case it was worse when he did.

As she stood at Euston Station, waiting to board her train, his name pinged onto her phone.

Thank you for telling me, Lina. If I came down hard on you, I apologise. I know it must have been difficult.

She thought for a moment before responding.

It was.

Then she hit 'send' too soon and had to follow it up.

Though of course it was harder for you to hear it. I shouldn't have told you at work.

Another distinct lack of response, so once she had boarded the train and found her seat she fired another message.

Do you have any questions?

He didn't reply straight away. She could feel his strain even as the train pulled out of the station, and she was well out of London before her phone pinged. She was on the receiving end of a frown from a fellow passenger for daring to not silence her phone.

I don't think it's fair on either of us to ask them.

She looked at his text for a very long time before she finally answered.

You can.

There was no further response.

The plan had been to sleep on the train, but instead she just stared out at the English countryside and wished he was there beside her, that she could have wrapped her arms around him and made things right between them...

Made it hurt less.

But today everything hurt.

The sight of the bridges over the Tyne always moved her and the accents were familiar as she headed out of the station to find her accommodation.

There was a café she knew, and her aunt was nearby.

This place felt like home...

Almost.

Everything was making her cry today, so much so that she had to duck out of her little bed & breakfast and buy an eye mask in the hope of looking normal for her interview the next day.

Oh, that.

Lina was torn, so torn.

It was a massive decision she was about to make. It was stay or go and it deserved her full attention—except she couldn't focus on that because it was a future without Garth that was killing her now.

She'd feel better in the morning, Lina told herself as she ate a sandwich she'd bought on the train and told herself to get some sleep. But Garth was on her mind the whole night through. So much so that she deliberately switched off 'Do Not Disturb' on her phone and kept leaping in hope every time it bleeped, only to find it was *just* the news—or rather not the news she was desperate for.

Garth.

She fell asleep with the agony of his features visible to her closed eyes, and the awful knowledge that she had caused it.

And she awoke to the same.

Interview day dawned and Lina was brilliant at putting on a brave face—it was an almost prerequisite for her job. Arm hanging off? Not a problem. Impaled on a fence? Nothing we haven't seen...

A shattered heart? Usually she could deal with that, except the diagnosis here was starting to look a whole lot like love, and these were uncharted waters for Lina.

She was tempted to be late for the interview, to sabotage all her chances, but somehow public transport decided to behave and she arrived with fifteen minutes to spare.

And they were all so welcoming.

'You were born here?'

'Yes.' Lina beamed, keeping her professional hat on and sounding upbeat. 'I spent most of my summers here. It's like a second home really…'

So why did her mind keep flicking to the four-in-the-morning feeling she got driving through London, and the laughter and camaraderie with her colleagues? Yes, even when she was paired with Perfect Peter. The many, many hospitals she attended, where everyone knew her by name, each one offering a different welcome but somehow never making her feel like the 'new girl'.

London, even if she couldn't afford it, even with all her issues, really was starting to feel like home.

Still, the interview went really well.

And the house viewing went even better.

There were two. One was a complete disaster, but there was one that she could actually afford. A two-bedroomed house with the steepest stairs ever, but the kitchen had been refurbished, and the bathroom was liveable, and there was a teeny garden out the back—not that Gretel would venture out.

But she could admire it from the window ledge.

Yes, it all went too well, because as she took the train from Newcastle up to the Scottish borders, a day later than initially planned, Lina knew that there could be no more putting things off and that choices had to be made.

The Borders were grey and sort of gothic, which perfectly matched her mood, and Lina loved it completely.

She booked into her little hotel and then wandered around the bitty shops and tried her level best to enjoy her getaway.

Bounce back, she told her heart. *Snap to it.*

She'd only spent one weekend with Garth, and by all accounts they were through, so he could have no bearing on the decision she was about to make.

Except, even with the lousy start it had been the best weekend of her life.

And breakfast at the café with Garth had been the best breakfast she'd known and she did not know how to explain to herself the pain of the absence of him in her life when he'd barely been in it.

It just felt as if he belonged there.

And even if they could never be, still she wanted to know how he was faring and to apologise for her handling of things, yet her phone remained stubbornly silent. And so she distracted herself by heading into a musty-smelling shop filled with old books and antiques, in her ongoing search for vintage ambulance models.

'We don't have any,' the man said. 'Pity you weren't here yesterday…'

'I was supposed to be,' Lina sighed, because that had been her initial plan before the interview had come up. He was carrying an armful of records that he was about to put on display, and once he had laid them out Lina found herself flicking through them.

There was a whole jazz collection section.

A whole world she'd never known!

'I'd buy that now if I were you,' the man said when he saw her looking at one. 'It will be snapped up.'

'Really?' Lina frowned.

It was, she was told by the man who turned out to be the owner, a piece of mint-condition vinyl by a famous jazz musician. She read the back and was sort of toying with it—after all, Garth had bought breakfast and dinner and she sort of wanted to close things on a better note. 'Is it for someone?' the shop owner asked.

'Yes, though I think he likes modern jazz…' whatever the hell that was! 'I don't know if he's got anything to play it on.'

'He'd want this, believe me…'

He was either a completely brilliant salesman or it would make the perfect gift—only Lina wasn't into sentimental gifts and anyway, they were over.

Except…

Perhaps she could send it to him, with a little note.

Or maybe a card?

Just to say that she had seen the vinyl and was thinking of him and hoped he was doing okay and that she was very *sorry* for her handling of things.

And *then* she could move on with her life…

Really move on.

It was a very expensive gift, as it turned out, and there was certainly no gift wrapping. He gave her an old paper bag and she carefully zipped it into her pack, and then she moved on to a coffee shop, which usually helped to lift her mood. But it just didn't today.

She had a vanilla and malt milkshake *and* a chocolate éclair, but nothing helped.

Nothing helped.

Not even pizza delivered to her room because she was too teary and jumbled to go out. Instead she was sitting in her little B&B bedroom and crying her eyes out. If this was love, she didn't want it, because it simply hurt too much.

Oh, why didn't he call?

Why didn't Garth say they could put it behind them, and work on it?

He didn't.

But, then, Lina thought, neither had she.

She passed another lonely night, and in the morning it was misty and grey when she pulled back the curtains. The temptation to close the curtains and climb back into bed was unfamiliar and worrying. Not that she tended to bounce in the mornings, but she had never been so close to taking to her bed.

Instead, she hauled on her clothes and then stood in the tiny kitchen and hard-boiled her eggs, and then made some sandwiches and a big flask of coffee, packed up her rucksack and checked out. The bus journey to St Abbs, which was to be the start of her planned walk, passed in a bit of a blur, but she was glad for the effort she'd made when she stepped off and walked down to the harbour. It was bracing and the air smelt of seaweed. The sky was grey, but the water was a deep, angry blue, while the fishing boats bobbed, and the lobster creels were all piled up at the sides.

She was glad to be here, Lina thought as she started the coastal walk.

She was through with men.

Only not quite.

Garth Hughes wasn't being added to the list of terrible mistakes. He had a heading of his own.

If Only.

Walking really was her de-stressor—the occasional good morning from a fellow human, a greeting from a dog, the wind in her face—this was how she sorted herself, Lina knew.

Concentrating on where she put her feet, or pausing to look at a magnificent view, it left her mind free to sort out the jumble of problems in the background, even if it dared not ponder the big one called Garth Hughes that seemed lodged in the foreground.

And later, sitting on a damp clump of heather, she knew that a decision had to be made—not about Garth as that felt too raw to deal with just yet. No, she had to make up her mind about moving and starting her life all over again.

She thought of the positives.

A tiny house of her own instead of sharing.

A patch of garden.

All these gorgeous walks a bus or train ride away.

A chance to advance her career.

She had some aunts and cousins nearby and she knew that paramedics were a friendly lot so her social life would be just fine.

Except...

She thought of little Michael, her soon-to-be god-son, and Brendan and Alison and, yes, Shona, when she wasn't being a pain. And Mum and her brothers and May, who had offered to speak with her before she made such a decision.

Yes, she should have spoken to May about moving, because she wasn't just a colleague, she was a friend, a huge part of her world...

And then there was London.

Beautiful London that felt as if it was her own when the blue hour came just before dawn, and the best cafés she knew and the hospitals and her history and all the people she loved...

She couldn't avoid thinking about Garth and having to face him if she stayed. But as awkward as it might be, bumping into Garth on occasion—and it would be awkward, that much she knew—it wasn't a big enough reason for leaving.

Lina hadn't inherited her father's knack for running away.

The fact was that she loved London.

Even if she couldn't afford it.

Even if it meant having to see Marcus every morning as she hard-boiled her eggs and wearing earplugs every time he and Shona had sex until she'd saved enough for her own place…

One decision down, five thousand to go, Lina thought as she hauled herself up and rather gingerly made her way down a track so steep that she had to hold on to the handles.

Imagine falling here, Lina thought. Imagine having to retrieve a patient who had fallen here…

And then she nearly found out exactly how it would be done because her heart lurched and her legs almost gave way beneath her. Garth was on the beach, waiting for her.

She was surely seeing things.

Up ahead was a guy, a large guy with dark, wavy hair, watching her walk towards him.

It couldn't be him because she knew he was working this weekend and she was in Scotland, for goodness' sake…looking terrible.

So terrible!

She had on khaki trousers and a big raincoat and massive boots, and she was wet and red-faced, and certainly not profile-photo-ready! But it *was* Garth and he was walking towards her and looking a whole lot more together than her.

'I thought I might find you here,' Garth said, and then smiled at her bemused face. 'Well, I thought I might find you here yesterday…'

'I'm running a day behind schedule.'

'I know,' Garth said, 'because I was here yesterday too…'

'Why?'

'Waiting for you. In fact, I really am starting to feel like a stalker.'

'You're nothing of the sort.' Lina smiled.

She tried to keep her heart under control, and to stop herself from jumping into his arms and pleading for this purgatory to end, but then she reminded herself that Dr Sensible probably had some things about Carrie that he wanted to ask and that was confirmed with what came next: 'I do have some questions I'd like to ask you, if that's okay.'

'Sure.' Lina nodded.

'It seemed wrong to ask them via text.'

'So you decided to rock up on my walk instead,' Lina teased, and was glad that he got her, because he smiled.

'Yes.'

There wasn't a lot of talking at first because they left the beach and found themselves on a fairly steep incline. Lina was glad of the silence just to get her head around the fact he was actually there.

And looking gorgeous, by the way!

His bum was fantastic and she sneaked a guilty look as she huffed her way behind and once, or maybe twice, she had to tell him to slow down. 'I'm not a walker walker...'

'That's right,' he said as he slowed down.

'I amble rather than ramble.'

So they ambled to the top and there she took a very long drink of water and then said, 'I am so sorry for telling you at work...'

'We'll get to that,' Garth said, like a schoolteacher temporarily filing away a misdemeanour.

For now they just walked, enjoying the bracing breeze and the seagulls swooping and calling, and the balm of nature.

'So this is what you do with your days off?'

'Pretty much.' Lina nodded. 'Well, not all of them, but it's my hobby, I guess. I came here as a little girl,'

Lina said, smiling at the memory. 'Well, the next village over. I remember having ice cream and feeding a seal...'

'With your parents.'

'Yes,' Lina said.

'You miss him,' Garth said, not as a question, more an observation.

'Not right now,' Lina said. What she wanted to say was, *I miss you*.

He was here, but no doubt it was to find out more about his late wife.

Their walk was interspersed with benches carrying plaques in memory of people who must have loved to sit and take in the stunning views too.

'Do you want to sit?' Garth suggested, and she nodded.

They were both shy and nervous, and though they knew this difficult conversation had to be had, they didn't dive straight in. 'I've got lunch,' Lina said as she opened up her rucksack, 'if you want to share it.'

'Sounds good.'

Egg sandwiches had never tasted so good, but he declined her coffee and stuck with his water, and they just sat, enjoying the feel of the wind whipping their hair and cheeks and the majesty of the rugged North Sea.

'How was your interview?' Garth asked.

She turned and her mouth gaped. Not the best look mid-sandwich, so she rapidly closed it and swallowed before croaking, 'How do you know about that?'

'I heard May giving you a reference, just before we went out...'

'Ouch.' Lina cringed. Maybe that was the reason that the mood might have been a bit flat at first.

'So, how did it go?'

'Brilliantly,' Lina replied. 'Too brilliant,' she then

sighed. 'I didn't know how to tell you about it. I mean, I would be the stalker if I told you on our first date that I was thinking of dropping my plans to move away on the back of one breakfast, one night out…'

'Probably,' he said, 'but, then, with the way we were that weekend, probably not.'

'I need to give Shona an answer.'

'Why don't you text her and say yes, it would be great if Marcus moved in, because Garth wants to move in too?' He smiled as she laughed and he didn't need to tell her he was joking. It was funny to picture Shona's face if she did, but way better than that was the return of his smile.

'I'm staying,' Lina said. 'I'm happy at work, I've got brilliant friends, and I'm sure, well, I'm determined to find somewhere that is affordable just for me, hopefully with a little balcony…' she thought for a daunting moment '…that doesn't mind a cat.'

'How's Gretel?' Garth asked as they shared a bag of crisps.

'Temperamental,' she said. 'But Shona is looking after her and I've bought her some extra treats to have while I'm away.'

'That's good.'

She turned and faced him, feeling a little braver now. 'I know you hate cats…' He looked at her and frowned. 'Carrie told me you did.'

'Really?' He blinked in surprise and then he smiled; she guessed he was replaying memories with his late wife. 'I don't hate cats, I just told Carrie that I did…'

She swallowed as he said her name.

'The thing was that her parents had this cat, Suky. Honestly, Lina, this cat had a face that could haunt houses. She was the scariest thing you've ever seen, and they were all over her… I just blanched when I saw her and then to cover said that I just don't like cats. However, that's not strictly true. I'm sure Gretel's beautiful.'

'She is.' Lina smiled and looked at him, and suddenly it wasn't so terrible because he had said her name, and told a little of his history, and they were still standing—or rather sitting—smiling at each other.

'I was going to tell you about her,' Garth said. 'When I went in to do all the paperwork, I was determined to do it that night, but then you threw a picnic in my lounge with Christmas pudding and everything, and the time just didn't seem right.'

'That's why you haven't had Christmas pudding in years.'

He nodded. 'It didn't feel as if there was much to celebrate. Lina, I had a head injury. It was six months of rehab and a year before I went back to work, and once I was back I chose to work over all the Christmases and New Years. I've moved around a lot since Carrie died, six months here, two months there, I learned pretty quickly not to tell anyone about it. There are too many questions, too many awkward glances and the assumption that I'm lonely or on the pull, and sometimes those assumptions were correct…' He was being very open. 'But then it was time to move on, and that meant taking a permanent position, which I have…' He looked over at Lina. 'I get what you mean about wanting your own place and putting down roots…'

'I've got a box at my mum's,' Lina said. 'I've never bothered unpacking it, but I will once I have my own place.'

'I never know what to do with our wedding photo, where to put it up, or if I should…'

'Of course you should.'

'It does tend to lead to an awful lot of questions,' Garth said.

Lina thought for a moment. His honesty was still so refreshing. She understood that a wedding photo on the wall wouldn't exactly help a fling or a short-term thing.

'I would have told you that morning,' Garth said, 'but then you walked out the door. Why?'

'Garth, I can't even make simple relationships work, let alone complicated ones. I thought you were keeping things light with me, just putting on a front.'

'What on earth made you think that?'

'Lots of things. Carrie told me you and your dad don't get on, but you told me the two of you were close…'

'Ah…' Garth looked ahead now, perhaps glimpsing how confusing it had been. 'We didn't used to get on. My mother died when I was very young and if ever there was someone not cut out to be a single parent, it was him. He wanted his career and it was boarding school for me. I did have a time of it growing up, but when Carrie died he came into his own and was really supportive, and I suppose I gave him another chance. We get on better as two adults.'

'Is he in Wales?' she asked. 'Is that where you'd been when you brought those cakes back?'

'No, he's just outside London. It's her mother who's in Wales. I visit Gwen a couple of times a year. Carrie's father died a couple of months after the accident. Gwen's never got over it and I doubt she ever will.' He looked over. 'It's hell seeing her, because just when I'm feeling as if my life is moving on, I'm back again, going through albums and watching wedding videos and talking about grandchildren that can never be…'

Lina swallowed.

'Carrie was pregnant,' Garth told her, and it was such

a relief that she wasn't the one telling him that. It was such a relief to let go of the stress of holding that knowledge and not knowing whether he knew. 'I wasn't supposed to know, but I'd seen the test and the champagne in the fridge…' He looked at her. 'Did she tell you?'

'Yes.' Lina started to cry, even though it wasn't quite her place to, but it was both a relief that he knew and she was so sad for what he had been through. And because she liked it that he cared about a lady who sat home alone with her memories.

'I do have one question,' he said, 'if you're okay answering it.'

She braced herself, and found that all the ropes holding her heart up were strong and intact.

'Was she scared?' Garth asked. 'I always worried that she was alone and scared.

'She wasn't scared.' Lina thought back and knew she had to be honest. 'Well, at first she was scared that she'd lost you, but you'd moved your arm and I told her I thought you could hear…' She let that sink in. 'Then she said she was worried about the baby…' Lina didn't look over to see his reaction, but she felt him squeeze her hand and gave his a squeeze back and then said, 'I told her we'd deal with the baby later and for now we were taking care of her…'

'Was she scared to die?' Garth asked. His voice was a husk and she could hear the years of dread and torment behind the words.

'I don't know that she knew she was,' Lina said. 'And I'm not making that up.' They looked at each other then. 'She was a doctor, I was a paramedic, so I guess we both knew, but it just… Somehow it was peaceful. She said she wasn't in pain and we talked right up to the end.' Lina said with certainty, 'She wasn't alone and she wasn't scared.'

They sat then for a moment, both lost in that night six years ago, both living it all over again.

'I understand why you couldn't tell me,' Garth said. 'For selfish reasons I didn't want you to have been there at the accident, and I'm not just talking about Carrie…'

'Then what?'

'I was embarrassed.'

She frowned, not understanding.

'I'm not now, but when you first told me, I hated that you'd seen me like that.'

Lina nodded, even though she had never thought of that until now, but a proud man like him would hate to have been seen rendered helpless. 'To be honest,' she said, 'I wasn't really paying much attention to you.'

They shared a very watery smile, but it helped dilute the pain of what they were discussing. 'Is there anything else you want to know?'

She held her breath, because she was scared, so scared that somehow he might blame her, that if he felt she'd not done enough, however misplaced, then it would surely be something they could never get past.

'I don't think so. I wish it hadn't been you but in the same thought I'm grateful that you were with her.'

They sat, listening to the whistle of the wind and the screeching of the gulls, but louder than that was the sound of her pulse in her ears as she waited for his polite smile and his careful words to thank her for laying his ghosts to rest.

To draw his neat conclusion and place a neat line under them.

For Garth to simply leave.

'Shall we walk?' he said, and Lina blinked. 'If we want to make it back before it starts getting dark...'

He was still here.

CHAPTER TWELVE

THINGS FELT LIGHTER when they started walking again. Though maybe, Lina conceded, that was because he was carrying her rucksack, but she felt her old self starting to filter back as her professional hat blew away with the wind.

'I need a drink,' Garth said as they huffed up a hill.

'I need an ice cream,' Lina said.

'It's freezing.'

'Then it won't melt.'

He laughed as they debated where they might eat in the village that would be home for the night. 'Come on,' he said. 'Almost there.'

They found a little Italian café and Lina got her ice cream and Garth had a ginger ale and cake. They sat outside in the thin winter sun, which was bracing but invigorating.

'So where are you staying?' Lina asked.

'There.' He pointed to the little hotel she had chosen for that night.

'It's the same one as me.'

'I know.' Garth smiled. 'I remembered you telling me about it and I decided to risk it…' He was honest. 'Lina, I can head back to London tonight if it's difficult for you.

I know how much you've been looking forward to this and I really don't want to ruin your days off.'

'It's not difficult,' Lina responded. They were back to where they'd been, before she'd remembered—or even better than they'd been, because now there were no secrets between them. 'It is cold though. I think I'm going to check in and try to warm up in the shower.'

It was a lovely little hotel and she registered in a matter of moments and they headed to the stairs. 'Do you want to come up?' she offered. 'I believe there's a kettle *and* biscuits!'

Her room was gorgeous, if very small, but it looked out on the water. It was hard to believe he had come all this way just to speak to her.

'Thank you,' Lina said as she took off her huge jacket, 'for coming all this way to talk to me, for clearing the air…'

'It's the nicest walk I've ever had.'

'Really?' Lina frowned, doubting that it was.

'Really.' He took her wool and khaki-wrapped body in his arms and she was back in her favourite space, somewhere she'd never thought she'd be again. 'I don't think I've walked properly since camp at school.'

She laughed and then just rested a while in his arms.

'I've missed you,' Lina told him. 'I probably shouldn't admit that, but I've really missed you.'

'I've missed you too,' Garth said. 'I do have another question.'

'Oh!' She pulled back from his arms, not sure she was ready for what was to come.

'Would you ever have got in touch?'

'We'd have seen each other at work,' Lina said, attempting nonchalance for all of five seconds, but then giving in. 'Yes. I'd have probably caved and called you tonight, or...' She went in her rucksack and pulled out a scruffy paper bag. 'Failing that, I was going to give you this, with a card, though I haven't bought it yet...'

'What would the card say?'

'I don't know.'

'Try?'

'That I panicked,' Lina said, and took a breath.

'And...'

'That I'm not very used to relationships working out, and I thought that this might be too much, but I'd hoped...'

He opened the bag and took out the record she had brought. He frowned and smiled as he turned it over in his hands. 'Where the hell did you get this?'

'At a vintage shop. The man said it was really rare and I should snap it up. I don't know if he was just playing me.'

'He wasn't playing you, Lina...' He smiled. 'This is amazing, thank you.'

'You like it?'

'I love it.' He looked at her. 'You hate jazz.'

'You don't, though.'

'If you knew how sexy this was...' He held her and they danced around the little room, and she could almost hear the music she hadn't even known existed thrum through her body, making her less shy.

His kiss was like a gentle eraser, wiping all the fears and the troubles of the world away, a caress to her soul that felt almost familiar, as if it couldn't be any other way and could only be him in whose arms she unravelled.

He took off her ugly trousers, and massive black boots, shredding her armour in the process. Then he let out a low laugh when he saw her stunning satin burnt orange bra. 'That underwear you wore really wasn't for me…'

'Nope…'

Garth brushed back the hair from her face and kissed her deep and slow.

He was ruining her, Lina thought as they kissed, because she wanted long walks with him and kisses like this, and…for ever.

Her skin was all blotchy and cold and red and it was nice to jump into bed and lie under the heavy blankets and watch him undress. 'I'm so glad you're here.'

'I'm very pleased to be here too.'

Garth was far, far too big for her tiny bed, but it made it nicer somehow. It was deep in winter and so it was dark already, even though it was only late afternoon.

His skin was cold and his kiss warm, his hands taking in the curves of her body. That ease and excitement from before had returned.

He kissed her neck, and the roughness of his jaw as it dragged across her cheek caused her eyes to screw closed at the bliss as her mouth awaited his.

'Open them,' he said.

She looked into navy eyes as he told her that her eyes were the greenest he had ever seen. 'You're beautiful, Lina.'

She was so new to that feeling, and in his arms so accepting of it, because he made it true.

His kiss made her both shiver and burn. Her hand crept down his body, touching, caressing, until she held him again and stroked him between them.

Warm, intimate and tender, till they both needed more. He turned her onto her back and lifted up, just so that he could look down at her as they made love. She didn't care that her hair was a knotted mess and that her cheeks were pink from the wind.

She tasted the salty skin of his shoulder as they made tender love.

Nothing else mattered as they took themselves to a place only the other knew and she had to hold onto those three little words as she shattered beneath him, because otherwise she might end up telling him that at the age of almost thirty she had, for the first time, found love.

And it scared her.

He lay on top, both of them panting, catching their breaths as the world came back in, and all Lina knew was that she could never go back out there—could never venture back into single land if this didn't work out.

'What?' Garth asked as she rolled away, but he tucked her right in against him. 'You've gone all silent again.'

'I'm just…'

How she wanted to emergency-text Shona, or Brendan, or even May!

An emergency pow-wow was needed ASAP, except she had to make do with her own troubled mind.

It was too soon for declarations surely?

'Just what?' Garth prompted.

'Hungry,' she settled for instead.

'Then we'll go and get dinner…'

She swallowed and then turned and faced him, her deepest truth a whisper away.

'What's wrong?'

'I was going to grab some pasta at the Italian, well, that was my plan, but…' She had to be very honest now. 'Garth, I feel like I have the cheat sheet on you.'

'The cheat sheet?'

'That I could tick all your boxes because I know

things about you, but I have to be me. It's tempting, though…'

'Lina, I have no idea what you're talking about.'

'Everyone keeps telling me what I'm doing wrong, how I need to be less assertive, wear a dress, be more this, less that…' They lay facing each other in the co-coon of bedding as she bared her soul. 'I want to keep you,' she admitted, 'and I'm scared I might use my su-perpower for evil. I live in jeans, I love pasta, I hate jazz. Remember the cat thing?'

'Lina,' he broke in, 'can I tell you something.'

She nodded.

'Carrie knew a different me.' There was a huskiness to his voice that told Lina how difficult these words were to say. 'And while I did used to say that I hate pasta, I would kill to sit and have the biggest bowl with her…'

She nodded, because that much she understood.

'The little things that once seemed to matter don't any more when you lose someone you love.'

'I guess.'

'It's true, because I guard my privacy more than any-one, but after you'd gone, I sat in the office and I spoke with May…'

'You told May?'

'I couldn't just keep on working.'

'Because of Carrie…' she said, running a hand through his thick dark hair, just so honest and warm and safe in this bed.

'Because of Carrie and because of you. May pretty much knew most of it anyway—she was on the interview panel after all, but I ended up telling her about you…'

It was the nicest break of confidence she had ever heard, that this gorgeous man had opened up to some-one about her.

'I'd love to share a bowl of pasta with you, Lina.'

She smiled, and then laughed. 'Do you know what, I don't even fancy it now…' She could hear the rain battering the window now. 'Shall we just get something sent up?'

'How about you let me take care of dinner?' Garth said. 'I could book us a table downstairs.'

'A *date* date?' Lina checked.

'Why do you think I'm here, Lina?'

To find out about Carrie, to resurrect them, to see if they were salvageable…but then he said something that made her heart go completely still, 'I'm here to fight for us.'

'Fight for us?'

'Yes…' He looked at her very seriously. 'I know we could have done things differently, on both sides, but I'm not going to let something as wonderful as we've found slip away…'

His words made her shake.

In fact, they were the words she had waited for ever to hear.

Someone who fought for her.

Fought for them.

Didn't just give up when things got too hard or too messy. Didn't just up sticks and walk away.

Except he was climbing out of bed. 'Where are you going?'

'To get ready,' Garth said. 'I'll meet you down there at, say, seven…?'

Lina nodded as she silently panicked.

She had a *date* date. A serious, proper date with a man she was—whisper—in love with, and who was possibly starting to feel the same, and she had *absolutely* nothing to wear.

There was no Shona and her wardrobe of many colours to draw on.

No high street to dash out to.

Nothing.

She gulped as she thought of May's words: 'We'll just have to work with what we've got.'

Not much!

There was her interview dress, but this wasn't an interview, because the questions had all been asked and answered.

And so she put on jeans but wore the nice black jumper she had worn for her interview and put on lip balm and wore her hair down.

That *was* Lina making an effort.

Apart from the violet dress, Lina realised, he hadn't seen her in anything other than her uniform or practical walking clothes, or bundled up in a coat and scarf.

And yet, she reminded herself, he still liked her.

He didn't seem to mind the wet and messy hair, and that she talked about work, and he didn't even seem to mind her egg sandwiches.

She was nervous. Like one of his awful jazz songs, her heart was going *boop-doop, doop-doop* as she made her way down the creaking steps of the little hotel, following the herby scents to the bar.

And there, waiting for her, standing up as she entered, like the old-fashioned guy he was, was Garth.

He wore black jeans, a black jumper, and he'd actually shaved.

'You look so handsome,' she said, and caught a whiff of cologne as they shared a brief kiss.

'You look stunning,' he told her, and the blaze in his eyes told her he meant every word. That this version of Lina was better than fine by him.

'Thank you.'

She was embarrassed, shy and pleased all at the same time.

She felt feminine and herself as they sat by a roaring fire in a pub, both drinking beer, Lina ordering crab on toast and him ordering an amazing-sounding pie that was topped with blue cheese.

And between mouthfuls and a little taste of each other's food and a whole lot of laughter, they talked.

They talked about Gretel's diabetes—and his eyes didn't glaze over. In fact, he took it just as seriously as he would if the cat were a patient, which delighted Lina.

She told him about her model vintage ambulance collection and he discussed in great depth his vast vinyl collection—her eyes did glaze a little, but that was possibly lust or the stronger-than-expected beer. And how warm the flat was, thanks to her radiator skills. But he still needed...

'Curtains,' Lina finished for him.

'Yes!'

'We know all this stuff about each other...'

'Except we know so little.' Garth smiled. 'I can't wait to get to know you some more, Lina.'

'I can't wait to get to know you either.' She smiled back and thought about it and then said it again. 'I honestly can't. I've never felt like this before, Garth. In fact...' She blushed at her own presumption. 'What are you doing next weekend?'

'Working. Why?'

'It doesn't matter.'

'Why?' Garth pushed.

She was finally brave, because his hand on her thigh made her so. 'Alison and Brendan have asked me to be godmother and they said I can bring someone... It's not a big deal.' She corrected herself. 'I mean, it's a big deal that they've asked me, but it's fine that you can't make it…'

'I'd love to be there.'

'Really?'

'I am down to be working,' he admitted. 'I actually had to swap things around to get these days off, but I'm sure I can sort something out with Richard…' He took out his phone and put in the date; it was just about the nicest thing he could have done for her. 'I'll do my best to be there, even if I can only get away for the service.'

That he would try meant the world. 'Thank you,' she said. It made a special day extra special.

'Lina, about you telling me at work…'

She felt her hopes suddenly plummet, as though the cable on a lift had snapped, Maybe he'd decided to ditch her in public and, no, she wasn't being dramatic. Lina had had two men disappear on her mid-dinner.

'You were right to…'

'Right?'

'Would Alison wait till Brendan's shift ended to let him know she was in labour?'

'No.'

'Life happens in real time,' Garth said, 'and I want my life to happen with you in it. I never thought I'd be happy again,' Garth told her. 'Not truly. And I don't mean that in a depressing way. Hell, I have a nice life, I just never thought I'd feel *it* again.'

'It?' Lina checked, because that was exactly how she herself had described it, this feeling that had descended the second she had walked into the staffroom and seen him.

The awareness that had knocked the breath from her when she had first taken a seat by his side.

But, more than that, it was the confidence he gave her and the acceptance, the moments of being herself, shared with someone who felt *it* too, enough to address the parts that hurt. 'I know you'll always miss her.'

'Yes,' Garth said. 'And I miss life for her, if that makes sense, but you make me happy, Lina, in a way I never expected to feel again.' He was serious all of a sudden. 'Lina,' he said, 'I can't get through dinner without asking. Will you marry me, please?'

'Pardon?'

'I know I should have a ring, but we can go and choose one together...'

'You want me to marry you?'

'Yes, please.'

'Me?'

'Yes you.'

'But we're only on our...' she counted '...second date. Or third if you count breakfast.'

'I don't need another to know I love you.'

'I love you too.' It was, as it turned out, as simple as that. 'I love you, Garth.' It was a relief to say it, to admit it, to kiss and confirm it, but there was just one thing weighing on her mind. 'You don't have to marry me, though. We can live together, we can—'

He pulled his face back, but held it in his palms. 'What aren't you telling me?'

Lina took a breath and looked into the dark pools of his eyes and knew that with this man she really could be honest. 'I don't want a big wedding. I don't want...' she made herself say it '...to ask my father and have him not come, or...' she swallowed '...if he does, expect it to be big, given he's come all that way...'

'Lina,' he said. 'Do *you* want to marry me?'

'More than anything in the world.'

'And do you want a big wedding?'

'It's just not me.'

'Fine,' Garth said, 'then we'll have a tiny wedding but, Lina Edwards, I am going to marry you!'

CHAPTER THIRTEEN

'ANY PLANS FOR your days off?'

'None,' Lina said, and to avoid meeting Brendan's eyes she looked out of the window. 'Well, I'm moving the last of my stuff into Garth's.'

'You two really are serious, then?'

'We really are.' She turned now and smiled. 'What are you up to?'

'We're moving Michael into his own room,' Brendan said. 'I'm setting up the monitor tonight.'

It was a busy shift and they ended up at The Primary at ten p. m. when they should have been signing off. 'I thought you finished at nine,' Lina said when she saw May.

'No rest for the wicked,' May muttered. 'Still, I can't complain. I've got the weekend away from this madhouse…'

Just another weekend, except Lina could not wait, because tomorrow—not that anyone apart from her and Garth knew—she would become Mrs Lina Hughes.

She felt a little guilty about not sharing her news with Brendan, but if she did, she'd only feel more guilty for not telling her mum and brothers, and if she told them it would mean telling her dad, who she was sure wouldn't come. Then there was Garth's dad and his new lady friend…

It would all get too complicated for words and so they had decided to keep it to themselves for now.

She crept into the flat at eleven and tried to ignore the Shona and Marcus love fest going on in the next room as she put on a face pack and did her nails.

'What are you up to?' Shona asked when they met in the hallway past midnight.

'I'm just having a shower to wash this conditioner out.'

It was exhausting being polished and elegant!

They'd gone shopping, but Lina had decided she didn't want an engagement ring. 'I'd have to take it off for work and I know I'd lose it…' And as well as that, they wanted to keep their secret a little while longer from the world.

So, instead of shopping for an engagement ring, they'd headed to the blacksmiths in Gretna Green and bought wedding bands that fitted together with the anvil mark hidden on the inside.

They weren't eloping exactly, but it came pretty close.

The morning of the wedding loomed and Shona headed off for her shift at the beauty clinic. When Lina safely had the place to herself, the *real* preparations began.

Using curling tongs, Lina livened up her hair and then did her make-up, as she did on occasion now. With the clock running away with itself, she cut all the labels and price tags out of her very expensive silk underwear and put it on.

This set of underwear was for him.

Well, for her too, but she couldn't wait to see his smile when he saw the gorgeous white velvet and tiny red bows. It was subtle—virginal sexy—and just so gorgeous that it was worth an entire Saturday night shift at The Primary.

The set had cost more than her dress.

Ah, but what a dress.

It was a gorgeous crisp white cotton embroidered with red roses and she had known the second she'd seen it that this was the one.

She slipped it on and struggled to do up the tiny zip at the back and then slipped into the heels she had worn for Michael's christening last week.

Garth was waiting for her, and walked towards her as she stepped out of the taxi.

It was a gorgeous registry office, beside parks and a river. It was a busy Saturday in London but here it was peaceful as they walked hand in hand to make their vows.

'Oh, Lina,' he said, because over and over she amazed him and in turn he took her breath away, for he wore a charcoal-grey suit and a grey tie with a shirt as crisp and white as the cotton on her dress.

'I'm terrified,' Lina admitted.

'But sure?' Garth checked.

'I have never been so sure of anything in my life.'

'You look beautiful,' Garth said, and he kissed her on the cheek so as not to spoil her lipstick, and, still hand in hand, they walked in together when their names were called.

The celebrant was glamorous indeed, with caramel-blonde hair and a stunning suit, and it made the day just a little more special to see her smile and the effort she had made.

'Just the two of you?' she asked as the seats in the

room remained empty and they had their two borrowed witnesses.

'Just us.' Garth smiled.

'That's all a marriage needs,' the celebrant said, and the formalities began.

The ring felt heavy and cool as Garth slipped it on her finger, but how right it felt to be wearing it, Lina thought.

And she looked at his expression as he examined his white-gold ring. There was that second, she knew, when he must have been thinking about the first time, but it wasn't a threat to her, just a poignant moment that meant they both knew how lucky they were to have found each other.

'You are now husband and wife.'

His kiss was thorough and her lipstick, along with her heart, was completely gone as she gazed at her husband and smiled.

They had hired a photographer to take a few pictures on a little bridge outside, and they headed there to stand amidst the geese and swans.

Except there, waiting for them, was the biggest surprise.

Trefor Hughes and his lady friend, as well as Lina's mum and her brothers, Richard and May and a few others from The Primary, and she hoped no one needed help because it seemed that half of her paramedic colleagues just happened to be there, having a picnic!

'She's got legs!' Brendan shouted as Lina stood, stunned, and everyone laughed.

'You did this!' Lina gaped and then turned to Garth. 'How on earth…?'

'I had nothing to do with this. In fact, I had absolutely no idea,' Garth said, staring in bemusement at the activities taking place. Blankets were being spread on the grass and corks were popping. Shona was there, with Marcus in tow. 'There's Boris…' Garth said, pointing to a man arriving with a wicker picnic basket and another wrapped gift that could possibly be more bubble bath and candles.

'Lina…' Her mum embraced her. 'I am so happy for you and…' she looked at her new son-in-law '… Garth, it's lovely to meet you.'

'It's lovely to meet you too, Jeanette.'

Her mum pulled Lina aside the first chance she got.

'You don't mind that we didn't tell you?' Lina checked.

'Of course not. I dreaded a big wedding and having to face your dad again and…' She rolled her eyes. 'He was asked, of course, but he was never going to come all this way for a picnic…'

It was the only teeny blot on a wonderful day. But then he called and it felt like the best gift.

'Congratulations!' her dad said. 'Your colleague Brendan called me on Wednesday. If I'd known earlier, I'd have tried—'

'Dad, it's fine, I didn't even know they were sorting out a party.' They chatted a little, and he even spoke to Garth before they returned to their surprise party.

There were nieces and nephews and Michael lying there, kicking his legs, and Brendan happily confided that of course he'd guessed that she was up to something.

'Alison took Michael out for the day and checked the marriage notices on display…' Brendan laughed. 'We thought it would take ages, but it was the first registry office she went to,' he said, proud of himself and his wife for carrying it off.

'How did you know?'

'Because I've never seen you so happy,' Brendan said,

'and I've never known you so reluctant to talk. I knew you were up to something.'

Of course he had.

Lina had known she had wonderful friends and that even during the lonelier times they had, in their own unique ways, all been there for her.

They were certainly here for her now, doing everything they could to make today an extra-special one.

There were egg sandwiches, of course, but they were cut in little triangles, and instead of tuna it was smoked salmon and cream cheese, and Les thoroughly approved of them.

There were little lemon meringue pies and scones with cream and jam and just the most gorgeous afternoon tea, spread out on the lawn with all the people they cared about and loved, and who cared about and loved them in return.

'You didn't think we'd let you get off without a little party, now, did you?' May said, pouring champagne. 'You're one of us.'

There were no speeches, no pressure, just love and laughter on a lazy spring afternoon, with children running and adults laughing. If she had arranged this party herself it could not have been more perfect.

And later, as the blankets were all cleared away and the happy crowd drifted off, everyone agreed it had been a brilliant wedding.

'You've got grass in your hair,' Garth said as he picked it out on the taxi ride home.

'Here,' he said, and handed her a gorgeous keyring and a key of her own. As she turned the key in the lock, Lina didn't get to step into her new home, instead he swept her up and she laughed as he carried her from room to room.

The lounge room windows had long, heavy amber velvet drapes, and the ones in the huge spare room were jade-green and in the bedroom, well, they were kingfisher-blue...

Then he put her down by their brand-new dressing table, where a bottle of champagne was cooling in an ice bucket. Leaning on it was an envelope.

Mrs Lina Hughes

'What's this?' Lina asked, turning the envelope over in her hands and looking for clues as to what it contained.

'It's our wedding present.'

Lina frowned and felt a little flurry of panic, because she hadn't got him anything. Well, there was the underwear, but that didn't count! 'I didn't get us anything.'

'Just open it, Lina.'

She peeled open the envelope and took out a smart navy wallet, and then swallowed when she saw that it was two plane tickets to Singapore as well as a booking for ten nights in a rather nice hotel.

'Singapore?' She blinked and just stared at the tickets that would carry her towards a father she wasn't sure wanted her, one who might make excuses as to why he couldn't fit her in. And almost pre-empting that, she started to make them on her father's behalf... 'What if he's working or—?'

'I'm sure we can have lunch with him,' Garth said. 'Or dinner...'

'But what if—?'

'I said on the phone that I'm looking forward to meeting him, and he said the same.'

It was such a relief to hear someone speak nicely

about her father—always it felt as if he was being criticised, yet Garth seemed to instinctively get that it simply didn't help matters. Still, as exciting as the prospect was, there was that nagging dread that, despite his words to the contrary, her father might not be so thrilled at the thought of spending time with her. 'What if he doesn't want me back in his life, Garth?'

'Then I'll take you to the rooftop bar and we can drown our sorrows in Singapore slings.' Garth smiled. 'But I'm sure that won't be necessary.' He could see that she wasn't convinced and though he couldn't be positive of the outcome, he knew one thing for sure. 'Lina, I get on with my father now a thousand times better than I did growing up. You're already ahead of me there. He gave you a great childhood…'

'He did.'

'And then the teenage years got all messed up, but I'm sure you can sort it out…'

He sounded so positive. He was a living example after all, and it helped to know that when she got off that plane in Singapore it would be with Garth beside her, and at that awkward first meeting with him Garth would be there too.

Maybe he was right. Maybe this really could be the start of a whole new relationship with her family on the other side of the world.

'I'll call him and tell him we're coming,' she said with a smile.

'Call him tomorrow,' Garth said, and she nodded and smiled again.

She frowned at an old gramophone and then laughed as he took out a familiar-looking old record.

'Am I going to ruin your night by playing jazz?' Garth said as he lowered the needle onto the record.

It was slow and melodious and beat into her blood as it danced through her veins.

He pulled down her zipper and kissed her shoulder as he peeled off her bra. 'I think white drapes for the bathroom,' he whispered, 'with little red bows.'

'Of course,' she replied.

He had made his home theirs, each room already holding a memory...

EPILOGUE

BRENDAN HAD BEEN RIGHT.

Lina would never, ever tell him that, of course, but the fact was Brendan had been right when he'd said that being a parent changed everything!

Martha Aileen Hughes had been born six months ago but she'd changed their lives long before that.

Lina had been working in the control room since she'd found out that she was pregnant and had been on maternity leave since she'd had her daughter, but she was returning part time and was back in the driving seat for the first time in what felt like for ever.

'Here…' Garth said, and handed her a lunchbox from the fridge, filled with egg sandwiches, a chocolate bar and a muffin, as she squeezed a last cuddle out of Martha before she headed off.

She was adorable.

Fat cheeks, fat hands and the biggest blue eyes, and a single black curl on the top of an otherwise bald head. She had them both besotted.

On her first shift back from maternity leave they were called out to an eight-month-old with respiratory distress and it was blue lights all the way to The Primary.

'Lina!' May said as she came in with mum on the stretcher holding the baby.

Except there wasn't time for a catch-up or to share photos of Martha, because one look at the baby and May was waving them through to Resus. 'Richard!' May called in a voice Lina knew only too well.

He was there in seconds, examining the little baby as Lina guided the shaky mother to Reception to register the babe.

Lina felt shaky herself.

Back in the ambulance she let out a breath. 'Nice work,' Brendan said, and then looked at her. 'The baby will be fine.'

'I know.' Lina nodded, because she'd already started to look better by the time they'd left. 'But Martha's cheeks were a bit red when I left and there's loads going around…'

'I'm sure Garth would call if there were any issues,' Brendan said.

'Of course he would.'

'And he is a doctor,' Brendan pointed out. 'Martha couldn't be with anyone more qualified…'

'I know all that.' Lina sighed.

'That baby was sick,' Brendan said patiently. 'Martha's just teething.'

'I know all that, it's just…' She rolled her eyes and gave in. 'It's different when you have one of your own.'

'Told you so!' Brendan couldn't help himself but after a triumphant smile he was kind. 'Maybe text him and check everything's okay.'

'It's two in the morning.'

So rather than wake Garth, she breathed her way through the rest of her shift, and chatted with Brendan about, well, everything really.

Well, not *everything*.

It had been on their honeymoon that Martha had been conceived, she and Garth were sure.

They had explored Bukit Timah Nature Reserve with her father and his family, and they'd been on a night safari with them too. And while it might not sound romantic to spend half your honeymoon with your long-lost dad and his family, it had been magical for Lina. And because it was their honeymoon, she and Garth had been on river cruises and, yes, there had been Singapore slings. It had been such a magical time they had decided they would soon come back for another visit.

This time with little Martha in tow.

Garth still drove over to Wales now and then and Lina stayed behind. It was bitter-sweet for Carrie's mum, of course, but she was a kind and gracious lady and had sent a card and a little knitted cardigan for Martha, which she would be wearing for her christening...

Speaking of which...

'Do you and Alison want to come for dinner next week, or lunch?' Lina invited, oh, so casually.

'Lunch would be better,' Brendan said. 'Michael's on a strict schedule...' He turned and smiled. 'Any reason?'

'No reason.' Lina smiled. Other than that they would be asking Brendan to be godfather, and they were also going to ask May to be godmother. 'It would just be nice to catch up out of work.'

It felt good to be back. But for Lina it had been a very long night and she simply could not wait to be home, and she wasn't relishing the long journey ahead.

Sometimes Garth just got it so right, because at the end of her first shift, when she was ready to dive into the tube, and itching, just clawing, to see for herself that Martha was okay, there he was, standing by the car with a takeout coffee for her, and undoubtedly a tea for him, and a paper bag, which she rightly guessed held almond croissants.

'How was your shift?' he asked.

'Long,' Lina said. 'It was good, though.'

But there was something she wanted far more than croissants and coffee for there, in the back, nestled in her little car seat, was a sleeping Martha.

Her little hands were sticking out of the blanket, the fingers splayed as if in surprise, and she was the sweetest sight for sore, tired eyes.

'She woke up at two and then at five,' Garth explained, 'and then wouldn't settle.'

'Do you think she missed me?'

'She did, but then she decided that I'd have to do and took her bottle, but rather than go back to sleep she decided to practise chewing her feet.' He laughed.

It was so brilliant to see his smile and to hear his laugh. Such a privilege to see the happiness return to his world and lightness revive his heart.

'Did you give Gretel her treats?'

'Yes, I gave Gretel her treats,' he said. 'She missed you too.' They drove home, chatting about each other's nights, then he parked the car and took the lift up to the apartment. He carried Martha as Lina wanted to shower before she had a much-needed cuddle with her daughter.

She turned the key and had to pause for a second for she just loved stepping into her home.

Their home.

Her own boxes had finally been unpacked and there, amongst the med-school pictures and their graduation and holiday photos and childhoods and their wedding photo, was another one...

The past wasn't hidden, and when Martha asked who

the other gorgeous bride was, they would tell her, of course.

It brought a lump to Lina's throat this morning as she passed.

She went straight to the shower, where she shed her uniform and came out wrapped in towels to the sight of Martha asleep in her cot and Garth undressed and back in bed.

Sunday morning breakfast with Garth really was the nicest treat in the world and they lay there, sharing kisses and conversation and eating their treats.

Safe in love.

* * * * *

HEALING
HER BROODING
ISLAND HERO

MARION LENNOX

MILLS & BOON

For Alison, whose love and knowledge
of beach and garden was a gift to us all.

CHAPTER ONE

SHE'D FORGOTTEN ABOUT WOMBATS.

Gina Marshall had been on Sandpiper Island for less than an hour before she remembered, and she remembered with a thump. Now she was standing on a gravel track surrounded by thick bushland, shining her phone torch at a wombat lying in front of her aunt's car. Feeling ill.

How hard had she hit it? Surely not hard enough to do major harm.

Gina had caught the last ferry to Sandpiper, arriving after dark. Her Great-Aunt Babs had organised her car to be left for her at the ferry terminal. Babs's car was a Mini, old, battered and tiny. The wombat was large. Gina had been lucky the car hadn't rolled.

Wombats had been a menace on Sandpiper roads for as long as Gina could remember. They were like solid, heavy logs. The locals knew and respected them, but Gina had forgotten. She'd braked when she'd seen the 'log', but she hadn't braked soon enough.

The wombat was now upended, lying on its back with its four little legs in the air.

One of its legs looked…bloody.

Uh oh.

She was in the middle of a national park, and this side

of the island was almost uninhabited. The dark and the enveloping bushland were enough to give her the shakes, but she needed to pull herself together. She was a nurse, trained in emergency medicine. Triage. Action. Surely she could deal with this.

'I'm so sorry I hit you,' she said, out loud. 'But what to do next?'

That was helpful. Asking the patient for a plan of action?

And the wombat clearly was unimpressed. It stared up at her, its little eyes unblinking. There wasn't a huge amount of blood, but it lay unmoving.

Head injury? Spinal injury? Was it lying still because of shock, or something worse?

How could you tell with a wombat?

Given a human, she should check its breathing, its pulse, its vital signs, but she knew enough about wombats to know that, unless the wombat was actively dying, she stood a very real chance of being scratched or bitten.

But she needed to get it off the road, and this was a seriously big wombat. She wasn't sure she could lift it, even if she was game to try.

Aaghh.

She stood in the middle of the road and tried to think of what to do next. She hadn't been on the island for years, and she had no contact details for emergency services. She thought back to the darkened little town she'd just driven from. She thought of the sole operator of the ferry terminal, switching off all the lights as he'd left, leaving the place locked and dark.

Black.

That was what the night was. Unwanted memories were suddenly all around her. A mountainside, impenetrable darkness, the stink of blackened ruins, and nothing, nothing, nothing.

This wasn't black, she told herself. She had the car headlights. She had her phone torch. But beyond their beams…

Get over it, she told herself harshly. Move on.

Her only choice was to phone her great-aunt. Babs was frail, with advanced heart failure, which was why she hadn't come to collect her in person, but she'd be waiting up for her to arrive. Babs could at least give her island emergency numbers.

And blessedly she answered on the first ring. 'Gina.' Her voice was acerbic, a bit annoyed. 'Are you on the island? Did you find the car? I told Joe to give you the keys. I expected you before this.'

'I found the car,' she said. 'But, Aunty Babs, I've hit a wombat.'

'You've what? Oh, for heaven's sake…'

This wasn't a promising start. Babs's tone held astonishment—and also immediate judgement. Sandpiper Island was the smallest of the Birding Isles, an hour's flight from Sydney plus a ferry ride from the biggest island in the group, Gannet. It had a population of about four hundred, mostly small-scale farmers or fishermen. It was known for its solitude—and for the protection it gave its wildlife.

'I didn't hit it very hard,' Gina said defensively. 'But I think I've hurt its leg, and it's not moving.'

'Is it conscious?'

'It's looking at me.'

'I imagine it is,' Babs snapped. 'It'll be terrified. Don't go near it unless you have to.'

'Right,' Gina said, just as dryly. 'Don't scare the

wombat. Got it. But apart from that… Babs, I need help. What should I do?'

There was a moment's silence. Then… 'You need Hugh.'

'Hugh?'

'Hugh Duncan. He's a doctor.'

'Don't I need a vet?'

'Of course you do,' Babs said, in that condescending voice Gina remembered so well. Gina had been thought of as useless from the moment Babs had met her. 'But Sandpiper's not big enough to have a vet. We don't even officially have a doctor—you remember we take the ferry over to Gannet if we get sick? But Hugh's worked for some foreign aid organisation—those doctors who go to war zones. Rumour is he was hit by a bomb. He has a gammy leg and he hates being disturbed, but he'll help in an emergency. If he can keep it alive until tomorrow, you can put it on the ferry to Gannet. There's a wildlife rehab place there. Meanwhile there's a rug in my car. Cover it so it doesn't scratch, put it in the car and take it to his place.'

In the dark? Gina thought. And then she looked back at the wombat and thought even if she wanted to—which she didn't—picking it up wasn't an option.

'I can't lift it,' she admitted. 'It's enormous.'

'Oh, for heaven's sake…' Babs's exasperation was growing. 'Ring him, then. He won't like it, but he'll come.'

'Isn't there a policeman or someone else? I mean, I'll stay until someone arrives but…'

'You could ring Joan Wilmot,' Babs told her. 'You must remember her—she's our local mayor, and our police. But she'll just ring Hugh, and then you'll have two people fed up with you. Three if you count me.'

'You're fed up?' Already, she thought.

'You should have been more careful,' Babs snapped, and Gina thought, I've come halfway around the world because you admitted you needed me, and I get a lecture before I've even arrived?

Suddenly she was thinking back to herself at fifteen, arriving on the island after her parents died, being gathered into Babs's arms and hugged as if she'd never be released. Then, half an hour later, she was being scolded because she'd set the table with the knives and forks on the wrong side. But even with Babs's judgement, she remembered staring down at the table and feeling a surge of something that could only be described as relief. After weeks of horror, Babs's scolding had somehow made her world settle.

At least briefly.

But that was why she was back here now. Babs was ill, but this was the same Great-Aunt Babs she knew. She'd be scolding until the end.

'So I have to ring this… Hugh.'

'I'll ring him for you if it helps,' Babs said magnanimously, and then spoiled it by saying: 'You'll only mix up the directions. I imagine you'll be on the track leading down to Windswept Bay by now. Up on Windy Ridge?'

'How did you know?'

'Because wombats are always on that track,' her aunt snapped. 'Stay where you are, and I'll ring now.'

'Babs?'

'Yes?'

'Ring me back and tell me if he's coming,' Gina said, trying—and failing—not to sound like a scared kid.

'I will,' Babs told her and sniffed. 'I remember you don't like the dark. You should have got over that by now, but you needn't fear. The only bogey man you need to worry about is Hugh Duncan.'

He did not want to answer the phone.

Dammit, he should have chosen another island. One with a medical service.

He'd come to Sandpiper because it seemed about as far from the world he knew as he could get. The island was ninety per cent nature reserve, ten per cent small farms. Most of those farms were on the other side of the island, centred around the only town. This side of the island was practically deserted.

He'd bought this place from a guy who'd seemed almost a hermit, and that was pretty much what Hugh intended himself to be.

He and Hoppy, the little fox terrier retrieved from the hellhole where they'd both been injured, had looked at the natural beauty of the place and thought, Yes! There'd been a few issues with Hoppy and the wildlife, but a three-legged, not very young dog posed little threat. Once Hoppy had learned snakes were for avoiding—and a bite from a blue-tongue lizard had helped—they'd settled well.

And then the islanders had discovered he was a doctor.

He'd never intended to be the sole doctor on a remote island. He needed his head read for not finding out the situation before he'd come, but once the islanders learned of his medical background, he was stuck.

He *could* refuse to help, and if it was something a ferry ride across to the excellent medical service on Gannet Island could fix, then he did. But in the three years since he'd been here, there'd been calls he couldn't refuse.

'Doctor, he's dying... Doctor, there's been a crash...'

So now it was ten at night and his phone was ringing. The islanders had learned his response to waste-of-time calls. He knew whatever it was would be unavoidable.

And then he saw the number on the screen, and he thought, Trouble.

Babs Marshall was eighty-four years old. She lived in the only other cottage on this side of the island, but, like him, she kept to herself. He saw her sometimes when he and Hoppy were on the beach. She'd be collecting drift-wood, or carting seaweed back to mulch her garden, but she never made an attempt to chat. She was private to the point of surliness.

Then, a few months back she'd had a major heart at-tack. She'd only survived because he'd noticed her lights hadn't come on at dark and he'd been worried enough to walk over and check—to find her unconscious, near death. After she'd come home from hospital, he'd or-dered her to ring him whenever there was the faintest need, so there was no choice about responding now.

'Babs,' he said briefly because social niceties were wasted on his neighbour. 'Problem?'

'It's Gina,' she said, sounding waspish. My niece.'

He relaxed a bit at that. Despite the best of treatment after her attack, Babs's heart was still failing, and there was little he or any other medic could do to help. When he'd seen her number on his phone, his own heart had sunk. But...niece?

This Gina must be the phantom niece she'd talked of when he'd worried about her living by herself. 'I've told my niece she's needed,' she'd said months ago, but he'd heard nothing since. So now...

'She's here? Is she ill?'

'She's just arrived, and she's hit a wombat on the

ridge track,' she snapped. 'She says she's hurt its leg, and it's not moving.'

Silence.

Apart from his and Babs's smallholdings, this side of the island was a designated nature reserve. Speed limits were strict. Wildlife was sacrosanct.

'She wouldn't have been speeding,' Babs said, seemingly following his thoughts. 'She's driving my car.'

He knew the car and he almost grinned. Babs's tiny car was almost as old as she was. The fact that it still went at all was a miracle, and if there was a choice between the car's speed and that of a lumbering wombat, he reckoned the wombat might win. But at night, on these roads…

Idiot.

'All right,' he said wearily. 'Tell her to bring it over.'

'Well, that's what I can't do,' she said, still waspishly. 'She's by herself. She says it's a big one and she can't lift it. Sometimes she's not very bright. She's also scared of the dark. I'd try and help, but she has my car. She just landed on the island tonight, and Joe took my car down to the ferry so she could drive here herself.'

'She's a mainlander?'

'She's been on one of those cruise ships,' Babs told him. 'She spends her life doing that—talk about a waste of space. Only now with the pandemic and everything, the cruises have stopped so she's finally come.'

Oh, great. The vision he had of the niece was getting worse every minute.

'You know I hate to bother you,' Babs was saying. 'But could you get her out of trouble? Not for her sake, you understand, but for the wombat.'

For the wombat.

He practically gritted his teeth.

But Hoppy was staring up at him in concern. The little dog had been pretty much his lifesaver over the last few years. If you wanted empathy, Hoppy was your dog. Now he had his head cocked to one side and his eyes were huge.

Hugh glanced back to his fire, his book—an excellent mystery, half read—the glass of whisky.

Then back to Hoppy, who was showing his concern in every fibre of his being. Another creature in trouble?

He was anthropomorphising, giving human feelings to a dog. Hoppy couldn't even hear what was being said.

He was still looking at him.

'Fine,' Hugh said, goaded.

'Thank you.'

He didn't bother replying, just disconnected and grabbed his boots.

'Keep the fire going and don't touch the whisky,' he told Hoppy, and Hoppy gave a tentative wag of his tail.

'Yeah, I know, it's a wombat and I have to help,' he snarled. 'But it's also a dingbat woman who spends her life on cruise ships. I'll help, but there's no reason I have to do it graciously.'

She was getting cold. She was also growing more and more nervous. There wasn't a light to be seen, and the dark was making her shiver. The ocean breeze, balmy during the day in this gorgeous, subtropical climate, was starting to bite through her cotton jacket. The trees were rustling around her, dark and looming.

The wombat was still on its back, its little eyes staring up at her. If she couldn't see its eyes following her, if she couldn't see it breathing, she might have thought it was dead.

'Which would have been easier,' she muttered and

then winced. 'Sorry. I didn't mean that. I'm very glad you're not.'

The wombat didn't appear to be worried either way. Its eyes were unblinking, looking up at her, judge and jury rolled into one.

'Babs said someone's coming,' she told him, and finally she saw headlights, coming up from the opposite side of the bay to where her aunt lived.

'Mr Jefferson's place,' she told the wombat, as if he might be interested. She remembered Jefferson from the two years she'd lived here after her parents died. He'd lived in a ramshackle log cabin set back from the beach, collecting *stuff*, wheeling and dealing in whatever he could get his hands on. He'd declared the southern end of Windswept Bay his half, and if she dared walk even one metre inside his perceived territory, he'd threaten to turn his dogs on her.

Babs had told her the National Park officials had moved in a couple of years ago and demanded he shifted his stores of suspect stuff. So this guy…Hugh…had taken his place?

A doctor.

Another hermit?

She stood and waited, and for the life of her she couldn't stop a tremor or two. She was all grown up now, not the scared fifteen-year-old who Henry Jefferson had terrified, she told herself. But still, as the car drew to a halt, leaving her in the full beam of its headlights, she found herself bracing, drawing herself up to her full five feet three inches.

Wishing she were back with her team, somewhere safe, somewhere like the wilds of Antarctica.

The vehicle was an SUV, solid, heavy, built for hard

work. The driver's door swung open and the driver stepped out.

All she could see was his silhouette. Big. Broad-shouldered. A dark shadow behind the headlights.

It was all she could do not to whimper.

Which was ridiculous. She'd spent the last few years working as a medic with a research team that travelled to some of the most remote places in the world. She was a nurse, and a good one, her extra training as a nurse practitioner having led to her career in emergency medicine. This guy was a doctor. Her professional credentials must surely put her as this guy's equal—or almost.

'Hi,' she said, and almost kicked herself as it came out as a quaver. 'You're Dr. Duncan?'

'For my pains. And you're Gina. Who's hit a wombat?'

There was such censure in the harsh, gravelly voice that she winced all over again.

'It was in the middle of the road.' She sounded small and defensive. For heaven's sake, she had to pull herself together. 'And I didn't hit it very hard.'

'You're in the middle of a national park.'

'I know. I'm sorry.' Why was she apologising to this guy? She'd already apologised to the wombat. 'It's hurt its leg.'

'*You* hurt its leg.' He came forward, limping a little, and she got a clear sight of him in the beam of his headlights.

He was indeed big, tall, with broad shoulders tapering down to narrow hips and long legs. He was wearing a stretched, faded T-shirt, old jeans and heavy boots. What looked like a scar was etched deep, running from the side of his mouth to the base of his left ear. He had short-cropped dark hair, a strongly boned face, shadowed eyes and a mouth set in grim lines.

He was pulling on leather gloves as he walked. He ignored her, just bent over the wombat and flicked on his torch.

The wombat turned its gaze to him. Like…she's hurt me, mate. Get me out of her clutches.

'I think I might have broken its leg,' she said. Damn, why was her voice so small?

'Let's see.' Amazingly his voice had gentled. He was running his gloved hands over the creature, carefully, taking his time. 'It's okay, mate,' he said in the gentlest of tones. 'We'll get you somewhere safe as soon as we can, but let's see what the damage is first.'

And then she was ignored. She stood back, feeling guilty and helpless and, okay, like a superfluous idiot. She had the feeling that if she got into her car and drove away, he wouldn't even notice.

Finally, he rose and headed to his car. 'Wh…what…?' she stammered, because for an awful moment she thought he might be about to drive away. But he snagged a heavy blanket from the car and returned.

'I don't think the leg's broken,' he told her, the harshness returning to his voice again. 'Lacerations, but not too deep. Gravel rash. He's lost a bit of fur. I reckon he's concussed, though. Hopefully nothing he won't get over with a bit of peace.'

'But…he's conscious.'

'You can be concussed and still conscious,' he told her, in the tone of one addressing someone a bit thick. Or maybe very thick.

She knew that. Why was she sounding so dumb? Dammit, she couldn't seem to help herself.

'I… What will you do?'

'I'll take him home, clean the leg and keep him warm and quiet for a day or so,' he said. 'We're lucky you're looking at a male. A female with young in her pouch could have been much more complicated. Hopefully I can bring him back here as soon as he's healed, with a warning to look out for idiot drivers who don't look out for wombats in a nature reserve.'

Ouch. She deserved it, she thought, but still ouch.

'I was driving slowly.'

'If you hadn't been driving Babs's car, you'd have killed him.'

'Then wasn't it lucky I was?' she said, a flare of anger coming to her aid. 'I didn't mean to. Babs's headlights are crap, and the thing was just…here.'

'It's a national park. It's allowed to be here. You aren't.' He stooped and laid the rug beside the wombat, then moved it effortlessly into its midst. Then he wrapped it and lifted it, as if it weighed nothing at all.

Once upon a time Gina had found an orphaned wombat, during a storm when she'd lived here. She'd had to care for it until the weather settled enough to take it over to the refuge on Gannet Island. It had been little more than a baby, yet it had felt as if it weighed a ton.

This one was maybe four times as big, and Hugh lifted it as if it were a bag of feathers.

'Is your car still drivable?' he snapped, and she blinked and then turned her attention to the front of the car. The fender was a bit bent, but it wasn't touching the wheel. A hammer tomorrow, a spot of amateur panel beating, and it'd be fine.

'It's drivable.'

'Then go slow. Being here after dark is stupid.'

Like she didn't know?

'I had to drive along the track,' she said defensively,

and was annoyed that she sounded sulky. 'There's no other way to get here. And Babs needs me.'

'She needed you months ago.'

Wow, talk about judgemental. She fought for something she could say to defend herself, but the reasons were all too complicated. Besides, he already had his back to her, moving the wombat to the back of his vehicle. He closed the door on it, and then turned back to her.

'Go, then. I'll stay and watch until I see your lights reach Babs's place.'

'In case I hit more wombats?'

'In case you've done some damage to the car you don't know about. I don't want to be called out again.'

'Gee, thanks.' But she was grateful. Sort of.

'Are you okay yourself?' he asked suddenly. 'No sore neck? You were wearing your seat belt?'

And that disconcerted her. He'd changed, as he'd changed when he'd spoken to the wombat. Suddenly she was the patient, and he…he had a duty of care?

He *was* a doctor, she reminded herself. He'd be doing what he had to do.

'I'm fine,' she said, a little stiffly, but was suddenly absurdly conscious of a desire to weep. It'd be shock setting in, she thought, and fatigue. It had been a huge journey, an endless road to get here.

'You're sure?' And he was striding back to her, torch in hand, shining its light into her face.

Seeing the fatigue? Seeing the trace of stupid tears? She blinked and blinked again.

'I'm sure,' she managed. 'Just…tired. And a bit sad about hitting the wombat.'

'Your aunt says you're scared of the dark.' His voice gentled even further, and she thought weirdly, He's seeing me now as he's seeing the wombat. As a creature to be cared for?

Haul yourself together, woman, she told herself, and she did. She managed a nod and stepped out of the glare of his torch.

'I'm not scared,' she told him. Which was, actually, a lie. 'My aunt still thinks of me as a kid. Thank you very much, Dr Duncan. And can I...can I pay you for the...house call?'

'I don't charge wombats,' he told her, and she thought she saw the trace of a smile. But it was only a trace. 'Go on,' he said. 'Take it slow, and I'll watch your lights.'

'Th...thank you,' she said again, and there was nothing else to say.

'Go,' he said, and she went.

CHAPTER TWO

'I'VE MADE DR DUNCAN a pie.'

'What?'

Gina stood in the doorway of her aunt's kitchen and tried to fight the sensation she'd been transported to another planet. Shock from last night's wombat encounter? The after-effects of months of struggle to reach her aunt? The faint remembrance of waking up here when she was fifteen, when the world as she'd known it had ended?

She'd arrived late last night and been hugged, fed and scolded pretty much in that order, then sent to bed as if she were nine instead of twenty-nine. Now she emerged to find her aunt surrounded by cooking chaos, surveying two pies sitting on the flour-strewn bench. The smell was amazing.

How long since she'd tasted home-cooked food?

'I got extra ingredients because you were coming, but he deserves a pie more than you do. Now sit down and get some breakfast into you. It is almost lunchtime, but I let you sleep. Nasty thing, travel, it does all sorts of things to your insides. I remember when I came here from Sydney, I couldn't sleep for weeks.'

That would have been when her marriage had fallen through, Gina thought. Babs had coped with it by fleeing everyone she knew, to live a life of an almost-hermit.

But if Babs wanted to put the effects of that forty-or-more-years-past journey down to jet lag from a one-hour flight from Sydney, why argue?

Why argue with anything? she thought as she pulled up a chair and sat.

Babs put the kettle on the stove, then opened the little fire door at the front, popped a piece of bread on a toasting fork and handed it to Gina to hold it to the flames. Which did something fuzzy to Gina's head. She was suddenly hit by the memory of doing this fourteen years ago, on that first awful morning…

'So you're to eat your breakfast and take the pie straight over,' Babs said, in a voice that brooked no argument. 'I have a basket that'll hold it steady.'

'Me?' Gina said cautiously. 'Take a pie?'

'I rang this morning. The doctor thinks the wombat will live. He's cleaned its leg and he'll keep it until it's healed enough to release. It's very good of him.'

'Very good,' Gina agreed faintly. 'Let me think about it when I've had coffee.'

'I only have herbal tea,' Babs said tartly. 'The idea of maudling your insides…'

'I like my insides maudled.' No coffee? *Aagh*.

'The doctors say I should take it easy on stimulants,' her aunt added virtuously. 'Though Hugh did say he didn't see how a nip of whisky or two would hurt. Mind, he's not my doctor—he's no one's doctor, really—but he did help when I was in trouble. Maybe I didn't tell you,' she said diffidently. 'But it seems he watches for my light to go on every night and that night it didn't. Not that he had any right—I hate the thought of anyone spying—but the doctors on Gannet said he saved my life. I was unconscious when he found me and I would have died, so I have to be grateful. And now he's helped you last night. So…finish your breakfast and go.'

'Fine,' Gina said meekly, and then the toast was toasted, and there was home-made butter and a jar of marmalade to die for. Babs sank into her crossword puzzle, as she'd done every morning for the two years Gina had lived with her, and the world settled.

And she had time to look at her aunt.

Babs was eighty-four years old and looked even older. After her heart attack she'd reluctantly given permission to Gina to talk to the doctors on Gannet Island.

'There's little we can do,' the cardiac specialist had told her. Gina had briefly outlined her medical background and the cardiologist had pulled no punches. 'The angiogram shows ischaemic heart disease, with blockages widely distributed in small arteries. She's been having angina for a while, though not admitting it, and with the amount of damage it's a miracle she hasn't had a major event before this. But with widespread disease, stenting or bypass can do little to help. We're putting her on maximum medication but there's no use giving false hope, and she understands. We've offered to send her to Sydney for a second opinion but she's refusing to go. And we concur—there's little they could do. She wants to go home. It worries us that she'll be so isolated, but we can't stop her. If you can come, we advise you to do it soon.'

Soon had turned into those four long months. At every phone call Babs had told her: "Don't worry. I'm fine. I don't know what the fuss is about." But now…the pallor of her face, the slight tinge of blue…

She wasn't fine.

'I want to stay here this morning,' Gina told her. 'Babs, I've come to be with you.'

'Well, there won't be a lot of joy doing that this morning,' Babs said with asperity. 'I've been up since five cooking, and now I intend to have a nap. And this pie needs to go round to Hugh now. If I've gone to all the trouble to make it, the least you can do is deliver it.'

Which was pretty much what Gina should have expected. Babs lived her own life. When Gina had lived with her, she'd fitted in at the edges, isolated, knowing Babs resented her presence. But maybe that was part of the healing, she'd decided later on. When she'd first arrived, shocked, bereaved, all she'd wanted was to hide. Babs had been there for her when she'd needed her, but there'd seemed little regret on either side when she'd left.

Babs was a loner. As, it seemed, was this Hugh.

'He won't set the dogs on me?' she asked nervously, and Babs snorted.

'He's not like Henry Jefferson. Those dogs of Henry's were appalling. Hugh does have a dog, but it's small. Three legs. Hugh limps himself. There's a story there but he doesn't talk about it. He doesn't talk about anything.'

'Do you ask him?' Gina found herself intrigued, but she already knew the answer. Babs's solitary existence didn't include gossip. She kept to herself and paid the same respect to everyone else on the island. Gina had found it frustrating in the past, and even more so now.'

'Of course I don't,' Babs snapped. 'What do you think I am? But he came here three years ago and rebuilt that cabin and he just stays there. He has a job he needs the Internet for, I do know that. He's had some sort of satellite dish put in—he offered to share it with me, as if I'd know what to do with it. He and that dog... I see them on the beach. Fishing sometimes. Watching the sandpipers. Mostly just sitting. He doesn't chat.'

Hoist in your own petard, Gina thought wryly.

'But he's the island doctor now?' she ventured.

'Not by choice,' Babs told her. 'Only because Wendy Henderson fell off the ladder while he was in the general store. She cut her arm and bled like a stuck pig. Hugh did all the right things. Then of course everyone knew he was a doctor, so they started using him. Only in emergencies, mind, we wouldn't dare ask anything else.'

'So last night…'

'Yes, you were an emergency,' Babs told her. 'And he never takes payment.' She hesitated. 'I did hear that his family is wealthy,' she conceded, as if admitting that she'd listened to such rumours was a crime. 'But rich or not, I intend to pay. So get yourself dressed and take this pie, and tell him thank you very much from me.'

'It was me he helped. I should have made it.'

Babs snorted at that. 'You? Cook? You think Hugh would think one of your pies was a thank you?'

She had a point. The life Gina had led was hardly conducive to learning to cook, and for the two years she'd lived on Sandpiper Island, Babs had hardly borne her being in the kitchen.

'Has your cooking improved?' Babs snapped.

'I…no.' Not much chance of that where she'd been living.

'There you are, then,' Babs said. 'So no more arguments. Go.'

Henry Jefferson's cabin had been built in one of the most beautiful places on the island, but Henry had done his best to destroy any vestige of beauty. The cabin had been a mess of faded timber and rusted iron. There'd been old car bodies, rubbish of all sorts strewn everywhere, and, guarding it all, three huge, snarling dogs.

At fifteen Gina had been far too terrified to go near

the place. Now she walked tentatively up the path from the beach—and stopped in amazement.

The cabin was gone. In its place was a house built of soft cream local stone. It was long and low, almost disappearing into the natural landscape. Its French windows and wide verandas opened out to give a slivered glimpse of the beach below. A huge wicker chair sat beside the front door, a dog bed beside it. Native bougainvillea, crimson, brilliant, twined up the supports at either end.

It must have taken a small army to have cleared Henry's rubbish, she thought, blinking. In its place were vegetable beds, a herb garden, a small greenhouse.

She stood, too astonished to move, and then a little fox terrier came tearing around from the back of the house, as fast as his three legs could take him. His yapping could have woken the dead, and with visions of the last dogs Gina had seen here she braced.

But the little dog reached her and crouched and rolled, fawning, his big eyes an unspoken plea of pat me, pat me, rub my tummy. He wiggled and wiggled, then, as she reached down to pat him, he smelt the pie in her basket.

She rose fast, but who knew a dog with three legs could jump so high?

'Hoppy!'

And here he was, limping around the side of the house. He was wearing a ripped T-shirt, stained trousers and heavy, scuffed army boots. The scar on his face looked almost menacing.

He was carrying an axe.

Whoa.

'I've brought you a pie,' she said, and for the life of her she couldn't prevent her voice wobbling.

He stopped dead, eyeing her as if she were some sort of alien.

Maybe she was, she thought. She'd certainly felt like that when she'd last lived here.

Sandpiper Islanders were…conservative to say the least. She remembered at fifteen, going into the general store with her aunt for the first time. The whole store had stopped, staring at her as if they were seeing some strange species.

Okay, she had been going through her punk period. She'd arrived on the island wearing black leathers, goth make-up and her huge Doc Marten boots. Her fiery hair had been cut boy-short, and dyed deep, deep black. At fifteen she'd been in full rebellion mode, and no one had warned her that her parents weren't planning to stick around to rebel against.

She'd even had a pet ferret, though by the time her aunt took her shopping Arsenic was…deceased.

Hit by a brick.

Fourteen years later she was almost past rebelling— she was even almost over Arsenic's death—but on board the ship she wore tough, expeditioner gear.

Her off duty clothes were pretty much the opposite.

So now she stood in what was, for her, fairly tame clothing. Sky-blue capri pants with glitter stars down the sides. An oversized windcheater, pink, with the same glitter stars. Purple, open-toed sandals. She'd caught her riot of copper curls back with purple ribbon—almost demure—and she'd kept her make-up to a minimum.

There was no need for this guy to be staring as if he were seeing a Martian.

'Babs made you a pie,' she said, her second statement coming out almost defiant.

He was still motionless, just looking.

Well. A cat can look at a king, she thought, anger coming to her rescue. While the little dog—Hoppy?—continued to leap for the pie, she did her own perusing.

The impressions she'd gained last night solidified. This guy was seriously big. Tough. Weathered. He was holding the axe in one hand and it looked as if it were almost an extension of himself. His grey, deep-set eyes were narrowed against the morning sun, and a scar marred the left side of his face. A laceration, but burns as well, she thought.

'Haven't you been told it's rude to stare?' he demanded, and she blinked.

'What?'

'You were staring.'

And that settled her. What was it with this guy?

'For some reason I always stare at guys who come at me with an axe,' she retorted. 'Stupid, I know, when what I should do is turn and run. So what's your excuse for staring? You think my pie is loaded?'

There was a silence at that. He'd be used to people staring at the scar, she thought, but, dammit, he'd spent almost a minute inspecting her from the toes up.

'Touché,' he said at last, but still he didn't move. His face was grim, unwelcoming.

'So what do you want me to do?' she asked, beginning to feel seriously fed up. 'Put the pie down and flee? I warn you, Hoppy'll take his share before you even reach it.'

'Hoppy!' he said, and the little dog ceased trying to leap for the pie, looked uncertainly back at his master and reluctantly made his way back to his side.

He was still staring. The silence was starting to seriously unnerve her.

'So now what?' she demanded. 'I put the pie on the

ground and back away with hands raised?' She was starting to think Old Man Jefferson had nothing on this guy.

And finally, he pulled himself together. 'I...sorry. Your hair looks amazing.'

'And your axe looks sharp.'

'You were looking at my face.'

'I admit, I was stunned by your mesmeric grey eyes, but, believe it or not, the axe took precedence.'

There was another moment's silence and then, finally, his face relaxed and his mouth twisted into a trace of a reluctant grin.

'I was chopping wood.'

'Right,' she said slowly. 'So you heard a visitor arrive and thought, Fine, I'm already armed.'

She got a long stare for that, but then he wheeled away and laid the axe on the veranda. 'Satisfied?'

'The warmth of your welcome is almost overwhelming. Come and get this stupid pie so I can leave. Believe it or not, it's a thank you for last night. Babs made it though, not me, so there's not the least need for you to feel grateful to me.'

'Babs's beef and mushroom pie.'

'Yeah, legendary.' She couldn't quite suppress a smile. Babs's pies had been one of her very few ways of comforting. She'd laid one on when Gina had first arrived on the island. Before Arsenic...

Don't go there. Instead she tilted her chin and met this unwelcoming toerag's look head-on. 'Luckily, she's made two. I'm going to head home and eat the other one right now.'

'What's she got to be grateful to you for?'

And that took her breath away. She went right back to staring at him, astonishment and anger doing this weird mix inside her.

He gazed calmly back. He might have been St Peter, she thought, grimly telling her she'd been judged and found wanting.

'What's that supposed to mean?' she managed at last, and his expression didn't change.

'You know she has end-stage heart disease.'

'As a matter of fact I do.' Anger was superseding surprise now. Anger in spades.

'So she had a massive heart attack four months ago, and there's little left to repair. She shouldn't be living alone, but four months ago she told me her you were coming. "My great-niece stands to inherit this house and land," she told me. "Of course she'll come." So what kept you? You figure wait four months and you'll be that much closer to inheriting?'

Whoa.

There was so much in that to stun her. So much…it was almost unbelievable.

She could, though, believe that Babs would say such a thing. She remembered the phone call to the hospital, a nurse holding the phone for her aunt.

Gina had been on the ship, off the coast of Cuba. The cardiologist had just told her what Babs's outlook was.

'I'm coming home, Babs,' she'd told her. 'It might be complicated—with all this stuff going on I don't know how long it'll take to reach you—but I'll get to you as soon as humanly possible. Don't you dare die before I get there. Do what you have to do to stay alive. I… I love you.'

And she supposed she did. Babs was, after all, the only family she had, the only family she ever intended to have.

You were supposed to love family, weren't you? Gina had learned the hard way that such loving got you nothing but pain. Babs would be the end of it, but for now, like it or not, the tugs of affection were still there.

And maybe deep down, Babs felt the same. For Babs, who didn't do emotion, who was an acerbic old lady who'd decided long ago that she needed no one in her life, who never accepted help from anyone, had choked on a sob. And then she'd pulled herself together.

'Good,' she'd said. 'With this pandemic I suppose you need a place to stay for a while.'

That was her way of saying Gina was welcome. The idea of Gina coming home because she loved her could never be admitted. That Gina was coming for practical reasons was something the unemotional Babs could handle.

And she could almost see Babs saying it to her seemingly also aloof neighbour—if they ever talked. *'My great-niece stands to inherit this house and land. Of course she'll come.'*

They made a great pair, she thought bitterly, and looked down at the pie in the basket she was carrying and had an almost irresistible urge to toss it straight at him.

Get over it, she told herself. She'd found herself loving Babs regardless of the lack of human connection, but it hurt, and she didn't need to feel anything for this guy.

'Here's the pie,' she told him and put the basket down on the ground. 'Thank you for last night. Goodbye.'

He was still watching her, his face now expressionless. 'You didn't ask about the wombat.'

Another judgement? She huffed. 'Babs told me it'll live.'

'Would you like to see it?'

And that caught her. She should stalk off, dignity intact, but she did, sort of, want to see the wombat.

Okay, she badly wanted to see it. She'd woken this morning remembering its beady little eyes.

It had also looked accusing, she thought. Who needed St Peter when she had Babs, this toerag *and* a dumb wombat with poor road skills, all three in judgement mode?

But seeing the little creature upright and healing... It might help.

'Yes,' she said grudgingly. And then, because she couldn't help herself, because she was weak and needful and she was totally pathetic, she added a rider. 'You wouldn't have coffee, would you?'

'Coffee.'

'Babs only has herbal tea,' she told him. 'Sorry, I know you think I'm beneath pond scum, but if you were to make me a coffee, I might even be prepared to forgive you for making stupid, cruel judgements about something you know nothing about. And will you stop staring at me? I know you have a scar on your face, and I know that's what you thought I was staring at, but I don't know what you're staring at and it's giving me the heebie-jeebies.'

'Your toes,' he said promptly, and she looked down at her toes and her world settled a little. She actually quite liked her toes.

'Ballerinas,' she tossed back at him and he blinked.

'What?'

'I've had two weeks' quarantine in Sydney. Two weeks stuck in a hotel room with only my computer and a kit full of nail polish to keep me company. Every toe has a dancer in a different ballet pose. Cute, don't you think? Arabesque, attitude, *croisé*, turn-out... They might be a bit wobbly—I had to plead to be allowed to order tiny paintbrushes online—but they're a work of art, even if I do say so myself.'

And she lifted one foot and held it out, inviting inspection.

He didn't move. He stared at her as if she were an alien. She put her foot down, tucking her cute little ballerinas away for a more appreciative audience. Though where she'd find one on this island…

He was still staring.

'Stop it,' she said at last. He'd lifted Hoppy—probably to stop him heading for the pie—and was cradling him loosely in his arms. He was stroking the little dog behind his ears, a gesture totally at odds with the size, strength and coldness of the man. 'Whether or not you're impressed with my artistic skills, I need to move on,' she told him. 'Yes, I'd like to see my…the wombat but I have more pressing needs. Give me coffee or tell me to go away.'

He sighed. He put the dog down and then had to make a lunge to reach the basket before Hoppy did.

'I'll give you coffee.'

'Gee, thanks. You are *so* neighbourly.'

'I am and all,' he told her. And then his face softened—just a little. 'But you're right, I am judging when it's none of my business. So, judgement aside, I'll give you coffee and show you the wombat.'

'You're all heart.'

'I'm not the least bit heart,' he told her. 'But I can show you a wombat and make coffee.'

CHAPTER THREE

HE DIDN'T WANT her here. He hadn't wanted to go to her rescue last night and he surely didn't want her sticking around here, drinking his coffee, checking his first-aid handiwork.

He had no choice. He took the pie inside—some things took precedence—then led her around the back of the house. She followed meekly. She probably would have liked a coffee first, he thought, but this was his place, his rules. He was wishing he had disposable cups—that way he could hand her coffee and say good-bye.

But wombat first. He led her to where he'd homed the wombat in a hastily made wire enclosure. He'd lined a wooden box with moss to provide bedding. The wombat, though, was currently not sleeping. He was lazily munching. He glanced up at them as they neared, gave them a beady little glare, as if to say, 'Back off, this is mine,' and then went back to his meal.

'What's he eating?' She stopped a few feet from the enclosure, and he gave her credit for knowing this was a wild creature and her presence would stress it.

Or was she scared of it? With those toenails, that was definitely a possibility.

He thought suddenly of a kid he'd had to sit next to

in grade school. She was pretty and pink, and a total airhead. 'She's just a bimbo,' his parents' chauffeur had decreed, driving them home after he and his nanny had answered the summons to the principal's office because 'one of these children is obviously cheating'. It seemed their arithmetic tests had been found to be identical. From the arms of her adoring parents, Pretty and Pink had tearfully confessed—and Hugh had been given a serve for 'aiding and abetting'.

'Don't teach him that word,' his nanny had scolded as they'd driven back to the family mansion. 'She's a muppet, Hugh. Cute on the outside but nothing but cotton wool inside. She can't help it—you just need to learn to stay clear. We'll ask your parents to sign a request to have you sit by someone else.'

They both knew that wouldn't happen—when were either of his parents around long enough to attend to such trivia?—but it was meant to console.

So yes, this woman was definitely muppet material, he decided, hauling his thoughts back to the present, but at least she seemed one with spirit. He was starting to figure she gave as good as she got.

'Sweet potato,' he told her. 'I checked the Internet. They eat native grasses and roots but foraging for them this morning seemed a bit hard. Wildlife rescuers drop sweet potato into bushfire areas and it's deemed safe. He seems to like it.'

'It's definitely male?'

'Didn't you notice last night? He's young, masculine and has attitude. He was still enough while I brought him here, but then he recovered enough to fight. It was a bit of a struggle to get that leg cleaned and disinfected.'

'Without an anaesthetist?'

'I wrapped him in a heavy blanket.'

'Much less risky than an anaesthetic,' she approved. 'But he's big. That's impressive.'

That was a strange statement for a muppet to make, he thought. He cast her a curious glance, but she'd crouched down, eye level to the wombat, who looked too busy munching to react. 'Hey, I'm sorry I knocked you over last night,' she told him.

The wombat glared and went on munching.

'He's not much of a conversationalist,' she mused and looked up at him. 'Does he have a name?'

'He's a wombat.'

'Yeah. So, does he have a name?'

'No.' He stared down at the wombat, who decided to stare up at him, almost accusingly. He thought of all the stray animals he'd met in war zones over the years, then he looked at Hoppy. You named an animal, you lived with the consequences.

'Then it's Hubert,' she said as the silence extended.

He thought, Please don't do that, but the thing was already done. Hubert went back to munching. 'Hi, Hubert.' Then to Hugh: 'So you decided not to send him to Gannet?'

'No need. His leg's not broken. I'll keep him quiet for a few days until I'm sure he's safe from infection, and then take him back to where you found him. The only people who use that track are Babs and me—and you. Babs and I don't hit animals. It'll be hoped you don't either.'

'You really don't like me, do you?'

'I don't like people. You want that coffee?'

'Yes, please,' she said and stood, abruptly. 'Thank you. I should stalk away now, but my need for caffeine is overriding my desire for dignity.'

'Fair enough.' He headed back to the house and she followed.

Hoppy tagged behind—with her. Usually Hoppy stayed at his heels. The fact that he'd fallen back to trail along beside this woman seemed almost traitorous.

Though she did have interesting toenails. Hoppy was almost at toenail level. If he was honest, he wouldn't mind a closer look at those toenails himself.

And that was where those thoughts had to stop. He practically stomped into the house, angry with himself for having his equanimity upset. He lived in his own solitary world and he liked it that way. He liked that Babs was the only other resident on this side of the island, and he didn't like that this woman was likely to be staying for a while.

Or was she?

'How long do you intend staying?' he demanded as he flicked on the coffee maker and put a couple of cups into the microwave to heat them.

But she was distracted. She'd reached the door but hadn't come in—he hadn't actually said come in, nor did he intend to. He'd take the coffee onto the veranda. But she was staring through the open door, looking at his state-of-the-art coffee maker with what looked like hunger.

'Proper coffee,' she breathed. 'Please don't tell me it's decaf.'

He had to smile at that. 'No chance. My coffee maker and coffee beans arrived on the island before my furniture. How do you have it?'

'Strong. You can make it milky? Oh, my!' She stood and watched with what almost looked like reverence as he made two mugs and carried them back out.

She didn't say thank you. She didn't need to. She accepted the mug in both hands and held it to her lips, savouring the smell before she tasted, and the look on her face was a thank you all by itself.

He watched in fascination as she took her first sip, as her face creased into what could only be called ecstasy. She closed her eyes and sighed, a long, drawn-out whisper of relief. 'If you knew how much I've missed that…'

'Since last night?' he said, astounded. 'You've only been here since yesterday. Are you so addicted?'

'Yes, I am,' she said darkly. 'And it hasn't been since yesterday. We're talking about months in quarantine, on the ship and on land. We're talking deserted airports and government offices, and before that… Faceless people in full PPE giving me polystyrene cups of lukewarm stuff that doesn't even taste like coffee. Leaving it at my door and sometimes not even knocking to tell me it's there, me finding it when it's stone cold.'

'Yeah?' He frowned. 'Your aunt told me you've been on a cruise. So you had to quarantine?'

'The whole ship had to quarantine. They took the passengers off, but the crew was stuck. Interminably.'

He'd heard such stories. The recent pandemic had left many ships' crews with no harbour prepared to take them. For some it had been a nightmare.

For this woman?

'You were crew?' Her aunt had said she was on a cruise. She hadn't said that she'd been working.

What as? He glanced at those toes and thought she could have been anything. A hostess? A yoga teacher? Someone pandering to the idle rich?

But without coffee. He had to suppress a shudder.

'Yeah, I have your sympathy now,' she said, and took another sip. 'And now Babs only has herbal tea. I need to take a mercy trip into town to see if I can find a plunger and coffee.'

She might be a muppet, but his nanny's words were still embedded. *'She can't help it.'* Maybe he could afford to be nice.

'I doubt if the store will stock them, but I have a plunger you can borrow,' he told her. 'It's my emergency back-up in case of catastrophic power failure. I also have back-up beans—a lot. I can grind you some if you like.'

'Really?' She took another sip, and another, and then sighed with pleasure and drained the mug. Then she carefully set the mug on the bench by the door—and turned and hugged him.

It was an all-enveloping hug, a complete, no-expense-spared embrace that hugged all of him. She was little, five foot four maybe, a good eight inches shorter than he was. To complete the hug she stood on her tiptoes. She wrapped her arms right around him, she held him against her and she just…hugged.

He'd never had such a hug. Or maybe he had—surely he must have—but if he had, he'd forgotten.

The warmth of her. The smell…something citrussy, fresh, nice. The way her breasts moulded against his chest, her head pressing into his shoulder, her hair brushing his chin.

He froze. He had an almost overwhelming desire to hug back but he wasn't stupid. This was entirely inappropriate. He should put her away. He should…

He didn't. He simply stood, frozen, and let himself be hugged.

And she took her own sweet time about finishing. This wasn't a hug to be cut short, and somehow he got the sense that she needed it, too.

There was such a strong urge to hug back. He didn't. He kept his head. Somehow.

And finally it ended. She tugged away, and stood facing him, smiling a bit sheepishly. For some reason there was a tear tracking down her cheek. He had an urge to put out his hand and wipe it away...

He didn't. Someone had to be sensible.

Why did it have to be him?

'Sorry,' she said at last. 'I know, you didn't want that, but you deserved it and I needed it. Babs told me you rescued her, you rescued me and now you've saved my sanity with coffee. Three rescues surely require a hug. And before you run screaming into the hills, I should tell you I've been tested and tested and tested before I've been allowed onto your pristine island, and if any bug escaped from me to you, mid-hug, then the only source is that stupid wombat. So there.'

It was a defiant statement and it made him grin.

'I'm not scared of bugs.'

'No. You look like you're scared of hugs though, so I'm sorry. I apologise for taking liberties and I won't take them again. Please, give me my coffee and I'm out of here.'

He left her standing on the veranda while he ground her some coffee beans to take with her. Again, he thought he should ask her in, but he didn't. Why should he? This place was his sanctuary, his place to escape the world. He did what he must to help the islanders—it seemed he had no choice—but his door was a boundary too far.

This woman was a boundary too far. That hug...

Why hadn't he hugged back?

What, hug an uncaring muppet with ballerinas painted on her toes? For the last few months he'd been watching Babs grow weaker. He'd known she was hanging out for her niece's arrival, and he'd been growing angrier on her behalf. He knew how much properties on this side of the island were worth—who better? With pretty much private beaches, with scenery to die for, with solitude assured, these were hideaways of every realtor's dreams. It had cost him a small fortune—and luck—to buy this place. When Babs died her beneficiary stood to inherit just such a fortune, yet she'd been left alone for far too long.

'She'll get here in her own good time,' Babs had told him, and the taciturn lady had refused to say more. If she'd agreed to give him contact details he might have phoned the muppet and given her a serve, but she hadn't so he couldn't. It hadn't stopped his anger building though.

And now she'd arrived, and she had ballerinas painted on her toenails—and she'd hugged him. And she'd felt warm and soft and she'd smelled of something faint but wonderful. Her curls had brushed his chin and he'd wanted…

He did not want. He told himself that fiercely as he tugged the spare coffee maker down from a top cupboard and started to grind coffee. It took time. He wished for the first time ever that he had pre-ground coffee to hand over, or a spare grinder, but he didn't and he'd promised. So he ground on, all the time aware of her sitting on the steps just through the screen door. Hoppy had stayed with her, and she was fondling the little dog under his ears, speaking gently to him, and Hoppy was just about turning inside out with delight.

Yeah, if she stroked him like that…

Get a grip, he told himself. It had been way too long since he'd spent any time with a woman, but he wanted it that way. Women meant emotional entanglement, and that was pretty much the last thing he wanted, now and for ever.

Finally, he headed out and placed the plunger and coffee into her basket without a word. She stared down at it and then beamed up at him, a wide, encompassing smile that said she had everything she wanted in this world, now and for ever.

A man could drown in that smile.

'I guess I'll see you on the beach some time,' she said, and turned to leave and he had a momentary urge to stop her. Easily contained.

'I don't go there much.'

'That's right, Babs said you keep to yourself.' She hesitated. 'But you didn't keep to yourself the night she had her heart attack. I'm very grateful.'

'Not grateful enough to come home. I can't keep looking after her indefinitely.'

'You won't have to,' she retorted.

'What, you're hoping she'll die soon?'

There was a stunned pause. She stared up at him, her eyes wide and increasingly angry. She opened her mouth to say something and then closed it with a snap. Thought about it for a moment longer and then spoke, tightly, her anger still obvious.

'You saved my aunt. You saved my wombat and you've given me coffee. I guess the least I can do is shut up when you act like a judgemental—and ignorant—toerag. But, no, I won't see you on the beach. I'll make very sure that doesn't happen. Enjoy your pie. Good luck with Hubert. Thank you.' And she wheeled to walk away.

And then his phone rang.

A couple of times a week, about this time, his half-sister phoned, like it or not. She was ten years older than he was and he'd had little to do with her growing up, but, since he was injured, she'd decided to move back into his life again, even if it was just by phone. She'd ring after dinner, her time, chatting inconsequentially about her kids, her dogs, her husband, her life in New York. He'd tried to cut her off in the past, but it always backfired—she'd ring back and ring back. So now the calls were just part of his life. She'd finish her dinner, make herself coffee—was that a genetic need?—and ring her brother. He'd get on with his day, her chatter a blur in the background.

She'd rung early this morning while he was tending the wombat—Hubert?—so his phone was still on speaker setting. Which meant the voice on the other end of the phone could be heard all over the yard.

Which meant Gina could hear.

And it wasn't his sister.

'Doc?' The voice on the other end of the line was frantic. 'Doc, we need help. Will you come?' The fear on the other end of the line was unmistakeable.

And there went his day. A wombat last night, his sister for almost an hour this morning and then Muppet. And now a medical emergency.

He wanted isolation. He craved it. Life, people, activity, gave him the shakes. He should be well over it by now, but he wasn't.

The shrinks in the army hospital he'd found himself in had done their best, but one of them had been honest. 'It might be something you just need to live with. Figure some way you can work around it. Give yourself time, Hugh. Be kind to yourself.'

Being kind to himself didn't include getting involved in other people's lives, but there was terror emanating from the other end of the phone, and he had no choice but to respond. 'What's happened?'

'There's been an explosion out the back of the town. A big one. One of Henry Jefferson's sheds. You know he stores all sorts of junk? There was a fire in the outer shed, the fireys were putting it out and wham. It's gone up, all of it, one big bang. You should be able to see the smoke from your place.'

He strode to the end of the veranda so he could look back across the island. Sure enough, there was a plume of black smoke rising in the direction of the town.

'Casualties?' he snapped.

'We dunno where Jefferson is.' The guy's voice was shaky. 'He might have been in the big shed; in which case he's gone. There're casualties among the fireys, though. We rang Gannet for help, but the chopper's out on one of the outer islands. They're rerouting the ferry but, mate, you're all we have. Please come. Oh, strewth, I gotta go.'

And the phone went dead.

An explosion. Multiple casualties.

His worst nightmare.

He could feel the shakes build up inside, but this wasn't the time for shakes.

'You're all we have.'

He had gear in the truck. Not nearly enough, but, after that first episode with Mrs Henderson's fall from the ladder, the doctors on Gannet had supplied him with a decent emergency kit. 'We know you don't want it,' they'd told him. 'And we swear we won't call you unless it's life or death, but can you keep it just in case?'

He'd kept it. He'd kept his registration up. When all was said and done, he was still a doctor.

He had no choice but to be a doctor now. Muppet was

staring at him, looking concerned, but there was no time for the niceties of farewell. He scooped Hoppy up and put him inside, then headed for the truck at a run. Swung open the driver's door. Gunned the engine into life.

And then realised that Muppet was jumping in beside him.

'Get out,' he snapped. The last thing he needed was a useless onlooker.

'I can help.' She must have heard the conversation.

'This is nasty. Get out!'

'I'm a nurse,' she told him, and he cast her an incredulous glance, his foot hovering on the accelerator.

'A nurse?'

'Yes.'

For heaven's sake, what was this? 'Your aunt says you've been swanning around the world on cruise ships for years. You think I want someone with no practical experience?'

'I have practical experience. Shut up and get going.'

'I'll drop you at your aunt's on the way.'

'Don't be dumb. Use me.'

And maybe he could. If she'd done basic training, no matter how long ago, she might be able to assist in some small way. But he glanced again at her and said the first thing that came into his mind. 'In those clothes?'

'Good point. Stop for a minute,' she snapped, and the sudden authority in her voice had him keeping his foot on the brake. 'Wait!'

And she was off at a run, up to the veranda to grab a pair of wellies he'd had sitting under the bench. Ten seconds later she was back. 'Go,' she said, and he hit the accelerator while she tugged on his oversized boots.

'You're right,' she said, even sounding approving.

'Explosion means rubble and I'll not add to your work. These'll feel weird but they'll let me move.'

It was all he could do not to stare. The muppet label—the useless bimbo he'd labelled her—had suddenly transformed. She might still look the part of muppet, but her voice was that of a clipped professional.

'Drive,' she said, and he did.

'Tell me what the set-up is,' she demanded as they hit the road. 'I missed a bit. Do you know how many casualties? How long before we can expect backup?'

What the hell...? 'What sort of nurse are you?'

'A good one.' The look she sent him was almost a glare.

'When did you last nurse?'

'Approximately two weeks ago.' Her voice held more than an undercurrent of anger. 'Did my aunt really say *swanning*?'

'She said cruising,' he admitted. Why did it suddenly seem as if he'd dug himself a hole and now he was digging it deeper?

'I've been in charge of medical services on a purpose-built expedition boat,' she told him, her voice still clipped with anger. 'We sometimes take well-heeled passengers, but that's to help funding for our research teams. Our ship's chartered by world environmental groups, to take scientists back and forth to the Antarctic, or occasionally into other remote communities. Sometimes we have a doctor on board, but mostly we don't. I've coped with everything from ingrown toenails to a guy who lost a leg in a winch accident. I managed to save him—as well as the guy with the ingrown toenail. I haven't coped with an explosion before, but I have coped with a fire in the engine room, with multiple burns. And before you make any more disparaging remarks about me being a waste of space and not caring about my aunt, for the last four months I've been stuck at sea because of the pandemic. Along with crews from scores of other boats. I haven't exactly been idle during those months, either, apart from the last two weeks in quarantine in Sydney. At one time I was the sole medic for five boats trapped in the one harbour. So can you accept that I might just possibly be of some help?'

Whoa.

He needed to concentrate on the road, rutted from recent rain. The last thing he needed was to get stuck, so he had to pay attention. But what she'd said...

For some reason he found himself focussing on the totally inane. 'Your toes,' he said stupidly, tangentially, and she stared at him for a long moment and then—to his astonishment—she chuckled.

'Yeah. Toes. How many nurses' toes have you seen in your lifetime, Dr Duncan? So are toes the litmus test on whether we make competent medics or not?'

'I...'

'When we were finally allowed to come home,' said, quite calmly now, 'they put us in quarantine in a hotel in Sydney. So I've had two weeks in one sparse hotel room, with half an hour supervised exercise a day. It's a wonder I haven't tattooed my whole body. Now can we get over my toes and move on? I believe I asked you... Casualties? Backup?'

And finally, the personal was left behind. Finally, he managed a gear shift, and she was an experienced medic and so was he, and they were facing what could well be a disaster.

Two medics. The weight of responsibility shifted a little.

He wasn't completely alone.

Muppet might even be useful.

CHAPTER FOUR

HENRY JEFFERSON HAD been a scrounger, a filthy-tempered wheeler dealer all his time on the island. Rumour had it he'd moved to Sandpiper because he'd done time in jail on the mainland. There'd been talk of drugs, and rumours that gangland figures had threatened him, but that was years ago. He'd settled on the island and surrounded himself with junk. Supposedly he hauled cars apart and sold parts and scrap. He also charged for collecting things like old sump oil and discarded tyres, organising for them to be taken off the island for legal disposal, but with this tiny population he couldn't possibly be making a living that way.

He'd been kicked out of Windswept Bay because the National Park authorities had discovered leakage into the pristine ground. He'd responded by moving to the site of an old whaling station, where his mess didn't seem to worry anyone.

There were rumours, though. Maybe drugs arrived on darkened boats and were stored for more clandestine boats to take away. Maybe he even manufactured drugs.

'He doesn't seem to be doing anyone any harm,' Joan Wilmot, the local cop-cum-mayor, had told islanders who'd worried. Joan's professional rule of thumb was 'anything for an easy life', and she could see no reason to trouble herself. 'The rumours of drugs are just rumours,' she'd told them. 'I'd need a warrant to search and I don't have grounds. He's well out of sight in Whalers' Bay, and he's doing useful work. Who else is going to get rid of that stuff?' But as they topped the last rise leading into the town Hugh thought Joan might be paying a very high price for letting sleeping dogs lie.

Henry's three sheds were a kilometre or so from the town, just back from the kelp-strewn Whaler's bay. You could just see their roofs from the high point of the island. He could see them now. Or he could see where they'd been.

The one on the lee side seemed almost vapourised. The others were a mass of flames. A brisk wind was pushing the smoke towards the coast, so he could see the mess that remained.

He could see the island's fire engine, parked well back. Firefighters were hosing flames. A cluster of people stood on the edges of the action, onlookers. A stream of vehicles was on the road, more people than could possibly help.

'Right,' Hugh said grimly as they reached the turnoff to Whalers' Bay. 'Hold onto your hat. I don't have a siren on this baby but the next best thing.'

One thing Gina had never experienced in her years at sea was coping with traffic. She hadn't expected it now. Sandpiper Island wasn't known for traffic jams.

The road from the town out to Whalers' Bay, though, was packed, with every islander headed in that direction. With the amount of smoke pouring out to sea there was no disguising something huge had happened. Some of the islanders would be desperate to help, and all of them would want to see. Cars therefore had banked up, inching slowly towards the mess.

Hugh shoved his hand on the horn, a massive blaring klaxon thing. He pulled into the wrong lane and put his foot on the accelerator. Woe betide anyone daring to come in the opposite direction. When the road narrowed, he simply hit the verge, lurching up the incline onto sand.

Gina had her seat belt on, but she held her seat like grim death. She didn't make a sound, though, even when a tree loomed and she was almost sure they'd hit it. They didn't. Hugh knew what he was doing. Every ounce of his being was focussed on getting where he needed to go as fast as possible.

And then they were there, swinging in beside the parked fire engine, and Hugh was out of the truck almost before it stopped.

She was with him. An explosion like this...burns... Every moment was critical.

A woman was running towards them, and she recognised Joan Wilmot. When she'd last seen Joan she'd been in her forties. She must be close to sixty now, but she didn't seem to have changed. Her hair was still a mass of steel-grey tight curls, her dumpy figure just as dumpy.

She was wearing an apron with pictures of poodles all over it. Wow, Gina thought tangentially. It'd take some emergency to get Joan here without taking time to don either her cop uniform or her mayoral robes.

'Doctor!' she said, and in that one word Gina heard real relief. And more. One word and she realised that responsibility was being handed over to Hugh. This type of situation was far beyond Joan's skill. Or anyone on this island, Gina suspected.

'How many casualties?' Hugh snapped, and Joan stopped dead and Gina thought she looked as if she'd been about to throw herself on Hugh's chest. But the snapped question stopped her. She faltered and then seemed to regroup. Years ago, she'd trained as a cop, and her training was still there.

'We think Jefferson's gone up with his shed,' she said, failing to disguise a tremor in her voice. 'He was here when I got here, trying to pull stuff out, and then it went up. But the fireys, too… The ones close to the shed…' She faltered.

'How many hurt?'

'F…four.'

'First things first,' Hugh snapped, looking over at a group of people clustered around the obviously injured. Even from where they were, they could see it looked bad. A couple of men had joined Joan now, listening— waiting for orders? And Hugh obliged.

'Priorities,' he snapped. 'Get everyone, and I mean everyone, back from the remaining sheds. They need to get the hell out of harm's way. Tell the fireys to let what's left burn. Heaven knows what's in that smoke, so their priority has to be clearing the area. Have someone contact Gannet, upgrade the need for the chopper, tell them to notify an evacuation team from Sydney. Then get someone with a motorbike sent down the track to get those cars off the road. Everyone clears off the track, parks on the verge, whatever, I don't care, but I want that track clear. Then I want four trucks, with empty trays, with rugs, anything you can find in the back to make them into makeshift ambulances.' He paused to make sure they were listening and got unanimous nods.

'Right. You…' He pointed to a guy holding a mobile phone. 'Phone anyone you can think of back in town. I want mattresses in the school hall, clean linen, a stack of it, and towels, from wherever you can get them. Tell people to raid their linen cupboards. I want a supply of boiled water by the time I get there, as much as they can boil, get it on now so it can cool. And I want cling wrap, lots of it, we'll need it to dress burns. Raid the store. So… Clear the crowd from the sheds. Contact Gannet. Clear the track and prepare four trucks for transporting the injured. Then prepare the school hall. Got it?' He was tugging gear from the back of his SUV as he spoke. 'Right, Gina, let's go.'

The island's fire truck was manned by volunteers, and only four had been able to get to the truck before it left the station. The rest of the team had only just arrived as the shed blew, so blessedly there'd only been four in the face of the explosion.

Plus Jefferson. He'd been in the shed when it had blown. There was no chance he was still alive now.

What on earth had been in the shed? Hugh thought as he strode towards the injured. Drugs? He must have been into some sort of crazy manufacturing process, but who would know?

Now wasn't the time for asking questions. He had people with major injuries, and no one to help but Gina.

But help was too mild a word for what she was doing. She'd climbed out of his truck, taken one look at what was before her and sorted priorities. As he'd finished throwing curt orders, she was heading for the group clustered around the people on the ground. His huge boots looked the only sensible thing about her, and even they looked ridiculous, but she strode towards the group with purpose.

'Let me through.' Her voice, normally soft and low, suddenly had the resonance of a sonic boom, and the clustered locals were startled enough to make way.

Four people were lying in the dust.

By the time Hugh reached her she'd already bent over the first casualty. She was doing a fast assessment— airways, heartbeat, bleeding. She was giving curt orders to one of the bystanders.

She glanced up at him as he reached her and nodded towards the two casualties furthest from her. Division of priorities was sorted in that glance. He left the first two to her and moved to the third and fourth.

He started his own assessment, checking airways, looking for wounds that could be bleeding out. Looking for spinal damage, head injuries.

As he checked the fourth—a woman with burns down the side of her arm, bleeding from multiple scratches, moaning with pain—Gina called him back, her voice low and urgent. 'Hugh, you're needed here. Compression chest injury. Breathing problems.'

Another plus for her. Conceding fast that an injury was out of her area of expertise and handing over fast. They did a swap of patients.

'Burns, lacerations, shock, suspect spinal injury on four,' he snapped as they passed. 'Three's stable for the moment.' With no time to learn names, they'd done what emergency workers did the world over. Patients were referred to as the number they'd presented as, or, in this case, distance from the truck. Names would be needed, for reassurance as much as anything, but not now when the absolute imperative was to keep people alive. 'Backup kit with drugs in the back of the truck,' he told her. 'Four needs morphine, ten milligrams. Three as well, but four first.'

Then he headed for the chest injury, heart sinking as he saw what he was facing. The guy must have been hit full on in the chest. A vicious impact wound. Whistling, laboured breathing.

Shattered ribs? A punctured lung? Tension pneumothorax?

The people around them were silent, appalled, and Gina's voice rose above the stillness. 'You!' Her pointed finger skewered the closest adult, a middle-aged guy wearing paint-spattered overalls and huge, tradesman-type boots. 'I want any container you can find, filled with water. Use the fire truck supply if there's no tap. I want water poured on this lady's arm, as much as possible while we work. Do it now. Does anyone know her name?'

'G… Gladys,' someone faltered.

'Right. Gladys, we have a whole team of people helping and we'll have you out of pain really soon. You…' Another guy was skewered by that finger. 'I want something to stabilise Gladys's back. There's a heap of junk over there—find me anything I can use as a rigid stretcher. Gladys, I need you to keep still to help with the pain. The rest of you… Someone who doesn't faint at the sight of blood, help Doc. Plus I want two people, one on each side of each injury. Decide who, and then don't leave them for a minute, even if Doc and I are with you. Stream water over anything that looks like a burn. We're working between four patients and we need to be able to move back and forth. If there's any problem breathing, yell for us to get back to you fast! If there are any other injuries—bystanders hit and you're not saying—please, go sit by the trucks and wait until we can see you. The rest of you, check on each other and yell if you need us. Hard. And get the back of those trucks ready for transport. Move.'

Ten metres away Hugh was working frantically. The

guy he was attending seemed to be dying under his hands—by the look of his chest, the lung had completely collapsed. If he wasn't to lose him he had no time for anything else, but Gina's voice said authority had been taken out of his hands. For a woman dressed as she was, for a…muppet?…to have a voice that held such power…

And blessedly, the people she'd yelled at reacted.

'You heard the lady. Move!' the painter guy was yelling. 'Rod, Wendy, Stuart, there's buckets in the cab. Tap's on this side. Chris, there's timber back there, come with me and we'll grab planks. I want fire blankets, dog blankets, anything anyone has to soften makeshift stretchers. I want more fire blankets on the ground here for the rest of the injured. Do what she said!'

But Hugh had to block them out. He was dealing with a deadly chest wound, rapid, shallow breathing, an obvious shift of the chest wall to the opposite side… It had to be broken ribs, a pierced lung.

But even as he realised his most urgent need, he heard Gina's voice again.

'Someone, grab one of the oxygen cylinders in the back of Doc's truck. He'll need it. And bring the second one to me. Fast!'

He had a colleague. More, he had an intelligent, intuitive medic who was not only swiftly assessing and treating, she was also aware of what he was doing.

This wasn't just a nurse with basic training.

Maybe he should stop thinking of her as Muppet?

Whatever. An older guy he recognised, Ron, the local fisheries officer, was crouching beside him. Another woman came up behind him, Nora from the pub.

'You want help here, Doc?'

'Not if you'll pass out.'

'Used to be in the army,' Ron said steadily. 'Not a

chance. And Nora has five sons. Bit of blood doesn't scare us.'

Three colleagues.

'Gina…' He called across. 'I need to relieve a pneumothorax. Nothing else.'

She got it. He needed to be totally focussed on what he was doing. She'd also know that with a pneumothorax he could use any help he could get.

'Go for it,' she called. 'But I'm needed.'

He knew that, too. Much as he wanted—needed— a trained colleague to help with a complicated, dicey procedure, leaving burns, shock and suspected spinal injuries to be monitored by untrained personnel was a recipe for disaster. He was on his own—but so was she.

'Stabilise and get 'em shifted,' he called. 'Into the trucks and out of here if you can. If the wind shifts and the smoke comes this way…'

He didn't need to say more. The remaining sheds were more smoke than flames, but the smoke was black and acrid. 'School hall's being made ready.'

'Right you are,' she called back and left him to it.

The guy with the pneumothorax—his name was Ray Cross, the fishery guy told him—couldn't be moved until he had his breathing stable.

For years Hugh had worked in field hospitals, coping with collateral damage from war in less than optimum conditions. He'd seen blast injuries before. He knew he was fighting the odds to give the man he was treating a chance of survival, so he was almost totally focussed on what he was doing, but there was still a sliver of awareness of what Gina was doing.

She'd already administered morphine. She'd made sure the burns were being washed with cold water and she was organising more water onto the trucks so the washing could continue. She was supervising moving her patients into the backs of the waiting trucks. Watching them every inch of the way.

She was giving orders to the two persons she'd allocated to each casualty. She was watching everyone like a hawk.

If she weren't here, he'd have had to let Ray die. He needed a hundred per cent focus to cope with a collapsed lung, but each of the other three had life-threatening injuries as well.

Ray's breathing was fast, panicked, his eyes rolling in terror. His skin was tinged with blue and his pulse was so thready it was frightening.

All Hugh's attention had to be on him. He had to trust Gina.

He did.

'Mate, something's hit your chest and broken your ribs,' he told him, his voice matter-of-fact, as if this were the sort of injury a half-decent doctor coped with almost any day of the week. 'That's let air into the space between your lungs and the chest wall, which is stopping your lungs filling. It's nothing we can't fix, though. I've just loaded you with morphine and that should kick in any minute. As soon as it does, I'll pop a needle in and let the air out. That'll take the pressure off your lungs, and things'll settle.'

'A needle…' The guy visibly quavered and Hugh almost grinned. How many times had he seen this—tough-as-nails soldiers, or, in this case, a trained firefighter, scared to death of a needle.

'It won't hurt a bit,' he lied, but actually it was almost the truth because so much more would be hurting that one needle wasn't about to make a difference. 'Let's get you fixed and then back somewhere clean. Our lovely new island nurse is fixing up a makeshift hospital where you can join your mates. You need to meet her. She's something special.'

And… 'A doc and a nurse,' Ray managed to whisper. 'Geez, Doc, we almost have our own medical team. Just like Gannet.'

CHAPTER FIVE

THE SCHOOL HALL had been made into a makeshift clearing hospital, and afterwards Gina marvelled that it had been done so fast. Apparently, a gym session had been going on when the call had come to say the hall was needed. The gym teacher had promptly turned the session into a hike to the beach. The townspeople had swarmed in, and by the time Gina and her convoy of trucks reached town, the place almost looked like a hospital ward. Mattresses on the floor had been made up with clean linen. Urns of water had already boiled, and some had been poured off to cool. Someone had thought of using trestle tables with camping mattresses on top to form makeshift examination tables.

By the time Hugh arrived with Ray, she almost had order.

Urgency was still there, though. Burns were the most pressing issue. She'd administered as much morphine as she dared and then worked fast to get the burns covered. Some were full thickness. They'd need specialist attention, but for now she washed and washed and washed again.

Water was always used to cool burns, and, as well as that, she didn't have a clue what had been stored in that shed. Some of these burns might well have a chemical cause. So she had teams gently pouring water until she had time to assess each. With her roll of cling wrap.

Cling wrap was a blessing when it came to burns treatment. Not only was it almost sterile, coming from the supplier in a roll that was wound so firmly it had to be almost airtight, it clung like a second skin, it moved with the injury, it covered exposed nerve endings—and medics could still see what was underneath.

So she covered the burns and left helpers monitoring colour, sensation and movement. Then she moved on to the next imperative. She had two patients with fractures, but Glady's arm was losing colour, only the faintest thread of pulse in the wrist showing that any blood was getting through.

Gina was looking at it with a sinking heart. Yeah, she had training in emergency medicine, but realigning a fracture on a burned arm…

And then there was a stir at the doorway and Hugh entered beside another of the makeshift stretchers. She saw the apparatus being held beside the patient—drips, plus a thin tube leading down into a container carried carefully beneath.

He'd performed a thoracostomy, then. Under these conditions. The concept took her breath away.

Thoracostomy to cope with such a wound, inserting a needle catheter to release the air trapped in the pleural space… She'd studied the basics during her post-grad training as nurse practitioner, but doing it in the field, with a patient with other life-threatening injuries… If Hugh hadn't been here, she knew the outcome would have been death.

But the fact that their patient was still alive and obviously stable enough to be transported spoke volumes. Hugh strode in now beside the stretcher but one look at him told her it hadn't been easy. His face was almost haggard. Haunted? Yet she glanced at the stretcher and knew his patient was alive.

And overriding her reaction to his expression was the knowledge that she had a doctor. Here.

For a fraction of a moment she let herself savour relief, finding strength in the knowledge that she wasn't alone. And then she opened her eyes and Hugh's gaze was on hers. Holding.

'Next?' he asked simply, and the haggard look had gone. It was replaced by an expression of determination. And of trust. One professional to another. He'd left it to her while he'd coped back there, and now he was deferring to her to decree priority.

She headed towards him, swiftly, so they could speak without being overheard, and for an insane moment she felt like hugging him. The expression she'd caught on his face... But it was gone—maybe she'd even imagined it—and there was no time for questions.

'Gladys,' she said. 'The lady firefighter. Her arm's burned, not too badly, but it's broken and I'm losing pulse in her hand. It's been pretty much colourless for five minutes. If you could...'

'I'm on it,' he said, but unexpectedly he reached out and gripped her shoulder. 'You're okay?'

'I'm not going to faint, if that's what you mean,' she said with asperity.

'I can't imagine you fainting.' His smile was a bit crooked, but it was still a smile. He looked past her, at her almost orderly 'casualty department'.

And unbelievably, that was what it looked like. Orderly. She had patients on the 'beds', three metres or so between them. She had two people with each patient, one on each side, watching, gently talking, touching if possible. Reassurance was a huge factor in treating shock, and leaving patients alone waiting treatment was a recipe for disaster.

She had a prep area—urns on a trestle table at the end of the hall, people pouring off boiling water to cool, people cleaning used equipment and linen. Chairs were set up there, too, and three women were attending a group of people with minor injuries. These would be people who'd been second to arrive at the fire, reaching the outskirts of the scene just as the blast hit.

She motioned to the ladies helping the injured. 'Meet our third tier of medics,' she said, following his gaze. 'Now you're here, you're in charge of the life-threatening, I'm on the urgent and these ladies are for the rest, with instructions to shout if there's the least chance of upgrade. Sensible ladies, all of them—they put their hands up when I asked if anyone had done any first-aiding courses. Directions are to gently wash everything, using heaps of water—heaven knows what was in that blast. Apply antiseptic, leave things open for us to check later unless it's actively bleeding, and refer anything suspect to me. There are lacerations, which they're putting pressure on until we can reach them. Ralph Henry has a foreign body in his eye, which looks serious. They've washed it and washed it and I have it covered—he's lying on the far bed waiting for you.'

Then she gazed down at the guy on the stretcher, drugged and only barely awake, but still alert enough to be watching her. Recognition obviously dawned. 'Hey, Ray,' she said and smiled. 'Remember me? I'm Babs's great-niece. I believe I dated your little brother for a whole six weeks back in eleventh grade.'

'Gina,' Ray breathed, and Hugh thought how close he'd been to death, how tricky it had been to get the needle where it needed to go. And also how much Gina had achieved while he was doing it.

'Hey, are you okay yourself?' Gina asked, and he realised she was talking to him. It needed only that—that she was worried for him.

'I'm needing to apologise for calling you a muppet,' he said faintly. 'But moving on. I'll see to Gladys. Can you keep an eye on Ray?' He glanced around the hall. 'As well as everything else you're seeing to?'

'Of course I can,' Gina said promptly. 'I'll delegate—delegation is my principal skill. We'll be right, won't we, Ray?'

'Bloody hell,' Ray muttered, his voice a thready whisper but amazingly it held a trace of humour. 'Maybe Mum and Dad shouldn't have told Luke you were a waste of space. Welcome home, girl. You know Luke's still available? You want us to set you up with another date?'

And then it was just sheer hard work, with more than a bit of skill on the side. Medics from Gannet Island, two doctors, two paramedics, arrived half an hour later. By the time they did, Gladys's hand was turning pink again, circulation restored. That had been a bit of tricky surgery, where Hugh had needed Gina's skill as a theatre nurse. Any lingering doubts as to her skill had dissipated in those fraught moments as he'd needed to focus to reposition the arm, as he'd fought to stabilise that tiny thread of circulation. She'd assisted as if she'd been twenty years a theatre nurse.

In the fraction of consciousness he had for anything but the job at hand, he'd been reflecting on his months of building anger at her, for not coming home to her great-aunt.

Babs could have told him, he thought grimly, but then Babs never said a word more than she had to.

And neither had he. He'd looked out for her, especially after he'd found her after her heart attack, but he'd never asked more than basic questions.

'My great-niece will come,' she'd said with asperity when he'd pushed. 'When she's finished gallivanting round the world on those cruise ships.'

Gallivanting. Wrong word. Whatever Gina had been doing for the past few years it hadn't been gallivanting. The skills she had… It almost looked as if she coped with emergency medicine every day of her working life.

And when the team from Gannet Island arrived, she greeted them smoothly, professionally—and even with friendship.

'Hey, Elsa!' she called as they arrived. The woman doctor from Gannet—obviously pregnant, but, like all of them, intent and focussed—stopped in her tracks. 'We've got some work for you.'

Elsa looked stunned. 'Gina? It's never Gina Marshall? Hey, you've lost your nose rings.'

'Bit of a nuisance where I've been working,' she said briefly. 'Frostbite's a problem and frozen nose rings are the devil. You guys know Hugh? He's caught up with a compound fracture—far end of the hall. Let me walk you through the rest.'

He was dressing Gladys's arm, stabilising so his work wouldn't be undone. One of the paramedics moved to assist, the rest listened to Gina's fast, incisive handover and then sorted priorities for themselves.

Wow, she was good. The new arrivals meant every patient was getting optimal field treatment within minutes. Hugh could finally relax.

Move back.

Stop being the chief medical officer in charge of a nightmare.

During all this time, memories had been swirling, the scene he'd just come from mingling horribly with memories of scenes he never wanted to recall. He'd fought to block them out and, somehow, he'd managed, but now... He felt sick.

But more assistance was pouring in. More medics. Police from Gannet. Joan had disappeared briefly. She now reappeared wearing her official policewoman's uniform, ready to take the officers from Gannet to the explosion site. Things were under control.

Sort of. One dead. Others with injuries that'd take months to heal. Traumatised islanders.

His own trauma? That had to be shelved.

He worked on, almost on remote control, doing what had to be done. The Gannet Island team organised evacuation. Blessedly the sea was calm enough to use the ferry. Ray and Gladys would both need skilled stabilisation before they could be airlifted to Sydney for the specialist burns treatment they needed, so they were to be ferried to Gannet. Three others would be flown to Sydney tonight, the two injured fireys plus Ralph Henry, who'd need specialist surgery if he wasn't to lose his eye.

'We should leave you with another doctor.' Marc, the head of the Birding Isles Medical Group, husband of Elsa, was looking concerned as they organised the evacuation process. 'But with this lot coming in, we'll be tight for staffing on Gannet, and you look like you have things under control.'

'We'll need replacement medical supplies,' Gina told him. 'We've used almost everything Hugh had.'

'There's no rush,' Hugh said grimly. 'That kit was for emergencies only, and I'm damned if I'm taking on something like this again.'

'Unless you have to,' Gina said softly, glancing at him, looking worried.

'We know you don't want to work as a doctor,' Marc told him, and reached out and gripped his hand. 'But we're bloody grateful you did. And you, too, Gina.' At some stage during the drama he'd been given a brief résumé of her qualifications, and there'd been no time for questions. 'What a godsend that you were home.'

'Yeah, all that luxury cruising and finally I get to use a bandage,' she said, with a sidelong look at Hugh. She grinned. 'But I'm with Hugh on this one. No more drama, please.'

'There'll be coroner stuff,' Marc warned. 'The police are up there now, poring over the site. Good luck to them finding anything of Jefferson's body but if they do...'

'Then we'll call you back,' Gina said, and Hugh caught her taking a sidelong glance at his face. 'You're a helicopter's ride away and Hugh's done enough. He doesn't need to cope with what remains of a low life who not only killed himself, but also put every islander at risk. Let's not ask more of him.'

Hell. How much did she understand? But Gina was fixing Marc with a look that said what she was saying was inarguable—don't mess with me. And Marc glanced at her and nodded.

'I can finish here if Hugh wants to head home,' Gina said. There were still minor injuries to be dealt with. A few of the lacerations had been pulled together hurriedly with Steri-Strips and could use stitches. There were probably others who might present when they thought the drama was over and they weren't being a bother. There'd also be shock to deal with.

'We'll cope together,' Hugh said gruffly, and Marc nodded.

'So you're a team—well, thank God for it. You don't know how much we've wanted a team out here. The island's too small for it, we know that, but with these injuries, that you were here today... You know you've saved at least one life and prevented long-term damage. May you both stay for ever—that's all I can say.'

And then he hesitated. 'But tomorrow...with this amount of minor injuries there are bound to be niggles to clear up.'

'I have Australian registration as a nurse practitioner,' Gina said briefly. 'Leave me equipment and I'll deal.'

'She's good,' Hugh said gruffly. Almost reluctantly. He heard the tone in his voice though and regretted it. 'Very good,' he amended. 'There'd probably have been deaths without her.'

Marc glanced at him then, assessing. 'And you'll back her up?'

More medicine. Ongoing minor stuff. Checking for infection. Stitches. Coping with delayed shock, or injuries that onlookers hadn't brought to their attention because they'd seemed too trivial in the face of what had happened to others.

He hesitated, for just a moment too long.

'I'll only call you if I need you,' Gina said generously, and he knew she'd got that he didn't want any further involvement. 'If I can have this place for an hour or so tomorrow morning, just to check...' She frowned. 'But it'd be good to have a doctor as backup if I need it. Isn't there any medical service on the island at all?'

'One of our docs comes over once a week,' Marc told

her. He hesitated, looking at the evacuation currently taking place. 'Our centre's good but it's not huge, and I suspect all available staff will be needed on Gannet. When we come, we use rooms set up at the back of the general store, but it'll be hard to staff it tomorrow.'

'Then I'll staff it,' Gina said, and then looked uncertainly across at Hugh. 'Um…backup?'

'I'll help if I must,' Hugh said, goaded. 'But we're not talking long term here.' He needed to get that out, even though he'd said it to Marc time and time again. 'It's time this island had a doctor based here.'

'Don't I know it,' Marc said. 'But you try getting a doctor to agree to working on an island with a permanent population of four hundred. Even a permanent nurse would be good.' He raised an eyebrow at Gina. 'Interested?'

'Hey, not me.' She raised her hands as if to ward him off. 'Let's not go down that road, especially when I've been on the island for less than twenty-four hours. I lived here for two years and that was enough. I'm here to look after my great-aunt and then I'm off again. But for the time being, I'm happy to help.' She fixed Hugh with a considering stare. 'So… Can I call if I need you?'

'Do I have a choice?'

'I guess not,' she said, cheerful again. 'Seems we're both between a rock and a hard place, professionals whether we like it or not. We should both have trained as belly dancers.'

'Belly dancers,' he said faintly.

'Okay, not you, but that was once my life's ambition,' she conceded. 'I see you more as a lumberjack, complete with axe. That'd let us both off the hook now—what use are lumberjacks and belly dancers when someone has an infected toe? But here we are, one false move in our career choices and we're stuck. So, moving on... Let's go.'

It was almost dark by the time they finished, and weariness was coating Gina like a thick grey blanket. It always did after drama.

But at least she hadn't been alone. There'd been frightening incidents during her time on the boats, times when she'd have sold her soul to have a doctor on hand. The engine-room explosion... Yeah, don't go there.

And then she glanced across at Hugh.

His hands were clenched on the steering wheel. His knuckles were white, and his face... The trauma...

The story Babs had told her had been scant. Foreign aid. A bomb. It must have been something truly appalling, she thought, and she wasn't thinking just physical injury. It seemed he'd run to Sandpiper Island to hide, but by the look of his face he hadn't run far enough.

So what to do? Leaving trauma in place wasn't Gina's style.

One thing she'd learned while working with expeditioners was that buried trauma surfaced when it was least wanted—or needed. She'd worked on scores of expeditions now, many dangerous, and almost all of them long. As lone medic—and often lone woman—she'd found crew members often began to depend on her as separation and hardship took their toll. After years of practice, she'd learned that when she sensed problems, the best option was to ask the hard questions early.

This man wasn't one of her expeditioners, but he *was* traumatised, and he was heading home to solitude. In her book that could be a recipe for disaster. So do something, she told herself, whether it was her business or not.

But what? After such a short acquaintance, demanding he tell all was never going to work.

But she knew a way that had worked in the past. Shared experience. The last thing she wanted was to talk about her own trauma, but exposing herself…making it about her fears… Maybe it was worth a try?

So she closed her eyes for a moment, letting herself return to a scene she'd tried hard to forget. Then, deliberately, she pulled the plug and let it out.

'I never thought I'd have to cope with something like this again,' she said, conversational, but almost to herself. 'All day I've been trying to block it out. I guess it helped today, having had that experience, but I have no idea…how do I process both these now?'

He glanced across at her. His hands were still clenched on the wheel. He looked as if he was in some nightmare place, but he could hardly not answer.

'What?' he demanded, gruffly, and she felt a tiny sense of satisfaction. This man held himself rigid, emotions running deep. The scars on his face weren't terrible. She suspected what lay beneath was.

And he'd opened the gates to trauma. Just a crack but maybe enough for her to wriggle through.

'I copped something like this a couple of years back,' she told him.

'Like this…'

She shrugged. Forcing herself to go on, opening her own can of worms.

'We were heading down to McLachlan Island,' she said, trying to sound matter-of-fact, as if the accident had been a simple part of her professional life, not something that haunted her still. 'There were twenty of us on board. The weather was atrocious—well, the weather's always atrocious down there. Then a fire started in the engine room. Four of the crew were in there trying to get it out, and bang. I still don't know what happened, but suddenly there were flames everywhere. Blast injuries. Burns. We got the fire out, otherwise I wouldn't be here talking about it, but then we were stranded, wallowing without an engine in appalling seas, with injured crew on a knife edge between life and death. It took twenty-four hours to get us airlifted off. Twenty-four hours where I'd never felt so alone. They all recovered, but a couple carry scars which would have been a whole lot less if I'd had your skills. So today I was thinking, I'm so glad I had your help. And I was so glad to be on an island and not another ship.'

'Yeah…'

'And I'm guessing,' she said, making her voice matter-of-fact, one professional to another, 'you're thanking your stars you're not in some combat zone as well. And now I can go home to one of Babs's pies and so can you. You and Hoppy will like that pie.'

There was silence at that. She'd risked having her nose snapped off—she knew she had—but it was a technique she'd used before when she'd coped with injuries in isolation. By obliquely talking about shared trauma maybe she'd normalised things a little, hopefully dragging ghosts out of the past to be put in perspective, so he could think of what lay ahead.

And maybe it was working. She watched his hands deliberately unclench on the wheel, then regrip with a hold that was more normal.

He still looked grim though. Well, maybe the man was always grim.

'McLachlan Island,' he said, and she thought he was deflecting attention back to her. Fair enough. She'd cop that and run with it.

'It's an amazing place,' she said. 'Stunning. It was such a privilege to be part of the team down there.'

'Why the hell didn't you have a doctor on board?'

'There's usually a doctor stationed down there,' she told him. 'My job was just to be on the ship as we took off a team that had summered over. I've done it before. Macca's awesome and I jump at any chance to go back there. The wildlife's breathtaking, of course, but it's also an amazing example of uplifted ocean crust. It's almost the only place in the world where oceanic lithosphere is exposed above sea level. The island's volcanic basalt, cooled below sea level, and that's created the most amazing oval-shaped pillow lava. The pillows have a glassy external margin because they cooled so fast. You should see them. The geological features…the plate boundary dynamics above sea level… Then there's this layered troctolite…'

And then she glanced at his face and saw…incredulity?

'Whoops, sorry,' she said. 'I forget some people aren't all that fascinated with rocks.

'Rocks.'

'I love 'em,' she said in satisfaction. 'Anything you want to know about rocks, I'm your man.'

'Muppet,' he said tangentially, and she frowned.

'Sorry. What?'

'I'm doing a rethink,' he admitted. 'I've been doing a rethink all day. It was the toes that did it.'

'So, muppet,' she said thoughtfully, and eyed him sideways. 'You said that before. You mean…bimbo?'

'I admit, to my shame, I meant bimbo.'

'Asking for it,' she said darkly, and he frowned.

'What?'

'That comes from a guy on my second or third expedition,' she said, feeling a twinge of satisfaction that—

muppet comment aside—she seemed to have pulled him out of his trauma-filled head space. 'We'd left Hobart, heading south, and had a day of calm, warm weather. You don't know how rare that is in the Southern Ocean. The guys were all in shorts and nothing else—they knew it was their last chance of warmth from the sun for maybe a year. I wasn't missing out either—I was on deck in my shorts and sports bra, soaking up the sun. But then above me, from the bridge, I heard one of the new expeditioners say, "Will you look at that bit of flesh? If she's not asking for it… What a…" Well, what he said next wasn't repeatable, but then he finished with, "I'll be into that before we reach McLachlan."'

He slowed. Swore. Looked across at her. 'That must have really upset you.'

'I wasn't upset. I was just mad.' She hesitated. 'Okay, demeaned as well. What I was wearing was far more modest than what the guys were wearing, and I pretty much expected the team and the crew to treat me as just that—one of them. But I didn't take it lying down.'

'Um…how did I know you wouldn't have?'

'Don't lie to me, Muppet Man. You know nothing of the sort.'

'Not a lie,' he said faintly. 'Okay, this morning I judged you and got it badly wrong, but now… What did you do?'

'I had to do something,' she told him, thinking, yay, she really had tugged him out of his trauma. Okay, he wasn't sharing what had happened to him, but maybe this was the next best thing. 'There were women on McLachlan who were wintering over, and they didn't need this scumbag causing trouble. Luckily, I realised he was talking to the skipper and Mike was a mate. I knew he wouldn't be tolerating that crap. But I didn't wait for his response, just hiked up there—still in my bra and shorts—and laid it on the line. And Mike backed me. The long and short of it was that the guy came back with us rather than staying on the island. He lost a job he'd angled for for years. So…' She slipped off her oversized wellingtons and lifted her feet so her toes rested on the dash. Her ballerina toes. 'There you go. Muppet, eh?'

'I'm very, very sorry.'

'Yeah, well, I had you down as an axe murderer when I first saw you,' she conceded. 'I'll nobly put muppet aside if you forgive the axe.'

'Maybe an axe is slightly more threatening than ballerinas.'

'I don't know.' She eyed her toes with consideration. 'The pirouette blonde has a bit of a menacing expression. I tried to change it, but it's pretty hard to tweak facial expressions when you're working on a canvas the size of a middle toe.' She hesitated. 'You know,' she added, quite kindly, 'if I were you, I'd watch the road. I hear there are wombats hereabouts.'

He almost choked and then he chuckled, and she grinned and felt insensibly cheered. After the horrors of the day…to make this guy smile…

And then he was pulling up in front of Babs's cottage and for some reason she felt reluctant to get out. They'd shared such a day. And besides…that chuckle… It seemed to have done something to her insides. She went to open the door but suddenly he reached over and put his hand on her arm.

'Gina, I'm very, very sorry about calling you a muppet,' he told her again. 'And I'm very, very grateful for what you did today. I couldn't have coped alone.'

She looked down at his hand, large, weathered, strong. And the twisting sensation inside her…she wasn't sure where it came from, or what to do with it. 'I suspect you've got pretty good at coping alone,' she said gently, and then she hesitated. 'Would you like to come in? I know Babs's pie is big enough to feed an army and you can save yours until tomorrow.'

'Thank you, but no.' All of a sudden, he sounded stilted, as if refusing invitations was a rote response. 'But I have Hoppy and I also have a wombat to see to. Responsibilities.'

'So you have.'

But still his hand stayed on her arm.

She glanced up at his face and saw the horror was still there. It had been helped by her silliness, helped by her waffle, she thought, but it was still there.

How important was human contact after trauma? she thought. There'd been a reason they'd assigned two people to stay beside every one of the injured. To be injured and alone…

And she looked up into his scarred face and thought, that's what he is. Tough. Solitary.

Injured and alone?

And with that thought came instinctive reaction. She couldn't help herself. Without thought she learned forward, put her hand against that scarred cheek—and she kissed him.

It was a feather kiss, a kiss of friendship, warmth, thanks. Nothing more. Or that was what it was supposed to be. It should have meant nothing to her. Or to him.

But the day had been too traumatic, and her heightened emotions were screaming at her that she wanted—needed?—to be closer. She wanted the reassurance of human contact—and maybe so did he.

And she never meant him to react.

But he did.

And maybe she shouldn't have been surprised. Who knew how much the horror of the day had brought back whatever was in his past? But she'd known it was there. Close enough to the surface to shatter reservations? To have him take what she needed as well?

For his hands caught hers and suddenly, without either of them seeming to will it, she was being kissed. Properly kissed. Deeply, strongly, with a fierceness born of who knew what?

And maybe it didn't matter. Maybe it couldn't matter, for her body was reacting with a heat, a need, a searing response to something she had no hope of explaining.

He felt...fantastic? No. Fantastic was far too small a word for what was happening.

Maybe she'd been stressed herself. Well, of course she had. She'd spent four long months trying to get off the boat, out of quarantine, back to a great-aunt who would never have admitted she needed her. Most of that time she'd felt alone. And today...she'd been pushed to the limit of her professional skills and she'd seen how close...

Don't go there. Just take what was offering, she told herself, and what was offering right now was this man.

His mouth. Oh, his mouth. The taste of him. The strength of his hands holding her. The heat. Her breasts were moulding against his chest, fitting as if she belonged. She was so close, and she wanted to be closer. To have a man hold her like this...

Not a man. This man. This wounded guy who smelled and tasted like the drama of the day. Filthy from smoke and antiseptics and dirt and sweat and what else?

'Gina!'

For a moment she didn't respond. How could she respond? She was far too busy. But the rap on the truck window and the harsh word was impossible to ignore. It was Hugh who reacted first, putting her back from him with what felt real reluctance.

He was reluctant? She felt like fighting to keep him just where she was.

'Gina?' The tap was insistent. It was Babs, of course, tapping and peering short-sightedly through the window.

'Uh-oh,' Hugh said. 'Sprung.'

'She's not wearing her glasses,' Gina managed. 'There's...there's hope for us yet.' She hauled herself further away from him—how hard was that?—and opened the truck door.

'Yep, me, Auntie Babs. I asked someone to ring you and tell you where I was. I hope they told you...

'Well, of course they did,' Babs snapped. 'I must have had fifty-seven phone calls telling me you were being of use to the good doctor. It's the first time anyone's ever told me you were useful.' And to Gina's astonishment she heard a note of pride in her aunt's voice. 'You'd better come in, the pair of you. Dinner's keeping hot.'

And she sensed Hugh stiffen. Pull back even further. Retreat into himself?

'I need to get home to see to Hoppy and the wombat,' he told her.

'Hoppy's here, and I've seen to your wombat,' Babs told him. She hesitated and Gina thought, wow, this was a big admission for a woman who normally would have walked on fire rather than get involved. 'It was the least I could do,' she admitted. 'When the whole island's been running around like headless chickens, that's my mite. And nothing more,' she snapped, as if Hugh might be about to take advantage. 'But your dog's here and he's been fed and your dinner's on the table.'

Gina glanced at Hugh and then deliberately climbed out of the truck. Something in Hugh's face…

He didn't need additional pressure.

'Hugh's tired, Babs,' she told her aunt. 'And we're both desperate for a wash. Let's just give him his dog and let him go.'

'I've his dinner ready for him. Look at the time, and I'll bet neither of you have eaten since breakfast. If you go home now, you'll have to heat my pie and that'll take time, unless you make it soggy by using one of those microwave things, and what a waste of my good pie. Don't be ridiculous, man. Come and eat and then get home to sleep. Dinner's going on the table now.'

And she turned and marched inside.

'I'll get your dog,' Gina offered. Hugh's face was set, impassive. 'She's just…like a bulldozer. You just have to learn to get out of her way.'

'Is that why you left the island?' he asked. The intensity between them was still there and she could almost see the effort he was putting into drawing back. Making things impersonal again.

But the question was anything but impersonal.

'There's a story,' she said, struggling to make her voice flippant. 'But now's not the time for story. Now's the time for pie and bed. You want me to get Hoppy?'

'No.' He climbed wearily out of the truck. 'Your aunt's right, it's more sensible to eat here. Sorry. I'm being ungracious.'

'You're not being ungracious. But you don't have the energy to get out of the way of the bulldozer. Welcome to my world, Dr Duncan, but only for the duration of the pie. Come on in, but I'll make sure she lets you go.'

CHAPTER SIX

HE ATE QUICKLY, as did Gina. They were both exhausted and Babs wasn't one for small talk. The pie was excellent, but it was a relief—maybe to all of them—when he left.

He took Hoppy home, slept, then woke knowing he couldn't leave Gina to cope with the day's medical needs by herself.

Actually, he could. He had no intention of working as a face-to-face doctor, ever again. Or face-to-face anything if it came to that.

The medical needs post explosion should all be minor. Any injury of significance had meant evacuation to Gannet, but for the population of Sandpiper Island that meant another problem. The Gannet medical facility was excellent but small. Their medical staff was limited—which meant there'd be no medic available to come back to Sandpiper to deal with any aftermath.

Well, that was okay. Gina had offered herself into the role of chief medic without a show of reluctance and had said she'd only call him if she needed him. With her experience she could well cope with lacerations, scratches, dust-filled eyes from the blast…

But on the morning after the explosion, Hugh lay in

bed listening to the crazy island birds with their raucous dawn chorus and he thought…he'd have to help.

He also thought—strangely—that he hadn't slept so well for years.

Which was crazy. The explosion should have brought past trauma flooding back. Instead he'd slept with the memory of a woman leaning into him, of her mouth touching his. Of her arms holding him as his had held hers. Of her breasts moulding against his chest.

How long since he'd had human contact?

He remembered waking in hospital when he'd finally been returned to Australia, months after he'd been injured. His mother had occasionally talked to him on the phone since he'd been able to speak, and, once he was back in an Australian hospital, she'd dragged his stepfather in to see him.

He remembered gushes of tears, and the sensation of overpowering perfume as she'd hugged him.

He remembered his stepfather standing back, camera pointing.

'Please don't.' He remembered saying it, but he'd already known it'd be useless. He'd seen his mother's social media posts since the accident—'My Hero Son'. He'd seen the mass of over-the-top emotion from her 'followers'.

The next day it had been as he'd feared, his picture all over the Internet: 'Wounded Hero with Distraught, Socialite Mother…'

It always had been all about her. His father had walked out when he was five—and who could blame him? Although if it were *his* son Hugh might have made an effort to stay in contact. But his father's sole interest had been in making money, and he saw Hugh rarely.

Andrew Duncan had been disgusted when his son

had decided on a career in medicine, scorning what he labelled as 'an idiot's idealist aim to save the world'. Thus, from the time he'd left school there'd not even been financial support, and Hugh suspected the only reason his father had finally bequeathed him his fortune had been that he hadn't had the imagination or forethought to think of an alternative.

Hugh's half-sister—the product of his mother's first marriage—had thus been Hugh's only real family, but Sophie was ten years older than he was. Their mother was so appalling that Sophie had left as soon as she could, without a backward glance to the little brother who'd thought she'd loved him. Even now he thought Sophie's phone calls were mostly due to what she saw as duty—plus gratitude for his decision to share some of his almost obscene fortune.

So he didn't do family. From an early age he'd learned that needing people was a weakness that left him exposed. He'd occasionally dated, but the trauma he'd endured over the past years had only solidified his need to be alone. He'd never felt the need to get close.

So hugging as a sensation of choice? Not so much.

He didn't even think he'd missed it.

Until Gina.

No. It had nothing to do with Gina as a person, he told himself. It was just that there'd been trauma and she'd been a warm body willing to share some of that warmth.

Hoppy leaped up onto his bed and attempted to snuggle under the bedclothes, and he thought that was what he'd needed last night. Hoppy.

But Gina…

The meal at Babs's had been stilted. Babs had been polite towards him, but there'd been tensions between Gina and Babs. Babs had asked him rather than Gina what had been happening. At times Gina had attempted to talk, but every time Babs had deferred to him. 'Is that right, Doctor?'

He thought of Gina complimenting Babs on her pie. Babs snapping, *'Well, you should remember it.'* Gina growing quieter and quieter.

He'd judged her for staying away for the four long months since Babs's heart attack, and it turned out that that judgement had been unfair. And now she'd offered to do all the minor medical stuff herself for the next few days.

'I don't have a choice,' he told Hoppy. 'I need to help.'

Hoppy eyed him with suspicion, maybe sensing the sequel, and Hugh almost grinned. Smart dog.

'Yeah, I know, that means you get to stay home and look after Hubert all by yourself. But sheesh, Hoppy, you've hardly had a day by yourself since we came here. She said she'd call if she needs me but it's not fair to leave it all to her. It can't hurt to help.'

It couldn't hurt? That was what he told himself as he made the call to tell Gina he'd pick her up and they'd head to town together. It was no big deal.

So he'd spend a few days working with a woman who'd held him as if she knew he needed it.

He hadn't needed it.

It couldn't hurt at all.

The idea that there'd be little work ended up being a pipe dream.

A notice had gone out via the island's grapevine— official and unofficial—that any minor injuries from the day before would be seen by Gina. Two minutes after they arrived at the set-up behind the general store, Wendy, the storekeeper, upgraded the online information to say Hugh would be on hand as well. The island therefore had a doctor plus a nurse, available for consultation. Half an hour later their list of patients was over a dozen long.

'You'll need to get a receptionist if this keeps up,' Wendy told them, but her smile of satisfaction said she was enjoying it.

'It won't keep up,' Gina told her. 'We're just in mopping-up mode.'

But the mopping up extended. Always one to look out for 'her people', Wendy took a liberal approach to what mopping up entailed.

They worked through a myriad of scratches, bruises. They also saw Alana, a fifteen-year-old girl who'd woken with tummy pains—her mum had thought the pain had been niggling for some time and Alana would be more comfortable talking to Gina than to the male doctor who came once a week from Gannet. It was a possible case of endometriosis, Gina thought as she listened to the history.

She ought to refer her on to the gynaecologist on Gannet—well, she would—but Hugh was right through the door and he was a doctor after all. She didn't want to exclude any diagnosis requiring more immediate intervention. She went in as a support person because Alana was nervous about male doctors, but Hugh had her smiling with relief that her pain was being taken seriously and there were things that could be done to help.

And then there was Marjorie Atwell, popping in because— 'Oh, my hand aches, Gina, these fingers are so swollen. I know you're only doing stuff from yesterday, but it hurts so much and it's a whole week before the Gannet doctor comes back.'

And so it went. They worked through the morning,

mostly separately, with Gina handing over anything beyond her ken. Sometimes together. But the emotions of the night before seemed to have wedged an emotional barrier between them.

They drove home speaking sparingly of the morning's work, almost rigidly formal.

And then they worked the next morning. And the next.

And then finally it was Saturday and their makeshift clinic was closed. The Gannet Island doctor was due to return on Monday, his weekly sessions resuming. Hugh could retreat to his shell again.

Hugh woke at dawn, made coffee and headed out to the veranda. This was awesome coffee. He'd invested a lot of thought and money putting together a world-class system—beans and equipment that'd be at home in the best urban coffee spots in the world. Mostly his wealth was channelled into the International Aid Trust he administered, but coffee was sanity.

He'd given Gina his back-up plunger and some decent, ground coffee, but for the last few days he'd been making two morning travel mugs instead of one. He'd picked her up on the way over to town, handing her the mug as she'd climbed into his truck, and they'd lapsed into appreciative silence as they'd driven.

It had helped. That dumb kiss had created tension between them, and mutual appreciation of coffee seemed a no man's land where they could put tension aside. He'd driven, she'd buried her nose in her coffee and he'd glanced across at her and seen her relax.

Which was a state he was starting to figure she didn't stay in very long.

He hadn't quite figured out the relationship between Gina and her great-aunt, but he knew there was tension. Sometimes when Gina came out of the house in the morning, her face was grim, and when she climbed out of the truck after work, he saw her almost visibly brace. He could probe, but it was none of his business. He could give her coffee—and thus seemingly a little time out—and that was all that was needed.

And today even that was over. He could retire to... his coffee?

Not entirely.

Hugh came from a family of immense wealth. His father and his grandfather before him had been huge property investors, and the fortune had grown far beyond one family's ability to spend it.

Even as a kid, though, the life choices of his over-the-top society-darling mother, or his miserly, money-obsessed father had held no appeal—especially as they'd never included him. When his father had died, he'd just finished training as a doctor—despite his father's taunts he *had* been intent on saving as much of the world as he could. To his mother's disgust he'd set up an International Aid Trust with the family fortune, and headed into war zones to personally do what he could.

After his injury he'd become more and more hands on with the Trust. He knew how aid agencies worked, and he knew where the money was needed. His home office was now set up as a control centre, where he coped with applications, with research reports, with the daily minutiae of making sure his wealth made a difference.

So there was always work to do there.

And then there was Hubert.

The wombat had been gradually healing over the week. For a couple of days Hugh had worried that the leg might become septic. He'd made a call to a vet on the mainland, figured the dosage of antibiotic and watched in satisfaction as the wound had responded. Today it was time to release him back into the wild.

Gina would like to help.

Gina? She was the one whose negligence had caused the injury. He was under no obligation to involve her.

Except every day this week she'd asked—sort of causally— 'How's Hubert?' He'd heard the anxiety in her voice when he'd told her of the infection.

It wouldn't hurt to let her know he was letting him go.

It wouldn't even hurt to let her join him.

Except…except…

Ghosts. Personal stuff. His background of solitude, overlaid now by the stuff that had him retired here, had him keeping his scars and his nightmares to himself.

She'd be drinking plunger coffee now. With Babs. Who, he'd already figured out, was resentful of Gina's presence, even though she needed her, even though Gina had spent four months battling to get to her. In quarantine. Drinking caterers'-blend coffee.

And she'd worked beside him this week, skilfully but also empathically. He'd even found himself enjoying the sensation of working with her. Maybe even of being part of a team again.

Yeah, let's put that aside, he told himself grimly. A team? Not going there. He set his mind deliberately back to his coffee.

Focus on the small things, the shrinks had told him as they'd tried to help with the post-traumatic stress that had hit him like a sledgehammer as he'd recovered physically. Good coffee. The feel of the sun on his face. The warmth of his dog. These were the things of sanity.

But Gina was drinking plunger coffee when, with just a small relaxation of his rules, she could be drinking barista-quality stuff.

And coming with him to let Hubert go?

That'd be more than a small relaxation of his self-imposed rules, but then, this whole week had dragged him out of his safe space.

Hoppy was looking at him, head cocked, seemingly questioning.

'Yeah, okay, mate,' he told him. 'I'll do it. But that's it. Just for today.'

Hoppy might crave company but he didn't.

He picked her up at eleven and she was dressed almost as she'd been the first morning when she'd brought the pie over. For the last few days she'd worn sensible navy trousers and a polo—the polo had even had a research-team logo stitched on the front pocket.

'These are work clothes for the team I'm usually attached to,' she'd said shortly when he'd asked. 'I'm not supposed to wear them off the ship, but who's here to notice?'

Nothing more had been said, but when she emerged from the house this morning looking more like…well, more like herself…he felt a smile grow somewhere in his gut.

She was wearing her pants with glitter stars and a soft white shirt, dotted with the same glitter stars. She'd twisted her curls into a demure knot during the week, but now they were caught back in a ponytail, with that same purple ribbon he'd seen on the first day.

She looked bright, eager…happy?

She put a basket into the back beside Hubert's crate, she bade Hoppy good morning and climbed in beside him.

'Hey,' she said cheerfully, shifting Hoppy and putting him on her knee. And then she looked at the cup holder in the middle. 'Coffee! Hugh Duncan, if that's not the way to a woman's heart I don't know what is.'

He managed a grunt in reply. He didn't have to enjoy this.

But he couldn't resist glancing down as she buried her nose in her coffee.

Sneakers. Purple but closed in.

'Sensible,' she said, following his gaze. 'I figured we wouldn't be letting Hubert out anywhere where open-toed sandals would be a good idea. Me, I'm touchy about Joe Blakes.'

Joe Blakes. The Australian idiom for snakes. It was still only spring, and the sun didn't hold much heat, but they'd still be around. They'd be a bit slower than in midsummer. Easier to step on.

So closed shoes were sensible, but he'd sort of wanted to see those toes again.

'I touched them up this morning,' she said, grinning, as if she guessed where his thoughts were going. 'I reckon I got the smile right.'

Oh, hell, he so badly wanted to see. He wanted to stop the truck and check them out now, right now.

Check all of her out. She looked amazing. Her smile peeped at him and he thought, why had he wondered if she might be miserable, trapped with her grumpy great-aunt? This woman didn't know how to be miserable.

Hoppy looked pretty contented to be on her knee, and why wouldn't he be?

'Hubert looks resigned,' she told him. 'Not happy, though. I suspect he was on a pretty good wicket at your place.'

'I've brought chopped sweet potato,' he told her, trying to focus on the road. 'I'll scatter it where we leave him, so he has a few days of tucker before he needs to go back to foraging for roots and leaves.'

'So he has a picnic, too,' she said, sounding satisfied.

'Picnic?'

'You should have seen Babs move when I told her where I was going,' she said. 'I got off the phone and told her I was heading out to release Hubert, and ten minutes later she had handed me a basket with sandwiches, cake, apples... "And don't come back until after my afternoon nap," she said. "You know I need my sleep."'

And there was enough strain in her voice then to give him pause. The happiness had backed off, just a little.

'So you and Babs...'

'It's not a marriage made in heaven,' she admitted. 'She needs me. I know she's getting weaker. It must have been a huge effort to make those pies on the first morning, because even filling sandwiches left her exhausted this morning, but she doesn't want to admit she needs help. I think it's almost been a relief to her that I've been out of the house every morning this week. But there is a need. I've come home at night and cleaned and coped with the laundry and done the day's washing up—she insists on cooking, but it leaves her too tired to face the sink. She doesn't comment. But I try and do the work when she's not around, so she doesn't have to face the fact that I'm helping.'

'She doesn't thank you?'

'She doesn't need to thank me. She kept me from foster homes all those years ago. I owe her.'

'But you're fond of her.'

'I guess I am.' She sighed. 'Yeah, okay, I am, and in a dumb way she's fond back. When I got home this time, she hugged me and I thought...' She hesitated. 'Well, I guess it doesn't matter what I thought. Or what

I hoped. She was landed with me when I was fifteen, she did her duty and I'll always be grateful. I'd have ended up in foster care if she hadn't taken me in, and I was in full rebellion mode. Heaven help me if I'd been placed somewhere I could have let out that anger and rebellion in full.'

'Anger...'

'Yeah.' She grimaced. 'You want to hear?'

He should say no. Her life was none of his business.

'Yes,' he said, and she cast him a speculative glance, as if she didn't quite believe him. And then she shrugged.

'So I was a wild child,' she told him.

'I imagine... Your parents' death...'

'I was wild before that.' She shrugged again. 'Okay, you're about to cop too much information but here goes. My parents were in love. Only not in love the way most couples are. They were practically joined at the hip. They met, they fell passionately in love and they stayed that way. They ran an air service, taking people to the remotest parts of Australia. They both had pilot licences and they worked as a team, catering, organising...you paid a mint for their services. They were the best.'

'So you...'

'At one stage in their early bliss they thought a baby would be wonderful,' she said, frankly now, without bitterness. 'Only when two people are obsessively in love, and with adventure as well as each other, there's not really time for a kid. They figured it out soon enough. They felt bad about it but not enough to include me. Until I was seven there was Grandma, but she died and then there was no one. Home was wherever they could park me. I learned early not to get attached to places because they always changed, and they hardly ever included Mum and Dad. When I was eleven, I was old enough for boarding school. And I guess I got lonelier and lonelier. Then…well, I won't bore you with all the trouble a rebellious teenager can get into, but I was a handful. So finally…'

She grimaced. 'Okay, I was maybe a bit too rebellious and I was kicked out of school.' She managed a wry smile. 'I had a pet ferret, you see. Arsenic.'

'Arsenic?' he said faintly, and she grinned.

'I'd like to tell you he was cute and cuddly, but he really wasn't—he was pretty much as grumpy as I was. And maybe a bit more smelly. But he was mine. Anyway, the school's housemistress found him and told me to get rid of him, and I said I would but of course I didn't. And then he got loose and found his way to the kitchen. Cook thought he was a rat and dropped a huge vat of soup. When they were cleaning the mess, someone found him and realised he wasn't a rat—and of course they knew whose he was.'

'Because he didn't actually look like a rat?' he ventured, and her irrepressible smile emerged again.

'Well, maybe not. When I first got him, I spray-dyed him with one of those non-toxic hair dyes. Purple. He looked great and I'm sure he liked it. I was trying to figure how to get him a nose ring to match mine, too. Sadly the colour had faded and there was no nose ring— hence the rat conclusion—but there was enough purple to make identification certain.'

She sighed and the smile faded. 'Anyway, the long and short of it was that I was expelled. Mum and Dad were away—of course. They were running an expedition in the high country—extreme skiing—and they got the call to get me. So they flew to Melbourne to collect me—did I tell you they had their own plane and they both had pilots' licences? Only they had to do it on the only day they had free, and the day was foul. We tried to fly back, but there was a storm, and the plane hit the side of a mountain. They died instantly. But not me. I…' She faltered and then forced herself to go on. 'I sat in the dark all night, waiting for someone. Anyone. I guess… It was a bit of a nightmare.'

There was a gap of deathly silence while he took that on board. 'A nightmare,' he said at last. 'That has to be an understatement.'

'It was grim,' she admitted. 'I still… I still have trouble being alone in the dark. Anyway, somehow Arsenic and I survived. I had a week in hospital, and someone finally contacted Babs. They told her she was the only person I had.'

'Oh, Gina.' He was imagining it, a terrified kid, injured, stuck, alone. 'I'm so sorry.'

'I'm over it,' she said darkly. 'Though I still have Arsenic issues.'

'Um?' he said faintly, and she managed a smile.

'I got him here,' she told him. 'One of the guys on the chopper who rescued me was great enough to keep him for me. He gave him back to me the day I left hospital. He didn't know I was being taken straight to the airport to come here. So I landed here with Arsenic hidden under my jacket—we were pretty good at the hiding by then. And at the start Babs was great. She hugged me as I got off the plane—which was a huge deal for Babs. Huge for me, too, even though it nearly squashed Arsenic. But then of course she found him. There was a bit of a yelling match, and the next morning when I woke up… well, she explained it all pretty reasonably. There are no ferrets on the island, and he was absolutely a prohibited import. The wildlife officers would have had pink fits if they'd found him. So she dealt.'

'Dealt?' he said, cautiously.

'A brick.' She sighed. 'At least it would have been quick. And I guess it was sensible, but me and Babs... It wasn't a great way to start a relationship.' She shrugged. 'Anyway, there it was. I was stuck with Babs and she with me, and, when I wasn't at school, I was stuck on this side of the island with an aunt who always let me know she was doing her duty by me. She told me that first morning, when I was so angry, so upset, that I was only here on sufferance, until I finished school. So that was it. I decided my best option was to study—there was little else to do. I would have loved to study geology, but there was never enough money—Mum and Dad had died broke. A teaching or nursing scholarship seemed the only options, so at seventeen I got a nursing scholarship to Sydney and Babs was overwhelmingly relieved to see me go.'

He thought it through. Thought of all the preconceptions he'd had of her. Felt ashamed.

'She really is a loner,' he said at last, because he couldn't think of anything else to say. Gina was speaking almost impersonally, and he sensed making it all about Babs might make it possible for her to go on. Her tone said sympathy wasn't required.

And he sensed right. She nodded.

'She surely is. Even now, when she's grateful to have someone staying—I know she truly is scared—she's relieved when I leave the house. Did you know she got jilted three days before her wedding? Grandma told me that. She's been a recluse most of her life. Just like you.'

'Hey.'

She raised her brows, the grimness of the story fading a little as she gave the hint of a teasing smile. 'What, you're not a recluse?'

'I just like my own company.'

'Fair enough.'

Silence. A long silence.

If he'd had to predict, he thought he was expecting questions. Tit for tat? *'What happened to you? Why do you have a limp? Why have you locked yourself away?'*

Instead she gazed ahead at the road and seemed to drift into thought. It was a restful silence, though. No pressure.

He was still thinking of a fifteen-year-old stuck on a mountain with her dead parents. Of a kid with a pet ferret. Of a brick.

Tit for tat? Fair enough.

Maybe it was time to break his silence.

He motioned to the little dog on Gina's knee, took a hand from the steering wheel and gave him a brief pat.

'I guess I was lucky my Hoppy didn't meet the same fate as your Arsenic,' he said slowly, and she nodded again, as if she'd been expecting this twist in the conversation.

'So he had quarantine issues?'

'Quarantine here was the least of it. One of my team scooped him up after I was injured and arranged to keep him for me, even transporting him back to Australia. When I got out of rehab, one of the people in my team presented him to me, everything arranged. I'd been treated by an army shrink, and maybe he'd told them how much I'd need him.'

He cast a glance at her and thought, hell, what was he doing, talking about the past? But after what she'd gone through...

'I was working with an international medical aid team,' he told her. 'We'd set up within a peace-keeping army base, in a country that'd been ripped apart by war.

We weren't working for the army but were there to look after traumatised locals. There'd been an arrangement that the defence forces would provide us with security, but that was getting harder as the peace negotiations broke down. The last few months were tough.' He was trying to keep his voice light, as if it were no big deal. As if he didn't still wake thinking of the things he'd had to deal with even before the bomb blast.

'Hoppy was a stray, a starving mutt in a village where needs were everywhere,' he continued, fighting to keep emotion at bay. 'He hung round our camp and decided I was his new best friend. Wherever I went he seemed to follow. A few of the nurses started feeding him. I didn't—I was hard-hearted enough to accept we'd have to leave, and his best bet was to attach to a local—but still he followed me. And then, the night of the explosion…'

'Bomb?'

'How…?'

'Rumours,' she said briefly. 'Am I right?'

'Yeah.' He didn't want to go further. Not the moments after the blast. Not waking to find the men who'd tried to protect him…

'So let me guess,' she said, gently though, with a smile that was teasing, but at the same time warm and full of empathy. 'Hoppy flew into your arms and shrapnel hit his leg, which was right above your heart. So he lost his leg, but his action saved you. And they gave him the military medal and a pension for life, and assigned him as your bodyguard for ever? Why isn't he wearing medals on his collar?'

'He'd lost his leg well before I found him.'

'No, don't tell me. I don't want to know,' she said, shaking her head so her gorgeous ponytail bounced on her shoulder. 'If he did, I'm sure it was for an action just as heroic.'

And he grinned. The awfulness of what they'd spoken of faded, just a little, and he glanced at her and he thought, She has such courage.

The determination to survive here, to put her head down and work for a scholarship to give herself a future, to accept the limitations of that future...nurse instead of geologist...

To find a career that was challenging—medic on an expedition boat... He'd seen her skills now and he thought her as competent as most doctors. Cool in a crisis. Decisive. Kind.

Kind. There was a word that hung.

All those years ago Babs had greeted a traumatised, bereaved teenager and killed her pet with a brick. And yet, years later, Gina had returned because Babs needed her.

He thought of the conclusions he'd reached when she'd first arrived, and he felt ashamed.

'I'm sorry,' he said, and she arched those expressive brows.

'What, because you won't let Hoppy wear his medals? You ought to be. Hey, isn't this the place where I hit Hubert?'

It was.

He pulled the truck onto the verge and sat. He wouldn't have minded a few moments to assimilate what he'd just learned, but Gina was out of the truck almost as it stopped. Moving on.

'You can't let him out here,' she said, looking around. 'Should we find somewhere safer?'

'It's pretty nice here,' he told her, climbing out after her. They were on the rise leading down to their bay.

The ocean was glinting sapphire in the distance. The view was spectacular.

'Yeah, but the road…' Gina said, worried.

'You know how few people use it. And wombats are territorial. They swap burrows with other wombats, but only one uses a burrow at a time. And they're aggressive, scent-marking their territory and defending it. Hubert's been gone for less than a week so his markings will still be fresh enough to keep others away. If we put him somewhere else, chances are he'll be encroaching on someone else's patch, and the last thing he needs is a fight-to-the-death with another wombat. So he's safest here. If you like, I'll make a couple of Beware Wombat signs and stick them on the road. Just to remind us.'

'Remind me, you mean,' she said darkly, and he grinned.

'I think you've learned your lesson.'

'Gee, thanks. Right, then,' she said briskly. 'Moving on.'

And wasn't that what they both needed to do? Hugh thought. Wasn't that what he'd been trying to do for years?

And hadn't it felt as though he'd succeeded?

His life here was pretty much how he wanted it. He had his house, his dog and a worthwhile occupation, making the Trust more useful. He was probably even doing more good than he had as a field doctor, and this way he could stay isolated. Yes, he had to step in and cope with the occasional medical crisis on the island, and that meant an intrusion into his longed-for solitude, but he could retire afterwards. To his quiet place where the nightmares could be held under control.

But Gina had her nightmares, too. The story she'd told him had been horrific, and he suspected he knew just a sliver of it. But she'd figured her own way of moving on. This island stay—her loyalty to an aunt who seemed to have barely done her duty by her—must be messing with it.

Which was her problem, not his. Surely?

So why did the way he'd felt as she'd outlined her story seem as if it was messing with his solitude as well?

CHAPTER SEVEN

THEY RELEASED HUBERT as far back from the track as they dared, within the confines of a territory Hugh had researched. 'I rang a wildlife official,' he told her. 'He'll be fine here.'

And it seemed he was. Hubert stood in his cage for a long moment when Hugh opened it, then stumped out, cast them a backward glare through his squinty little eyes—that glare had to be for her, Gina thought—and then waddled firmly into the undergrowth.

He'd done with them.

'You'd have thought he could have said thank you,' Hugh said as he scattered hunks of sweet potato round the entrance to a couple of empty burrows.

She grimaced. 'He probably said thank you to you when I wasn't watching. He hardly has anything to thank me for.'

'But maybe the island as a whole does,' he said, thoughtfully. 'If it hadn't been for Hubert's accident you wouldn't have been at my place when that call came in. You wouldn't have come with me—and you saved lives.'

'Not me, mate,' she retorted. 'You're the hero.'

'Can we not use that word?'

She glanced up at him and saw the wash of revulsion, quickly repressed. And thought...hero.

It was a word thrown around in the military, she knew. On her expeditions she'd met a few ex-soldiers, and she'd learned a bit about their worlds. One incident stood out. A guy in his late fifties who'd spent thirty years in the military had been reading a news report when she'd been with him. He'd snorted and thrust the offending article aside.

'Another of our guys gets it,' he'd snarled. 'Lost his arm and guess what, the media's calling him a hero. That's what you get, and it's supposed to make you feel better. I went to a shrink once when there was stuff in my head I couldn't deal with, and the first thing she said was never forget you're a hero. As if that helped when what I was never forgetting was…well, let's not go there.'

He'd stomped away, and a few hours later she'd found him curled in his bunk with a migraine that had lasted three days.

'I'm sorry,' she told Hugh now, softly. 'That was insensitive. Anyway, enough, this day's great and as long as the islanders don't produce any more medical emergencies, we're free. Or at least I am, and I hope you are, too. Because that basket in the back of the truck contains our picnic. "Stay away as long as you want," Babs told me. Me being close makes her fidget. She'll be forced to wear some of it, though. She knows how sick she is. She wants me there, but she doesn't. The fact that I'm coming back and forth, that there's someone sleeping in the house with her, is enough.'

'Her only other option's a nursing home.'

'She knows that. From the notes she allowed me to read from the cardiologist on Gannet, she shouldn't be alone at all, so she's graciously—or almost graciously—conceded to have me here. And she's grateful underneath. I think. I scrubbed the floor before I left, and she sat on a chair in the corner and supervised every sweep of the mop. Boy, I did a good job, too.'

'I bet you did.'

'So, picnic…' she said, and he thought, *Picnic.*

Like Babs, he wanted solitude. Company did his head in.

Sort of.

He glanced at her and she was smiling, but behind her eyes he saw what looked almost a challenge. As if she guessed how he was feeling.

'Otherwise you can drop me off before the turn-off to Babs's and I'll head to the beach and watch the sandpipers while I eat it myself,' she told him. 'There's too much for one, but maybe the sandpipers will help. Or the seagulls if the sandpipers are fussy. Babs would prefer if I spend the day away, but I don't mind being alone.'

She said it brightly, but he had a sudden vision of a fifteen-year-old kid, next to a crashed plane, in the dark. *'I don't mind being alone…'*

'I'm not knocking back a picnic,' he said, because there was no choice. And what was there in the word picnic that was making warning lights flash in his head?

It was that kiss. A kiss that meant nothing.

A kiss that had to mean nothing.

'We'll have a picnic,' he said, and caught himself. It had come out a growl. 'Sorry.' He sighed. 'That sounded grumpy. A picnic would be good.'

'Hey, I'm used to grumpy. I'm living with Babs, re-member? But where?' she said, looking round, consid-ering. 'Maybe not here. Hubert's not going to be happy until he has his home to himself again.'

That makes two of us, Hugh thought, but he didn't say it, and even as he thought it there was a part of him that was yelling, 'Liar'. The thought of spending more time with this woman…

Yeah, those warning lights were definitely flashing, but there was enough stuff beyond for him to step right through.

'There's a waterfall about a kilometre's walk from here,' he told her. 'You can walk in along the side of the creek. It's not a bad place for a picnic.'

'Hey, I know it.' She sounded surprised and suddenly delighted. 'I used to hike there sometimes to do my homework. Or just to lie in the sun.' She wrinkled her nose. 'It's a bit of a hike though.'

And he got that, too. He'd seen that flicker of a glance at his leg. The bomb had shattered his knee, making his leg permanently stiff. She was worrying about him?

'I can do it,' he growled.

'Of course you can,' she conceded. 'Possibly because you're not wearing purple sneakers designed for looks rather than action.'

'But you were worrying about my leg.'

'Ooh, who's being touchy?' That cheeky grin popped out again. 'If you know the waterfall then you must know the track, so I'm assuming you're tough enough to cope. But I had to touch up my ballerinas last night and I worry about my girls in these flimsy sneakers. You tell me if it's too much for them and stop making it all about you.'

He had to grin. He looked down at her sneakers and he thought about her ridiculous toes—and he kept smiling.

'I guess these sneakers have enough tread to keep me safe,' she conceded, moving on. 'And if we sing all the way any snake will skitter before us. So if we're both okay… You want to go or not?' She glanced back at the truck where Hoppy looked hopefully out—he'd had to stay in the cab while they'd released Hubert. 'Hoppy's waiting, and three legs or not, gammy leg or not, ridiculous sneakers or not, I reckon we could all make it.'

'Fine,' he said, goaded. 'Don't blame me if you break an ankle.'

'My ankle's fine,' she told him. 'All of me's fine. You worry about you and I'll worry about me.' Her smile faded a little and she added a rider. 'Isn't that the way I suspect it's always been for both of us?'

It took half an hour to wend their way along the winding creek bed, through bushland and finally to a clearing where water cascaded down a rock face to splash into a pool below. Huge willow myrtles—native willows—spread across the pool, casting it into dappled shade. The trees were flowering, which meant their tiny white blossoms were drifting downward in the gentle breeze, floating on the water's surface. Moss grew on the rocks around the pool, forming vibrant green cushions.

Gina remembered the first time she'd found this place. The rocks in the background… The water cascading… It had become her own private sanctuary, worth the couple of hours' hike it had taken to get here from Babs's.

But from where they'd parked the truck, the route was much shorter. Not that it would have made much difference, she thought. Yes, Hugh's leg was stiff, there was a perceptible limp, but he strode strongly, and she had a feeling he was holding back in deference to…her toes? To the fact that he thought she wasn't up to it?

Well, maybe she wasn't. The last four months had been a progression of shipboard confinement and quarantine, and her muscles seemed to have turned to jelly. But there was no way she was even thinking of huffing.

Hoppy was tearing along in front, impatiently checking when they were too slow. A three-legged dog and a guy with a wounded leg… She had her pride. But when they emerged to the clearing, she fought back a sigh of relief.

Then she stood and soaked in the sight before her. And felt, for the first time since she'd arrived on the island, a sense of coming home.

'I'm so glad you found this place,' she managed, struggling to keep her voice from sounding puffed.

'I was glad to have found it, too,' he told her, a hint of a smile telling her he knew darned well she'd been struggling. 'Hoppy and I have pretty much explored all this side of the island, but we were here for six months before I found this place.'

'It was nearly a year before I found it,' she told him. 'But from then on it was mine.'

'And here Hoppy and I have been thinking it's ours.' He quizzed her with a smile. 'So do we toss for it, or do we share?'

'Share,' she said, because suddenly she felt happy.

Happy. There was a deep word. For all the expeditions she'd been on, the amazing things she'd done, the life she'd lived since her parents died—or maybe even before—there'd been few moments where this sensation had hit, the knowledge that right here, right now, she was simply extraordinarily happy.

And with that came an impulse impossible to ignore. 'I'm going in,' she told him, and kicked off her sneakers and started unbuttoning her shirt.

'Swimming?' he said, sounding startled.

'Why not?'

'It'll be cold.'

'Chicken,' she said, stripping off her jeans. She was wearing respectable knickers and bra—or almost respectable. They were a matching set, soft, turquoise lace with cotton panels hiding the important bits. She owned a bikini that was more revealing than this.

But Hugh was gazing at her as if…she was a coiled snake?

'Um…you have a problem with this?'

'No,' he said faintly. 'No problem.'

'But you're not coming in? Boxers or jocks? Respectability rating, one to ten?'

'Ten,' he said, just as faintly. 'But have you felt that water?'

She had. She'd swum in it almost every day when she'd lived here. It came from somewhere higher on the crags that formed the volcanic island's centre. She'd tried to find its source and realised it ran underground, where it stayed cold, all year round. But that wasn't stopping her.

'Hey, once upon a time I did a winter solstice Antarctic swim,' she told him. 'Compared to that, this is sissy stuff. So I'm ready, whether you're coming or not.'

And she turned and dived in.

She didn't even gasp.

He expected to see her surface, spluttering with shock from the hit of ice-cold water. He *had* swum in this pool, when he was alone, when it was a whole lot hotter than it was today. The initial immersion had taken his breath away.

Gina simply dived in and swam as if she hadn't even registered the cold. She looked sleek and confident, slicing easily through the water as she headed for the falls themselves. The film of tiny white flowers floating on the surface parted before her and closed over again as she continued.

During the walk her hair had been caught in a loose ponytail, but she'd set it free as she'd pulled off her shirt. All he could see as she swam was her back, barely covered by her gorgeous lingerie. Plus a mass of auburn curls streaming over her shoulders.

That was enough to take a man's breath away.

She reached the falls, twisted and turned to face him, water streaming from her hair. A fine mist was floating over her face, but he could see that she was smiling. Laughing. A water sprite finding her home?

'It's amazing,' she called. 'Come on in.'

'It's freezing.'

'Not once you get wet,' she called, using the age-old phrase every smug swimmer used after they'd done the hard yards of that first jump in. She grinned and duck-dived—and disappeared.

He and Hoppy were left standing on the bank. Hoppy whined.

Did he think he should be jumping in to save her?

Why wasn't he jumping in?

It wasn't that he didn't want to. It was just…

A boundary he had no intention of crossing.

If he dived in… He'd be diving into what?

He could see her again now, just. She'd dived right under the falls and was behind the sheath of water tumbling over the cliff. There was a rock ledge behind the falls; he'd found it when he'd swum here before. You could pull yourself out of the water and sit and look out. She did for a moment and then slid back into the water again.

He got that. Despite her nonchalance, this water was really cold. Hopping out and hopping back in again would be murder.

He watched her duck-dive, then surface, right under

the wash of the falls. She trod water, letting the water cascade over her. She held her face up to it, letting it stream down, then she held up her hands and twisted, turning slowly under the water's flow.

She looked almost ecstatic.

Did she have any idea what she was doing to a man?

Hoppy was whining, running back and forth to the water's edge, looking out at Gina and then frantically back at him. Do something, his body language said. Save her.

'She's not drowning,' he told Hoppy, but he was starting to feel as if it was he who was at risk.

Of drowning? It didn't make sense.

This was a nurse. A colleague. She was here temporarily, for family reasons. There was no reason he should feel so threatened. There was no reason he felt as though his foundations were being hauled from under him.

Hoppy had stilled now at the water's edge, staring back at him, his whines becoming desperate.

'Chicken,' Gina called, and he knew that was exactly what he was.

'Rather be a chicken than a dead hen,' he called back, the response every kid knew and used for their own protection.

'Scared of drowning?' she called, and he thought, yes, he was.

Drowning in what? His own fears?

She was laughing, still twisting, the water coursing down over her. She was so lovely. She was so… Gina.

Enough. He kicked off his boots, then hauled off his shirt and trousers.

'It's not cold at all,' Gina called, laughing.

'Liar.'

'You're right, I am,' she called back. 'Don't trust me

at all.' And she duck-dived again, disappearing under the surface of white flowers.

She could surface anywhere, he thought. She swam like a seal, totally at home in the water.

Don't trust me.

He didn't but he had no choice.

Chicken or a dead hen?

What the hell. Dive.

She surfaced and he was six inches from her nose. Gasping in shock.

Yeah, well, it was icy. It had taken every skerrick of resolve not to gasp when she'd dived in, and she was pretty proud of herself that she'd managed it. So now she heard his shock and she chuckled and duck-dived again.

She surfaced on the far side of the pool, which felt safer. Her knickers and bra were a bit too revealing. It was probably a bad idea to show this much skin to a guy who seemed to have been living in almost solitary confinement for years.

Not that she was worried about herself, she decided. She'd been a member of some heavily masculine-based teams over the years, and she'd held her own.

And if something did happen…

Yeah, well, she was twenty-nine years old and this guy was gorgeous—and she'd be leaving the island anyway.

Except why was there this niggle that she was playing with fire?

So what to do?

Swim, she decided. This was hardly the temperature to be frolicking in the shallows anyway.

The pool was narrow by the waterfall but widened into a long stretch before narrowing again to tumble over rocks at the far end and reform a creek. It was perfect for swimming lengths, and that was what she needed to do.

Despite the cold she needed to cool off. Not her body—that was tingling in the icy water. She needed to cool her thoughts, which were diverting to places they had no business diverting to.

Or maybe it wasn't such a divergence. Maybe the attraction—and maybe that was too small a word for it—had been building since she'd met this man. A whole week of seeing him every day…

After four months of loneliness.

Or a lifetime…

Well, she wasn't going there. Loneliness was something she'd been born into and stepping outside was far too high a risk.

She'd remembered the happiness and hope when her parents had picked her up from school that last appalling time. They were angry that she'd been expelled, that she'd messed with their plans, but her dad had always been a rebel. When they'd got her out from under the headmistress's eagle eye, her dad had said, 'Yeah, well, you are our daughter. Maybe it's time we took you into the family business instead of leaving you to the care of others.'

She'd sat in their little plane and she'd held her ferret and she'd felt a surge of something she'd never felt before. Hope?

And then after the nightmare of the crash, Babs had greeted her off the plane and actually hugged her. For a tiny glimmer of time, once again she'd held hope that here was a safe haven.

And then she'd woken to Babs explaining the brick.

Well, she wasn't going down that road again, and the

attraction she had for the guy swimming beside her had nothing to do with any long-term need.

But short-term desire?

She swam and she thought it wouldn't hurt to try dragging him out of his solitary state for a while. Who knew what hurt had been inflicted on him besides his obvious wounds? But over the years she'd realised that superficial connection helped. It helped her. Her nursing. Being part of expedition teams. Being needed…

She'd watched Hugh this week and he was a fine doctor. And this island needed a doctor. When Babs died she'd leave, but in the meantime…maybe it wouldn't hurt to drag this guy into being needed.

And then he swam a bit too close and his arm brushed hers and she forgot all about conniving plans to rescue anyone. She started to think…well, nothing really.

She just felt.

They swam on but closer, lapping silently back and forth. She was a decent swimmer herself, but she could almost feel him holding back to match her, stroke for stroke.

And the awareness of his body…the brush of his arm against hers as they stroked in tandem…

She was forgetting how cold the water was. She was forgetting pretty much anything but how close he was to her. It was a kind of merging, this tandem swimming, their arms just brushing as each stroke drove them forward.

She was speeding up. There was so much force within her and it had to find somewhere to go. She was swimming and swimming, pushing herself on, but unconsciously—or consciously?—willing him to stay with her. The line between sense and instinct was blurring. She was feeling the heat from the brush of his body. Feeling the force of him…

And then, finally, as the pace quickened to the point where she felt as if she might explode, they reached the waterfall again. As she twisted into a turn she surfaced, and her shoulders were caught. Two strong arms held her close. Held her safe. Held her…

And then he kissed her.

Of course he did. This was the culmination of what seemed almost inevitable. It was so…perfect.

The water was streaming over their faces, but neither noticed. He was tugging her close as he kissed. Her breasts were moulding against him.

The strength of him… The heat, the taste, the need…

Dear heaven, she wanted this man, and she wanted him with every fibre of her body. She wanted to be closer. Closer!

Ever since that first kiss her body had been aching to be closer. She was old enough, mature enough, woman enough, to accept this for what it surely must be: pure sexual attraction. There it was, and there wasn't a thing she could do about it.

Just don't be stupid, she told herself now, in the tiny part of her brain that was left to form such sensible thoughts. She'd drilled that into herself over her lifetime. Be safe. Make no commitment.

But surely…surely…

But suddenly decisions weren't in her side of the court. He was pulling away and it felt as if part of her was ripping. He was still holding her but at arm's length; he was smiling into her eyes, but she saw a hint of trouble.

'Gina, we can't.'

'Why can't we?' How she managed to get her voice to

work was beyond her, but she managed it. Water was still streaming over both their faces, and maybe her words should have come out as a gurgle, but instead it was a rock-solid question.

His hands were still holding her shoulders. His smile had died but his eyes were on hers.

'I didn't...'

'Well, I did,' she said, suddenly sure of where she needed this to go. 'If you think I carted that picnic pack all the way here just to carry sandwiches and fruitcake, you're very much mistaken.'

There was a moment's stunned silence. 'You planned...'

'Nope,' she said and was proud of how calm her voice sounded. As if it was no big deal. Which it wasn't. Was it?

'I didn't plan. But a girl can hope.'

'So...'

'Half a dozen condoms...packed under the sandwiches,' she told him.

'Half a dozen,' he said faintly, and she grinned.

'Yeah, but we need to get home by dusk.'

'Gina...'

'Up to you,' she said simply. 'But I'm in if you're in.'

For one long moment he held her gaze. His eyes were dark, fathoms deep. Questioning.

'Hey, no strings,' she said, a bit too quickly as his gaze intensified. 'We're consenting adults. I don't do long-term commitment. I'm based nowhere, and when Babs dies, I'll be gone, so no expectations. But if you don't want...'

'If you knew how much I wanted,' he said, his voice ragged.

'Well, that's excellent,' she said, and her own voice wobbled a bit. 'Because I want, too.'

And then, somehow, they were out of the water, onto the mossy bank. Entwined.

Hoppy waffled off into the undergrowth to explore, casting the odd reproachful look back. This was boring. He wanted some excitement.

He was doomed to be bored for a very long time.

CHAPTER EIGHT

HE MUST HAVE SLEPT. Not for long, surely, for the sun was still warm on his naked skin.

It wasn't as warm as the woman curved against his body.

His arms were around her, even in sleep. The gorgeous curve of her naked back fitted perfectly against his chest. Her curls were still damp, and they brushed his face.

He'd slept holding her.

What sort of oaf went straight to sleep after making love with such a woman? A woman who'd offered herself with warmth, generosity, with an open heart…

Open heart?

Don't go there.

He must have stirred because she did, too, stretching like a cat, her body shifting from his as she did, and he was aware of an absurd dense of desolation. Of loss.

She'd only moved six inches.

'I slept,' he managed, regretful. 'I'm sorry.'

'Hey, I did, too,' she told him, pushing herself up to sitting and smiling down at him. Her damp curls twined across her face and, oh, that smile. It was enough to make a man's heart melt.

There he went again. Heart.

No.

'Don't you dare be sorry,' she told him. 'Unless it's because not all of that little pack of six are going to see the light of day this afternoon.'

'Gina…'

'Or ever,' she said, a bit too quickly. 'You don't have to say no strings. I told you, I'm the last one to want 'em. Rings on fingers, home and hearth, they're for other people, not for me. What I do want, though, is lunch. I'm famished.'

She reached for her shirt and buttoned it back over her gorgeous breasts, then snagged her panties. Somehow in those first few moments she'd managed to flip them onto a nearby bush, and the wispy lace must now be almost dry.

She'd planned this?

Half a dozen condoms…

She was now kneeling beside the picnic basket, fishing through its contents. 'Egg sandwiches,' she said in satisfaction. 'On Babs's home-made sourdough. Yum.'

'Did Babs help you plan this?'

That stopped her. He'd spoken without thinking, and he heard the unvoiced implication in his question.

She sat back on her heels and looked at him. He'd pushed himself to sitting and was hauling on his trousers. Putting distance between them?

Yes, he was.

'Wow.' A crease furrowing her forehead. 'You're angry because I packed egg sandwiches? Nope? Then I guess it's the condoms?'

'I'm not used to…'

'Being seduced. Neither am I,' she said frankly. 'This wasn't seduction, Hugh. This was the build-up of a hell of a week. A hell of a few weeks for me. I needed it. I needed you. More, I believe you needed me. Not for ever, not for anything past this moment, but there was a need. So if you think packing condoms was a sin, then guilty as charged. And if you think packing egg sandwiches was also part of some deep, dark plot to drag you somewhere you don't want to go, then that's double sandwiches for me. I might even share with Hoppy, who doesn't seem to be looking at me with the same sort of judgement you are. Scarlet woman? Go take another cold dip, Hugh, and let me get on with enjoying myself.' And she picked up one of her sandwiches and headed across to the bank of the pool. She sat on the moss, dipped her legs in the water and bit into her sandwich. With her back to him.

Whoa.

He felt…slapped.

No. It was he who'd done the slapping. He thought of her background, of what she'd told him of her life, and he felt small. She was lovely, fun, exuberant. She was accepting life with all its challenges. More, she was embracing it.

She'd embraced him.

He glanced at her now and he accepted, without reservations, that what she'd given him had no strings attached. They'd made love as part of a glorious morning. She'd given him such a gift…

She was expecting nothing.

He thought of relationships he'd had in the past. There'd always been expectations.

With Gina…she'd shared her body with joy. A gift indeed.

He fished a sandwich out of the basket and went and sat beside her. They looked out over the pool and he tried to get his thoughts together.

'I didn't mean…'

'You did mean,' she said, but serenely now, and a little bit muffled because she was enjoying her sandwich. 'I can pick judgement when I hear it. So here's a question. Why is it okay for a guy to keep a condom in his wallet but not okay for a woman to slip a pack into the bottom of a picnic basket?'

There was now no anger in her voice. It was just a question.

Moving on.

'I'm very glad you did.'

'There wasn't one in your wallet?'

'I didn't bring my wallet.'

'Because you had no intention of sex?'

'I had no intention of…anything.'

'Really?' She twisted and faced him. 'No intention of anything, ever again? Just how badly were you hurt, Hugh?'

'I wasn't…'

'Well, you were,' she said, calmly. 'That's a vicious scar on your leg—yes, I saw it—and that burn on your face must have taken months to heal. But I wasn't asking about those hurts. What's the worst?'

How had he got here?

He didn't want to be here. He didn't want questions. He wanted nothing more than to be left alone for the rest of his life.

But here she was, a woman he'd just held, a woman who'd offered herself to him, who'd loved him with generosity and passion, a woman who carried wounds herself…

A woman he'd hurt by inferring some sort of ulterior motive. He hadn't accused her out loud, but she'd heard the insinuation. He'd seen the flash of hurt before the anger.

But she'd come out fighting, and then she'd put it aside, moving on. More generosity.

Something inside him was twisting and it was twisting hard.

What's the worst?

'I was a medic in a war zone,' he said, heavily, and the words felt as if they were being ripped out of him. 'I misread a situation. It was a trap, a bomb, planted just outside a family home. An old lady with a baby in her arms, kids by her side, came to our camp, pleading for me to see her sick daughter. Said she'd been in labour for three days. The sergeant in charge of camp security told me to leave it—ordered me to. We were supposed to treat within the security of the camp, not go outside. But how could I say no? So I overrode orders, and the sergeant caved and sent backup with me. I went in first, cautious, but there was a woman in the house, and she *was* in labour. I thought how can it be a trap? And then it blew—a ring of home-made explosives, around the house. I survived—just—as did the women and kids in the house, but my backup didn't, including the sergeant I'd disobeyed. I took them there. I killed them.'

'Oh, no. Oh, Hugh, that sucks.' She touched his hand, a fleeting touch, an acknowledgement of what he'd just told her. She hesitated for a moment and then said: 'I'm guessing you'll have been told time and time again that it wasn't you who killed them—you must know it—so I dare say it's no use me saying it again.'

'It's not,' he said shortly.

'Okay, I won't say it,' she said and touched his hand again—and then took another bite of her sandwich.

Moving on again? Which sort of seemed…shocking.

What had he expected? Raw sympathy? The kind he'd had in spades? Probably not judgement—he surely had enough in his own eyes to be going on with. But every time anyone learned the story, he'd see shock and horror, and endless, endless sympathy.

He could still hear the words of his trauma counsellor resonating after all this time. 'The horror will fade over time. You need to be kind to yourself. Forgive yourself and move on.'

Forgive... It was a heavy word, and in the counsellor's eyes he could see she thought he could.

He also saw she felt he needed to.

'It's not fair,' Gina said, across his thoughts. She was gazing over the waterfall, reflective words faintly muffled by sandwich. 'This fate stuff. You do the best you can and then, *bang*—fate. And you're left with the consequences. Scars fathoms deep.' She looked down at the remains of her sandwich and took another bite.

'I'm not sure whether hiding yourself away on Sandpiper is the way to deal with them, though,' she said thoughtfully, 'but who am I to judge? I spend my life on adventure cruises and maybe that's running away, too. Running from the thought of ever wanting a home. Other people seem to want homes, but they scare me stupid. Putting down roots only for them to be torn up again seems just plain stupid. Who wants that sort of pain? But once again, who's judging? Except you, judging me for packing condoms.'

The twist in conversation was so unexpected he blinked. 'I didn't judge.'

'Yes, you did but I'm over it.' She headed back and fetched the basket, hauling it over to set it between them. 'Have another sandwich. Hey, there's beef and mustard down here. Hooray for Aunty Babs. I'm going to eat two more sandwiches and a slab of fruitcake and then I reckon it's time to go home. Time to move on. Right, mate?'

And he got it.

Mate.

She was no longer the woman he'd just made love to. In that one sentence, with that one word, she'd turned them back into colleagues.

Friends?

She'd put a type of barrier in place, and he thought maybe it was a barrier that she needed as well as him.

He should say something. What she'd just given him... Warmth, passion, generosity.

Acceptance.

Time to move on.

'Yeah,' he said, striving for lightness. 'One more swim though.'

'Not me,' she told him. 'It's freezing.'

'Not once you get in.'

She grinned. 'Liar,' she told him. 'But you go ahead. I've jumped into deep water once today and I'm not doing it again. And actually...maybe I should remind myself not to do it again, ever.'

They trekked back to his truck pretty much in silence. Hugh fell behind, just a little, allowing Gina to set the pace. The track along the creek bed often widened, giving them room to walk side by side, but neither of them felt like it.

It didn't feel wrong to be separate, though, Gina thought. What they'd shared... She couldn't regret it. It had been a magic day and she felt a bit like the cat leaving a cream bowl. The memory of his body merging with hers...the feel of him, the taste, the strength...

it'd stay with her, she thought. She'd hold it for as long as she could.

But she would move on.

Babs. How long would she be needed here? She was forcing her mind to the practical—which was really hard when Hugh was right behind her. But she needed to be practical, so she attempted to haul errant thoughts about sexy males into a more useful channel.

If she wasn't to spend her time figuring how she could jump the man behind her, how could she fill the days until she could leave?

This week had been busy and in some ways that had been a blessing. Yes, Babs needed her. She'd watched her aunt clench into herself as the pain of angina hit. She'd seen her fear, but she'd also seen the almost fierce determination to stay in control. To keep her precious independence for as long as she could. Until now, Gina had left the house each day, giving her privacy, and for Babs that seemed a blessing. She wanted Gina here, but she didn't want her close.

So where did that leave Gina?

And the way she was feeling about Hugh… How could she back off?

She had to. She'd leave the island when Babs died. What else could she do? Stay, settle, wait for the next catastrophe?

It didn't have to be a catastrophe, she told herself, and for a moment she let herself indulge in the fantasy of a future here. With Hugh?

With a man who was as damaged as she was, but whose method of dealing meant closing out the world rather than embracing it? Pigs might fly. Reaching out to the next adventure was the only safety she knew, the only security that didn't scare her witless.

Hoppy ran forward and brushed her ankle with his nose—as if just checking. Behind she heard Hugh's steady steps. The slight falter from his limp.

His limp wasn't stopping him. The strength of him almost seemed an aura.

If she feigned a fall and said she'd hurt her ankle he'd be strong enough to carry her back to the truck, and she found herself smiling as she considered the temptation. To be carried in this man's arms…

Um, not. She'd pretty much seduced him already, she told herself. She needed to leave him alone. That seemed to be what he wanted.

But then she thought…yeah, but was it what he needed?

She'd reacted calmly to his story, sensing he didn't need her horror, but images kept playing in her mind. Hugh, doing what he thought right, and paying with a lifetime of remorese. Hugh, with all the time in the world to regret and regret and regret.

Which made her heart sort of…lurch.

This was one gorgeous man. He was an excellent doctor, he was skilled and kind, and if she'd been in the market for…

Stop, she told herself sharply. Don't go there. She had no thoughts of trying to share his solitude.

But maybe, maybe she could help. Maybe she could kill two birds with one stone—or whatever that analogy was.

They reached the truck, she climbed in and she made her decision.

'I've decided to keep the clinic open,' she said as he started the engine. Hoppy had leapt up onto her knee and she was hugging him—maybe to give her the courage for what she suspected might well be a response of wrath.

'You've what?'

'I know, it was only to be temporary until we cleared the backlog from the explosion, but Babs doesn't need me...'

'Babs does need you.' And there it was, the hint of returning hostility.

'She might need me, but she doesn't want me,' she told him. 'She caught me looking at her last night and hit the roof. "What are you staring at?" she demanded. "Figuring how long it'll take me to die so you can get out of here?" I was, in fact, figuring whether I'd have the courage to offer to cut her hair. I went ahead and offered, and she told me where I could put my haircut. "I'll die with my hair the way it is," she told me. "Who'll be looking at me in the meantime? Not you, miss, leave me alone."'

'Ouch.'

'Yeah, so I went into my bedroom and touched up my ballerinas,' she told him. 'But I can't do that for ever. So I figure I'll ring the guys on Gannet and tell them I'll keep on working here, in the clinic, for as long as Babs doesn't need me. Even if it's only for a few weeks it'll be a help. The locals tell me the once-a-week doctor's visit from Gannet fixes the urgent stuff, but day-to-day stuff a competent nurse practitioner could deal with often doesn't get done. Mind,' she said, casting him a cautious glance, 'a doctor on board would be great as well.'

'Sandpiper doesn't need a doctor.' It was a growl.

'You know it does. Marc, the guy I spoke to on Gannet, says there are all sorts of problems they can't fix. It's an elderly population. People are ill at home. Depression, minor ulcers, diabetes, leg cramps, niggles, things people think are too minor to get an appointment and wedge into a crammed once-a-week doctor's visit. Until they escalate.'

'So you'll fix that?'

'I can stop them escalating and I can refer to the weekly doctor if I can't.'

'Until you leave.'

'It's better than nothing,' she said, defensively. 'And who knows how much good I might do? Mind, a doctor on call would be so much better. It's really hard that there's no one.'

'So what?' he said, his anger obvious. 'You'd haul me in even further than I am now? For how long? And then you'd leave, and I'd be stuck with expectations.'

'Well,' she said thoughtfully, 'would that hurt? You have a great veggie patch, but how many veggies can one man eat?'

'Gina…'

'Yeah, I know, it's none of my business,' she said. 'But it seems such a waste.'

'Like you, wandering the world on cruise ships.'

'Hey, I fix people.'

'People who are putting themselves at risk. All you're doing is enabling them.'

'And having fun in the meantime,' she threw at him. 'How much fun are you having?'

Silence.

'Well,' she said at last. 'I'm going to keep on running the clinic. You can do what you want.'

'And if Babs gets sick while you're on the other side of the island?'

She took a deep breath. 'What choice do I have? Do you think either Babs or I could cope with me hanging around her house waiting for her to get worse?'

'That's an excuse.'

'It's not an excuse,' she snapped. 'But even if it was…
you know what? I can head to the far side of the island
with a clear conscience, because I know you'll be here,
brooding over your veggies. And I also know that one
phone call and you'll come, Dr Duncan. Because you
care. I know you do.'

'And if I help you, then I won't be there for Babs.'

'That's an excuse and you know it. Babs isn't counting on me, and I'm not counting on you. I'm talking
about morning clinics only, and if you were around to
help…'

'I won't be.'

'Then end of discussion,' she told him and folded her
arms and then had to unfold them because that made
Hoppy uncomfortable. The little dog squirmed and wrig-
gled and reached up and licked her nose.

And it helped. She hugged Hoppy and the tension she
was feeling eased.

'Hey,' she said, hauling herself together. She'd pushed
where she had no business to push, and she needed to
back off. 'Sorry,' she said. 'That was out of line and it's
no big deal. I'm not trying to blackmail you into anything you don't want. You sort problems your way and
I'll sort mine. I need people and work and fun to keep
the demons at bay. If Hoppy and a veggie patch full of
zucchinis do it for you, then so be it.'

'I can't stand zucchinis,' he said tangentially, and
she grinned.

'Really? Then don't go near 'em, Dr Duncan. Don't
go near anything that makes you fearful. And maybe,'
she said thoughtfully, 'that might include me.'

CHAPTER NINE

HE WAS AWAKE on Monday morning feeling bad.

Blackmailed?

Conflicted.

This morning Gina would be heading across to the clinic to do what? There was no emergency work left.

But he knew there was a need. And he also knew there'd be people lined up to see her.

Because she'd done her homework.

The island had a social-media information feed. It showed basic stuff like tide times, community meetings, whale watching, anything the islanders needed to share. Yesterday there'd been a simple post, stating Gina's qualifications and her willingness to see any minor problems. She'd added a disclaimer—her work was backed by the Gannet Medics, but her expertise was that of a nurse practitioner only. Also, the service she was operating was only temporary, available while she was visiting her aunt on the island.

Every islander would read it and understand. They'd also get the inference about being backed by the Gannet Medics. Her offer didn't include him.

Because he was to be left in peace. To water his vegetables?

Gina would be busy; he had no doubt. Because of

her association with Babs, she'd be considered enough of an islander to trust, and everyone had either seen or heard of the work she'd done last week. He'd done a decent stint in family medicine straight after his training, and he knew what sort of work she'd be getting. Mums worrying about babies, teenagers with teenage angst, farmers with stuff they considered too trivial to bother a doctor with, elderly islanders who just wanted to talk. Maybe there'd be underlying medical issues and maybe there wouldn't be.

But she could deal, and she could point anything urgent to the visiting Gannet doctor.

Who came once a week, for half a day.

It wasn't enough. Dammit, he knew it wasn't. He knew she'd be uncovering problems that needed a doctor.

Until now islander problems would have stayed uncovered until they grew serious enough to need urgent care. Or people would struggle on alone.

There was a need.

But he didn't want to be needed. To go down the medical path again…

It was as if there were a brick wall stopping him. One instant where his response to need had seen such tragedy…

'Time to move on. Right, mate?'

Gina's words were replaying in his head, and he couldn't get rid of them. He headed out to the veggie garden and spent an hour or so taking his frustrations out on weeds. He had an online meeting with the administrators of the trust this morning. He could get the asparagus bed sorted and then head online.

He was doing good. The Trust was doing good, and this separation was what he needed. Doing what concerned him and blocking out everything else.

Ignoring the needs of the locals?

Blocking the fact that Gina was doing something he wouldn't.

He couldn't. Dammit, it was fine for Gina, he thought savagely. She could play nurse and in a few weeks she'd pack up and leave without a backward glance. No long-term commitment at all.

Except she wouldn't be playing nurse, he thought. She'd be being of use.

As opposed to him. Who needed perfectly weeded asparagus beds?

'But if I go,' he said, savagely, out loud, 'there'll be no way I can walk away after a few weeks. She's using this to fill time, to stay out of Babs's way until her aunt really does need her. What she's doing is just a convenience.'

Except she cared.

And he knew that was true. He'd watched her during the last week. He hadn't been able to fault her professional skills, and he'd been impressed with her empathy. Her kindness.

He thought of the expeditions she'd been on, and he thought the expeditioners would have been lucky to have her.

But surely they didn't actually need her. It was their choice to put their safety on the line.

As it had been his choice, working in conflict zones?

He thought of the village where he'd been stationed before the explosion. The locals had been traumatised by years of fighting. He'd been attached to an international peace force, trying to sort an ongoing reconciliation.

They'd been successful, too, but not until after he'd left. Not until there'd been more deaths.

That last scene was still in his mind now, the peacefulness of that small village. The old woman coming towards him, tears in her eyes. Pleading.

The consequences…

Back away.

He rose and stretched, brushing the dirt from his hands. Hoppy was looking up at him, head cocked, enquiring. Troubled?

Because he'd been talking out loud?

A little dog with three legs. A dog who deserved to see his days out in this place of refuge, of peace, with a garden, a beach, sun on his face…

Yeah, but Hoppy had loved his day with Gina. He'd practically turned inside out with all the new smells, the picnic, the stuff going on.

'We don't need stuff going on,' he told Hoppy, and Hoppy looked at him as if he didn't believe him.

'Well, I am doing stuff,' he told him. 'The trust's doing good and it needs competent administration.'

Yeah? Hoppy didn't say it but he had his head cocked to one side, enquiringly. Hugh could almost hear the response. *So what, mate? Two hours a day? Is that all you can give? You know Gina's not just down there to fill in time. She wants to do good.*

Do good. The unspoken words sounded hollow.

'So remember where trying to do good gets us,' he told Hoppy, his voice almost savage. 'If we crack now, I'll be stuck as Sandpiper's doctor for ever.'

And once again, a silent question seemed to come from the little dog. *Would that be so bad? You still have current registration. What's stopping you?*

'It's not why we came here. Dammit, she *is* blackmailing me.' He was staring at Hoppy, who was staring straight back, and when he said that the little dog seemed to flinch.

Possibly because of the anger in his voice. Anger at Gina?

At a woman who'd held him. At a woman who'd offered her body with love and with laughter.

Not with love, he told himself.

Kindness? Even pity?

Who wanted kindness and pity? If that was what it had been, he could stay right where he was, stopping her intruding into his world.

But it surely hadn't felt like kindness or pity. It had felt like...joy.

Was that what was holding him back? The thought of a woman who sensed what he needed, who somehow seemed to see inside his head?

Was it fear that was holding him back now? Fear of commitment to the islanders?

Fear of the way he was reacting to a woman who seemed different from anyone he'd ever met before?

'So does that make me a coward?' he demanded of Hoppy, and Hoppy looked blankly back at him. No judgement?

All his judgement was within.

Gina's clinic would be operating until twelve. He could hardly help her. He was due to be online in half an hour. Trust business.

'That's a cop-out,' he said, out loud again. He glanced across towards Babs's cottage. Thinking.

He hadn't come to Sandpiper to be a doctor. He didn't want to be one.

But he was one. When Babs had needed him, he'd been there for her. When the explosion had happened, he'd been called.

How big was his veggie garden? How big did it need to be?

She'd done it. She'd got under his skin. She'd guilted him...

Hoppy was still looking at him. Bemused?

Was Gina guilting him?

She'd done no such thing. She'd just said it as it was.

'How much fun are you having?'

The question had been thrown at him with a teasing smile. *Fun.* She thought it would be fun to treat the islanders' minor complaints.

But suddenly he was thinking of his early years of medicine, of a dumb incident during his stint in family practice. Sunday night, late. He'd been on call all weekend and had finally headed home to bed when the phone had rung.

'Me wife's got an earache, Doc,' the voice on the other end of the phone had said. 'She'll never sleep.'

'Okay,' he'd said, thinking longingly of his own sleep. 'Do you have a car? I'll meet you at the clinic in fifteen minutes.'

He'd dressed and driven back to the clinic. The guy had arrived ten minutes later, climbing out of his car to greet him. 'Hiya, Doc.'

'Where's your wife?' Hugh had asked, and the guy had looked at him in astonishment.

'You never told me to bring my wife.'

He'd waited for another half an hour for the guy to go home and fetch his wife. He'd done what had to be done and then gone home to bed, gritting his teeth in frustration. But as he'd drifted towards sleep, he'd found himself laughing, and the next day the incident had been shared with the entire clinic staff. Their shared laughter and good-natured teasing—they'd even added a line to their answering machine recording: *Patients are ex-*

pected to arrive in person unless otherwise stated—
stayed with him still.

'How much fun are you having?'

He stared down at Hoppy, who looked blandly back at him. No help there.

His decision.

It had been his decision to move here, his longing. His head had been in some nightmare place and he couldn't deal with more inputs. He'd walked out of that last counselling session and decided he needed to get away, from everyone, from everything. He'd run.

How long could he keep running?

'How much fun are you having?'

He headed indoors, back to his desk. To what had been almost his only contact with the world for the last three years. He logged on, then hovered, his fingers poised to press the keys to admit himself to his trust administrators.

Hoppy had followed him in, but instead of settling beneath his desk he stayed sitting, watching, as if there were questions still to be answered.

Gina would be in the clinic by now. Treating odds and sods. People with earache. People who might even need the additional expertise of a doctor.

The Trust administrators would be waiting.

Fun.

He thought of the competent men and women he'd employed to run the Trust, people who, over the last couple of years, had been trained to know exactly the direction he wanted the Trust to take.

He *could* go help Gina.

'But I wouldn't be doing it for fun,' he told Hoppy. 'I'll be doing it because it's selfish not to.'

Yeah, right. Hoppy's bland gaze said it all, but the decision had been made.

He sent a brief message to the administrators, then rang Gina.

'Hugh?' Her voice sounded wary.

'You're at the clinic?'

'I've already seen six patients.' Her voice held a note of pride.

'Do you need me?'

The question hung. A cautious silence. Then...

'Of course I do,' she said seriously, quietly. 'Two of the people I've seen need to go on to Gannet to see a doctor. But if you came...'

'I'll come.'

Another silence.

Then, as if she were forced to be truthful even though she worried about the consequences, she said: 'Hugh, if you come... I do understand what you're facing. If... when Babs dies, I'll leave the island, but you could end up stuck with this for ever.'

'I've thought of that.'

'It's a big ask.'

'That didn't stop you asking.'

'Suggesting,' she said, and he heard the trace of a smile. 'I only suggested.'

'Like you suggested I jump into ice-cold water. Called me chicken.'

'And look what happened when you jumped,' she said, suddenly sounding happy. 'But come on in, the water's fine. And I and every Sandpiper Islander will be very pleased to welcome you in.'

'So...is that what you wanted?' he demanded of

Hoppy as he disconnected, and Hoppy jumped up on his knee and licked him, nose to jaw.

'Gee, thanks,' he muttered. 'Between you and Gina, I'm lost.'

CHAPTER TEN

Babs was growing more and more frail. Even though she didn't want Gina hovering, her condition continued to decline. She was weak, she was constantly tired, but she was also fiercely independent. When Gina dared ask, she had her head bitten off for her pains.

Still, she knew Babs wanted her to be there. The night she'd had the full-blown heart attack must have been terrifying. If Hugh hadn't noticed her light hadn't gone on…if he hadn't cared enough to check…

There was a reason that every time she felt up to it Babs was still cooking pies for him. 'Give this to the doctor if you see him,' she'd say nonchalantly as Gina left for work. And there'd often be pie for Gina as well—which was pretty much the only way Babs had of signifying she was grateful for Gina's presence.

There was no other way, though. Gina learned fast not to offer to help, to stay out of her aunt's way. But the need was there.

A month into her stay she came home after clinic and Babs was still in bed. That day Babs conceded she might just accept help taking a shower.

But the independence remained. 'Can I ask Hugh if he could pop in after clinic, just to have a listen to your heart?' Gina asked, and almost had her head bitten off for her pains.

'And waste his time? I don't know how you managed to drag him into treating the whole blessed island, but if he thinks he's treating me he has another think coming. He'd probably charge like a wounded bull...'

'I'm sure he wouldn't.'

'Then it'd be charity, and do you think I need that? Butt out, girl. Help me to shower and that's it.'

The next morning, Gina worried about heading across to clinic, but Babs almost pushed her out of the house.

'If you think I want you sitting here like a vulture, waiting for me to die, you have another think coming. It makes me nervous enough having you here at all. Get out and make yourself useful somewhere else.'

So she did, but that day the clinic was abnormally quiet. Since they'd started there'd been a constant stream of islanders wanting help. Both she and Hugh had been needed more than they'd anticipated, but bad weather was forecast for the next few days. The islanders were busy getting outdoor tasks done, preparing for one of the storms that happened too often for comfort on this remote, wild island.

She only saw one patient who needed Hugh. He'd taken to doing his administrative stuff—some Trust he talked of—in the back room of the clinic, so he could be at hand when needed.

'Rosemary Harvey's here,' she told him. 'She has an ulcer on her leg that's looking nasty. It needs debridement. She'd been seeing one of the Gannet Island doctors and was thinking about taking the ferry over, but with this weather forecast the ferry's not running. Can you do it?'

'Of course.' They were almost absurdly formal in this

setting. It was as if the swim and what had come after had pushed them to a boundary that neither wanted to cross. That neither *could* cross.

But this morning he hesitated before he went to see Mrs Harvey. 'Gina, tonight…this storm's threatening to be frightening. Babs's cottage isn't exactly a fortress. Would you both like to spend the night at my place?'

She blinked. An offer of accommodation…

With Hugh.

She'd been figuring what they'd need for the debridement. For some reason she didn't want to look at him.

'That's very thoughtful,' she managed.

'I'm very thoughtful.'

'Yeah.' She managed to turn and smile. 'It seems you're getting more and more thoughtful. Mrs Harvey practically bounced with delight when I suggested you might help with her leg. It's not just Babs who thinks you're the best invention since sliced bread.' She caught herself and added hastily: 'Your patients, I meant.'

'What else could you mean?'

'I…nothing.' Dammit, what was it with this man? He had her totally off balance. And here he was, asking that she spend the night with him.

Um…what? Spend the night with him? Whoa. That her hormones had taken the offer of a night's accommodation and decided to fling a wild party inside her treacherous head was totally dumb. He was offering to accommodate her ailing aunt during the storm, and she was the accompanying baggage.

Even that seemed pretty good to those treacherous hormones, but she clamped them down—she'd give them a good talking-to later—and geared herself for refusal.

'Babs wouldn't have a bar of it,' she told him. 'She's

ridden out storms before. We have storm shutters, lanterns, plenty of supplies. We can batten down for a couple of days. You think Babs would accept help if she wasn't desperate?'

'I know she wouldn't. But you?'

'I'm nowhere near desperate.' She managed a glower. 'But I will head home early if it's okay with you. I'll stick around and help with the debridement and then batten down the hatches.'

She wasn't desperate?

She wasn't, but the thought of Hugh's solid, dependable house grew more and more enticing as the evening wore on.

And Babs grew worse.

When she got home from clinic, she found her aunt curled up in bed, ashen-faced, her covers drawn up to her chin almost as if she was trying to hide.

'Pain?' Gina asked, trying not to panic. Her aunt's face was deathly pale and there was a tinge of blue around her lips.

'Just…no…just getting hard to…'

'Let's hook up the oxygen cylinder and call Hugh,' she told her.

'No!'

'Babs—'

'I won't have help. I don't need it. I don't need you.' When Gina lent over to put her fingers on her neck, to feel her pulse, Babs grabbed her hand as if to push her away—but then she clung.

'I'm glad you've come home, girl.'

'I'm glad I came home,' Gina said softly. 'Babs, let me help. Let Hugh help.'

'For what? To live longer? I don't need it.'

'The oxygen…' Hugh had set it up for her when she'd come home from hospital and shown her how to use it.

'Okay, the oxygen,' Babs conceded, as if it were a truly magnanimous concession. 'But nothing else. And can you stop those shutters banging?'

That was easier said than done, Gina thought. The shutters were old and rickety, and they'd had no maintenance for years. She'd fastened them as much as she could, but the wind was building to gale force.

She thought of Hugh's house, hunkered in the landscape, looking as if it was built to withstand an apocalypse. She thought of the limited things she could do to help her aunt.

Hugh was a phone call away. He'd come, she knew he'd come. He'd take them both over there. He'd know how to help Babs.

But this was Babs's call. This was her aunt's house and it was her aunt's right to call the shots on her treatment, on what she did and didn't want. For so many years she'd lived alone—apart from those two strained years where she'd had to put up with Gina. Gina had to respect that.

So she foraged in the storeroom and found hammer and nails and went out and nailed the shutters closed. She'd have to pull the nails out in the morning but then… what mattered was tonight.

A couple of slats were missing on the shutters. Grit was being blasted at her while she nailed, and she sent up a silent prayer that nothing would get through to crack the windows. There was so little Babs would let her do, but she could do her darnedest to give her peace.

Then she went inside, bullied her aunt into drinking a mug of hot, sweet tea—or at least a portion of it—then stoked up the fire and settled beside it.

She didn't go to bed. She hadn't nailed the shutters on her bedroom and maybe she should have, but she wouldn't have slept anyway. She didn't like storms. She didn't want to be here.

She'd tried to pull up a chair and sit by Babs, but Babs had told her in no uncertain terms to take herself off. 'If I'm dying, I'll do it alone,' she'd managed.

'Please, Babs, let me call Hugh.'

'Get out of my life.'

So she sat and stared into the fire and thought… Well, she tried not to think. Right now the world was just too unutterably bleak. Every now and then she rose and opened Babs's door a sliver, listened to the labouring breathing, softly asking… 'Babs? Do you want me to come in?'

'No.'

Oh, that breathing, though.

There was nothing she could do, but sleep was impossible. Outside the wind was a series of shrieking gusts. The little cottage seemed to be shaking on its foundations.

And then, at three in the morning, the lights went out. No electricity.

There was the faint glow from the fire. She focussed on that, holding to its glow to keep panic at bay. The dark, the storm…

'It's okay,' she said, out loud. 'We have lanterns and candles in the kitchen. You're a big girl, Gina Marshall. You can cope with this.'

But it was with trembling hands that she fumbled for the lantern and headed for Babs's room. Babs had left the bedside lamp on—that would have gone off. She needed to check.

She opened the bedroom door and stilled. Every time

she'd checked—every twenty minutes or so—she'd heard that laboured breathing.

Now there was nothing.

Her own heart seemed to stop. She closed her eyes for a moment, knowing but not knowing what had happened. Finally, she made her way to the bed, set the lantern down, put her fingers on the old lady's face.

Death had slipped quietly into the room.

Her aunt looked as if she were sleeping.

She was gone.

Hugh had been dozing by the fire, but only lightly, and he was awake when the lights went out.

His place was secure. Nestled into the side of the hill, built of stone and with double-glazed windows and secure shutters, nature could throw its might at his house and it wouldn't move. Inside the living room, with the fire blazing in the hearth, he could almost imagine the storm wasn't happening.

Except it was happening. He should be in bed, but a deep sense of unease had him not even trying to sleep. Across the bay, within sight from his living-room windows, he could see the faint lights from Babs's home. And Gina's home.

Usually the lights there went off at about eleven. Tonight though, they'd stayed on. Babs's shutters were old, slats were missing, and he could still see the chinks of light.

As the night wore on his sense of unease only deepened. His place was safe. Babs's cottage—not so much.

It would have weathered countless storms in its past, he told himself. It would weather another.

But why were their lights still on? Because the roaring of the storm was making them nervous?

He could go over and check, but he wasn't wanted.

Babs didn't want him.

Neither did Gina.

So why was he aching to head over there and cart them bodily back here? Would that suit his own macho image of keeping the women safe? Save the helpless?

He thought of Gina and decided helpless was hardly an adjective that fitted. She was competent and she was fiercely independent.

As he was. Independent was the way he liked it. It had been the way he'd intended to stay for the rest of his life.

Had been? Why was he talking in the past tense? It should be present tense, he told himself as he tossed another log on the fire. He was still independent.

Hoppy was asleep on his fireside rug. He stirred a little as the new log caused sparks to fly. One eye opened to check Hugh was still there, but once that fact was verified the eye closed again.

Hoppy was the only creature who needed him, Hugh thought, and that was the way he liked it.

Except…it was no longer quite true.

He'd been working at the clinic for a month now, and he'd already realised the growing dependence he was creating among the islanders. It wasn't just from the islanders, either, he conceded. Two days ago, he'd fielded a call from Marc, the head of the Gannet Island group. 'We don't have a doctor spare to do a clinic next Monday,' he'd told him. 'But you seem to be operating well over there. Can we leave scheduled clinics to you from now on? Can we depend on you?'

He'd almost refused, but then he'd thought why not? It was happening anyway.

Dependence.

At least he still had this place. His solitude. Nothing could interfere with that.

Except there was a storm and a battered cottage and two women…

There was Gina.

He sat on, staring into the fire, thinking he should go to bed. Glancing out occasionally towards Babs's cottage.

And then the lights went out.

That wasn't a big deal. This was some storm, and the electricity connection from the far side of the island was tenuous. He thought of flicking onto his backup power, but he should go to bed, anyway.

Instead he found himself back at the window, staring once more across to Babs's place.

The lights had gone out there, too.

Fair enough. It was three in the morning. They'd probably both be asleep, not even noticing.

But he was suddenly thinking of Gina, fifteen years old, on the side of a mountain in a storm. In the dark. She hated the dark.

'She'll be asleep,' he said out loud, straining to see the outline of the cottage through the driving rain.

And then he saw a chink of light. Babs's shutters were ancient, falling to bits. He'd offered to fix them, but she'd snapped his head off. 'They'll see me out. I don't need help.' So now he watched as light filtered out, faint. A lantern, moving from room to room?

From living room to Babs's bedroom.

So Gina had been up, too, sitting in the living room as he was. Lighting the lamp when the power went out. Taking it into Babs's room to check.

Staying there.

He knew the set-up in Babs's house. He'd been in

there when she'd had the attack, and a couple of other times when he'd insisted on checking her after she'd come home from hospital. He'd even insisted she give him a key. Now he stood and watched, waiting for the light to disappear, or to move back to the living room. Gina's bedroom must be the small back room and he wouldn't be able to see the light if she'd gone back there. Or she could leave the lantern in the sitting room and go back to bed.

Instead the light stayed in Babs's room.

The wind was blasting in from the ocean and rain had turned to a driving sleet. The light from Babs's cottage was a glimmer only, occasionally disappearing as sleet mixed with blowing sand.

He watched on. Ten minutes. More. The light didn't shift. Still in Babs's bedroom.

Maybe they were sitting talking, he thought. Maybe they were taking comfort by being with each other in the storm.

He thought of Babs and he thought, Ha! There was no way she'd concede she needed comfort.

Okay, maybe he had it wrong. Maybe it had been Babs in the living room, Babs taking the lantern back to her own bedroom. Maybe Gina was sound asleep. Why was he worrying?

Except he was.

He could phone.

He didn't want to phone. What he wanted was to head over and check, and the urge was growing by the minute.

Would either of them appreciate him pounding on the door at three in the morning? Babs would tell him where to go in no uncertain terms if she thought he was interfering. And Gina? Maybe he'd be told off by both of them.

If Gina needed him, she only had to lift her own phone, he told himself. He knew she wouldn't hesitate if she thought he could make things easier for Babs. The safest—the most sensible—course was to stay where he was. To not interfere unless asked.

But still…what was he risking by finding out?

'Scared of drowning?' They were Gina's words, thrown at him as a dare.

Scared of showing he cared?

Same thing.

He was suddenly back in a war zone, listening to a woman pleading for help for her daughter. Hearing the sergeant in the background. *'We can't afford to care.'*

This wasn't a war zone. This was an old lady with a heart condition and a woman he…

A woman he…what?

No. Don't go there. *There* was a step too far.

But he looked out into the night again, at the flickering, distant light, and suddenly he knew that, like it or not, he'd already taken that step.

He was thinking of Gina as a child of neglectful parents. He knew she'd have had a similar childhood to his, without the advantages of riches. Of nannies who were at least paid to care.

He was thinking of her as a teenager, alone after an appalling plane crash. Then he was thinking of her arriving on the island, only to be told she was here under sufferance.

But she'd conquered. He was thinking of her courage, her humour, her inimitable spirit.

He was thinking of the way she'd held him, of the way she'd given herself, no strings, with love and with laughter.

Did those words go together?

Love?

No strings?

He was feeling 'strings' now, and he was feeling them in spades. The amazing thing was, though, that they didn't feel terrifying.

They felt right.

Hoppy was awake and at his feet, looking up at him, puzzled. Hugh was standing by the door. The storm was raging outside and Hoppy's look said: 'You have to be out of your mind.'

'So maybe I am,' he told his little dog. 'But we're in this together, mate. How about we vote? You're probably more sensible than I am right now, so you get two votes to my one.'

There was a cop-out if he'd ever heard one, because Hoppy knew his duty. He sighed and put his nose against the door.

He'd be thinking, as dogs did, that Hugh was simply insisting he head outside to relieve himself before they both slept. But Hugh gave a rueful smile.

'Not a bathroom break, mate. I have a feeling it might be a break of a completely different kind.'

A break from solitude? From armour? From staying aloof for ever?

He thought of Gina and the defences she'd built for her own protection, and he thought it wasn't just he who needed to think about a whole new future. But if he was willing to share his isolation…

'Who am I kidding? She might not even open the door to us,' he told Hoppy as he opened the door and the wind almost blasted them back into the house. He picked up the little dog and tucked him under his arm. 'But Babs might be ill, and she might need us for practical reasons. And the rest… Why not give it a red-hot go?'

CHAPTER ELEVEN

SHE SAT IN the weak light cast by the lantern. She held her aunt's hand and felt the warmth slowly fade.

She felt sick. Cold.

Empty.

This, then, was the end.

She thought suddenly of that hug she'd had from Babs, all those years ago. She'd arrived on the ferry, shell-shocked, alone, bereft, and her aunt had hugged her. She remembered the wave of relief she'd had, the feeling that here was someone who cared.

The feeling of coming home.

And then, the next morning, the realisation that the hug had been an aberration. That there'd be no more displays of what Babs called sickly sentimentality.

But still, that hug had stayed with her. The hug had been why she'd made such an effort to get back to the island, and there'd been another when she'd arrived.

She was all Babs had, and Babs was all she had—and now there was nothing.

There was nothing for her here. She wasn't about to live in this cottage for the rest of her life, doing morning clinics, trying to pretend it was home.

Home was a fantasy. She'd always known that. Forgetting it, even for a moment, caused nothing but heartbreak.

So now what?

One step at a time, she told herself. Don't look too far into the future. So…

She could call Hugh, she thought, but then…why? She knew he'd come—he'd assured both her and her aunt. But Babs was gone. There was nothing here for Hugh to do.

There'd be time enough to call in officialdom in the morning, she told herself, because surely that was what Hugh was. The island doctor. There should be a funeral director on the island as well, or someone who acted as such. He or she could wait until morning as well.

And then? She allowed herself to think a little past the next few days. To a flight back to Sydney? To job opportunities? To the next adventure?

Why did it leave her cold?

She shivered. She should go to bed, but still she sat, taking the last vestige of comfort she could from the fading warmth of her aunt's hand.

She was crying. These were stupid tears that she knew Babs would have scorned. She dashed them away with her spare hand, but they still came.

She hated crying. She'd learned long ago that tears achieved nothing. They just made her feel appalling the day after, and the day after was for planning how to move on.

Tomorrow…

Stop crying!

And then a knock sounded above the wind. Or maybe it was just a part of the storm. She ignored it. It seemed just too hard to move.

It seemed impossible to release her aunt's hand from hers.

But then the bedroom door opened. 'Babs?'

And it was Hugh. He was standing in the doorway, a huge shape behind the glow of the lantern he carried. He was wearing a vast, all-weather coat, and a sou'wester hat casting his face into absolute darkness. He was so deeply in shadow she shouldn't even know it was him, but she'd know this man, even without words.

She didn't move. His lantern was lighting the room now, with a glow far stronger than the lantern she'd been using. He crossed to the bed and held the lamp high, taking in the sight of Babs's face, peaceful in death. Of Gina still sitting, her hand still holding.

And then he set his lantern down. He crouched beside her and gently, gently, he disengaged her fingers from Babs.

And then he took her into his arms, and he hugged.

When the trap had been sprung, when the bomb had exploded, Hugh's world had seemed blasted to pieces. His body had been wounded, but the physical wounds had been nothing compared to the shock and regret that followed. What had been left was a dull, grey void where, once upon a time, caring had been.

Now he held Gina, and somehow, in some way, his world seemed to settle.

The caring flooded back. The feelings he'd had watching the flicker of her lantern through the storm solidified into certainty.

For as he gathered her against his chest, as he felt her initial rigidity, which seemed to last less than a heartbeat, as he felt her let go, sink against him, burrow her face into his shoulder, let his arms embrace her, hold her, he felt as if...

He'd come home.

This, then, was his home. His peace.

Gina.

He was crouched on the floor and she was in his arms. He was cradling her as one would cradle a child. Holding for as long as she willed it.

He felt her sobs falter, fade, turn to desperate sniffles.

Somewhere in one of the cavernous pockets of his massive coat he'd have a handkerchief, but for now it didn't matter. The front of his coat was enough. Her face was buried against his chest, as if she needed the reassurance of his heartbeat.

This woman…

He loved her.

The knowledge came, a bolt from who knew where, but it was sure and strong, and with it came a feeling of wholeness. Of wonder. Of a future?

He'd tell her. He must tell her, but for now all he could do was hold her.

Gradually he felt her body relax, but still he held her, and she let herself be held. The moments passed and he thought she was taking time to readjust to this new world.

A world without an aunt who'd refused to love her.

A world without an aunt whom she'd loved, regardless.

And finally, finally he felt her regroup. She sniffed and sniffed again, then pulled back, just a little.

He still held her, but he could see her face now, swollen with weeping.

Lovely.

'I've… I've made a mess of your coat,' she stammered, and he smiled. All the tenderness he could muster—maybe more tenderness than he knew he had—was in that smile.

'There's a storm outside and this is a raincoat,' he told

her. 'Two minutes outside your backdoor and who needs a washing machine? Love, I'm so sorry.'

Love. Where had that word come from?

He'd never called a woman love.

It felt right.

But she hadn't seemed to notice. She closed her eyes and then opened them again, tilted her chin, visibly fighting for composure.

'She didn't call me,' she said bleakly. 'I knew she was fading, but she wouldn't let me sit with her. I was in the sitting room. I said, "If you have any pain…"' She broke off and he could hear agony in her voice.

'Hey, I'm looking at her,' he said, gently as he held her. 'She died in peace, love. Not in pain. She died secure in the fact that you were just through the door. She died knowing she had a family.'

'She wasn't…she didn't want…'

'She never admitted she wanted,' he told her. 'That wasn't Babs's way. But she did want you home. When she came home from hospital and I suggested she might move closer to help, she snapped my head off. "My niece will come," she told me, with all the assurance in the world. "She'll come when I need her." And so you did.'

'She never wanted me.'

'You know she did.'

There was a long silence. He held her close, waiting for the acceptance he knew must surely come. Outside the wind was screaming. A piece of roofing iron had come loose and was banging with every gust. The whole house felt as if it were trembling, as if any minute it could end up in Texas.

'Let me take you back to my place,' he suggested, but she shook her head. Finally, she gathered herself, tugged away and he let her stand.

'I...no. Thank you, Hugh, but I can't leave Babs. I'm so glad you came but I'll be all right now.'

And once more he had that vision of a kid on a mountainside, alone. *'I'll be all right now.'* How many times had she told herself that?

'Gina, there's nothing more you can do for her.'

'Except stay. Hugh, I can't leave her. Tomorrow... there'll be things... I can't think, but when the storm passes...'

'Then I'll stay with you.' He thought of his own house, warm, solid, safe. He thought of this place, rickety, cold, the fire stove never able to throw enough heat to negate the draughts blowing in through a thousand cracks.

An ancient house, with a dead woman.

The place where Gina was.

Of course he'd stay.

'You don't need to.' She was almost visibly regrouping. Pulling her fierce independence around her. 'I can cope.'

'You don't need to cope.'

'But I can.' She didn't sound sure, though. She sounded bewildered. 'I guess... I should sleep.'

'Could you sleep?'

'No,' she said frankly. 'But I'll stoke up the fire and sit the night out.' She hesitated. 'How did you know to come?'

'I saw the light from the lantern. It shifted into Babs's room and stayed. I thought...' He stopped and Gina nodded.

'Thank you,' she whispered. 'I...it means...it meant a lot. That you found her the first time. That you came tonight. You're a good neighbour.'

'I want to be more than that.' He said it flatly, definitely, and in those words was a declaration. Her eyes flew to his and held.

'H… Hugh.'

'Let me stay, Gina,' he said gently. 'I can't bear you to be alone.'

'I can't…'

He put his hands on her shoulders and met her gaze full on. Her face was swollen from weeping. Her hair was tousled, a riot of tangled curls. She was wearing some sort of jogging suit, faded pink, baggy, old.

He thought he'd never seen anything so lovely in his life.

'I think you can, love,' he said. 'For tonight, let yourself admit that you need me. Let me in.'

There was a long, long silence. The whole world seemed to be holding its breath. And then finally, finally that breath was expelled.

'For tonight,' she whispered.

'For now, let's accept that's all either of us can ask.'

'Oh, Hugh,' she said, and he felt the strength drain out of her. Her shoulders slumped and that fierce, determined courage seemed to drain away.

He tugged her closer, held her tight, feeling as if he was holding her up.

'Gina, for tonight…let me take care of you,' he said gently, and she put her face up to be kissed, as if it was the most natural thing in the world.

As it was.

This was his woman.

He'd come home.

She woke and she was in his arms. She was cradled against him, spooned against his chest. She was being held as if she was the most precious thing in the world.

Outside the sounds of the storm persisted, but the intensity had faded. There was water dripping down her bedroom wall. That'd be from the loss of the roofing iron. This old house was on its last days.

It didn't need to last any longer.

She should think about her aunt, whose body lay in the big, cold bedroom at the far end of the house. Of Babs, who'd slipped away to somewhere where she needed no one.

Of Babs, who'd sworn to need no one. As Gina had.

She should think of her own future. Of what she'd do now.

But right now, her mind wouldn't go there. It was as if something inside her had given her this place of peace. Instead of thinking of trouble, of emptiness, of grief, she lay in Hugh's arms and let herself savour this moment of peace. Of safety. Of warmth.

Of love?

No. This man was as independent as she was, she thought. He was trained in the same way. You did what you needed to do to stay independent. You never let your hard-won armour open, you never allowed anything to pierce your self-sufficiency.

He'd held her all night. Just…held her.

But for a moment she lay and let herself dream, of what life could be like if she turned within his arms and held him and told him…

What?

That she'd fallen in love?

She didn't fall in love. That was for movies and story books. Real life was practical. Real life was for holding on to your defences, to prevent pain ripping in. You could be fond, you could enjoy, you could find warmth and laughter and friendship. But you held that armour closed.

And with that thought, reality returned. When Hugh stirred and his arms tightened, when she turned into him and saw his eyes, gravely questioning, her heart twisted—as if there were a loss here that was too great to bear?

She hadn't lost, she told herself fiercely. She'd never taken in the first place.

'Love?' he said, and there it was again, that twist, sharp as a knife.

'Hey,' she whispered, shoving down unwanted emotion with every inch of her being. 'Good…good morning.'

Keep it light, her inner self was screaming, and something in her gaze must have got through to him.

'Good morning to you, too, love,' he told her. 'I guess it's not, but we can hold to this calm for a while longer.'

He smiled at her, a warm, embracing smile that was a declaration all by itself, and she had to fight to keep the surge of stupid hope at bay. She knew this man now. He operated on the same basis as she did. A hard shell deep within, armour to be protected at all costs. But caring was still there.

This was all this night had been. Caring.

Love must be different.

He hauled his arm out from underneath her and glanced at his watch. 'Five a.m. The world's not awake. There's nothing we can do yet. Can you sleep again, love?' His arms tightened. 'You know, this bed really is too small.'

It definitely was. It was the bed she'd slept in when she was fifteen. The bed of so many nightmares.

She'd hated this bed. She'd hated this bedroom.

She lay squashed now, in her too small bed, and she thought it had its advantages. Hugh was holding her close. He had no choice, but close was good.

Unless she let herself believe that close could cure anything.

'Gina, you can't stay here.' Hugh was awake now, and he must be aware of the water dripping down her wall. Of the broken shutters. Of the knowledge that this was the end of her time here. 'You'll need to stay at my place.' His arms tightened around her again—possessive? 'Hoppy and I have a king-sized bed, and I suspect he'll be as happy to share as I would be.' He hesitated. 'As I…will be?'

'Hugh…'

'I know,' he said, softly, against her ear. 'It's too soon to think of anything past today, and today will be bleak. I just need you to know that you're not alone. That at the end of the day Hoppy and I will be here. Love, you won't be facing this by yourself.'

'I can cope.'

'I'm sure you can,' he told her. 'You're one amazing woman.'

'Yeah,' she said dryly, fighting down something that felt like panic. That line…*you're not alone*…it felt like a siren song. She needed to block it out.

She was thinking suddenly, stupidly, of her aunt, all those years ago, greeting her from the ferry. Of a hug. Of the overwhelming sense that she was no longer alone. That she had a home to go to.

And then the next morning, the brick…

'Gina…' Hugh was watching her face, troubled. 'Love…'

'Please…don't call me love.'

'What, never?'

'I don't… I can't…'

'I didn't think I could either,' he told her. 'But right now—'

'Right now I might get up and start…'

'Start what?'

'I…' She was flailing for answers. 'I'm not sure. Where's Hoppy?' she managed.

'Hoppy's out by the fire stove,' he told her. 'Sleeping as the world's sleeping. And Babs is gone. You've done everything she allowed you to do to keep her last days secure, and there's nothing more you can do for her. The world will break in soon enough—it has to—but for now…' Those dark eyes were so gentle, so loving that she felt as if she could drown. 'For now, my love, my beautiful Gina, let me hold you close. For these next few hours…maybe let's both believe that what we have right now might be for ever?'

Hugh slept again but Gina didn't. She lay awake, co-cooned in his arms, maybe even half asleep, but she was in some dream of a twilight world. She should feel safe in his hold, but Babs's death was raw, the storm was still blowing, and in this twilight world Hugh's arms couldn't keep her from the nightmares she'd had over and over. Nightmares that had their basis in reality.

The loneliness of a childhood being passed from one carer to another. Of having no control of when and how goodbyes would occur.

The night on the mountain with her parents.

Babs's hugs and then the certainty of yet another goodbye.

In her dreams she felt as if she was swirling, the sensation leaving her breathless with fear. Of having no control. Of clinging and being torn again.

Hugh's arms still held her, but as the morning light finally filtered through the broken shutters the nightmare was still with her. Hugh's arms couldn't keep her safe. No one could except herself.

So somehow, she had to stay in control. She couldn't allow herself to hope.

Somehow, she had to be the one who said goodbye.

At nine o'clock Hugh hit the phones. Trees and power lines had come down over the track leading to this side of the island and they needed to be cleared before the outside world could break in. Hugh bullied Gina into eating some breakfast and then went to help.

When he finally returned, Gina was on the roof, hammering down a sheet of roofing iron. The wind hadn't died completely. She looked a tiny figure, up there banging in nails.

A convoy was behind Hugh's truck, consisting of the island's policewoman, the island's funeral director, a couple of other burly islanders and a truck full of chainsaws.

As they arrived, Gina clambered down her ladder and the look she gave him as he headed towards her was closed. It was as if their time apart had cemented what she knew she had to say. What she had to believe. She folded her arms defensively, a gesture that said back off.

'Gina, stay off the roof.' It was the policewoman who snapped it, not him. 'The boys here'll make the place watertight.'

'I will,' Hugh growled, but she shook her head.

'There's no need. I can do it.'

And then bureaucracy took over. The funeral director—a local farmer with a double role—was officious, dotting every 'i', crossing every 't'. He was intent on treating Babs's death as unexpected, which would have meant an autopsy and a coroner's report, so Hugh had to once more switch to doctor mode. Yes, he'd been treating Babs, yes, this was a pre-condition, her death was very much expected. When finally Babs's body was carried out to the funeral director's van, when finally the guys on the roof finished nailing—they hadn't taken no for an answer—when the policewoman left with her pile of forms, Gina retreated still further.

'Come home with me,' he told her, but she shook her head.

'I can't,' she said simply. 'Hugh, you've been wonderful, but I need to be alone.'

'Gina…'

'Please, Hugh, I mean it. Please leave me be.'

And that was that.

CHAPTER TWELVE

BABS'S FUNERAL TOOK PLACE four days later, in the island's
only chapel, at the edge of town, on a headland where
mourners could gaze through the stained-glass windows
and see the glimmer of the ocean beyond.

Gina sat alone.

There were any number of islanders who would have
sat with her. In the weeks she'd been on the island she'd
been accepted as 'one of them'. She'd accepted their con-
dolences with gratitude and warmth, but she'd stayed in
Babs's house and she'd refused all offers of company.

Including Hugh's.

Hugh had offered to be with her during the service,
but she'd simply said, 'Hugh, thank you but I need to
do this by myself.' When he'd arrived, she'd welcomed
him at the chapel door as she'd welcomed everyone who
attended. She'd smiled at him and held his hand for just
a touch too long—but then she'd shaken her head, as if
recalling something she should have known.

Then she'd walked to the front pew and sat, solitary,
her hands clasped tightly in her lap. Plain navy trousers
and white shirt. Her hair tied in a plain navy scarf. Part
of her uniform? Part of the Gina who was moving on.

The Gina he knew had been tucked back inside some

tight, hard shell. Something had happened to her the night Babs had died.

Or was it the night he'd called her love?

Babs's body was to be taken to Gannet to be cremated, her ashes then to be scattered on the beach she loved, so there was to be no burial. He watched Gina's face as the hearse disappeared and saw a pain so deep she couldn't hide it. He wanted to hug her. He wanted to take her pain into him.

He couldn't. He wasn't wanted.

It was the height of irony, he thought savagely. He'd held himself to himself for so long and now, when a woman had come into his life and broken through his barriers, her own armour was holding them apart.

The hall next to the chapel was being used to serve refreshments. The sight of Gina's strained face was killing him, but he couldn't leave. He stood and drank insipid tea and talked inanities to the islanders—and, okay, sometimes they weren't even inanities. She'd done this to him, this woman. She'd drawn him into a place where he felt himself caring for the whole damned island.

But her face... He watched her deflect sympathy and he thought, She's withdrawing, as he watched.

Would she leave? The thought made him feel ice cold, but what was there to make her stay?

And then his phone, turned off during the service, rang into life again. He excused himself to the fisherman who'd been explaining the complexities of his bunions to him and headed outside.

'Yes?'

'Doc?' And from the phone he heard terror.

'What's happened?'

'It's... Doc, this is Harry... Harry Whitecross. My wife, my Jenny, she's thirty-four weeks pregnant. We were heading over to Gannet next week to stay with her mum until bub's born, but half an hour ago she started bleeding. A lot.'

He stood on the hall steps and his mind stilled. The emotions playing in his head faded into the background as medicine took over. He was no obstetrician, but in years of working with overseas aid, he'd seen plenty. Bleeding in late pregnancy… A lot of bleeding…

'Is she in labour? Is she having pains?'

'No. No pain, Doc, but the bleeding's getting worse. More'n a period. Much more. We rang Doc Ellen, the obstetrician on Gannet, but the doc who answered said she's gone to a family wedding in Sydney. They said they'll send the chopper with help as soon as it's available, but meanwhile to ring you. Doc, she's scared. Will you come?'

This much bleeding…this close to term… Scenarios were playing in his mind, none of them good. He was already looking out at the car park, figuring how he could get his truck from behind the bank of parked cars. Being blocked in was the price he'd paid for coming early.

But he'd have to go. A significant bleed in late pregnancy… There was no way they could wait for the chopper, for evacuation to Gannet, to technology, to surgeons, to a hospital facility.

'Tell me where you are.' He mentally gave up on his truck—it'd take twenty minutes and a public announcement to get it out. But Gina's—or, truthfully, Babs's—Mini was free. As chief mourner she'd parked in the reserved spot.

'A farm two K south of town,' the guy on the end of the line was saying. 'The gate on the left at the end of Blainey's Road. Doc, can you ask Gina…? I know it's her aunt's funeral, but Jenny's terrified and at least she knows Gina. She's almost an islander.'

He glanced back in at Gina, surrounded by mourners, white-faced, stressed. Almost an islander? She wasn't, he thought, knowing she'd reject the label.

But even if Harry hadn't asked for her to come, Hugh knew he needed her. In every one of the scenarios in his head, he knew he couldn't do this alone. He was about to stress her even more.

'Tell Jenny to lie still,' he told Harry. 'Keep calm and see if you can keep Jenny that way, too. Tell her we're on our way.'

He was already heading inside. Heading for Gina.

The elderly farmer in front of her was balancing tea and scones with jam and cream in one hand, wringing her hand with the other.

'She didn't mix much but she was one of us,' he was saying. 'She must have been so pleased when you got home. I'm so sorry for your loss.'

It was pretty much what she'd been hearing over and over, any time these last few days. She was so tired she wanted to sleep for a week.

She wanted to leave.

At least she could. In her purse she had a slip of paper with details written after a call yesterday. An escape route. It didn't make her feel any less empty, but at least it was there.

And then Hugh was at her shoulder, touching her lightly on her arm. 'Gina?'

She turned, almost bracing. What was she expecting? That he'd put his arm around her, that he'd support her, that he'd declare to the islanders that he cared?

She didn't want it. She couldn't want it. But instead

she saw his face and knew that whatever he was here for, it wasn't that.

'Emergency,' he said curtly. 'Jenny Whitecross. Late-term pregnancy, bleeding. Sorry, Gina, but I need you.' He turned to the farmer she'd been talking to. 'Mate, could you spread the word that we've been called away? No drama but we're needed in a hurry.'

'Yeah, of course,' the farmer said quickly, and then patted Gina on the arm. 'You go where you're needed. Aren't we all lucky you came home?'

Home? Gina thought bleakly as she turned—with something of relief.

Not so much.

Hugh told her fast what was happening. They grabbed gear from his truck, shifted it to Babs's Mini and then headed to the Whitecrosses'. Gina drove as fast as Babs's ancient Mini allowed.

Feeling desolate.

She wanted to get off this island. She wanted to stop grieving for an aunt who'd never loved her. She wanted to stop caring for islanders, when this island wasn't her home.

She wanted not to feel…what she was feeling…for the man by her side.

But for now, everything had to be put aside in the face of Jenny Whitecross's need.

And then they were turning into the farmyard. Harry was bursting outside to greet them, and medical need took over.

Jenny was in the main bedroom. She was lying super-still. She looked young, not much more than a teenager, fair-haired, pale, swollen with pregnancy. Obviously terrified. Her eyes were wide with fear, and the towels under her told their own story.

Gina took one look at the blood, and her heart sank. This was way beyond her.

Since she'd finished her training, she'd been working on expedition ships. In that role, she'd coped with everything that a team of fit young men and women doing crazy things could throw at her.

Complications of late pregnancy, not so much.

But Hugh had dumped his bag by the bed and was holding Jenny's wrist, stooping so his face was at her level. He at least was exuding an air of calm.

'It's okay, Jenny. We're here now. You know that I'm a doctor and Gina's a nurse. We have all the skills you need to see this through. Harry tells me you're thirty-four weeks pregnant. Is that right?'

'I…yes.'

Gina flipped his bag open and handed him his stethoscope. He fitted it, not above Jenny's heart, but lower.

'Let's listen to bub,' he said and there was a deathly silence while they all waited.

'Let's get a drip up,' he said to Gina before removing the stethoscope, and his eyes met hers. The look lasted only for a fraction of a second, but she got it. Trouble. Weak heartbeat? Foetal distress? He wasn't saying. Why terrify Jenny still further?

Jenny's fingers were curled into white-knuckled fists, bracing for the worst, but Hugh pulled the stethoscope away and smiled straight at her.

'I can hear the heartbeat. Your baby's safe, but I suspect it wants to come out. Soon.'

And the woman seemed to sag. 'Oh, God… Oh, thank God. But why…? The blood…'

'Have you had a fall? A sudden jerk?' He'd be thinking about placenta abruption, Gina thought, the ripping of the placenta from the wall of the uterus. He was feeling Jenny's tummy now, gently figuring foetal position.

'N…no.'

'Nothing that could have bruised anything inside?'

'Harry's been cosseting me so much,' Jenny whispered. 'He won't let me near the cows. I've hardly been allowed to carry more than a cup of tea. There's been nothing.'

'That's great.' He smiled a reassurance. 'But something has to be making you bleed. While we figure things out, Gina will set up a drip. That'll keep up the fluids for you and for bub.'

And that had Gina fighting back her almost instinctive panic and starting to act like the medic she was. She was pulling saline out of the bag, figuring where they could hang it, organising swabs and syringes. 'We need to counter that bleeding,' Hugh was saying. 'The docs from Gannet will bring plasma, but for now saline will do the trick. Jenny, have you had an ultrasound during your pregnancy? Have you had prenatal checks with the obstetrician on Gannet?'

'I…at twenty weeks,' Jenny whispered.

'We were supposed to go back at thirty,' Harry muttered from behind them. He was leaning against the wall, arms crossed, looking as terrified as his wife. 'But the appointment was the week of the explosion. Dad was one of the guys hurt. He's okay now, but with all the drama… I've been working his place as well as ours, and Jenny reckoned everything was fine. I worried, but she reckoned we could put going back to Gannet off.'

'I get that,' Hugh said calmly, as if time didn't matter. Which Gina knew it did. 'So the ultrasound at twenty weeks... Do you remember? Did they say anything about the placenta?'

There was a moment's pause. Finally, it was Jenny who answered, and she sounded horrified.

'I'd forgotten. Ellen said it was a bit low. She said not to worry though, it'd probably fix itself, but she'd check it again before the birth, just to make sure. I didn't think it was anything to worry about. There's a picture, if you like. We stuck it on the fridge.'

Wordlessly Gina headed out to find it. The grainy black and white image was in pride of place, right in the centre of the fridge. She looked at it and winced, then headed back and handed it to Hugh.

Yeah, the placenta was low. Not low enough to cause problems, though. Mostly such positioning would resolve as the pregnancy progressed, leaving the cervix clear.

But if it didn't... If it had slipped still further, and the pressure from the growing baby had caused a tear...

She watched Hugh's face. Impassive. Calm. As if he didn't concede this was the emergency it was.

She didn't need to have heard the heartbeat herself to know this baby was in peril, and Jenny, too. Deadly peril.

'Jenny, I think I know what the problem is,' he said, laying the image aside and taking her hand. 'The placenta has shifted down rather than to the side, so it's blocking the birth canal. The baby's...'

'A girl,' Jenny breathed, and Hugh nodded.

'Great,' he said, as if that helped. 'Your little girl is lovely and big, and she's almost ready to be born. But that's what's causing you both problems. She's been growing fast and, because she's nice and big, she's starting to push downward. She's exerting more and more pressure on the placenta, and my guess is that's what's causing the bleeding. And the bleeding won't stop until the pressure's taken off. If she pushes any harder it might get a whole lot worse. So, Jenny, to keep her safe, to keep you both safe, we're going to have to deliver her. Now. That means you'll need to trust us to perform a caesarean. At thirty-four weeks she should be fine. You'll have your daughter and things will be okay.'

'A caesarean…' It was Harry, his voice rising in panic.

'Yes,' Hugh said, and his voice was firm, sure, implacable. He glanced again at the bloody towels. 'And we need to do it now.'

'But where? Can we get to Gannet in time? There's no hospital here. How can you do a caesarean?'

Hugh still held Jenny's hand and his eyes didn't leave hers. His words were still firm, with certainty and confidence behind them.

'Gina and I can perform a caesarean right here, Jenny. We have all the skills necessary, plus the equipment and the drugs to do it without causing you pain. Right now, you have a healthy baby, but if she's pushing down enough to make you bleed then she needs to come out. She can't come out naturally with the placenta in that position, and if we leave her in there the bleeding will only get worse. Both of you will be in trouble. Gina and I can have her out in no time, and instead of being scared, instead of bleeding, you'll have your daughter in your arms. Will you trust us to do that, Jenny?' He glanced back. 'Harry?'

'Oh, Harry,' Jenny breathed.

'There's no choice, is there, Doc?' Harry said heavily.

Gina thought, This guy's a farmer. He'll be used to delivering calves; he'll know more than most the danger his Jenny is facing.

'There's no choice,' Hugh said evenly. 'But you're in good hands. I'm not an obstetrician, but I've been working as a crisis doctor in war-torn countries for years, and I've delivered many, many babies. And Gina here has all the skills to help me. Jenny, we won't put you to sleep. I have the right anaesthetics in my bag to give you an epidural—a spinal anaesthetic to block out any pain. You'll be awake the whole time, awake enough to see your daughter born. But, Jenny...' He allowed himself another glance at those towels. 'We need to move now.'

'She's not ready to be born.' Jenny's voice rose in panic.

And then, amazingly, Hugh's face creased into a smile. 'Sorry, Jenny, I hate to tell you this,' he said, gently but, oh, so firmly, 'but this is not your decision. It's your daughter's. It's your little girl who's pushing who's causing you to bleed. It's your daughter who's decreed she wants to be born, and she wants to be born right now. She has a mind of her own. So...would you like to meet her face to face? Fifteen minutes, Jenny, and you'll have your daughter in your arms.'

'But thirty-four weeks...'

'And she's a big 'un,' Hugh said, still smiling. 'She's raring to start her life, right now. Will you let us deliver her?'

'Oh...'

'You have to, Jen,' Harry said urgently, heading to the bedside and taking her other hand in his. 'We've had premmie calves before. We know how to handle them, and this is our daughter. Let the doc make you both safe, love.'

'Gina...' Jenny looked wildly up at Gina, fear and indecision warring. And Gina got this. Women the world over had looked to women for advice during childbirth.

Little did Jenny realise that Gina had less experience of birthing than anyone in this room.

But now wasn't the time to say so. Now was the time to haul the cloak of ancient women's business around her, to put all the gravitas she could muster into her response.

'You don't have a choice, Jen,' Gina told her. 'Now she's messed with her placenta she can't stay inside. And Hugh...' She glanced at Hugh. 'I've seen this guy at work and he's the best. It'd be more convenient for us if we had a nice bright hospital theatre, with all the bells and whistles, but this way you'll have your baby at home. At home where you belong. But she is making you bleed, Jen, so we need to move now. Hugh's a doctor in a million. I'd trust him with my life. Will you trust him with your daughter?'

'If it was you...if it was your baby...'

Fat chance of that, Gina thought, but she didn't let that show in her voice. 'I told you. I trust Hugh.'

And Jenny searched her eyes for a long, long minute—and then seemed to cave. She took a ragged breath, looked from Gina, then to Harry—and finally she looked to Hugh.

'Yes, please,' she whispered.

'That's what I wanted to hear,' Hugh told her, and Gina could almost see the tension he was under. 'Right, Jenny, right, Harry, it's time we introduced you to your daughter.'

For all the confidence he showed, he wasn't confident. He never was. Obstetrics wasn't his thing.

It was true he'd delivered babies, scores of them. Usually in war- and famine-type settings. Almost always as a measure of last resort, a woman in desperate trouble, her family at their wits' end, finally bringing her to see the 'foreign doctor'.

Usually by the time they came he was lucky to save the mother. Dead babies…he'd lost count.

And this little one…despite the confident face he'd assumed when he'd talked to Jenny, she'd been bleeding for at least an hour. He'd listened to the heartbeat and he'd heard unmistakeable signs of foetal distress. It had nearly killed him to take the time to reassure, to ask for permission to operate. To waste precious seconds.

He knew from past experience that there was no other way—to operate on a patient rigid with terror was a recipe for further disaster. But he'd looked at the amount of blood and he'd had to almost physically restrain himself from moving to crisis mode. He'd been reaching the stage where he'd have had to bring terror into the equation—*If you want a live baby we have to operate now!*

But Gina…

'Hugh's a doctor in a million. I'd trust him with my life. Will you trust him with your daughter?'

Until she'd said that, things had hung in the balance. Jenny would have finally agreed; the bleeding, her husband's terror, sheer physical weakness would have superseded everything and he'd have been allowed to operate. But Gina's words had settled things. The panic in the room had dissipated.

'I'd trust him with my life.'

She was moving swiftly now, as was he. She might not be trained specifically in obstetrics, but he knew she'd interpreted his silent message. And she'd know the risks.

They'd wordlessly decided to operate here, in the bedroom. Moving Jenny, putting more pressure on that placenta, could be a disaster all on its own. Gina was manoeuvring a surgical sheet over the bedding, talking to Jenny all the time as she explained what was happening, shifting her as little as possible while she set the bed up to be as clinically impregnable as she could. He had the drip organised now and was organising the epidural. A signal to Gina, a quick explanation of what he intended, and they rolled Jenny, oh, so carefully onto her side.

Then there was an excruciating wait for the anaesthetic to take hold. He left his stethoscope on her abdomen, willing that heartbeat to continue. Gina had a tray set up beside him and was ordering Harry to put towels in the stove to warm. 'Like you're about to warm a lamb, but this will be one very special lamb,' she told them, making the couple both smile.

Then she looked at the curtains hanging over the window, jonquil-yellow, soft, new.

'Hmm,' she said. 'How much do you love those curtains, Jenny? Can we use them?'

'They're washable,' Jenny said faintly. She was beyond asking for reasons. 'Use anything you want.'

And two minutes later the curtains had been rearranged, one end still on the hook at one end of the window, the other propped up by a curtain rod leaning on the wardrobe at the other side of the bed. Settled to hang across the room, over Jenny's chest. To stop Jenny or Harry seeing the moment of incision.

A makeshift privacy curtain.

'There,' she said in satisfaction. 'Harry, that's just in case a little cut as we bring your daughter out makes you feel faint.'

'I wouldn't faint,' Harry said in indignation.

'Then you're a stronger medic than I am,' Gina retorted, grinning. 'The first caesarean I watched, as a trainee nurse, the dad had to scrape me off the floor.

There's nothing like a wee bit of blood to make you feel woozy, and this is your Jenny. So you stay on Jenny's side and I'll stay on Hugh's side. Then in two minutes we'll hand your daughter over and no one gets to scrape anyone off the floor.'

And Jenny even managed a smile at the look on her husband's face—and she was still smiling as Hugh swabbed and then made the incision and lifted one small, indignant baby out into the world.

Half an hour later the chopper arrived from Gannet, and Jenny and Harry and one healthy baby girl—big for dates, almost healthy enough not to need the specialist neonatal equipment that came with the doctor and specialist midwife who'd arrived with the chopper—were airborne, heading for hospital.

A couple of carloads of islanders arrived just as the chopper left. Where they'd got their information, who knew? But they came prepared to take over.

'We'll look to the cows and the farm,' a big-bosomed, middle-aged woman told Gina and Hugh. 'And we'll clean up inside. You guys have just given us a brand-new islander. You've done your work, now we'll do ours.' They dispersed to their self-appointed roles and there was nothing for Gina and Hugh to do but pack their equipment and leave.

'Do you want to go back to the hall?' Hugh asked as they loaded their gear. There'd still be islanders there for the remnants of the wake—weren't there always?

'You need to pick up your truck,' Gina told him. 'I'll take you.'

'Sure.' He glanced across at her. Her face, relaxed, almost happy as the baby had been born, was still carrying the echo of a smile. 'And then you'll go home?'

And the last vestige of smile disappeared.

'This isn't my home,' she said softly. 'This never was my home.'

Babs's Mini was parked in the driveway of the White-cross's farm, high on a ridge overlooking the sea. From here they could see almost all the way to Australia. Was that where she was looking?

'You'll go back to Sydney?' he asked, cautiously.

'Maybe.'

'I thought you might stay. Babs's house…'

'Babs hasn't left the house to me,' she said flatly. 'She left it to the Wilderness Society so the land could be an extension of the national park.'

That stunned him.

But maybe it shouldn't. Babs had been a loner. She hadn't wanted Gina to be here. Why would she make it easy for her to stay? She'd implied she'd be leaving it to Gina—had that been a ruse to get her here?

Gina would have come anyway, he thought. He knew this woman.

'I'm sorry,' he said, stupidly, searching for better words and not finding any.

'Don't be.'

'But… I imagine you'll be able to stay as long as you want, though,' he said. He knew the National Parks people—they'd be rapt that Babs's land had come under their care, but they'd hardly want the cottage.

'I'm leaving tomorrow.'

Tomorrow. The word seemed like a hammer blow.

'Why?' he managed, and she shrugged and gave a hollow laugh.

'I have a living to earn. And I don't belong.'

'You could belong,' he said cautiously. 'You know,

when Jenny was in trouble…she wanted you because she thought of you as an islander.'

'I'm not an islander. I don't belong…anywhere.' She shrugged and he saw her almost visibly regroup. 'I don't stay in any place too long. I don't get attached. Like you…haven't we learned the hard way not to form ties?'

'I am forming ties,' he said, still cautiously. He was figuring it out himself. 'Since you've come, ties seem to be happening all over the place.'

'You were acting as emergency doctor before I came.'

'But I didn't care then. I care now.'

His words emerged before he knew he intended to say them. Before he knew them for truth.

But it was true. Before Gina had come, he'd emerged from his shell when it was imperative, and then he'd escaped, back to his refuge.

But for the last few weeks he'd been interacting with the islanders on a daily basis. And today… He'd watched Harry's face as he'd held his newborn daughter, and something had twisted inside him. The cold, hard knot that had served him so well since he'd left the crisis medicine he'd been doing for so long seemed to have softened, unravelled. Leaving him exposed?

And looking at the woman beside him…he was even more exposed.

Since he'd been injured he'd carefully, consciously built himself a barrier where he couldn't care, but some time in the last few weeks that barrier had been broached.

He did care.

A lot.

'Don't go,' he said, urgently now. 'Gina, what we have here…we could build on it.'

'You mean as medics?'

And that set him back. As medics? Or as something more?

It was far too soon—he knew that. He needed time to let the knots unravel further.

To care still more?

For the last few weeks he'd been coming to terms with Gina living a stone's throw away. With Gina being at their makeshift clinic. With Gina's skills, her kindness, her laughter.

With Gina.

When the bomb had exploded something deep within had been blasted out of him. Trust? Emotion? He wasn't sure what, only that what was left had seemed a dark void that couldn't be filled. He'd felt like an empty shell, without whatever it was that had made life worthwhile.

Hope? Yes, that had been destroyed as well, and he hadn't been able to figure why. It had nothing to do with physical injuries. The shrinks had talked about the cumulative effect of years of fieldwork, of seeing the worst. They'd explained it, but they hadn't cured it. There hadn't been any chance of healing. All he'd been able to do was lock himself away.

But then he'd met Gina and his world had expanded. But it had expanded safely. He had no intention of giving up the peace, his quiet patch of island, his retreat from a world of pain, but she'd just been *here*. She'd added to his peace.

He'd started to…love?

'I don't think it is…just as medics,' he said, measuring each word, trying to figure what he meant himself. 'Gina, what I'm starting to feel for you…it needs more time. Both of us need more time, but all I know is that I want you to stay. If Babs's cottage doesn't work, then maybe we could share…'

But he wasn't allowed to finish. 'You mean I could retreat to your place?' It was a snap, and it left him stunned. He watched her face, tried to figure what she was saying, tried to figure what he was feeling.

She shook her head, seemingly trying to figure what she was feeling. Maybe the same as him? But their two worlds weren't meshing. 'I'm done retreating,' she told him, still with that harsh edge to her voice. 'It never works.'

'It can.'

'Has it worked for you?'

'Has running worked for you?'

'Is that what you think I'm doing? Running?'

'From pain? Maybe I do.'

'Then that makes two of us,' she said, and her voice softened. There was a moment's pause, a long one, where they both seemed to regroup. 'Sorry, Hugh,' she said at last. 'It was a great offer. At least I think it was going to be a great offer. To share your hideaway until we see what the future brings. The thing is that, for me, hideaways don't work, and in the end they cause more pain. This thing called home... I don't know the meaning of the word. How can I get attached to something...?'

'Something you're afraid of?'

'Maybe I am,' she said, still softly. 'So the two of us are at opposite ends of the spectrum. You're using the word home to describe somewhere you can hide from the world. I'm thinking the world is the place I can escape from needing any such thing.' She took a deep breath. 'You're a lovely man, Hugh, and we've had fun. I know you can build something good here on the island, some way back into what you need. But me...it scares me. If I put down roots, they'll only be torn up again and I can't... I couldn't bear it.'

'We could take a risk.' For that was what it felt like, a step into the unknown, but a look at her face told him she wasn't prepared to take it.

There was a long silence. A chasm impossible to bridge?

'So you'll get a job in Sydney?' he said at last.

'I won't.' Her chin tilted. 'I had an email yesterday— from the team I've worked with before. Travel's opening up again in this part of the world. A group's leaving in two weeks, a team of thirty, travelling down to summer over at McLachlan Island. There won't be a doctor on board. Not many doctors are prepared to spend six weeks travelling between bases on the Southern Ocean, so they've approached me again. I've said I'd go.'

'In two weeks.' He felt winded.

'Yes.'

'And then?' He was trying to get his head into some sort of order. So many conflicting emotions.

What he wanted, more than anything, was to step forward and take her into his arms. But something was holding him back. Something rigid, unassailable.

What he needed was an open heart, a surety that he could offer this woman the home and hearth she needed.

He had that. A home. A hearth.

She needed more.

There were so many emotions circling his brain. The birth he'd just witnessed had left him exposed. He'd seen the absolute love between the couple inside the house they'd just left. He'd seen the joy. But he'd also seen the terror that had gone before. They'd come so close.

If he managed to hold Gina… If she were to be pregnant with his child… If she took risks on his behalf…

'No.' She took a step back and managed a wavering smile. 'Hugh, don't beat yourself up and don't feel bad on my account. My world is what it is, as is your isolation, your need for escape. I can't help you and I can't continue to share. I've bullied you into helping me at the clinic and I hope you keep that up. I hope you become a true islander, that this place becomes your home and you and Hoppy can live happily ever after. But meanwhile, I'm off to find more adventures. I hope the world will open up again and I can have fun.'

'Is that what you want?'

'Yes,' she said, a trifle defiantly, but then she softened. She took his hands, then leaned forward and kissed him, very lightly, on the lips. And then she retreated before he could reach out and hold her.

'It's been good,' she said as she stepped back, and only a slight quiver in her words let him see the vulnerability behind the façade. 'I've done what I could for Babs, and so have you. I've even had a good time here, but it's time to reclaim what we both need. Hugh, I think…' She took a deep breath. 'I think I've come very close to loving you, but I don't need a refuge. I can't… I can't want a home.'

'Gina—'

'Don't say any more,' she begged. 'I need to go.'

CHAPTER THIRTEEN

SHE LEFT AND there wasn't a thing he could do about it. He kissed her goodbye at the ferry. She kissed him back, she held and clung for one long, sweet moment, and then she pulled away. There were tears in her eyes, but she lifted her duffel bag and turned and boarded the ferry without a backward glance.

She'd sorted Babs's belongings, distributing them among the islanders and to the local charity shop. As far as he knew she'd taken nothing for herself.

The size of her duffel was smaller even than the kit bag he'd carried on fieldwork.

She travelled light.

She travelled alone.

It was early morning when the ferry left. He'd driven her to the terminal. Now he headed to the clinic. It was half an hour until his first appointment. He stood and gazed at the space Gina had organised. At the state-of-the-art coffee maker she'd ordered from the mainland as 'essential supplies'. At the chair she'd used in the outer room, neatly pushed back under the desk.

There was not a personal thing on the desk. She'd left nothing.

And then the first patient arrived. It was Holly Cross, wife of one of the firefighters injured in the explosion.

Ray was home from hospital, doing well, but Holly was still holding up the farm. She had a laceration on her leg that was starting to ulcerate.

'Bloody cow kicked me,' she told him. 'Been too busy fussing over Ray to worry about it. So Gina's gone. You gonna miss her, Doc?'

'We all will.' It was all he could say. She let it be, and they talked of Ray and cows and life in general until he was almost done. He'd debrided the edges of the wound, cleaned and dressed it and was organising antibiotic.

'We guessed she wouldn't stay,' Holly told him conversationally. 'Her bloody aunt. You know I went to school with Gina? Babs told the teachers, that first day... "She's only here until I can find someone else to take her. Do the best you can with her but if I can find someone on the mainland to take her, I will." We all heard it. Gina had just lost her parents, and what sort of a welcome was that? It's a wonder she came back at all.'

'Yeah.' He felt...grim was too small a word for it.

'And the word is you're nutty on her,' Holly said, still in chatty mode, as if what she was saying was no big deal. 'There's been bets on whether she'd stay but I reckon she's been kicked too often. It'd take more 'n romance to get a woman like that to trust enough to put down roots.'

Had their...attraction...seemed so obvious? 'Holly...'

'Yeah, it's none of my business,' Holly said blithely. 'Ray says I'm always butting in where I'm not wanted. But you know, Doc, we managed without you before you came, and we could do it again. So, if you ever wanted to, I don't know, head off for any reason...' she glanced out at Hoppy, who was doing his normal thing, settled on a bench on the veranda, overlooking his world '...the Gannet doctors could deal here again, and there'd be a bunch of people lined up to look after your little dog. Me first in line. For a cause like that...'

'A cause...'

'Persuading her to come home,' she said softly, and she gave a rueful grin. 'Yeah, I know, my advice isn't wanted, but I'm all for happy endings. You guys saved my Ray and if there's anything we can do...'

There was a loaded silence where he tried to figure something to say—and couldn't. Finally, she held up her hands, as if in surrender.

'I know. Back off. I've said my bit, and it's over to you. See you later, Doc, and thanks.'

And she was gone.

He stayed still until the screen door slammed after her. Until he heard her car head away down the road. Until the silence settled over the empty clinic.

He had someone else booked in, but they were running late. Dammit, he wanted them to be here, now. He needed to keep busy.

Instead he headed out to the veranda and stood looking out over the valley to the sea. He scratched Hoppy idly under his ear and Hoppy looked up and whined, as if he knew something was wrong but didn't know what.

He knew what.

Gina, heading off to the Antarctic with a team of strangers. Gina, moving from one place to another, as she'd done all her life.

He'd asked her to stay.

'It'd take more'n romance to get a woman like that to trust enough to put down roots.'

He'd put down roots, though. He'd settled on this island and he had no intention of leaving. He'd seen enough of what the world held...

Gina was out there, in the world.

She could be happy here, he thought. They could be happy. With his work, with this little clinic, with his house, secluded from the world...

His escape...

He'd asked her to escape with him, he thought. To stay safe.

But as he gazed out over the valley he thought suddenly, *Define 'safe'*.

He'd come here to escape from horrors, from nightmares, from things the world had thrown at him.

For Gina, escape meant something different. He thought back to what Holly had said:

'Babs told the teachers, that first day... "She's only here until I can find someone else to take her. Do the best you can with her but if I can find someone on the mainland to take her, I will..."'

Gina's nightmare wasn't what the world could throw at her. Gina's nightmare must surely be being rejected.

Hell.

A truck was pulling into the parking lot. Here was his next patient. He'd be busy for the rest of the morning. He had online work to do this afternoon and then there was his garden. Life could get back to normal.

His safe life could stay...safe.

Without Gina.

'Hiya, Doc.' The elderly farmer climbed out of the truck, stiffly because of advanced arthritis. 'Lost Gina, hey? Just lucky for us you're staying.'

Lucky.

He struggled to collect his thoughts. He was needed here. He wasn't the waste of space Gina had thought he was when she'd first arrived.

But Gina...

She'd be at the airport at Gannet now, heading off to Sydney to join her boat. She was gone.

'Hey, you with us, Doc?' the farmer asked, and he caught himself.

'Sorry, mate. Just thinking…of what comes next.'

'My toe's what comes next,' the farmer told him. 'I reckon I might have gout.'

'Let's have a look, then,' Hugh told him. A gouty toe had to take precedence.

And then what?

Things were changing inside him. Stirring. Liberating?

Frightening?

'Nothing to be frightened of,' he said out loud and the farmer looked at him in alarm.

'What, me toe? You're not about to chop it off, are you, Doc?'

And that made him grin. 'Nope,' he reassured him. 'I'm definitely not. But there might be other things that might need a bit of tweaking.'

'Other things about me?'

'Other things about me,' Hugh told him, still grinning. He put a hand on the man's shoulder. 'Okay, mate, enough about me. Let's look at this toe and then go from there.'

CHAPTER FOURTEEN

Sydney, November 18th.
Australian Ship Icebreaker Two.
Departure: eight a.m.
Final team meeting before boarding.

GINA WAS STANDING to the side, watching as the team oversaw their belongings being loaded onto trolleys to be taken on board. This wasn't just personal gear. Each member of this highly skilled team had a specific purpose for being here, so there was research gear to be loaded, as well as the massive provisioning.

She'd been onboard already, setting up her clinic, making sure she had things as safe as she could make them.

Which was never very safe. The Southern Ocean was one of the most treacherous places in the world, and she'd made this trip before. The seas tossed the boat around as if it were a flimsy toy. Almost every expedition resulted in minor injuries—and sometimes major ones.

She was good at her job, but she wanted to be better. These projects were chronically underfunded. It'd be great to have a doctor on board with them, but it was hardly ever possible. The responsibility was hers.

And then there was a stir at the doorway and the team leader entered. Erik Andersson was a burly, bearded hulk of a man, weathered by years of just this type of work.

He was followed by another man. Gina glanced past Erik—and then she froze.

Hugh.

'Guys, listen up.' Erik's voice, trained by years of seagoing, boomed across the departure hall. 'We have a passenger who might just become a crew member. This is Dr Hugh Duncan. He's on board as a passenger until we reach Hobart, taking the two days to test his sea legs. If we can all be nice to him and his stomach's kind, then we have ourselves a doctor for the trip. If he gets seasick, we'll chuck him off at Hobart, but if everything goes right, Gina, we have you a colleague.'

He gripped Hugh's shoulder and chuckled, the deeply satisfied laugh of someone who'd just made his team a whole lot safer. 'So... You guys doing the steering—can you keep away from any nasty waves that might make him squeamish? The rest of you, I want you to make him welcome, and, if possible, don't give him any work at all. Let him think it's all a holiday until we get nicely clear of Hobart.'

What followed was a raucous cheer. Every team member knew he or she was taking a risk heading into such a remote environment. Many of them knew Gina and trusted her—she'd worked with this team before—but having both a doctor and a trained emergency nurse made them all much safer. There was a surge forward to greet him.

But Gina didn't...surge. She couldn't seem to do anything but stand exactly where she was. Her body felt frozen.

'Gina.' Erik's voice boomed out over the noise. 'Doc tells me he's worked with you before. His references say he's good. You gonna agree and let us keep him on board?'

And everyone turned to her.

'I might,' she managed, fighting desperately to find words. Her eyes caught Hugh's and held, and what she saw there... Don't think it, she told herself desperately. Just...respond. Somehow. 'I saw him fix a wombat's leg once,' she managed at last, and somehow she dredged up a grin. 'If he can do that, then maybe he can fix the stuff we might throw at him.'

There was general laughter, and then the skipper of the boat announced boarding and Erik took Hugh to introduce him to the senior crew members.

She needed to supervise the medical gear. It was lucky she'd done this before, because she was working on automatic.

Hugh was here.

The hour before departure was always frantic, almost everyone using the guaranteed stability of harbour to unpack precious research equipment. Gina spent the time sorting medical supplies, trying to get her head to work...and failing. Erik seemed to be towing Hugh around the boat introducing him to everyone. She could hear Erik's voice booming in the distance, Hugh's muted replies.

And then the engines thrummed into life and she could hear no more. She finished what she was doing, then went up to the deck and stood in the bow as the boat left the harbour. Her mind seemed to have gone blank. So many questions.

She stood in the bow and waited.

'Hey.'

He came up behind her and put a hand on her shoulder. Inevitably. That he was here… It'd been a shock, but somehow she'd known that what was between them couldn't end with her running away.

She hadn't been running, she reminded herself. She'd been sensible.

She'd been doing what she needed to keep herself safe. So how to keep herself safe now?

'H… Hey.' Her voice didn't come out right.

'Pleased to see me?'

'What…what have you done with Hoppy?' It was a dumb question, but dumb questions seemed all she was capable of. He was so near. He was so… Hugh.

He was wearing tough seaman's clothes. She thought of him working for so many years in foreign crisis zones. She thought of Erik, presented with Hugh's credentials. Erik would have hired him in a heartbeat.

Tough didn't begin to describe this guy.

'Hoppy's pretending he's a cattle dog,' he was saying, while she deviated to wondering what was happening with her heart. It was thumping as if it were trying to jump out of her chest. 'He's staying on Holly and Ray Cross's farm, happy as a pig in mud. Ray's still recovering, so Hoppy alternates from lying on Ray's bed or day couch, or fitting in as one of their pack of farm dogs. He's forgotten he only has three legs. He's forgotten he was even wounded.'

There was a moment's hesitation and then his voice softened. 'And that's why I'm here,' he said gently. 'I figure it's time I forgot as well, but I've figured… I've finally figured I can't do it alone. I'm hoping I might find someone to help me.'

'Yeah?' How hard to get her voice to work? It was

coming out as a ridiculous tremor. 'So you jumped on a boat to the Antarctic? To try and find someone?'

'I had inside information,' he admitted, just as softly. 'I knew that the woman I wanted to spend my life with was already on board.'

And her crazy, jumping heart forgot all about jumping. It seemed to still. It seemed to almost stop.

'Hugh…'

'I don't get seasick,' he told her.

'Wh…what?'

'I talked to Erik,' he said, because she couldn't think of a single thing to say past that one lone syllable. 'It wasn't fair to join his crew without letting him know the situation. I told him we've worked before. I also told him I had every intention of asking you to marry me. The last thing he wants is conflict within his team, so we have a deal. This boat docks in Hobart in two days, before heading south. If either of us is the least unhappy about the situation then I get off then. And I will. He's more than happy to take a chance in order to get his team a doctor, but there's to be no pressure on you. You say the word and I'll do my best imitation of pale and wan and leave the boat. They'll think I'm a wuss, but there's the end of it. But it does mean I need to lay my cards on the table right now.' He hesitated and then his voice softened still further.

'Gina, when you left Sandpiper, I felt like part of me had been wrenched away. It took a while for me to figure out, but I finally have. You want me to explain?'

How on earth could he explain? For that matter, how could she? All she knew was that when she looked into his eyes some part of her that she hadn't even known had been missing seemed to flood in and make her…complete?

It didn't make sense.

'I don't think there's anything to explain,' she said, struggling desperately to find words. 'Nothing's been wrenched away. Sandpiper is your home.'

'It's not my home.'

There was a moment's silence and then he took her shoulders and turned her to face him.

For some reason there was no one else in sight. Often when they left harbour the bow filled with team members, but they were completely alone. It'd be Erik, Gina thought randomly. If Erik knew what Hugh intended… He was a softie at heart, a born romantic. He had a wife he loved to bits—Louise was a research scientist in her own right and she was on board now. Erik thought the rest of the world should be as happy as he was.

She could just see him engineering this.

'Gina, look at me,' Hugh said, and her swirling thoughts centred. Somehow. He was gripping her shoulders and she looked up at his face. Her gaze was held.

His eyes were dark, serious. Loving?

'We have it wrong,' he said.

'Wrong?'

'This whole home concept,' he said softly. 'I left the crisis team wounded, and thought I needed to retreat from the world. That's what I figured home was. A place to hide, to lick my wounds, to stay emotionally distant. And you…' His voice gentled so far, he had to tug her closer to hear. 'I might have this wrong—tell me if I have—but for you the concept of home is scary. It seems to me that every time a home's been offered to you, it's been snatched away. As a kid you seemed to have been tossed from one place to another. Then your parents were killed—your only security. You came to Sandpiper when you were crushed, and, instead of saying welcome home, Babs told you right at the beginning

that it wasn't home. That she had you under sufferance.
I imagine you spent those two years trying desperately
not to make any ties, not to build any sort of connection
that would hurt when you left again.'

She stared up at him, stunned. 'Hugh…how can you
know…?'

'I don't *know*,' he said, just as gently. 'I'm guessing, but when you left, I had a heap of time to guess. I
also had time to figure how much I lost when you got
on that ferry and disappeared. But you know what finally did it?'

'How can I know?' Her voice was a thread.

'I guess you can't,' he told her. 'But it was Hoppy. The
night after you left I went home, or where I thought was
home, and I sat in front of the fire and Hoppy jumped up
on my knee and almost purred. And I thought, without
Hoppy, this place would be totally bleak. It wouldn't feel
like home. And then I thought, what's the definition of
home? You know the saying *Home is where the heart
is*? I'm going to add to that. I'm going to say home *is*
heart. Because that's what I'm feeling, Gina. Like it or
not, I want my home to be you.'

'Hugh… I don't…' She got the words out, but that
was all she could manage. Her voice trailed to nothing.

'Yeah, it takes time to get it,' he said, drawing her in
to hold her against him. She let herself be drawn, feeling
the strength of him, the warmth, the surety. 'But there's
another quote, my love, that my grandma used to read
me when I was a kid. Ruth to Naomi. "Whither though
goest, I will go." Grandma used it when she was talking
about love. More, she used it to talk about what home
meant, and it's taken me all these years to finally understand. Gina, if you'll let me, I would ask you to allow
my home to be you. And if you could find the courage,

if you could find the trust, more than anything in the world I'd like your home to be me.'

'I don't…' She was stuck in some repetitive loop, unable to get her voice to say anything else.

'No pressure,' he said, resting his head on her hair and holding her close. 'Love, I've figured it out for me. My home is people. My home is my dumb Hoppy dog. And I would love, more than anything in the world, for my home to be you. But if you don't want it, I won't turn into some crazy stalker, following you to the ends of the earth. I'll head back to Sandpiper and get more and more attached to old Joe Carstairs' piles and Mrs Barker's bunions. Because somehow you seem to have opened that door to me, and I love it, too. But equally… I've talked to Marc on Gannet and he agrees Sandpiper needs a decent medical service. I can help fund it. They'll advertise for a doctor to live there, which will free me, so that if you want… "Whither though goest, I will go."'

'Even to the Antarctic?' It was a faltering whisper.

'I plan to grow a beard,' he said solemnly. 'I've seen adventurers with frost dripping from beards a foot long. Would you love me with a frosty beard?'

'Oh, Hugh…'

'You know, you're going to have to think of something else to say but, "Oh, Hugh,"' he told her, kissing the top of her head. 'No pressure, love, but if you think your home could be me…'

He put her away from him, just a little, so he could look into her eyes. She searched his and what she saw there…

Home.

Hugh.

And with that came a flood of warmth so great it almost overwhelmed her. Here was love, here was peace, security, wonder.

'So what's it to be, love?' he asked gently. 'Shall I hop off at Hobart or will you be stuck with me for ever? Stay or go, love, it's up to you.'

And with that she felt that fragile armour finally crack. More than crack. She looked up into his eyes and it dissolved as if it had never been.

'Yes, please,' she managed to whisper. 'Who...whoever thought bricks needed to be bricks and mortar? Everything I want in the world is right here, right now.'

His smile deepened. Softened. 'You mean it? I haven't even brought out the big guns yet. Gina, I've arranged for the world's best coffee machine to be installed in the galley. Call it a bribe, but there it is.' The warmth in his eyes was a caress all by itself. 'So, my love, with or without my coffee machine... Will you marry me?'

She choked on what could have been tears, could have been laughter. He had to ask? Her Hugh?

'Yes, please,' she said simply and then there was no need for words. She was swept into his arms, against his heart, and she was kissed.

And then she found out the whereabouts of all the team who usually gathered in the bow to watch the ship leave harbour. There was a massive cheer from above, so loud it made them draw apart enough to look up.

The wheelhouse was crowded. Here was her team, every one of them cheering, clapping, laughing with delight.

'Erik reckoned if we had a happy ending we had to share.' Hugh was chuckling, still holding her but looking up at them with a smile a mile wide. 'Reckon we've supplied it?'

'Reckon we have,' she managed and smiled and smiled. 'But only if you kiss me again.'

'Anything you say, ma'am,' he said promptly. And did.

EPILOGUE

Sandpiper, autumn

IT WAS THREE WEEKS after *Icebreaker Two* had docked back in Sydney. Just enough time to find a wedding dress, organise the formalities and plan a simple wedding on Windswept Bay.

But a simple wedding, with just Hugh and Gina, the celebrant and the two witnesses necessary for legal reasons, was never going to happen.

Because the island celebrant was also the mayor and the island's policeman, and when had Joan Wilmot ever been discreet? They'd landed back on the island to find the organisation of the wedding had been taken out of their hands.

'Sorry, guys,' Joan told them. 'You asked me to find a couple of witnesses and suddenly I had a queue of everyone on the island. I knew you wouldn't want to offend anyone, so I thought, lesser of two evils, give them their heads.'

Which meant the beautiful Windswept Bay was dotted with picnic rugs, beach umbrellas, tables laden with food and drink, all centred around a magnificent homemade arch strewn with what must surely be every rose on the island.

For, whatever Gina and Hugh's definition of home might be, the islanders had their own ideas. They'd heard of Gina and Hugh's plans by now. There'd been talks with Gannet Island medical centre. It seemed there were medics interested in what Gina and Hugh were offering, a base on Sandpiper at prearranged times, intermittently staying in Hugh's magnificent house, in return for medical coverage while Hugh and Gina—and occasionally Hoppy—headed off on yet another adventure.

Gina and Hugh would be Sandpiper medics, with backup so they could be anything they wanted. Even a geologist, if she'd like to go back to study, Hugh had told her, though she'd kind of figured by now that she liked being a nurse.

And she'd very much like being Hugh's wife.

Their adventures might need to be curtailed in the future anyway, Gina thought serenely, as Holly Cross fussed about her veil, and smiled and smiled, and then declared the bride ready for the short walk down to the beach. To where Hugh was waiting.

Or maybe she had her definition of adventures wrong.

Down on the beach, under the magnificent arch, Hugh stood and waited for his bride. Hugh, resplendent in a dark suit—who knew he even owned such a thing? Hugh, his deep, dark eyes smiling and smiling as he watched her make her way towards him. Hugh, who she loved with all her heart.

Hugh, who was her home.

Adventures needing to be curtailed? Maybe not so much. Lately there'd been an urge…not yet but soon… and when she'd mentioned it to Hugh his eyes had flared, with love and with hope.

And excitement.

An adventure devoutly to be wished? Spending the

rest of her life with this man? Loving him? Carrying his babies. Maybe adopting another dog or two, rescuing the odd wombat, helping islanders in need?

What greater adventure could a woman want? A career, a base and a man who loved her, as a husband and a friend.

And then she reached his side. He took her hands in his and he kissed her—surely that was for the end of the ceremony, but who cared? She kissed him back and knew that whatever the path their lives took, here was her heart.

'Ready, love?' he murmured as Joan coughed and raised her formal sheet of vows meaningfully.

And Gina smiled and smiled, though maybe there were tears in the mix as well.

'I'm ready, my love,' she whispered back, and she gave him one last hug before they turned to the celebrant to be pronounced man and wife.

'Oh, my love, welcome home.'

* * * * *

COMING SOON!

We really hope you enjoyed reading this book.
If you're looking for more romance, be sure to
head to the shops when new books are
available on

Thursday 16th September

To see which titles are coming soon, please visit

millsandboon.co.uk/nextmonth

MILLS & BOON

THE HEART OF ROMANCE

A ROMANCE FOR EVERY READER

MODERN
Prepare to be swept off your feet by sophisticated, sexy and seductive heroes, in some of the world's most glamourous and romantic locations, where power and passion collide.

HISTORICAL
Escape with historical heroes from time gone by. Whether your passion is for wicked Regency Rakes, muscled Vikings or rugged Highlanders, awaken the romance of the past.

MEDICAL
Set your pulse racing with dedicated, delectable doctors in the high-pressure world of medicine, where emotions run high and passion, comfort and love are the best medicine.

True Love
Celebrate true love with tender stories of heartfelt romance, from the rush of falling in love to the joy a new baby can bring, and a focus on the emotional heart of a relationship.

Desire
Indulge in secrets and scandal, intense drama and plenty of sizzling hot action with powerful and passionate heroes who have it all: wealth, status, good looks…everything but the right woman.

HEROES
Experience all the excitement of a gripping thriller, with an intense romance at its heart. Resourceful, true-to-life women and strong, fearless men face danger and desire - a killer combination!

To see which titles are coming soon, please visit

millsandboon.co.uk/nextmonth

MILLS & BOON

Coming next month

REAWAKENED AT THE SOUTH POLE
Juliette Hyland

Helena Mathews put Kelly Jenkins's shoulder X-rays on the light box. Carter still couldn't believe his eyes. If it hadn't felt ridiculous, he'd have pinched himself. Not that it would do any good. This wasn't a dream.

She was truly here. At the Amundsen-Scott South Pole Station. The odds were astronomical. This was a situation that one saw in cheesy movies. Not actual life.

Time had been exceedingly kind to Helena. Her features were more refined now, but the beautiful young girl had transformed into a stunning woman. The long blond hair she'd worn in braids was shorn close to her head in an adorable pixie cut. It was a cut that her parents—particularly her mother—probably would have hated, just like she probably disliked the small diamond stud in Helena's nose. But both seemed to suit the woman standing next to him.

And some things hadn't changed. Like her jade eyes or the full lips that barely stuck out in a pout. Kissable lips.

Carter shook himself as he stared at the light box. He needed to pull his shaken core together. Seeing Helena was a shock, but it changed nothing. He wanted to believe the lie, but his heart hammered against his chest, denying that anything about this winter assignment would be the same.

For the first time since he'd ended his engagement, he felt like he was at a crossroads. In those broken moments he'd sworn he'd never step off the isolated path he'd chosen, and nothing was going to change that. Yes, Helena was here, but that didn't have to mean anything significant for him. She was just another medical professional wintering at the research station.

Except…

His brain cut that thought off before he allowed it to wander.

Crossing his arms, he studied the X-ray. It was Kelly's shoulder that mattered right now. Not the soft woman standing inches from him.

"I don't see any breaks, Carter."

His name on her lips sent a wave of unwelcome emotions through the darkened corners of his soul. Light poured into places that had been dormant for years. Home…it felt like home. Warm, welcoming, supportive. All the things he'd taken for granted. All the things he did not need.

Home.

Continue reading
REAWAKENED AT THE SOUTH POLE
Juliette Hyland

Available next month
www.millsandboon.co.uk